THE BACK GATE TO HELL

A NOVEL OF THE LATE ROMAN EMPIRE

EMBERS OF EMPIRE
VOL. III

Q. V. HUNTER

Eyes and Ears Editions
130 E. 63rd St., Suite 6F
New York, New York,
USA 10065-7334

ISBN 978-2-9700889-4-3

This novel is entirely a work of fiction. The names, characters
and incidents portrayed in it, while at times based on historical
figures and events, are the work of the author's imagination.

eyesandears.editions@gmail.com

1. Hunter, Q. V. 2. Constantinopole 3. Roman Empire 4. Late
Rome
5. Historical Fiction 6. Action and Adventure 7. Syria 8.
Espionage Fiction
I Title

TO OUR 'ROCK,' P.

Also by Q. V. Hunter

The Assassin's Veil, Embers of Empire, Vol. I
Usurpers, Embers of Empire, Vol. II
The Wolves of Ambition, Embers of Empire, Vol. IV
The Deadly Caesar, Embers of Empire, Vol. V
The Burning Stakes, Embers of Empire, Vol. VI
The Purple Shroud, Embers of Empire, Vol. VII
The Treason of Friends, Embers of Empire, Vol. VIII
The Prefect's Rope, Embers of Empire, Vol. IX

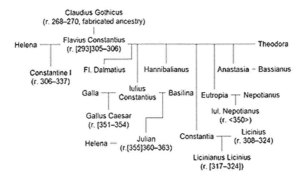

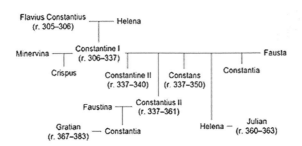

THE CONSTANTINE FAMILY

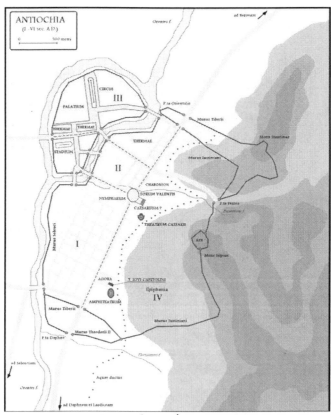

Antiochia, 4th Century

TABLE OF CONTENTS

Chapter 1, The Vigil at the Bridge

—Evening, Oct 10, 353 AD—

No one celebrates my birthday because no one knows the date, least of all myself. I was born to the wife of an obscure Numidian mule trader who sold both mother and child into slavery for domestic service in Roma some twenty years ago.

Since then, I had earned my freedom by spying for the Roman army on religious suicide 'martyrs' terrorizing my native province. That action won me a new career as an imperial agent, so I suppose I could have dug up the details of my sale in the Roman market in archives somewhere. But even if I cared, there was no way to recover the exact date of my birth.

For that matter, I now had much more important things on my mind. The civil war between the Western and Eastern halves of the Roman Empire was over. The Emperor Constantius II was in control of the entire civilized world. Certainly, the Persians and nomads to the east didn't count as 'civilized' in our minds. Since ridding the field of all usurping generals and family contenders except for his younger cousin, the Caesar Gallus, Constantius' reign seemed supreme at last.

So the celebration of any anniversary or birthday in the court of Constantius was a major event.

But as I crouched in the darkness that cold October night by the river Rhodanus, I certainly knew one thing. *If* I had known the date of my own birth and *if* I had ever celebrated it, I certainly would not have asked for prisoners-of-war as presents.

I had learned that emperors are different. Emperors like that sort of gift, particularly the ones with a nervous, suspicious disposition like Constantius. Toadies and careerists anxious to please the throne rush forward, offering surprises in shackles.

I'd taken up the job that day of inspecting the road licenses of all traffic heading through Arelate's gates facing the eastern bank of the river. I'd caught a few forgeries and let a few others pass with an understanding wink or minor bribe. I was *biarchus* class in the *schola* of agents, the *agentes in rebus*, and I'm sure the more junior man I took over for knew full well that I had a secret purpose in mind. We agents were trained not to ask each other too many questions.

Road inspection wasn't my real concern. Since midmorning I'd been waiting for Constantius II's 'anniversary presents' to trudge into view. It had been a long and futile watch. Now I just crouched under my short cloak in the lowering autumn dusk. I'd found a comfortable spot in the soft grass under the tall stone tower linking a pontoon bridge to its twin on the western shore. I didn't draw the attention of people leaving Arelate to cross the bridge, but from time to time I poked my head around the tower and cast my eyes upstream, checking the bend in the northern road that skirts the river.

If my informants were right, a prisoner convoy must appear any hour now. Whether by boat or road, I didn't know. I'd paid dearly for the little intelligence I had. It was a highly sensitive political operation and all the convoy routes were a closely guarded secret. Demobbed soldiers, outlaws, and highborn desperados still loyal to the failed uprising attacked such convoys to free their friends and family from the tortures awaiting them. These unfortunates were the defeated dregs of tens of thousands of fighters led by idealistic military rebels and their kin against Emperor Constantius for control of the West two years ago. Their leader General Magnentius, the self-proclaimed 'barbarian' emperor, had killed himself rather than be taken prisoner.

I'd been there. He'd impaled himself on my sword.

Some of his followers, many of them well-heeled Roman aristocracy, had fled by boat across the Sea of Adria to hide in Greece. Others, especially from noble families of Gallia, had wagered they stood a better chance of finding sanctuary across the water in colonial Britannia.

They'd made a fatal mistake. The Emperor's cruelest hound, Paulus Catena, 'Paul the Chain,' had dogged their fleeing wagons northward, month after month, across the sleeve of water that separated the port of Bononia from the broad mouth of the Thamesis River, then up past the civilized outpost of Londinium and the coastal Roman colonies and right into the Celtic wilds.

I knew the swarthy Catena's reputation. In Sirmium, I'd seen for myself the Hispaniard's experiments in torture techniques copied from the Persians. In escaping his sick contrivances, I had even inflicted a nearly fatal wound on his own throat. So I knew that his anger with the House of Manlius to which I had belonged as a slave still ran deep and fierce. If Kahina, the last Manlius matron, staggered along with the other prisoners arriving in Arelate tonight, I braced myself for the worst. I would be grateful she still breathed, whatever her condition. Her five-year-old son, Leo, must have his mother back, even if she'd been crippled by Catena's chains or blinded and scarred through his notorious sadism.

The river lapped at the shore just inches from my boots. I carried the standard protections of peacetime duty, not battlefield maneuvers. In the cuff of my right boot, I'd also fixed the small swivel knife issued at the Castra Peregrina headquarters to all *agentes*. I looked more harmless than I was.

Most of the dwindling wagon traffic was rumbling in the other direction, out of Arelate and over the bridge, returning for the night to the farms and little workshops that supplied the townspeople. The exodus of day workers who lived in the simple suburbs finally sputtered out in this last hour of daylight.

I accosted the sleepy driver of a lumbering wagon carrying little more than empty crates back from a day at market.

'*Evectio*? *Diplomata*?' I reached out for his papers, either a one-time license or a yearly pass, and glanced around the vehicle. The red dust and broken pottery sherds in the wagon bed identified him as an *amphora* salesman.

I wondered what else the sullen scoundrel might have smuggled past the taxman inside his big wine containers that morning. He showed me his certificate to use the *Cursus Clabularis*, the state road reinforced for heavy ox-drawn cargo, military trains, and the like. It was all in order. I let him move on.

The sinking sun relinquished me to my lonely vigil in the tower's shadowy chill. Not for the first time I wondered whether my information was wrong. Had I missed something vital? Had I paid the eager tattletale too little?

A sudden roar at my back broke the pregnant silence of my watch. In the arena ten minutes' walk back into the city, thousands of Arelatians were cheering the last Games of the day with animal pleasure. Soon, streams of spectators would be filing through the heavy Circus arches and back into the dusky streets. How quickly most of them had forgotten the disruptions and deaths of war! How little they agitated now for reform or new blood. They didn't care that Emperor Constantius was marking thirty years since his investiture as a boy *caesar*. They only loved him for offering entertainment for yet another day.

Was Constantius even attending tonight's festivities in his honor? I had never seen the Emperor smile, much less relax or let down his guard. During any ceremony or procession he kept his large, expressionless eyes fixed on the far horizon. He never lowered his gaze or turned his head to take in the masses of ordinary people lining the streets. Even addressing his beloved troops, he saw everyone and at the same time, registered no one.

Some said Constantius never even blinked.

The boisterous Magnentius had always liked the Games, the winners and the losers grappling in the sand or racing within an inch of their lives. Most of all, he loved the spectators who bet on them. He saw himself as one of life's contestants. He needed the applause and acclaim from ordinary people. He shared their dreams, their fears, and their superstitions.

Constantius professed to be an Arian Christian, but had postponed actual baptism. He might, like his father, submit to confession only on his deathbed. He was a hard and practical man. Instead of relaxing at the Games this evening, the Emperor was more likely to be concluding some pressing business with his Principal Council, the *consistorium*, before the anniversary party began and he received his 'presents.'

Perhaps Constantius simply felt he could not afford to blink.

After all, he was the last of the old Constantine's sons still standing. His brother Constans had killed the eldest, Constantine II, and then died during the revolt of Magnentius.

I was just about to abandon my spot for the second day running when my heart leapt at the sight of a thin black line of forms descending a distant hill. Were they human? Were they bound together? Were these the prisoners? Or were my eager eyes fooled by a mirage made by a line of mules or returning field workers?

Of course . . . of course, I smiled to myself, noting the hour and the falling light. As always, Paulus Catena was shrewd. He wasn't taking any chances. Courtiers said Constantius was ruled by fear of yet more challengers, more usurpers surfacing from the sea of unrest in the West, or popular generals making a name for themselves on the eastern front. Catena was bringing his prisoners in after dark and at the very last minute. He would do everything he could to avoid the slightest public show of lingering sympathy for the civil war's survivors.

After all, Magnentius' gold coins still circulated from palm to palm. Perhaps secret support for reform circulated with them.

My breath quickened, just as it did before an actual battle. Years of suppressed devotion and longing rose up in my breast. I could taste my emotions like a hungry man salivates at the smell of a hot meal. Perhaps Kahina would come into view within the hour, within the half hour, or even in the next ten minutes or less. Why was that line moving so slowly? It might mean the end of years of worry and deception.

After the massacre at Mursa had ripped apart our lives, killing her husband the Commander Gregorius, all I had to cling to was her wedding ring carried back by a stranger to the family's house in Roma. That ring proved she had survived the war, if not the elimination of loyalists. It hung on a cord around my neck along with two rings I'd rescued from a man's severed hand on the Mursa battlefield. I had sworn that someday I would return that treasure to the widow of Magnentius' *magister officiorum*, Marcellinus, slain underfoot by Constantius' mounted cavalry. I had sworn that someday I would also see that wedding ring back on Kahina's finger.

But the widow Marcellinus and all their family had been wiped out in Catena's purge. Had Kahina suffered the same fate?

People said that we *agentes in rebus* didn't owe allegiance to any emperor, only to the Roman Empire itself. They showed us respect as we carried out our duties, but behind our backs they said we were nothing but troublemakers, spies and that peculiar insult that haunted our heels, '*curiosi.*' They said we were as corrupt as our predecessors in service, the self-seeking *frumentarii*. But I knew better. However cold or impartial our actions, we were still men of honor with hearts and memories. Our 'bribes' were mere tips compared to those demanded by the *frumentarii* and our missions often as noble as they were invisible.

I sat there listening to the mighty Arelate oak gates behind me squeaking closed on their iron hinges and blocking out much of the evening's torchlight. Now the deepening darkness cloaked me better than my thin riding garment. I would wait for the mysterious line to arrive.

Finally I heard them, or rather I heard their leg shackles dragging heavy chains along the paved road. The convoy was about a hundred feet away. As they drew within fifty feet of the tower the wind shifted and the stench of pain, blood, and weeks, perhaps months, of being denied a civilized Roman's daily bath, hit my nostrils.

Finally they came around a curve and within my view. They marched at a forced pace across the bridge and right past the tower where I lurked in the thick grass of the shadowy bank. There were at least three hundred of them, and possibly more, all linked by iron in ranks six abreast.

A former slave always remembers how to move unnoticed. I waited until the convoy had cleared the tower and remounted the slope with my hood pulled low over my forehead. The two guards at the rear had relaxed and were no doubt anticipating their reward—pay, dinner, and a soft bed. During the long weeks' march southward, they might once have been on the alert for an attempted breakout or rescue. But tonight they could see the finish line and they weren't worried, not now, not within minutes of their final destination. They hadn't detected me in the dark and I slipped in among the stragglers at the convoy's tail and slowed down my steps to match their leaden pace.

The prisoners kept their own eyes lowered. If I hadn't known that at least some of these pitiable folk had once presided over lavish banquets in their suburban villas and important councils or town *curiae* in Hispania or Gallia, I would have thought them peasants from the meanest hovels. Tonight their jewels, fine robes, and ceremonial armor were gone. Some of them bore the cuts of Catena's whips, still red or suppurating from neglect. Worse, all of their pride was stripped away for good.

Together we halted but by then, I'd hunkered down low and from the center of the back ranks of the cortège, I had worked my way up through the rows of the first few dozen prisoners. It was touch and go footwork, dodging the dangerous chains while checking each set of downtrodden features layered with grit and dried tears. Once the documents carried by one of Catena's lieutenants had been cleared with the city's sentries up ahead, our long line waited while the huge gates swung back open.

We moved forward again, passing under the arch, always six by six. I kept my face well covered as we passed the *agentes* post from which all mail was registered and dispatched and all licenses for the *Cursus Publicus* issued or checked. My colleagues knew me well at that little porter's lodge. Although they might hail me only in innocence, I couldn't afford discovery until I'd found Kahina and got her to safety.

Where was she? By all accounts, this was the very last prisoner convoy. This pathetic column of wraiths was my last hope. I was determined to search the face of every female in that procession with brown hair. We were trudging up one of Arelate's main streets now. The stall awnings had been rolled up and the streetside butchers, tailors, cobblers, and schoolmasters had retired for the day. The normal languid activity of evening now pervaded the streets. The ramshackle balconies of the cheaper apartment buildings leaned over tavern tables spread along the sidewalks. Conversation bounced from windows above down to groups of happy neighbors dining after the Games that marked any imperial holiday, religious or secular.

As the prisoners' train approached the cheerful revelers, a pool of tavern lamplight revealed the horrible condition of the captives passing row by row. The carefree chatting dropped off as the customers averted their faces with embarrassed glances away from these miserable souls. Any dormant sympathy was stifled by the ferocious expression of Paulus Catena and his lieutenants riding past on their heavily armored horses under imperial banners marked with the Constantinian logo, the Greek letters, 'Chi Rho,' starting the name Christ.

By dogged stealth, I had now reached a row of women chained together. I saw Kahina's hair at last, thick and chestnut, peeking out from under a torn shawl of hand-woven flax. It was the sort of covering she would have picked up in Britannia, perhaps the gift of a kind woman giving shelter to the refugees. The shawl's fringe lifted in the October wind that came in off the sea just to the south and defied even the city walls at this time of year. My heart leaped with it and in my haste to move forward through the tired ranks, I tripped on the next chain at my feet.

'Watch your step up there,' one of the guards at the rear shouted at me. I took it slow again and marched along without hope of another lunge at the shoulder I saw bobbing under the chestnut hair.

I had no idea what to do when I did reach her. My information about the convoy had come only the night before last. I carried no tools for smashing apart shackles. Of course I'd thought about it all through the long day, but I had assumed Kahina would be linked to no more than one or two other women who at an opportune moment could be scurried around a corner or down a narrow alley in the dark.

Yes, Catena was shrewd indeed. Six prisoners manacled by the ankles as a single flank posed a big problem, even in streets still crowded with people enjoying the lingering gaiety of the holiday.

I was closer to her now, navigating the chains with patience and agility, hoping no prisoner I jostled would have the energy to look me straight in the eye and turn me in. These captives were more than docile. Their passivity and indifference frightened me more than their leg irons. They walked like souls summoned up from Hades who had abandoned all hope of ever returning their five senses to the life around them. Perhaps that was exactly what they were.

For the first time I felt a chill dampening my excitement at a reunion. I had imagined Kahina wounded or weakened, but I could not imagine a Kahina, as dazed and emotionless as these walking dead, returning to mother Leo.

I reached the chestnut head drooping under the rustic cloth. Hoping not to shock her, I softly called, 'Kahina. It's Marcus. I'm here.'

She didn't dare turn her head, what with the ready whips ahead and behind us. The head nodded and I had to fight back my excitement.

'Kahina! Keep close to me. I'll get you out of here.'

She lowered her head. I knew she'd heard me.

'Wait for me to signal. We'll have to take everyone linked to you with us, as soon as I see a chance. But I'm ready and armed.'

She turned and spat right into my face. Then she pushed me hard and I fell back into the row of women tramping behind us, tumbling onto their sagging breasts and empty stomachs. Chains rattled as the next cluster of woman cried out in protest at this final indignity. The angry eyes glaring at me weren't those of Kahina. Her twisted, bitter expression was all that I deserved for taunting a strange woman with the hope of escape when we were less than ten minutes from the Imperial Palace walls.

'What's going on down there?'

One of the lieutenants from the front reined in his horse and waited for us to reach his position. We continued toward him along the narrow street's makeshift walkway set over the sewage gutters. Now the mounted guard was heading back toward us.

His horse's hooves clopped along with care to avoid breakage on boards meant for sandaled feet, not horse muscle. He was still about half a block away. At the first chance I saw, I dodged out of the convoy on the far side, tossing back my hood and coolly sitting down opposite a startled drinker halfway through his beaker of diluted wine. I smiled and grabbed his pottery goblet to toast his health. I held his bleary-eyed stare with a frozen smile and never turn my face toward the dregs of humanity trailing past our table.

The horseman reined in his mount and peered down into the ranks of prisoners. My chestnut-haired prisoner was nearly into the city forum by now. With reluctance, the guard turned his horse back to rejoin his fellow lieutenants at the front of the convoy.

I darted back into the procession, wondering how to finish my search when a hard-fingered grip yanked back my shoulder.

'Marcus? Marcus Gregorianus Numidianus?'

Now it was my turn to keep my eyes fixed on the open forum ahead of us. Without the alleys and sidewalk taverns as cover, it would be harder to move in and out of the prisoners' file across such an exposed public space.

'Marcus, tell me, is that you?'

The man with the pleading tone was speaking with an educated accent I glanced back over my shoulder, keeping my hood well over my features.

'Who are you?'

'Titus.'

'I don't know you.'

'Yes, yes, you do. I was a tribune under Gaiso's command.'

I took a deep breath. I played for time.

'I don't remember you. What is your full name?'

'Titus Gerontius Severus. You *must* remember me!'

Titus.

Yes, now, I did recollect a Titus Gerontius Severus riding alongside the indomitable Commander Gaiso, Magnentius' *magister equitum*. Yes, my mind's eye recalled Titus, a formidable horseman, training the cavalry *tirones* to wheel and charge, to mount in full armor and dismount in one graceful dance. With over fifty thousand dead in one day on the fields of Mursa, it was likely that none of those eager trainees had survived but it was not the fault of Titus or his instruction. I knew he was far from a bad fellow.

I also realized that this desperate and doomed man held a sword over my own head.

For this very Titus had ridden with Commander Gaiso and the rest of us under the rebel Magnentius' orders to hunt down and capture the despised young Emperor Constans. While Constantius was busy fighting back Persian incursions in the Eastern Empire, Constans had driven the Western Empire into the mud of corruption, inflation, degradation and finally, military revolt. The usurper Magnentius had intended to arrest him, with me carrying the necessary legal papers as *agens*, and to drive him into exile.

The plan had gone fatally wrong. Cornered in the most eastern reach of the mountains of Pyrene, the panicked Constans had made a last lunge with his ceremonial sword for Gaiso's back.

By instinct more than political decision, I'd saved Gaiso's life from ambush—and killed the Emperor Constans, the youngest of Constantine's heirs. Accused once of this crime before the Emperor Constantius himself, I'd been cleared, by a lie, as a favor owed to me.

I couldn't count on someone lying for me twice. I was determined to avoid Titus.

'Marcus!'

I tried to pull away but his scrawny fingers pinned me down. Even without turning to face him, I felt the manacles holding his wrists together biting into my shoulder.

'Marcus, you're an honorable man. You knew Gaiso for an honorable commander. Say that you know me!'

I turned despite my fears. I did know him—barely. He had been a handsome man in the Gallic mold. Now there were large pouches under his bloodshot eyes, deep creases down the once-cheerful cheeks, and a scrubby beard flecked with gray masking blistered lips. I remembered how that mouth once glistened wet with a hearty glug of wine from a goatskin sack. He was limping badly. As I glanced away from his distress, he heaved up a glob of viscous green phlegm that betrayed sick lungs.

That brief encounter had delayed my escape from the procession and now it was too late. The convoy had entered the Arelate forum and we were crossing the hundreds of yards of polished marble paving that spread over the level space from the steps of the Christian basilica—once a fine temple to Jupiter—to the main baths and municipal offices and around to the colonnaded stone roof that sheltered permanent stalls and stands for vendors. A leather tarpaulin kept the moist night air off the public 'weights and scales table' where every market morning busy housewives double-checked the probity of their butchers. The baths were quiet and the tall church doors locked up tight.

But the forum wasn't empty and the prisoners were exposed to the scrutiny of any onlookers as they crossed the wide space illuminated by a few oil lamps and overlooked by memorial statues on their plinths.

Titus fell silent as we paced up to join the hundreds of prisoners already halted outside the exterior gates of the imperial compound. The anniversary celebration party would be well underway by this hour and the Emperor was no doubt eager for the 'presents' that signaled the end of three years of bitter civil strife.

I was trapped in my own subterfuge. It was impossible now for me to slip out of their ranks without being spotted until we were actually inside the imperial reception rooms.

'Yes, Titus, I do know you, but please, this is dangerous. I'm searching for the wife of Commander Gregorius.'

'Why? Do you have papers for her release? Is there any hope for the rest of us?'

'None. Is she here?'

'Will Catena torture us again?'

'The Emperor has little appetite for that kind of spectacle, but Catena won't be denied his triumph.'

'You're right,' a familiar, if strangled, voice whispered a few feet away. 'I won't.'

With the tip of his long *spatha*, Paulus Catena hooked my sword belt and jerked me out of his cortège.

'Marcus Gregorianus Numidianus.'

I pulled off my hood and looked straight into his face, with its features oddly mismatched for so powerful a physique. The eyes were not the same size nor evenly placed. One sat closer and lower to the small, pointed nose than the other. He had a mouth too small for his heavy, black-stubbled jaw. I was used to this jumble of elements making up the nasty face of Catena, but if the face was familiar, something was wrong with his voice box. His throat was wrapped with a fine red wool scarf. Now I knew why our *schola* master Apodemius had warned me that Catena's voice would not recover from the garrote I used to escape him in Sirmium. If he sounded this hoarse, I must have left an ugly scar.

Catena yanked me up to him with one tight, burly fist. I saw the chin bristles under his helmet strap. My nostrils filled with the smell of road and horse rising off his long cloak.

'You escaped my interrogation in Sirmium too soon. In Mursa, you ducked a conviction on charges of imperial assassination on the back of a falsehood. How kind of you to join your fellow traitors so obligingly now.'

'I have a job serving the court,' I bluffed. 'Who's to say I'm not doing it?'

I tried to reach for the papers identifying my status as a mid-ranked *agens* with the right to stop any traffic and check any road licenses and much more, but his deadly blade grazed my fingers.

'Don't test me with petty protocol, slave-boy.'

'As I recall you started as a wine steward at the Emperor's banquet tables, then you wangled a receivership up in the provinces. What kind of notary imprisons men up to their neck in tubs of their own shit for the fun of it? Don't get haughty with me, Catena. I'm a freedman now.'

'You're Numidian scum,' he rasped, 'and your powerful protectors lie dead back in Mursa or trapped by barbarians up on the Rhenus. I don't know what you're doing here, making trouble with my prisoners, but I can report you to your headquarters for overstepping your puny authority.'

'I hear you know a lot about overstepping authority.'

It was a lethal shot. I saw I'd hit a hidden mark. Catena's campaign to hunt down Magnentius' followers in Britannia had led one noble governor to kill himself. The notary's leer dropped away and now the only thing left was the core of evil in his lopsided pupils.

There was a difference between our two kinds of loathing. I survived, despite nightly sweats and days of fear, to protect the souls of those I loved. Catena had survived his battles fuelled only by some insatiable lust for yet more cruelty that was destroying his soul, bit by bit.

'Get out of there.' He pulled his *spatha* away, and its blade sliced right through my sword belt. He stepped back, waiting for me to make my escape.

'Don't leave me, Marcus,' Titus pleaded. 'You were there. You can testify on my behalf in there.'

We were now marched as one through the outer courtyard of the Imperial Palace. I saw Catena's rage fighting to explode out of that pinched face of his.

As we inched forward, he recovered the reins of his horse and handed them to an aide with a jerk of his head in a gesture of dismissal toward me. With this strange capitulation of his, I realized in that second that I was dangerous to him and not the other way around.

'You *want* me to leave, Paulus Catena? That's all I need. I'm staying for the party,' I said.

'You have no invitation,' he sneered.

I shook my head and tapped the insignia on my breast. 'You forget, Notary, an *agens* never needs an invitation.'

Chapter 2, Chinks in the Chain

—THE IMPERIAL AUDIENCE ROOM, ARELATE—

There were many reasons why people called the *agentes in rebus* the *curiosi* when they thought we weren't listening. (Of course we were always listening.) Since my recruitment into the service, I'd learned that to do my job well, I mustn't care about popularity. We *agentes* inspected roads, but also accounts, dispatches, registers, and customs forms. We were authorized to stick our noses into other people's business and to report corruption too egregious to ignore.

We were also automatically cleared from prosecution for any action—no matter how offensive to law-abiding citizens—if performed in the course of our duties. We were trained to arrest both the lowborn and the highest of officials. If justice must be done, or at least must be seen to be done, we *agentes* were the men to carry out the job. We captured and brought back absconders for trial. Depending on the sentence handed down, we might also escort the disgraced offender into exile or to the place of his execution.

The Master of Admissions at the palace in Arelate knew me well enough. So when I appeared at the curtained doors to the imperial audience chamber a mere minute or two before Catena led his gruesome trophy collection forward, I got through with a respectful nod.

I slipped into the glittering assembly to find my place as junior in grade to Ahenobarbus, the senior *agens* attached to the

Constantius II court. In principle, Ahenobarbus was under the authority of the Emperor's Master of the Offices. In practice, everyone knew he and I both reported to and spied for the head of our service back in Roma and as protocol dictated, only Apodemius answered for our *schola* back to the *Magister Officiorum*.

The chamber was jammed tonight with hundreds of courtiers, most of them *illustri*, that is, illustrious heads of the great central ministries and the military commanders of the various prefectures. I spotted a few privileged *spectabili* and *clarissimi* from the slightly lower ranks of imperial service as well. To my relief, the most powerful Lord Chamberlain of the Empire, the silky eunuch *Praepositus Sacri Cubiculi* Eusebius, was noticeably absent tonight. By last report, he was moving between Mediolanum and Sirmium and I for one hoped he would take his time.

'Eusebia's here,' Ahenobarbus muttered to me, lifting one of his coppery eyebrows. In honor of the celebration tonight, even the imperial women had ventured from the isolation of their luxurious suites. Constantius' new Macedonian bride sat in a part of the audience hall sectioned off from us lowlier mortals by a waist-high grille filigreed in gold and silver. Her predecessor, the daughter of Constantius' half-uncle Julius Constantius, had lain in her grave for less than a year, but no one knew the cause of death.

And no one asked.

The new Empress watched the audience from under lowered eyelids. Intimates said Eusebia said little but missed nothing. When she did speak her mind, it was only to caution and temper her jittery spouse.

Tonight Eusebia sat as quiet and observant as I'd always seen her on the rare occasions she graced official events. She was dressed in the ornate, heavy style of the Eastern courts that Constantius favored. Yet under her jeweled diadem and thick, embroidered robes, she looked drawn with worry. She managed only a tentative smile to one arrival after another paying their respects in front of the grille. Arelate's society ladies whispered to each other underneath their fashionable veils. *How much easier Eusebia's life would become once she had borne Constantius an heir . . . This anniversary party marked only another month of disappointment and apology for the unlucky imperatrix . . .*

Apart from her ladies in attendance, Eusebia's sole companion for the evening was the Emperor's sister, Helena. I'd only seen this very young woman once before and then only by accident as she was trailed by a dozen chaperones down a corridor in the imperial palace at Mediolanum from a morning meeting with her priest-confessor. Modest and plain, with heavy-lidded eyes similar to her elder brother's, the poor thing could hardly have anything in her life to confess but some said the sacrament of penitence was the high point of her day.

Tonight Helena peeked out at the gathered invitees from under the same festooned black braids and curls worn by her older sister, the *Augusta* Constantia off in Antiochia. But the spit and fire of Constantia was nowhere to be seen in the younger girl. Helena sat slightly behind her sister-in-law tonight and appeared to know no one, for nobody greeted her. It seemed to me that of all the remaining Constantines, Helena wielded no power—or at least, not yet.

Would we even lay eyes on Helena again before the Emperor celebrated his fortieth anniversary of rule? Who might she be married off to before another decade rolled by? Her vicious sister had been harnessed to Gallus, their own younger cousin, but the world was running short of Constantines worthy of this pale and pious youngster.

There might once have been a passel of relatives waiting in the wings had it not been for her brother Constantius' reaction to the great Constantine's death—the wholesale massacre of any male relatives close enough to challenge his reign back in 337. The corpses included Constantia's first husband, his own brother-in-law and cousin, the General Hannibalianus as well as the older brother of Gallus, the imprisoned young man just excavated from house arrest to play Caesar of the East.

The Constantines enjoyed a messy family history. Whether celebrating that history was worth all the finery and fanfare of this party was a silent question no guest would voice this evening.

I finally dared to scrutinize the Emperor himself, sitting on a wide golden *cathedra* in a carapace of heavy purple and gold robes. His expression was as impassive and joyless as ever.

At a signal, the musicians tinkering and plucking away in the corner of the vast room finally fell silent, all but a lyre player accompanying a panegyrist no one was listening to. The Master of Admissions announced Paulus Catena. The Hispaniard wasn't a popular companion at the best of times and I scanned the reaction to his defiant appearance tonight. He hadn't changed out of his rough travelling trousers or soiled tunic. I suppose he meant his garb as a sort of sartorial rebuke to Arelate's elites who let hardworking fanatics like him mop up the Empire's enemies.

His gesture didn't pay off. The notaries and priests, ministers of finance and the Privy Purse, principal tribunes, and the *quaestor* with his legal briefs to hand, the Master of the Offices and the Prefect for Gallia standing next to the Praetorian Prefect, and all the other members of the Emperor's 'sacred' *consistorium* weren't looking chastised at all. Yes, just as I suspected, they were all turning their barbered, perfumed heads away in embarrassment from the filthy notary standing in the center of the hall.

'The Chain' seemed oblivious to their distaste as his lieutenants herded in his grisly 'gift,' dragging their ragged heels and torn hems, across the sparkling mosaic floor to the space just beneath Constantius' raised dais.

At 'shushing' from the guests, the lyre player and his droning soloist finally shut up and fumbled with their music sheets.

But the Constantines themselves stared straight at the prisoners. They might have been boring into their enemies' souls in search of repentance. This pitiable gaggle was the painful residue of a mighty force that had outnumbered Constantius at Mursa until a fateful last minute defection by General Claudius Silvanus had tipped the balance.

And suddenly I recalled my very last glimpse of Titus Gerontius Severus hurtling across the plains of Mursa into the cloud of dust and blood that left men gagging for breath and relief. Tonight he huddled among these men and women being lashed by Catena's henchmen into a bundle as tight as fish in a net, all three hundred or so pressed into one indistinguishable block of coughing, scratching, limping and bleeding torment.

How far he had fallen!

The desperate Titus scanned the ranks of officials and guests but he couldn't spot me. His appeal still lingered in my ears, but it would be folly for me to speak up for him. Nothing could be more foolhardy for my career than to turn defense witness during a ceremonial punishment of decided treason. If I knew what was wise, I should remain only what I was, a silent *agens* hoping for promotion to *centurion* status within the next few years. And any promotion could come only after my assignment to the rebel courts of the Magnentius faction had faded from official prejudice.

Only a fool in my position would speak up for Titus.

I listened to Catena's obsequious greetings and presentation of the prisoners with close attention from behind Ahenobarbus' protective shoulder.

Catena greeted the Emperor as a civilian should, genuflecting before the dais and then kneeling to kiss the hem of the imperial cloak in 'adoration of the purple.' As part of his formal presentation, he then held out a gold-threaded cloth laid across his palms in the symbolic gesture of offering.

Constantius answered Catena's presentation in that same rigid formality I'd first heard when he addressed thousands of troops on the Sirmium battlefield.

'We thank you for this anniversary gift, Paulus Catena. This costly civil war is over at last. We ourselves have made many sacrifices to preserve the unity of the Empire supreme. We have always put the interests of our own family second to the needs of the great Roman state, as have you, a loyal citizen.'

At Constantius' speech, Paulus Catena allowed a very slight smile of pleasure to escape that mean little mouth. He longed for two sounds in life—praise from the Emperor's lips and screams from those who challenged his personal ascent. He sighed with audible pleasure as Constantius continued:

'Let everyone present know that the Imperial Notary Paulus Catena has endured both hardship and danger as he travelled with insatiable appetite to avenge the assassination of my late brother, the Emperor Constans. We have read Paulus' reports sent from the mountains of Hispania, the northern coasts of Gallia and finally, as far as our colonies in Britannia, as he hunted down the last of the rebels supporting the tyrant and usurper Magnentius. We congratulate you, Paulus Catena, on your persistence and devotion to our throne.'

There was a murmur of reaction from the assembly but no applause.

'And we add this,' Constantius went on. 'Everyone here will recall that out of Christian charity, while standing on the very battlefield of Mursa littered with more than fifty thousand bodies, all of them soldiers of our Empire, we offered amnesty to any rebels not directly responsible for our brother Constans' brutal murder.'

The answer to this was much dutiful clapping.

I had seen this clemency on the battlefield for myself, although I would have phrased it differently. After the suicidal debacle at Mursa, Constantius had extended a blanket amnesty to the Roman Army of the West out of justifiable terror of losing the Empire altogether. Without the survivors of both sides rejoined into one fighting force, no one would be left to defend Roma against the upgraded Persian forces of the Sassanid monarch, Shapur II.

Of course, on a night like tonight, Christian charity sounded much better than military commonsense.

Catena shifted and scraped the precious mosaic floor with his hobnailed marching boots.

'These traitors deserve their punishment, *Imperator*, particularly one Titus Gerontius Severus who rode with the notorious Gaiso to assassinate Emperor Constans at the foot of the temple named after your own grandmother Helena. I tracked him up the eastern coast of Britannia all the way to Camulodunum.'

'Which one is the man?'

Catena yanked Titus by his chains from the center of the crowd, dragging forward his five cowering companions by force.

'This one, *Imperator*.' Catena gestured his lieutenants to unshackle Titus. I could see the onlookers' revulsion at Titus' pitiable condition, all the more visible now that he was isolated from the mass of pustulous, bleeding companions.

The lieutenants threw Titus down, sending him sprawling across depictions of Christ and his Apostles pieced in mica and gems into the floor.

'Did you ride with Gaiso to Vicus Helena?'

Titus lay silent, panting with fear and exhaustion, as the Emperor waited.

'Speak up, Citizen.'

Instead Titus started coughing, expelling blood onto the mosaic. I realized now that Titus was more than just enfeebled by his long trek from the Britannic sanctuary. He was dying. I sighed and looked down at my insignia for comfort. There was all the less reason for me to risk everything to save a man crossing the threshold of death.

Titus refused to perjure himself but he must hope for a peaceful end. He had seen enough of Catena's methods. He knew confession might bring a kinder demise. Why not confess?

'I can make him talk and with his account, you will at last have the truth.'

At that, Catena drew his sword and made a long, deep cut across Titus' bared calf muscle. The prisoner's leg twitched and spurted more blood all over the glittering floor.

The audience gasped at this action in such a setting and certainly not the gesture itself, for these were spectators hardened by years at the Games. Titus whimpered and tried to move his limb, but it only opened its grievous wound wider.

'You will never walk again. Tell the Emperor what you saw and who was with you, or next, it's an ear.'

21

Titus laid his cheek on the floor, tears streaming from those bleary eyes, but there was great nobility in his silence. One could feel that the Arelatians perceived it.

We waited as Titus trembled on the floor and tried to suppress his coughing. Then I watched with horror as Catena drew his sword back again and sliced off Titus' left ear. He tossed the bloody morsel at the feet of the Emperor. A noblewoman at the front of the assembly cried out. Two others fainted and were supported by stewards out of the reception hall.

At a slight signal, the Empress Eusebia, *Augusta* Helena, and their ladies rose from their seats. With imperious hands, they pulled their weighty robes clear of any more flying butcheries. They departed by a private exit curtained out of our sight.

The partygoers had come for a celebration, no matter how unfestive under the heavy eyes of their Emperor, but they came with an appetite for good eating and drinking, not the torture of an aristocrat. I thought of Titus' respectable clan back in Roma and its long line—all destroyed by his political favoritism for the barbarian reformer who failed to keep the West. Somewhere in the former capital stood the Gerontius townhouse, its garden atrium lined with ancestral masks and protective pillars topped by the *Lares*, their house gods. That house and all the clan estates sat abandoned now to the depredations of scavengers, political opportunists, and real estate speculators.

Titus looked up in his agony. His glance found my staring eyes. He nodded almost imperceptibly, as if I would understand, and then it occurred to me that Titus' silence was more than noble pride. Was he protecting *me*? After all, I was Constans' true assassin. Merely on instinct and training had I defended the leader of our arrest party, the Lieutenant Commander Gaiso from Constans' lurching ambush, but I was still his killer.

It was a terrible realization and if true, I couldn't let Gerontius lie there to be dismembered as a grotesque 'party turn' any longer. As the bastard son of Commander Atticus Manlius Gregorius, I was only one-quarter Roman aristocracy but I had enough nobility to recognize it in Titus' silence. And the other half of my blood was that of a Numidian ex-slave—not quite so strict with the truth. I could not let Gerontius' sacrifice go unanswered, but from me, it was going to demand a much bigger lie, a dangerous lie, to save him further mutilation and humiliation.

'I request permission to speak,' I whispered to Ahenobarbus.

'I advise against it, Numidianus.'

'I can't let this proceed.'

'Stay silent. We *agentes* are unpopular enough.'

'If so, then there's nothing to lose.'

Thus, within a few seconds of my impulse, I heard myself announced as a material witness to Catena's charade of an 'interrogation.'

I touched my sword in military salutation.

'I was present at the Temple of Helena on that day, *Imperator*, commanded by Gaiso to facilitate the journey to arrest and bring the Emperor Constans before General Magnentius. I was the *agens in rebus* in charge of carrying the licenses for use of the *Cursus Publicus* and all state services for the military party.'

The Emperor turned slightly to regard me, but only an inch, with that stiff neck moving his whole head as if he were one single block of stone.

'Yes, you are Numidianus, the African agent, the Manlius' freeman. We recall that in the aftermath of Mursa, you were accused by Paulus Catena of the very murder itself, but cleared of that charge by our trusted general, Claudius Silvanus.'

'I was. Now I must bear witness that this Titus took orders from his superior officers as a loyal soldier of the Empire, but that he had nothing to do with the murder of your unfortunate brother. He should not be in chains at all, much less tortured for sport. Your amnesty, in all its Christian kindness, should be applied to the case of this honorable citizen.'

Catena glared at me. I could not retreat.

'I rode with Gaiso. I witnessed the death of Emperor Constans. I do not recall the presence of Titus Gerontius Severus.'

That was strangely true in a way that did me no credit. I'd ridden within a few feet of the skilled boar hunter Gaiso with little care for the cavalry detachment that rode behind us. I had exchanged no words with Titus on that determined chase. Between meals eaten in the saddle and hard galloping along the earthen track running alongside the paved southbound state road, I'd wasted no precious time in conversing with men more experienced than myself.

Today, Titus had not denied being there and I'd jumped to the conclusion therefore that he was guilty. Yet, now I could not remember seeing him with us and in that sense, I was sticking to a kind of truth. My own confusion about his role emboldened my defense.

Croaking with frustration at my intervention, Catena retorted, 'And I maintain, *slave-boy*, that you may not recall this man riding in your company because you were too busy running your own sword through the Emperor Constans to notice anyone else.'

I saw Constantius heave a weary sigh, but it only provoked Catena to continue.

'We still have only the word of the absent and possibly *absent-minded* General Silvanus to counter reports I received within weeks of the Emperor Constans' murder.'

There was a murmur of appreciation from an audience who loved a good rhetorical flourish. They were in danger of giving their favor to Catena merely for his cheap turn of phrase. I was now in personal danger.

Constantius shifted very slightly in his chair. The ill-fated Gaiso had died in the churned-up mud of the Mursa plains. His death had cheated the last son of Constantine of any public retribution. No one knew how much the cold breast of Constantius had ever harbored real affection for his dissolute youngest brother, but pinning the guilt back on me would finally bring this imperial story to a more visceral and satisfying end for the chroniclers of his reign.

I had to fight back.

'Your reputation, Paulus Catena, arrives before you and lingers in bitterness long after you leave.' I turned to the recoiling guests. 'Why is this man nicknamed "The Chain?" I will tell you.'

Declaiming to the Emperor himself was well beyond my rhetorical experience. Slaves were trained in silence, observation, and discretion. *Agentes* were schooled in interrogation, surveillance, agility, stamina, and strength. Nobody expected an *agens* to decorate the entertainment of an imperial celebration by making speeches. But I'd dug myself in too deeply now to wriggle back to safety behind the minor officers watching me with open mouths. Aghast at my folly, Ahenobarbus was staring at me with dismay.

I spread my hands in imitation of the great Cicero himself. As a child, I'd spent long hours reading speeches to the blind patriarch of the Manlius household. The Senator had loved to hear my high and childish voice imitate the elocution of his beloved 'Consul Chickpea.'

'The chain, of course, refers to Catena's habit of dragging his captives and suspects such as these before you in chains. It's the sort of recreation better suited to a common warden of the imperial jails, not the sort of taste usually linked with a state notary, no matter how elevated.'

Catena shifted from one boot to the other, not sure whether he enjoyed his notoriety and cruelty publicized in such a venue.

'Catena is skilled in questioning people under duress. He always seeks answers,' I risked a smile, 'but rarely the truth. Might I remind the Emperor of reports from our Britannic colonies, reports that this Catena's campaign of terror swept up hundreds of *innocent* colonists? His ferocious and unjust purge, according to independent accounts, outraged the *Vicarious* of Britannia, a man whose loyalty to your reign, *Imperator*, was doubted by not a single citizen. Catena's rampaging bloodlust provoked this deputy, one Flavius Martinus, to threaten his own resignation in protest. But Paulus Catena refused to listen to reason and desist. Worse, in a sort of frenzy, he tried to silence Martinus by falsely accusing him and all of Roma's senior officers stationed across Britannia of treason. In desperation, the respected Martinus attacked Catena with his sword but thanks to his handy lieutenants here, his attack failed. The despairing *vicarius* then committed suicide.'

I turned away from the Emperor to confront the brutish notary. 'Do you deny these reports, Paulus Catena?'

I was playing to the crowd in the cheapest fashion. It was a dangerous gambit. Hearing my unexpected accusation, the partygoers' questioning reactions rushed at me from all sides of the reception hall like those river waves that had lapped at my boots only hours before. Their curiosity buoyed me a little through my trembling.

I was risking that Constantius, preoccupied with incursions over the Rhenus border and the eastern frontiers, had *not* read such detailed reports from Britannia relayed to him by our *schola* in Roma. But even then, no emperor could afford to admit ignorance in public. I myself had pored over these reports in my search for any clues to Kahina's fate. Instead, I had discovered tales of Catena's wanton irresponsibility and barbaric reprisals.

Until tonight, Catena's one-man devastation of Britannia had been my private ammunition to use. Now it was spent. Had I hit the target?

'May I continue, *Imperator*?'

The heavy head gave me a slow, single nod.

'Paulus Catena, is your nickname not also a reference to the chain of lies, unfounded accusations, and whole nets woven of falsehoods that you twist around the innocent to lengthen your so-called "traitor lists?" These are chains with chinks and many of the links are weak. Even among those mercifully free of his physical abuses, Catena's campaign of recrimination has been destroying Roma's noble reputation across the entire island of Britannia. He has sown bitter resentment in innocent men and women who lost their land and lives under his tortures. Such resentments spread political instability and nothing has roiled the reign of the House of Constantine more than internal unrest. I conclude my statement tonight only by urging that the sacrifice of *Vicarius* Flavius Martinus made in protest of Catena's crimes not go unrecorded by the citizens of Arelate and of our entire great Empire.'

I staggered a little, slightly shocked by my own performance. I knew the late Senator Manlius would have been proud of me.

He would have risen to his feet and cheered my eloquence, but no one applauded me tonight. Hundreds of gaudy shocked faces gaped at me standing there alone before the Emperor.

'He speaks the truth, great Constantius,' a bedraggled woman shouted from the front ranks of prisoners. 'Yes, some of us followed the Usurper Magnentius. We paid with our land and our families' reputations. But hundreds of Roman colonists who aided us, fed and sheltered us in our flight across Britannia, did so not out of love for Magnentius, but out of desire to heal the wounds of the Empire.'

She emboldened a woman chained to her who raised her own voice. 'Some of those Romans had never heard of Magnentius, *Imperator*, apart from seeing his profile on the coins issued from this very city. Where is the justice when this brute Catena tortures and kills those good and innocent Romans of the north while the people of Arelate who minted those very coins dress up and dine tonight off your imperial plate?'

Catena grabbed a whip from one of his lieutenants. He lashed its sharp tail straight across the faces of the two protesting women.

Constantius leaned his head back into his high, stiff collar and rested against the low back of the carved *cathedra*. He said nothing. His imposing silence emanated from his dais as if he had sent forth an invisible rank of sentries to caution the guests, group by group, even as far as the most distant cluster at the back of the room.

The partygoers turned as rigid as their ruler. The celebration itself, if it had ever got underway, was well and truly over now. For Arelate was one of the Western Empire's most prominent centers of coin production and distribution. The imperial mint managers who had overseen the striking and pressing of those Magnentius gold *solidi* were sure to be present tonight, standing in their bleached tunics and festive garlands only yards from where the prisoners crouched and cowered.

'We desire an end to all recriminations,' Constantius said at last. 'We thank you for your anniversary gift, Paulus Catena, and for the loyalty which prompts *us all*.'

His eyes came to rest on me. He lifted a right hand laden with rings. 'Now release these prisoners to what homes and families remain to them.'

The Emperor rose to his full height, not as tall as his father but imposing enough, and disappeared through the private imperial exit.

He did not seem to have had a good time at his anniversary party.

His most senior councilors followed him out. Though Ahenobarbus gestured that he wanted a word with me, I shook him off with a feeble excuse and made for the fresh air of the forum as quickly as I could.

⚖⚖⚖

When the moon was well up in the sky, I searched for Titus among the former prisoners. I found the largest group of them huddling close together outside the Arelate walls, eager to evade any more of Catena's impulses. They had limped as far as they could on what little scraps they'd got begging on their progress toward the gates.

I was glad to see that some Arelatians had shown enough kindness to hand them old blankets, fresh water, and some cooked food scraps. Perhaps Constantius' oddly cold compassion had inspired some Christianity after all. I rather suspect that rumors of the woman prisoner's accusation about the city mint had travelled through town and struck a chord of guilt.

Along with a few others too weak to walk unaided, Titus had been carried on a makeshift litter and laid close to the riverbank. I knelt at his side. A middle-aged fellow-prisoner was bathing his wounded ear hole with acetum. As she worked, he grimaced but suppressed all cries of pain. His leg was already bandaged but it was obvious that Titus would never need to walk again. If Charon, that mythical porter carrying the dead across the River Styx, had beached his boat on the shore a few feet from where I knelt, I would not have been surprised to hear him call Titus Gerontius Severus' name for the next crossing to the Underworld.

'I must ask you some questions, Titus. I beg you to tell me whatever you can.'

'Yes,' he rasped.

'Did you see the wife of Commander Atticus Manlius Gregorius among the refugees?'

'I think I did once, among the refugee ladies from Aquileia.'

My breath leapt into my mouth. 'Was she wounded or hurt?'

'Neither, but very worn and hungry.'

'Where is she now?'

'I don't know. I am so cold, Numidianus.'

I fetched more cloaks to spread over the trembling tribune.

'When did you see her last?'

'Who?'

'*Domina* Kahina.'

'I heard Catena seized her, along with other relatives of the leadership hidden by villagers outside Londinium. But it was only a whisper of a rumor, nothing more.'

So Catena had got his hands on gentle Kahina. It was the nightmare that had haunted me now for months.

'What else can you tell me?'

'Let him rest,' the woman tending him scolded me.

'Catena . . .'

'Catena what, Titus? Tell me!'

'If the prisoners have any strength or beauty left, he sells them for cash. That's why all you see here are the residue, the useless ones. He sends the men to a dealer for castration and slavery in the East and the women—'

'Sells where? To whom?' I wanted to shake him, but his pupils were rolling back into their sockets.

'To a middleman.'

'But that's illegal for a court official, even Catena, to sell citizens without trial into slavery! He must have help.'

'Yes, I heard him tell a lieutenant on the journey . . . once . . . an officer in the East . . .'

'What officer? What about an officer?' I grabbed my neck cord and untied the knot to remove one of Marcellinus' rings. I pressed it into Titus' skeletal hand. 'This ring should be enough to pay for your medical care, your transport home, and a new life. *Live*, Titus, so that we can meet again.'

He clutched the ring and smiled his thanks. 'You mean to pay for my honorable burial and plaque, I think.' Then his fingers fell open and dropped the ring back on my knees. 'Keep it. I won't need a burial ceremony. There's no one left to mourn me.'

I pocketed the offering with reluctance. I sat with him until the end. His companions tied his corpse to a boulder and we rolled it into the Rhodanus. Some of the Christian cultists among them said prayers.

'Marcus Gregorianus Numidianus?'

It was one of the most junior recruits to our *schola*, a young man just out of training who worked at the porter's gate of the Arelate palace. He was learning the shortcuts to registering letters and the turnaround procedures for the circuit riders. With a grimace, he pulled a packet of expensive vellum out from under his sword belt and pressed it into my hesitant palm.

'Sorry about this, Numidianus.'

It was a summons from the Emperor himself.

CHAPTER 3, THE LONELIEST THRONE

—THE EMPEROR'S PRIVATE OFFICE—

Since the horrible events at Mursa, I had not enjoyed one single good night's sleep. I never told others about the dreams that sent me covered in cold sweat bolting upright on my pallet. I tried rinsing my face in a basin and returning to bed but again and again the bloody fingers and detached heads kept calling to me and there I was carrying the fatally wounded Commander in my arms toward the medical triage tents that seemed to retreat farther away from us with each painful step.

When I woke up, my arms were empty and my heart was full.

At least I had not been sent off to Persia like some survivors. As an *agens*, I was not a soldier nor exposed to Constantius' 'Persian cure' for the legions that had fought against his forces. But even among those of us who had escaped reassignment to the dangerous Eastern front, the scars of Mursa persisted. I even heard talk among the *agentes* back at the Castra in Roma of suicides by Mursa survivors or inexplicable deaths of happily married veterans who had returned from the horrors of Pannonia to be found one day hanging by a rope in their barracks or plunged on their own sword.

Sometimes I gave up on sleep and read Virgil until daybreak. Other nights I strolled through empty streets listening to the silence of the citizenry at rest.

The night of Titus' death I tossed, as restless as ever, but with more reason. The man who sat closest on this earth to his

Christian God had summoned me by name. It couldn't be a good omen. I didn't sleep that night at all, knowing that at the next morning's *prima* hour, I should be standing outside Constantius' private office, an innermost sanctum I'd never imagined breaching before.

More than once during my night of staring at the ceiling, I considered using the jewels hanging around my neck to buy myself passage on the last boat of the autumn season heading down the Rhodanus out of Gallia and straight back to the North African plateau. I had once passed myself off as a seasonal olive harvester in order to spy for the endangered Empire. I could easily do it again to save my own neck.

An hour before dawn, I hadn't convinced myself that I had the courage to run. It would mean abandoning not only my *schola*, but also all hope of protecting the honor of the Manlius House and its heir Leo. Was a life in disgrace worth living?

The fuchsia dawn lined the eastern horizon. The glowing disk of the new day, as blood-red as a pagan's ritual offering, followed. I shaved, washed and put on my cleanest tunic shirt, straightened my riding trousers, rubbed down my boots and buckled on my sword belt. After a feverish night of imagining journeys south, north and east, it seemed I was going to keep my appointment with the Emperor after all.

It was what a Manlius—even a bastard Manlius—expected of himself. And I admit I was curious to see how the man who reigned over the known world actually conducted his working dawn.

On his hunting tours from the courts of Mediolanum to Treverorum, the younger emperor Constans had never even glanced at paper work. State treasure was for his spending, not budgeting. Soldiers were for escorting him, not him leading them. And prisoners-of-war were for buggering or in his case, vice-versa. He had started his reign off well, but eventually had eyes only for the attractions of his German prisoners, tall blond archers who accommodated his tastes with contempt and vigor. The disgust and professional indignation of the imperial army had overflown the goblet of loyalty and ended in his downfall.

Mornings with Magnentius had been more routine. In the rebel court of the Usurper, I'd personally collected the barbarian general's dispatches and then funneled them, sealed, and marked 'urgent, state business' straight into the imperial postal system in the safety of a high-speed relay rider's pouch. Of course, before sending, I read most of the supreme soldier's blunt and practical directives on the sly. I made coded notes for my own superior, Apodemius, who was monitoring the divided Empire back in the *agentes'* headquarters, the Castra Peregrina, in Roma.

If the self-proclaimed barbarian emperor guessed I spied on him each morning, he didn't seem to care. Perhaps the rough field commander in him hoped that my channel of intelligence would check the ambitions of the manipulative sponsor behind his throne—a formidable Gallic nobleman and the new *magister officiorum*, one Marcellinus.

At least Magnentius and Marcellinus had been made of flesh and blood. Marcellinus' salvaged rings around my neck reminded me of mortality and ephemeral power every day.

Constantius II was my third emperor and unlike the other two, he seemed carved from granite. Perhaps that's why he was the last man holding the Empire together. Even when travelling in the West, he was a sovereign styled in the Eastern mold. Hierarchy, ceremony, Arianism, and above all, bureaucracy ruled him as much as he ruled others. His private secretaries, always standing in his presence, prepared his letters and public orders with tight-lipped formality. They handed these documents addressed, sealed, tied, and resealed to the Master of Offices for registration by Ahenobarbus, as imperial protocol dictated.

No matter where he worked, Constantius saw enemies in the woodwork, the braziers, and the wall hangings. I knew Ahenobarbus had a Hades' time of it getting information extracted back out of these packets wrapped in everything short of imperial armor for the use of our own master Apodemius. I assisted Ahenobarbus often, melting down imperial wax seals, copying secret dispatches and personal letters, before resealing the packets for posting off. We carried out such espionage well clear of Constantius' wing.

In short, there could be no good reason for me to penetrate the inner sanctum of worldly power. The only explanation must be that Catena had gotten to the Emperor later in the evening and produced more evidence that I was the long-sought-after assassin of the Emperor's brother Constans.

As I waited for clearance past one palatine guard after another, the corridors grew narrower, the rooms more sumptuous, and my nervous heart more constricted. I envisioned Catena enduring weeks of marching those embittered, diseased prisoners southward through Gallia and driving them harder with each mile to arrive in Arelate in time for last night's anniversary reception. Then, instead of winning laurels for his grueling devotion, he'd heard himself exposed for turning a whole Roman province against the throne.

I was stupid and vain. I'd let that surge of truth-telling inflate into a bombastic imitation of senatorial oratory. My recruiter back in North Africa had warned me against showing off in front of the wrong people. It was useful for a slave to have read an entire library out loud to a blind Senator, but if that slave couldn't keep his mouth shut, his education was no use for working undercover.

The Emperor received me after I had spent half an hour fighting my nerves outside his door. I bowed low and kissed the hem of his robe and removed myself to kneel at the foot of his dais.

'We don't have much time,' he said, ignoring my salutation. 'We recall you were at Mursa and carried important messages of negotiation to the rebel camp.'

'It was my privilege, *Imperator*.'

'You served at the court of the Tyrant on the orders of your *schola*?'

'I graduated from riding the Sirmium route in the *equites* class to reach *Circitor Upper Class*, running communications and traffic in the court at Treverorum. After that I was reassigned to Aquileia on the orders of my superiors and promoted to *biarchus* for services during the events at Mursa.'

I avoided naming Magnentius.

'Do you always follow orders, Numidianus?'

'Yes, *Imperator*. I am a loyal servant of the Empire, first and last.'

'Something we have in common. Then who ordered you to speak out last night against all custom and protocol? Ahenobarbus?'

'On the contrary. As my superior, he advised silence.'

'Then sometimes you do disobey.'

'My conscience did not permit silence.'

'So you say.'

Constantius betrayed nothing. His expression was as ungiving as those masks poured from molten gold or silver and then attached to fancy parade helmets. Such disguises transformed cavalry officers into attendants worthy of the gods— cruel, humorless, and omniscient. In the last, I was not far wrong.

'One of our secretaries has provided us with the registration file sent from the *schola* on the occasion of your attachment to this court. You are from Numidia Militaris, once a slave owned by the Manlius clan in Roma, and manumitted from *voluntarius* status after a successful reconnaissance mission to suppress the Donatist schismatics. Are we correct?'

'Yes, *Imperator*. I was serving as the private bodyguard to the wounded commander Atticus Manlius Gregorius before my liberation and subsequent recruitment to the Castra Peregrina.'

'Which is why Paulus Catena refers to you as "slave-boy"?'

'Catena and I both suffer nicknames, *Imperator*. We both serve the Empire. But apart from crossing paths in Treverorum and Sirmium in the course of our duties, that is *all* he and I have in common.'

One imperial eyebrow lifted, cracking the perfect visage for an instant. The Emperor turned that implacable head to the secretary scribbling in shorthand at a rostrum to the right of his long gilt table.

'We also have—where is it? Yes, here we have from your file a report on your discreet assistance to the Lord Chamberlain Eusebius during the civil war.'

'Yes, *Imperator*,' I whispered.

My heart sank past my scabbard to my boots. Constantius was referring to a mountain of *dis*information that our spymaster Apodemius had sent in my name to the powerful eunuch in the East over the course of nearly six months. I'd escaped Catena's tortures in Sirmium with Eusebius' help. In exchange, Eusebius had asked me to spy on my own service. By writing these memos to the eunuch over my signature, Apodemius had seen an opportunity to control the intelligence flow but read the wrong way this morning, exposure of that deception could mark me a traitor. It was a risk Apodemius had taken on my behalf with glee.

So soon I would be exposed as disloyal as well as disobedient.

'The Lord Chamberlain is in Antiochia now, advising the Caesar Flavius Claudius Constantius Gallus. Eusebius reports that Gallus is learning the ways of statecraft quickly and that our subjects love him. We hold the Lord Chamberlain's opinion in high regard.'

'As do we all, *Imperator*.'

At this point did more lies matter? In fact, Eusebius was a crafty, oily practioner of intrigue who accumulated other people's land, bribes, and secrets like society ladies collected Christian charity causes and scent bottles.

Eusebius also collected scent bottles.

A steward approached and murmured, 'Paulus Catena is waiting outside, *Domine*.'

'We'll need him shortly,' Constantius said.

I braced myself. So, the 'reward' for my defending Titus was to be administered by one of the most sadistic men I'd ever met. If it came to it, I was prepared to die honorably, but not slowly. It was best I used these last minutes well. I would drop to my knees and beg the Emperor for the immeasurable honor of a swift execution at his own hand. A death that was good enough for his imperial uncles and cousins was certainly better than anything Catena had devised for me.

'You spoke out of conviction last night?'

'I did, *Imperator*. And I am prepared to die for the truth, just as Vicarius Martinus died.'

Constantius curled the corners of my file papers with a manicured finger. 'Do you know a certain Lieutenant Barbatio? Served with him in Numidia, I believe?'

I nodded, almost too startled to speak. 'Uh . . . yes, yes. We served in the *Legio III Augusta*.'

'You see, we have a problem, *Agens*.' That immaculate finger tapped the marble table. 'We suffer from a question of trust.'

There was a long pause, perhaps worse for me than for Catena waiting in the corridor to dig his three-pronged steel claws into my flesh.

'Our sister, the *Augusta* Constantia, also sends us lavish praise of her young husband.'

He muttered, almost more to himself than to any of us waiting to do him service. 'Do we believe our sister? She holds us responsible for the death of her first husband. She'll probably teach Gallus to hate us, too, but at least they're both family. While we rule, they rule.'

'May your wise rule be eternal, *Imperator*.'

Constantius ignored my whimpering flattery.

I felt my bowels shift with fear as I heard Catena's impatient conversation with the guard echo off the tiles outside. I closed my eyes and remembered Titus on the floor the previous night. Catena would not start with my ears.

'But we hear other stories that are not so reassuring . . . from the Captain of the Palace Guards in Antiochia—none other than this Barbatio. His reports are full of incredible stories, perhaps because he wants General Ursicinus, our *Magister Equitum* based in Nisibis, and not the Caesar Gallus, to administer the East. Ursicinus has crushed a Jewish rebellion in Diocesarea, Palaestina to our great satisfaction but perhaps the General overestimates our gratitude.'

Barbatio had never been the brightest of officers. To imagine him plotting with a powerful general did him almost too much credit.

'Please, don't look surprised, Numidianus. We are not. Oh, we get letters from Ursicinus, too, and from another man, of high repute and lesser self-interest. They are saying that Syria is roiled with discontent, hunger, and scandal. They are suggesting that our cousin Gallus is a complete failure as Caesar.'

Bewildered by the Emperor's digression, I glanced around at the scribes and stewards attending this audience. Their faces remained impassive. If I hadn't seen the senior scribe's *stilus* working away, I would have thought them all, he included, stone deaf to Constantius' extraordinary confidences.

Constantius went on, gazing hard at a large polished pillar to his right. 'If we were to listen to our Empress Eusebia, it seems that the only man in the Empire we should trust is a man we've never met. He's in Roma. Of course, we have no wish to ever visit that sickly, rotten place, clinging to its pagan ways and outmoded prejudices. Why honor it with our presence?'

I remained on my knees, my head bowed and my heart unsure how long my little breathing time might last. The Emperor shuffled through my file. He drew out another vellum order, sealed and ominous-looking.

This was it.

'So Marcus Gregorianus Numidianus, we cannot spare *Agens* Ahenobarbus from his duties. He's essential to the chain of communications here and he'll move with us on our northern campaign against the Alemanni. We want you to carry this letter to that man in Roma and guarantee that no one, we repeat, no one *including yourself*, reads its contents. We know the games you *agentes* play but I believe you are a singular man of conscience. In this case, you will deliver our message personally, you will wait while this man reads it, and then you will personally ensure its destruction at his hands. No copies will be made and no registration recorded.'

I'm sure my eyes were as round as that pillar. I rose to my feet, keeping my head still lowered in submission. Stumbling forward, I kissed the purple hem of his cloak. I was afraid this hard man would see the tears of relief welling up and read my inner guilt.

'If his reputation serves him well, your *magister* in Roma will know what to do, leaving us free to concentrate on pushing the barbarians back into their mountain caves.'

With a wave of his hand, he indicated a side exit where a sentry stood poised to escort me from his divine presence.

'Take that door. If we were you, we would not seek the company of Paulus Catena again.'

'Thank you, *Imperator*. I am overwhelmed by the honor you do me.'

'We're already running late,' he sighed to his senior scribe. To my astonishment, he actually shook his head very slightly from side to side. 'There is no time. There is never enough time.'

That night I left Arelate for Roma, travelling by the fastest horse in our relay stable. I stopped for meals and fresh mounts in Forum Julii, Genua, and Pisae. Then I stormed down the coast straight for the former capital.

I arrived at last at the Porta Aurelia. I was unshaven, exhausted, and red-eyed from road dust but giddy with the fresh sea air filling my lungs with freedom. The Emperor's packet was safe inside my shirt. For once in my career as a trusted *agens*, I actually hadn't peeked at the contents.

Well, at least not yet.

CHAPTER 4, COLLECTING RUBBISH

—THE TAVERN AT THE PORTA AURELIA—

For as long as I'd been returning home to Roma from missions abroad, Verus had never been late to our rendezvous point, not once, whatever the day or the gate. If I were coming from the northeast, the old *dispensator* of the Manlius townhouse would be waiting on bustling Via Nomentana and trying to resist the attractions of the *Taberna Porta Collina* until I arrived to pick up the tab.

If I were arriving from the northwest, he would wait for me at a drinking spot near the Porta Aurelia. That's where I registered my presence in Roma today, as every *agens* was required by law to do on entering or exiting the city. The formalities done with, I hastened on to the Tavern of the Seven Sages.

But Verus was nowhere in sight.

I'd quenched my thirst with some good wine and forestalled ordering a second round, hoping for the old man to appear. I couldn't wait forever. After all, I had an emperor's letter to deliver. People were snacking at food stalls all around me or already digesting their meal in the midday sun. The drunks were sunk into the cocoons of the vendors' awnings overhead, trusting their safety to rickety poles staked into the hard-packed street.

I finally gave in to the second drink. Verus had yet to show his wrinkled face with its winking eyes. With the coming of autumn, the clocks were moving from 'summer hours' to the shorter 'winter hours', but however you timed it, he was more than an hour overdue.

I greeted a few riders breathless and dusty from the road just like myself and finally retreated with my cup to a small table in the far corner. From there I might spot Verus amidst all the bustling serving girls and raucous customers. The noise was deafening as travelers, tourists, and traders exchanged road tales that got taller with each round.

I admit I was worried. The Manlius *domus*, once bustling with reputation, rigor, and riches, had shrunk to an aristocratic shell presided over by the Commander's nephew-by-marriage, a louche and venal character named Clodius.

Only the levelheaded Verus was on the job to keep order for the child Leo until Kahina could be found and returned to her rightful place as matron.

'Numidianus! It's been a long time!'

A hearty man slapped me on the back and threw himself down on the empty stool opposite. He smelt of leather, sweat, stew, and sex. He was a decurion with the *Ioviani* I'd known during the war. I suspected he'd just come from the brothel next door where the good-natured girls were partial to couriers and soldiers . . . and everyone else.

'Cornelius? A welcome sight! I'm glad to see you here! You survived to screw again?'

Cornelius looked a shabby echo of his pre-civil war self. His sword belt was shiny with years of wear. A clumsy needle had stitched secondhand trim of frayed embroidery to his tunic sleeves with mismatched thread.

He seemed as energetic as ever. 'Forty years old next year and still up to it! And making up for lost time, right, Delicia?'

The waitress brought us some snacks and dodged his pawing grasp with a tolerant wink.

'It was a stupid war, Marcus. I'm not sorry it's over. I've got one more year until retirement—my pension, my bonus, the officers' association payout, the funeral fund allowance—and with all that you can bet I'll cut a fine figure back home.'

He leaned across the table. 'Don't be surprised if you read about a town councilor named Cornelius before too long!'

'The Emperor's amnesty was kind to some.'

'That eunuch-lover had no choice. Could he imprison the entire Western Army for desertion and still see off the Persians?'

'All right, then, the *Fates* were kind to many and you deserve it.'

I thought of Commander Gregorius dragging himself bound to sword and shield through the gore-strewn mud until he died in my arms. The Fates had been cruel to some far nobler than Cornelius.

'Have a drink on me.' I signaled Delicia to refill our cups—diluted wine for me, full strength for Cornelius. 'Do you see many others on leave?'

'Some leftovers of the *Herculiani* . . . I cross paths with some of the Mursa survivors from the *Ioviani* when I come to town. I exchange a coin for a word of thanks with the wounded that beg down in the Subura.'

'Poor devils.'

Cornelius shuddered. 'To live without a leg or a hand? I'd fall on my sword first but the city's so crowded now with foreigners and war refugees, where would I land?'

'Where to next?'

'Those Alpine brutes Gundomadus and Vadomarius have moved down off their mountains and cut off our main transport arteries. Now they're grabbing good land. Unless Constantius does something about it fast, they'll keep it.'

'And you're going to help them back up the mountainside?'

'To their crags where they can go back to doing it with goats! Come here, girl, give me a cuddle.'

Cornelius was popular with the ladies, low and highborn alike. Certainly he was always practicing his skills. Perhaps I rolled my eyes at his vulgarity, because he protested, 'Come on, Marcus, you know the saying, "Every soldier is a lover"?'

I laughed despite myself. 'Ovid said every *lover* is a *soldier*.'

Cornelius shrugged off my pedantry. 'I leave the books to you. Either way, I conquer you every time, don't I, my squealing, sighing little Delicia?'

He gave the serving girl a violent squeeze and a brass coin from his pouch. He relinquished her back to her duties only after extracting a promise of an hour with him later. They would frolic on her alcove bed out back without so much as a curtain to shelter her modesty.

'I have a soft spot for this old bull,' Delicia explained. She laughed as she lifted the hem of her tunic just a little to flirt with me. 'He always remembers my name. Are you as considerate?'

'No woman for you, Marcus?'

'Cornelius, you know I like women as much as you do. I'm searching for one now, the widow of my former commander, Gregorius. Remember them?'

His hand shot up to cover one eye in a reference to the Commander's empty socket.

'I remember him all right but I remember her better. The graceful *Domina* Kahina with a North African accent on her lips, just like yours, and a desert girl's lilt to her hips. I saw her once in attendance at the court of Magnentius when we reported for duty in the south.'

It would seem prudish to scold him for taking liberties, so I just nodded. Through no fault of her own, the humbly born Kahina had risen high in the Roman world and now fallen just as far. Ribaldry at her expense from a goodhearted soldier was the least of the insults she might be suffering now.

'Cornelius, listen. I heard there was some kind of slave trade run by an officer hiving off the best prisoners from Magnentius' refugees for private sale.'

'You and I both know you're talking about Paul the Chain.'

'Do you know where he sends them? Who handles the traffic? There's a middleman, but I heard the man who decides their final destiny is an army officer in the East.'

'Don't you people have lines of inquiry?'

'The army knows its own best.'

Delicia brushed past just then, whispering, 'It's a busy afternoon.'

Cornelius wasn't missing his opportunity with the girl. 'I'll ask around.'

He was good company. With regret I watched him head off to Delicia's charms but at that very moment, Verus finally appeared. He was lugging a travel bag and panting hard as he tossed it under the table on the floor and looked in all directions.

'Isn't my lady here?'

When I said Kahina hadn't returned with me from Arelate, that yet again she had not surfaced among the miserable prisoners, the old servant forgot himself and burst into tears. He'd been waiting many long months now and trying to hold things together until her return. Sobbing with disappointment, the poor fellow reached under the table and loosened his leather sack.

I looked inside and saw Kahina's brush, gold combs, a silk *tunica*, an embroidered blue *stola*, and a soft woolen *palla* to warm herself in the autumnal evening chill. He'd also brought her inlaid toilet box full of vials and clever silver tools for plucking, pinning, and curling. From the bottom he fished out a pair of sandals he'd bought for her with his own savings, 'So that my mistress would be able to hold up her head in style as she rode home, not like some of these refugees I've seen who skulk back in bloodied rags and all.'

He had mustered this toilet bag for her behind Clodius' back after accompanying the busy socialite to the home of a patron. We were expected now to return to the *Domus* Picenus to collect Clodius from his afternoon's call.

'He's nothing more than rubbish,' I blurted out. 'Why can't the creep get home on his own?'

'Gracious, Marcus, you still ain't no man of fashion, for all your travels! No one moves through the streets of Roma these days without their house attendants dragging behind them like a bunch of Circus animals, as many as they can pay for—whole armies of'em! That Clodius is constantly making the cook, the gardener, the laundrywoman, the messenger boy and me drop our chores, wash our faces, and put on fancy hand-me-downs to march alongside his litter like a bunch of clowns in one of them Greek farces.'

'He's lost his mind.'

'Well, if he has lost his mind, so has the whole city. Everybody's doing it. They're waitin' for us now, all but tethered up outside Picenus' house.'

'I'm heading straight to headquarters to deliver an urgent packet,' I said. 'You can come with me if you like.'

'I don't mind tagging along. After that, we collect "the rubbish," so to speak, and then you have a treat in store. The little boy's living with us now, finally home from Ostia with his nurse Lavinia.'

I'd scarcely taken in the joy of Verus' last statement when I was plunged into the crowded streets, trotting after the agile old man, to see what changes had come over my childhood city.

We marched at a good clip for the Castra Peregrina waiting atop the Caelian Hill, nestled south of the Palatine and Esquiline Hills. Sticking to the lower elevations we had to cut through some of the busiest intersections of the city.

It gave me a chance to see Roma under the new Prefect Orfitus. The grander byways leading toward the Forum were ankle-deep with refuse and clogged with beggars. Roma's famous water network of sewers, public fountains, and private wells was falling foul to blockages. I could smell the stink rising beneath the soles of my boots.

As we moved southwards toward the fashionable hills of the city, I saw more than one display of the kind Verus described. A society lady in her litter passed us coming down from the Palatine. She waved a white baton in her hand, imitating an army commander directing troops with his sword, only the 'forces' trotting after her were more than a dozen servants and slaves right down to a scullery maid with hands still reddened from the scrubbing board.

As we crossed the Forum itself, so nobly used in ancient times for Republican oratory and Imperial glory, we stumbled into the frantic aftermath of some huge public disturbance. From one end of the Forum to the other, all I saw were overturned vendors' tables, broken *amphorae*, ripped bits of clothing and traces of blood cluttering the grand space. Some forty officers of the Urban Cohort were overseeing a cleanup with the help of firefighting *vigiles*, keen to get any flammable rubbish safely out of the way as soon as possible. Slaves under their direction scampered this way and that, sweeping and lifting the detritus of violence into carts for moving off.

Verus shrugged as we picked our way through the mess. 'They been at it since dawn. There was a big riot last night over wine supplies for the poor.'

'Why isn't there enough wine?'

'Why isn't there enough of anything, Marcus? The countryside is rich enough.' He sneered and pointed at the debris underfoot. 'We was all near famine a few months ago, and it being harvest time, how does that big shot Orfitus account for that, I ask you? They should get after those scoundrels that inherit *annona* tickets and scalp them to the genuine poor. Orfitus may be some hoity-toity lawyer, but he ain't no prefect worth his salt. Some even say he's no better than an embezzler hisself.'

'But you had the farms sending in our supplies, didn't you? You yourself didn't go without?'

'I'm standing here to tell the tale, ain't I? We got deliveries of fruit and meat every week driven in as usual and the cook shared it out as best she could with needy neighbors until that Clodius caught her at it. It broke your heart to see the children's corpses lying there in the market alleys every morning.'

'Why doesn't Orfitus do something about it?'

'Well, he ordered all the foreigners to leave the city, so lots of decent folk got driven away, but you can bet some three thousand dancing girls got their dispensation to stay in town, all right.'

When we reached the Castra, I had a disappointment in store. Apodemius wasn't there to receive the Emperor's letter. I explained to his secretary that I didn't dare trust it to anyone else, on the orders of Constantius himself. The secretary gave me an appointment with the old man for midnight.

Verus and I kept going now, dipping back down through the crowds and then climbing again, leaving the begging and hawking hordes behind us. We ascended the steep, tree-shaded streets that led up to the Picenus house on the Esquiline, not too many streets from the Manlius house.

The meager collection of Manlius servants crouching in the shade of dusk heaved a visible sigh of relief as we strode into view of the gated entrance. Some thin music, only a couple of lyres and a single flute, toiled away behind Picenus' walls. I was hungry now and hoped that the banquet table held some scraps for a latecomer, even one wearing the *agens* insignia that always opened doors, but rarely prompted a sincere welcome. I didn't expect any warm hellos.

How wrong I was.

'Marcus Gregorianus Numidianus, my true friend. You're looking a little thin, but you're safe!'

A refined young woman addressed me, her quiet assurance cutting right through the frivolous hubbub. She stood there, still slight but more regal than ever, smiling up at me. If custom had permitted the embrace of a society noblewoman by a freedman-turned-*agens*, I would have swooped her into my arms with relief at her unexpected appearance. There were no salutations in the lexicon of my *schola* that expressed my emotions.

For there, wearing a long gown of cerulean blue linen fixed with precious sapphires at both shoulders, stood Justina, the virgin Empress of the deposed usurper, Emperor Magnentius.

She laughed as she witnessed the disbelieving tears sprouting from my eyes.

In this season of bitter reprisals, I had returned Justina untouched by both husband and politics to Roma with private unease. As a child-bride given by the proud house of Vettius to the 'barbarian' ruler of the West, she had received a vulgar gold wedding ring from the burly general, but seen little of him after that.

Still, there had been no guarantee she would be politically safe in Roma. Her disgraced father had committed suicide on the strength of ambitious dreams that reached Constantius' ears. Her protective brother Cerealis was nowhere in sight.

'Where's *Domina* Kahina?' I asked her. 'Have you had any word since she fled Magnentius' court?'

'Lost to us all. She fled to safety in the north—'

'And might have been sold into slavery in the East.'

Her hand covered her mouth in shock. 'Were they not given sanctuary by friends in Londinium?'

'It seems the long arm of Constantius would not leave them to their exile. Do you know anything useful, anything at all?'

Justina shook her head, and led me along one side of the colonnaded atrium toward a reception room where the raucous sounds of betting could be heard over the rattle of dice. Despite the political winds battering many aristocratic families of the former capital, this was still a beautiful townhouse in the best of taste. We passed a sparkling clean fountain splashing at the center of the garden, neat marble benches in good repair studding the walkways and the wax masks of noble ancestors gazing down from the walls leading beyond the atrium to the dining room and gardens at the back end of the house.

A few late flowers still perfumed the air. I was almost ready to forget all the squalor outside those privileged gates and to believe that, at least here, gracious Roman values of old still survived.

'Do you live here, *Domina* Justina?'

'Not permanently, I suppose, but my mother and brothers fled to the countryside and left me to this uncle-in-law for the winter,' she said.

'Will you remarry?'

She laughed. My question was probably on everyone's lips. 'My prospects are somewhat dimmed, to say the least, by my years as an empress on the wrong side.'

I ignored her wry expression. 'But you were a child, left virgin by all that. Surely the Vettius name still stands in some stead? What's more, you're a Constantine generations back. Isn't that high enough repute for any girl?'

'Just enough to determine that, come the spring, I'm invited to Sirmium to serve as a lady-in-waiting to Marina Severa, the wife of Tribune Valentinian who is fighting the Franks in the north. There are some lingering political ties, you see. His father Gratianus Major gave hospitality to Magnentius in Pannonia.

Constantius confiscated his lands and forced him into retirement in Cibalae as punishment. However, Valentinian broke with his father and now collects his reward. Joining his household will help to restore my good name.'

'A sad end for Gratianus, a former governor of Britannia.'

She laughed a little. 'Not a sadder end for a little girl the oracles once predicted would found a dynasty?'

'Who knows? You're still very young, *Domina* Justina.'

She looked at me over her bejeweled shoulder with a rueful smile. 'We are lucky simply to be alive, Marcus.'

She stopped and turned to face me. 'Why are you here? I hope you don't deliver bad news?' Her sharp query shattered our small talk. She had dramatically improved her imperious tone from the days when her childish orders provoked giggles from her ladies-in-waiting.

'To collect the nephew of the late Commander Gregorius. I believe he's in there, gambling with the other guests.' I now spotted Clodius in the crowd, grimacing from a fresh loss. I pointed him out to Justina.

'Oh, him. He's one of worst of the sycophants who wait for my uncle to die. I can hardly believe there's a blood tie to the upright Gregorius—'

'You are as perceptive as always. Clodius is a nephew of the late *Matrona* Laetitia who was carried off in 347 after a long illness.'

She nodded. 'He's here every day, like so many feckless young men, flattering and fawning over my uncle, hoping for a big handout when the will is read.'

'Is our host suffering from ill health?'

'In his body, but not in his mind, which is where so many of these parasites misjudge their chances.'

Before she could explain further, we arrived on the scene. Half a dozen young men leaned around a dice table and were hooting, booing, or crying out with greedy relief as their fortunes waxed or waned at a toss. Clodius hung back now, merely watching. I guessed he'd lost all his money and was trying to cover his embarrassment by pretending he was just taking a break. He saw me coming through the archway.

'Freedman Marcus! You've come to drag me away from my pleasures!' My appearance offered him a timely excuse out of the game, but he greeted me warmly enough to convince his friends.

'Are we going to lose you now, Clodius?' an old man cried in a dry quaver from the corner of the room.

I saw another cluster of perfumed and coiffured youths part ways so that Clodius could take his leave of an elderly patrician in a simple tunic and indoor cloak reclining against some cushions. This must be Picenus himself, judging by Clodius' belabored farewell, while rivals stood by listening with visible impatience.

'Until tomorrow, illustrious mentor!' Clodius shouted as he followed me back through the atrium and out the front gate. I glanced back at Justina who stood as motionless as a fine statue on the paved walk circling the fountain.

She waved a small hand in farewell.

Our exit was less than graceful. Clodius had drunk too much to proceed out of the gates with a steady gait. Verus offered a discreet arm to lean on. They made an odd pair, one dressed only in a short hemp tunic worn thin with washing, the other gussied up in a set of garments I assumed represented the latest in Roman folderol.

His cloak sported gold-embroidered animals—rabbits, deer, stags, and ferrets—running around the hem. I tried not to laugh as its fringe of tiny tassels caught on the doorframe. He righted himself, yanking at a multi-layered array of diaphanous silks pulled askew off his pale shoulder. He lifted his hands in an exaggerated fashion to show off his gossamer layers of raspberry, turquoise and emerald. The whole get-up must have cost a fortune, which I knew he didn't have.

'Look at our battered old litter,' he muttered as he lurched into the street. 'See how high-roofed everyone else's litters are? The first thing I'll do when old Picenus croaks is get one of those.'

I surveyed the collection of visitors' conveyances parked against the townhouse wall. Some of them had roofs elevated to absurd heights to tower over the traffic as they moved through the crowded streets below. As it was, I was relieved not to see any place made for me in the Manlius litter. Clodius' amber hair oil was overpowering.

'And we ought to have more attendants,' Clodius whined as he clambered in and gave the signal to head home. 'Oh, don't look at me like that, Marcus. I actually won today, for a change, though I pretended to hang back to give others a chance. You arrived just in time for me to get away with most of my winnings.'

Verus and I led the rest of the household on foot, the tired majordomo still carrying his sad bundle of Kahina's finery and spotless sandals.

I paid little attention to the march home nor to the petty bargaining Clodius conducted with the ten or so neighborhood rascals he'd hired to pad out his cortège for the day. All I could think of was that at last I was going to meet Leo, the heir to the house, Kahina's son, and unbeknownst to all but his mother, my very own child.

I'd given up my claim to the unborn boy, knowing the life my ex-master would offer Kahina and her offspring was far superior to anything an ex-slave or even a junior recruit to the *agentes in rebus* could provide. The sacrifice had gutted me and broken Kahina's heart. I forced her to stick to her Numidian family's promise to wed her to the mutilated war veteran and keep the fruit of our innocent affair our secret. So I was the bastard son of an aristocrat who unknowingly mistook his grandchild for his own offspring.

But to my mixed emotions, Kahina had since shed her provincial girlish memories of our tryst. Under the guardianship of the family patriarch, the late Senator, she had blossomed from a countrified serving girl of the desert into a graceful and loyal Roman matron. She had come to love the Commander and to rear the child without a murmur as the clan's long-desired issue.

Our silence had bound us in pain, but our love for the noble Gregorius and hope for the Manlius line eased the deception. So late in his life, the Commander had been able to abandon the distasteful plan of adopting Clodius as his heir in favor of paving the way for the long-desired baby son in the crib.

In the end, I could look on in good conscience. The baby's blood was indeed Manlius blood, only delayed by a generation. I told myself that the canny old Senator who'd educated me through long years of reading aloud to him in his study would have approved. All I had to do was keep things in place until Kahina returned and Leo was old enough to learn the truth and take up the reins of his inheritance.

I now saw that inheritance was more in jeopardy than ever. I ushered the shabby litter past the sprawling fig tree that marked the Manlius property and helped Verus slide the rusting bolt closed behind us. The gates needed new planks and the tree needed pruning. Clodius disappeared for his bath. I took stock of the interior in his absence.

Clodius had redecorated the public reception rooms since Kahina's departure for Aquileia to join her husband in the court of Emperor Magnentius. Instead of graceful deities and a trio of Fates, pornographic acts involving animals in garish tempura gamboled across the salon past the fading classical border of black, red and white that still circled the ceiling. The new mural job was cheap and already flaking off.

In the *triclinium* of old, a painting of a lush garden with flitting birds and painted fountains glinting with sunlight had enlivened dining for the military friends of the Commander and the gossiping matrons visiting the ailing *Matrona* Laetitia. Now I saw a painted scene, the Rape of the Sabines, with misshapen features and vivid genitalia. Adults might laugh, but I hated the idea of young Leo drinking in such spectacles on a daily basis.

The ancestral masks and house gods had disappeared. I could only hope that Verus had stored them safely out of the reach of the drunken vandals Clodius called his friends.

And the expense? Up close the rooms' gaudy new hangings turned out to be loosely sewn from cheap fabric. The cushions weren't custom-made but the sort of thing picked up in lots of six from the Subura stalls. One was already popping its stuffing. The entire decor shouted 'Clodius'—showy and shallow.

'If you want to see the library, it's all locked up,' said a small, clear voice.

Leo stood in front of me, five years' worth of pudgy, sticky little boy.

'Have you ever been inside?' I asked him, gulping hard at the sudden sight of his brown curls, his mother's limpid eyes, the strong little legs and that high brow that came to him straight from the old Senator's ancestors.

'Verus showed me, but only once. It's filled with Grandpa's books.' Leo glanced around as if ready for his nurse to summon him back. 'Are you another friend of Cousin Clodius?'

'More a friend of Verus. But I'll dine with Clodius tonight. Have you had your supper?'

Just then Lavinia called from the kitchens. Leo excused himself with, 'I have to feed Festus.' He toddled off on bare legs browned by years of playing in the sun of Ostia. The Manlius family kept an apartment in the port town for overseeing their dock holdings. Leo had been hidden away there during the civil war, safe and invisible from political retributions.

Now I prayed he would be just as safe back here in Roma. In fact, once I had reported to Apodemius tonight, I would visit the Castra's temple to Jupiter Redux. The now-neglected altar was blackened by hundreds of years of sacrificial flames lit by grateful returning soldiers. I would offer my own prayers for the boy's protection and Kahina's return.

'Reminds me of his mother,' Clodius said an hour later.

He had condescended to share his evening meal with me now that I was a freedman but balked at including Verus. 'Personally, I don't see much Manlius in the child, all brown and rough and raw as a little barbarian. And to think someday he gets it all.'

He sniffed displeasure as he knifed another piece of honeyed fowl.

'Or what's left,' I said, helping myself to the food. 'Come on, Clodius, you can tell me. Nobody's listening now. How much have you mortgaged, you rascal, and how did you manage it?'

He preened at my comradely tone. 'It's not easy without the deeds, but people around town, the old-timers who've known me since I first joined the house, are too embarrassed to call *everything* into question. They lend against a share in the dock revenues or ask for repayment in wine and foodstuffs coming in from the farms down in Sicily. I manage, but the big debts could only be met by selling off capital assets—'

'Yes?'

His eyes narrowed over the lip of his goblet. He'd told Verus to break out the good tableware, not so much to share with me as to show off. 'Perhaps I've already said too much. You forget your place.'

'I'm an *agens*. It's been certified by the very best that I know how to keep secrets.' I actually winked at him and hated myself for it.

'I'm sure you do,' he said, sucking on a roasted wing. 'All you slaves are lurkers and eavesdroppers by nature.'

'How much are you in the red?'

'I lost track. Creditors would probably confiscate the whole place the minute I turned my back, but even if I'm not the precious heir to the Manlius estates, I am a nobleman and I have a reputation to uphold. So I stay put until I can leave in style. I gamble and often win. I borrow from Lucius to pay Rufus.' He waved a greasy morsel from side to side.

'Can you keep it up? Until you leave, I mean.'

'Hard to say. These are difficult times. The civil war left everything up for grabs. A lot of the old families are in trouble and unloading whatever they can flog. The glut of antiquities and treasures is sending the market through the floor. I'm managing to keep this place presentable as best I can until things recover.'

'So I noticed.'

'I've half a mind to break down the door to that bloody library and offload it to the bookseller, but the prices for even first editions has collapsed, so what would be the point, even if Verus could find the key?'

'The market should recover in time. Just be patient.'

'Oh, I am, Marcus. You know me. I waited most of my life to be named the Manlius heir. Instead I find myself babysitting that little brat. You bet I'm patient.'

'What are your plans for the boy if *Domina* Kahina can't be found?'

'Oh, I'm not waiting for her! Once this legacy from old Picenus comes through, I'll escape this rotting city. I'm thinking of starting over. With some serious money in my pocket, I might head eastward. I'll leave it to Verus to see to Leo's schooling.'

'I can keep an eye on him if you like, at least until his mother returns.'

'Oh, she's dead, I'm sure.'

I blanched at his casual tone. 'Surely you haven't told Leo that?'

Clodius winced. 'Oh, of course not. I tell him *Mama's on a long vacation.*'

'His future should be planned. I have a bit of salary to spare for a tutor.'

'I couldn't care less if you recruited him as a tiny spy, as long as Picenus favors me with some of that fortune. I'm expecting the will reading soon, possibly even this week. I've been hanging around the old coot for over a year now, praising everything from his meager table scraps to his boring taste in music.'

Clodius dipped his sticky hand in a bowl of lemon water and dried it off in the folds of his fetching salmon-colored tunic.

'And if Picenus bestows you nothing?' I lowered my eyes for fear Clodius would detect my alarm that he might siphon off everything around us down to the last glass fingerbowl.

'Oh,' he smiled with a sly satisfaction that shot me through with inexplicable alarm. It was the sadistic expression I'd seen as a slave when Clodius kicked me hard as he left a room where I stood in attendance.

'The boy is my back-up plan, you might say. With his mother gone, no one could stop my profitable solution to him as well, but I'm not a monster. One does such painful things only as a last resort.'

A chill fell over our conversation. I couldn't weasel anything more out of Clodius that night. He headed out again to carouse with his friends. I got Verus to unlock the Senator's library and together we dusted down the shelves and tables. I ran my eyes down the familiar scrolls and codices, knowing I'd spot any thefts. The volumes were all there, my old friends Cicero, Homer, Horace, Virgil, Pliny, and Plutarch. Verus left me alone to browse among the dusty pages. As I ran my eyes across some beloved stanzas, I heard the old Senator's crotchety voice scolding me, 'Not so fast, child. Don't read like a parrot. Measure your words and digest their meanings.'

I must have sat for more than an hour by a single oil lamp on the low plastered bench the Senator had had molded right into the wall so my short legs wouldn't dangle while I read. Now my knees stuck up around my ears and the old rug that covered the platform seat was moldering.

It was well after dark when I finally replaced the crumbling, mildewed volumes, relocked the heavy door, and returned the key to Verus with a word of advice to heat some braziers to dry out the room.

As primitive as the gesture might seem, I also went to the nursery. Reassuring the startled Lavinia that I meant no harm, I checked the boy's breathing as he slept. I dared to place a hesitant finger on his moist and unlined brow. I pushed back his soft brown curls. His long lashes were like little feathers lying on his plump cheeks. I assumed that no one observed my tender gesture, but I was wrong. From his pile of straw in the corner of the tiny room, the pet rabbit Festus, wakened by my tread, watched me with red eyes.

For many minutes I felt an elation and pride in my boy beyond all my soul's previous experience. I could have stood there all night. But as I left for the Castra, that bursting happiness already sensed a stealthy foreboding creeping like a shadow toward my heart.

Chapter 5, Decadence Training

'Do you know what's in this?' Apodemius was pulling apart the intricate packet from the Emperor, breaking the imperial seal with no more reverence than he would show a difficult oyster. A distant basilica outside his office window chimed the sixth hour. The half dozen field mice, *apodemi*, he kept as pets skittered around their cage for a minute and then settled down.

'No, *Magister*. The Emperor expressly ordered me not to take an advance look, to wait while you read it, and then to ensure its destruction.'

'Pity you're so conscientious. You know these top-secret things are hard on my arthritis,' he quipped, working away at the expensive leather strings with his knobby, twisted claws until I rescued him. I cracked the thick vellum communication open from its casings.

His office hadn't changed much since my last debriefing. The basin and liniments waited on a side table for the deaf masseur who tended his gnarled limbs. I saw the same lumpy Egyptian linen cushions, the worn leather chair, and the locked iron box where the most sensitive documents were squirrelled away.

His nightshift secretary knocked and entered with another item of mail, a box wrapped in thickly embroidered damask cloth and tied with gold string.

'A present from Jason of Syria, *Magister*. It arrived earlier this evening,' he murmured.

Apodemius took the elaborate gift, raised one eyebrow and muttered, 'I can't put a face to the name . . . thank you. All right, Numidianus, let's see what's so urgent you haven't shaved in three days.'

He eased himself down behind his long, wide desk under the map of the Empire pinned to a huge piece of cork on the wall behind his head. I continued to stand and used his silence to gaze up at the positions of the pins that indicated the locations of legions, agents, and other important traffic. I noticed a lot of military congestion along the thin pen line that marked the Rhenus to the north of us and the Danuvius River to our north and east. In the distant Eastern Empire, thick clusters of pins marked the position of Shapur II's Persians poised along the border of yet another doubtful truce.

'Numidianus?'

'Yes, *Magister*?'

'Open that box and see what this Jason of Syria has sent me.'

'Certainly, *Magister*.'

It didn't take my sturdy fingers long to unwrap a gift of dried figs soaked in a honey and liquor syrup, garnished with crushed pistachio nuts.

'My gods, my gods,' Apodemius murmured at the Emperor's letter. 'Have you eaten?' he asked with a brighter note in his voice.

'Yes, *Magister*, at the Manlius house.'

'Well I haven't. Sweetened figs, are they? Slide them across.'

He kept reading Constantius' fat message, stopping once or twice to lay the pages in his lap as he fished out a paper from one of the many piles on his desk, ran a finger down a list of names, and then returned to the letter.

'Take a stool, Numidianus.'

'Thank you, *Magister*.'

He continued reading and absentmindedly fingered one of the succulent figs.

He looked up at me at last and smiled. 'It's a rare day our Emperor reaches beyond his sycophantic council for a fresh viewpoint.'

'He said the Empress Eusebia thought very highly of you.'

'Which must infuriate the Lord Chamberlain no end. Years ago I did her Macedonian family a favor. In any event, this may be the most important request I've ever received straight from the throne. You may consider it a privilege to have carried it.'

'Thank you, *Magister*.'

I rose to leave, already thinking of the clean bed waiting for me in the barracks on the other side of the Castra's parade ground.

'Where are you going?'

'To bed, *Magister*.'

Apodemius chuckled. 'Sit down, Numidianus.' He picked off a bit of fig and held it through the bars of the mouse cage.

'Are you hungry, Clarissa? Now, Numidianus, concentrate on what I'm going to tell you before I destroy this. The Emperor has received worrying reports about the rule of his precious Caesar Gallus. The stability of the Eastern Empire is at stake if these disparaging tales are true, but naturally he doesn't want to credit any of it. He wants to believe the Lord Chamberlain's and Constantia's reassurances that Gallus is doing just fine.'

'Gallus is his own flesh and blood.' I wasn't thirsty, but I was still a little hungry after all. Clodius' pigeon wings had been more bone than meat.

'A very cool variety of flesh and blood, those Constantines. Constantius is no fool. No one in his position can ignore such warnings. The last report to Constantius included the account of the execution in Antiochia of a highly popular young man on possibly false charges laid by none other than the *Augusta*. His death seems to have tipped the scales of popular feeling against the House of Constantine in some quarters.'

'That sounds quite serious, *Magister*.' I hoped there would be a bit of chickpea stew left in the canteen for me before I hit the pillow.

'Precisely. We labor under a sovereign who sees usurpers leaping out at him from the corner of every dining room, not to mention the least village of every province. I wonder if he even trusts his wife at this point. He must be able to depend on his

Caesar, his own cousin, to keep the peace in the East while he pacifies the Alpine frontiers.'

'Understood, *Magister*.'

I shifted nervously on my stool. Apodemius' agent network in the East was constantly under pressure from the Lord Chamberlain's own intrigant circles. The eunuch Eusebius' intelligence resources east of Sirmium were much stronger than those of our *schola*. The two men were hardly enemies, both seeking the strength of the Empire before all else, but I'd say they were definitely rivals—like two sides of one imperial coin.

On the obverse, Apodemius was the ascetic, wizened head and on the reverse, Eusebius definitely the greedy, spidery tail.

'So I want you to spend a few weeks here at the barracks. Brush up on your poisons training and your spoken Greek—I know, I know, your reading is fine—but you'll need to get your street Greek fluent now in order to move around Antiochia. Have you completed the specialist Eunuch Course?'

I closed my eyes for an instant as I realized what he was implying and then pulled myself together. I had not, I replied.

'You'll be attached to the court of Caesar Gallus and the *Augusta* Constantia, but keep in mind that this court is a sham—a powerless stage on which he's left to amuse himself. I'll make it clear to our senior *agens* in Constantinopolis that your job is only a short-term investigation. Leave the routine Antiochia mailroom and road control to his network.'

'But surely this kind of inquiry touching on the reputation of a Caesar would be carried out by someone higher ranked under his personal direction?'

'It's none of your business, Numidianus, but I can tell you that all of Constantinopolis Station's senior agents are busy with something a lot more sensitive.'

'More sensitive than a Caesar?'

Apodemius faced his map and pointed without comment to one pin, vulnerable and stark, poked deep into the cork well behind the Persian lines. I took a deep breath. Domestic problems were only the Empire's dirty laundry compared to military intelligence on which the Empire's very survival depended.

'Besides, this shortage of manpower works to our advantage. Nobody in that protocol-obsessed court in Antiochia would dream that such a low-ranked agent as yourself would be taking on the Emperor's private request to spy on his own cousin.'

'Thank you, *Magister*.'

I wasn't sure what I was thanking him for. Antiochia was farther east than I'd ever been and too far from Leo and Roma for my liking. I hoped my expression didn't betray my dismay. I was wrong.

'Stop sulking. Was Arelate so very thrilling? I didn't think so. This is not a long mission, just a very important one. There are five powerful dioceses of the Eastern Empire in play. All you have to do is assess the political success of the new Caesar. Surely any schoolboy could do that!'

'Yes, *Magister*.'

No doubt Apodemius' idea of a *difficult* assignment was spying on the gods themselves.

'May I ask the source of these worrying reports? The Emperor mentioned an officer named Barbatio, now Master of the Guards in Antiochia. I knew Barbatio in Numidia in the *Legio IIIA*.'

'Yes, he's one source of the stories about a murdered boy, Clematius, but possibly not the only informant.'

Apodemius checked a list of names on his desk. 'You'll also meet the Prefect of the Palace, the haughty noble Thalassius, and the Governor of Syria, a certain Theophilus. Then there's the *Quaestor* Montius with his law books, and of course, your old friend, the Lord Chamberlain Eusebius.'

'I thought he stuck to Constantius these days.'

'To climb the mountain passes on campaign? The question is, are some of them, or all of them, conspiring to build a false case against Gallus? Alternatively, are these sources risking Constantius' displeasure by daring to tell the truth in the interests of the Empire?'

'Where do I start?'

'With the *Comes* of the East, a man I know, named Honoratus.'

'I understand, *Magister*. But this sort of mission may take time. Constantius seemed impatient for reassurance. He's preoccupied about the Alemannic invasions.'

'Take enough time to get it right. An incriminating report based on untested falsehoods would bring you close to treason yourself. Of course Constantius hopes for good news, not bad, but I could not defend a job badly done.'

'No, of course not.'

'Make friends at the court. Sound out all these officials in a discreet, modest way but especially study up before you leave here on the world of eunuchs and their little ways. The court in Antiochia is infested with them at every turn. Luckily, Eusebius already thinks you're his double agent and I'll brief you closer to your departure about all that.'

'I'll do my best,' I said, with a sinking heart.

'Please avoid angering the *Augusta*, which I gather isn't easy with such a volatile woman. She'll remember you from Treverorum, won't she?'

'I suppose she will,' I said, remembering her attempts to seduce me.

'—Which is one good reason I shouldn't send you, so be very careful. Find out why this young society boy Clematius was executed, whether he was guilty of the charges, and if not, who trapped him in a net he couldn't escape and why. I know these are trying times and we are talking about a prefecture of the *East*, yet one hopes some concept of Roman justice still survives in that fetid climate.'

'How will I report to you?'

'I won't be so very far away. As I say, we have an important operation planned out of the base station at Constantinopolis. If it succeeds, we will have penetrated the Persian front with a valuable conduit for intelligence on their rear guard.'

I was finally free to leave. I had actually reached the door when there was a strange squeak. Apodemius lifted an oil lamp off his desk and turned his stiff shoulders around to peer through the cage at his pets. One of the animals was quivering, all four legs sticking into the air. A second later, it was dead.

Apodemius sighed. 'And one more thing, Numidianus. While you're cultivating all these important sources, don't forget the value of information from friends in *low* places, such as poor Clarissa here.'

He opened the cage and dropped his mouse by her tail into the bin he kept for fruit rinds and discarded paper. Handing me the box of lethal figs, he said, 'Please show these to the Poisons Master tomorrow morning.'

He drew his woolen shawl closer over his bony shoulders and chuckled, 'Jason of Syria, indeed! I can *always* put a face to the name.'

⁂

Language training at the Castra was more amusing than in ordinary classrooms. The dry texts and dusty metaphors that bored schoolboys to tears in the open-air sessions of the Roman streets were banished from our tutorials. *Agentes* needed information—fast—and we got more secrets from streetwalkers, gladiators, Circus workers, tradesmen and tax collectors than scholars or high-ranked priests. Our contacts weren't always refined people.

My Greek vocabulary needed a lot of work to bring my spoken skills to the level of my classical reading, but my mission to Antiochia wouldn't be undercover, just in the honest guise of a visitor *agens* from the West. From dawn onwards, I practiced my Greek with Pallo who always enlivened lessons with puns and riddles to relieve his own boredom as much as ours.

'What is the house you enter blind and leave with sight?'

'A school, Pallo. Try again,' I cajoled.

'What work can no one ever finish?'

'His autobiography. Give me one I don't know.'

We continued bantering in good spirits until the Greek words came as easily to my tongue as to my eye.

Poisons Class was little more than a refresher course. Since the first time in that classroom, I'd seen a fellow student collapse by making a mistake, not to mention having witnessed a beloved mentor drink a fatal dose of henbane in the field. I'd seen army medics use doses to relieve pain and bestow blessed oblivion on the wounded. I took poisons seriously and was already a good student of antidotes.

However, my afternoon lessons were far less comfortable. For some years, the Castra Peregrina had trained *agentes* heading for Eastern service in the origins, customs, and secrets of the eunuch class. Over the decades these men had insinuated themselves higher and higher into society's ranks, expanding their duties beyond bathing and barbering the royalty to outright rule in the bureaucracies east of Pannonia.

Our instructor was a eunuch himself. The formidable Einku was a tall and handsome Ethiopian who'd been gelded as a young slave in the household of a lascivious Roman society woman, after his beard had begun to sprout and he proved capable of acts of love. She bought and groomed men like Einku for her carefree pleasure. Roman law forbade such crimes but there existed a small illegal market for this niche demand. We all knew the famous rebuff to a maddened cuckold, 'Do you ask, Panychus, why your Caelia only consorts with eunuchs? Caelia wants the flowers of marriage—not the fruits.'

Einku had bought his freedom with his earnings from that grateful lady's bedside. Somehow he came to the attention of the Castra's chiefs. Apodemius and his colleagues were wary of eunuchs in general—and for good reason. They formed a brotherhood unto themselves and any of them might be a spy. However, Einku was patient, modest, and conscientious. He proved his worth. The rest of the *schola* teaching staff now held him in high regard for his candid and thorough instruction.

None of this made his lessons pleasant to follow, starting with Lesson One, 'Definitions of a Eunuch.' The first evening, I was sent back to my barracks room carrying a text over a hundred years old by the jurist Ulpian to memorize the differences between eunuchs. There were men made eunuchs by

Nature and men reduced to that state by *thlibia*, tying up the scrotum and cutting off its life juices until it dropped off or hung useless, or by *thlasia*, where the testicles were crushed until they popped out of their sacks which were cauterized back closed with a hot iron.

The next afternoon Einku showed me useful but disturbing illustrations of the medical effects of castration on young boys—the high voice, the elongated, fragile, bending limbs and the soft deposits of fat on the breasts and hips—versus the manlier attributes of late-eunuchs like himself.

The third day he unveiled his own genitalia to help dispel the fearful curiosity and unspoken fears he said the eunuchs in power liked to exploit when dominating normal men. Even if his phallus had once pleasured a desperate Roman lady, the shriveled testicles, flat and useless elicited my pity.

'Do not feel pity, and do not judge any eunuch's character by his state,' Einku advised. 'Some of the kindest and most erudite men in the Empire are eunuchs, while others well deserve their reputation for avarice and intrigue. Some have neutered themselves out of an extreme devotion to follow the teachings of their Christian savior, while others are victims of war and slavery. You must judge a eunuch as you would any other man.'

I was happier the next afternoon when Einku kept his clothes on. We moved on to the vexing question of the place of eunuchs under Roman law, including the difficult question of whether they kept their masculine rights after castration—especially if they were married men maimed as prisoners or injured in war.

Einku also discussed the culture of priests who had made themselves eunuchs when their devotion to the Great Mother God or to the Christian cult of chastity carried them too far. Their self-mutilations could provoke state prosecution on grounds of legal assault or even murder, for Roman law viewed castration as a social death from which no man could recover.

There was more to learn—about typical Eastern court relations between eunuchs and men and between eunuchs and women—with Einku reminding me that our late emperor Severus had called eunuchs 'the third sex.'

In his frank lessons, which both intrigued and repelled me, Einku discussed varieties and degrees of sexual desire among these men robbed of the capacity for penetration and their hapless and their often-unsatisfying means to sexual release.

'There are men who enjoy being violated and they are not always eunuchs. They are called *cinaedi*.'

Einku paused and looked at me for a moment, waiting for my comment. I realized he was alluding to the Emperor Constans, whose degradation at the hands of German prisoners-of-war had offended the Roman military's pride to the extremes of rebellion.

I said absolutely nothing, but thought, *ah, so I'm known within my schola as the assassin, whatever the courtiers around Constantius believe.* I wasn't worried, though. Our own brotherhood protected bigger secrets than that.

By the end of the week, Einku had covered his subject only too well. He ticked off my papers and cleared me as ready for service in Antiochia.

As our last lesson drew to a close, I asked the question that had been bothering me all week.

'What is the Lord Chamberlain?'

The powerful Eusebius' heavy jet necklaces and bronze anklets were fixed in my memory, as well as his scents and incense.

'All we know is that he is called *androgynos* by members of the Emperor's family who must cope daily with his growing authority,' Einku said. 'Be very wary of him. From everything we hear of his greed for land and authority, we assume his sexual appetite is channeled into a need to divest others of their property and status. Constantius II is a feeble prince who fears his generals and distrusts his ministers but the triumphs of his arms serves only to establish the reign of eunuchs over the Empire. Eusebius grows richer in power and assets every day.'

The Reign of Eunuchs . . . Even Apodemius had never uttered such a dangerous phrase. It would be blasphemy to be heard repeating it beyond the protected walls of our headquarters.

Thanking Einku, I left feeling this was the real enemy of our empire, the dying vitality that the distant Franks and Goths and Persians smelled like the whiff coming off an old whore's boudoir.

♇♇♇

I'd finished ten days of study. Now I was back in Apodemius' office for a final briefing. He was never at his best before the dinner hour. His arthritis crippled him in the morning and troubled him in the afternoon. Only by evening had his joints worked themselves free.

I found him lying on his long massage table under a threadbare towel, being rubbed and kneaded by his deaf masseur.

I'd worked hard at my training, so his greeting disappointed me. 'I've just received a formal complaint by a high-ranked official about your overstepping your authority during a formal court reception honoring the Emperor on the day of his anniversary.'

'I can explain that, *Magister*, if you'll let me read the complaint.'

'You'd have to ask my friends there,' he said with a laugh, pointing to his mice. 'I gave them the letter from Paulus Catena to serve as a cage lining for their tender paws. Now, concentrate on those documents, over there on my desk. That's the pile. They're copies of the "intelligence" I sent the Lord Chamberlain in your stead as his "counter spy".'

I studied the sheaf of papers he indicated, while his man continued to work at the knotted joints with some pungent liniment distilled from rosemary and laurel.

After a few dispatches, I began to perceive Apodemius' overall scheme. While I'd been posted to the court of Magentius,

69

he'd reported *almost* the truth, always a day or two too late for Eusebius to act in time. As an *agens*, I'd been well positioned to leak the build-up of forces rallied by the general-usurper against Constantius. Pretending to be me, Apodemius had inflated the numbers and sped up the legions' movements subtly enough to succeed in spooking Constantius into inaction. The Emperor had believed Magnentius to be so over-fortified for the Battle of Mursa, he'd made a last-minute offer to the barbarian to keep Gallia and rule it as Caesar—anything to avoid pitting Roman legion against Roman legion in a civil showdown.

Apodemius' distortions might have kept the Empire at peace, but for two unforeseen factors: the ambition of Magnentius who'd gone too far to seize the offered compromise and retreat, and General Claudius Silvanus' last minute defection to Constantius, tipping the balance of forces over to the Constantine heir.

I finished reading through 'my leaks' to hear Apodemius say with a shrug. 'One can't say we didn't try.'

'It almost worked. If the peace had held, fifty-four thousand men would be alive today, thanks to your deceptions here.'

'You don't read anything there you can't explain to Eusebius under interrogation?'

'Nothing. It's so close to the truth, just more so.'

'The best kind of disinformation, my boy, is the all-but-truth bent in the right direction.'

I folded the sheaf of papers. If I had felt reluctant about the coming mission in Antiochia, the memory of those corpses killed in a day stiffened my conscience. I was lucky to serve. I looked over at him. 'And what is the desired direction now, in Antiochia, *Magister*?'

'I wish I knew. If Gallus and his cousin-bride are the victims of slander, we must protect them by exposing their accusers. Those conspirators will try to silence you to save themselves, so watch your back.'

'But if the reports of incompetence are true?'

'If Gallus is a failure as Caesar or Constantia is poisoning his reign, then they're weakening the East. The Persians will pluck it like a ripe and rotting fruit off the branch. If Gallus can't maintain his rule, then we must deliver the bad news to the Emperor before the Persians see their opportunity—or before the royal couple add you to their list of victims.'

'But if I understand, this is just a case of one single man executed, rightly or wrongly?'

Apodemius pulled on a loose thread of his towel. The thread rippled back and forth across the fabric.

'Clematius was a respected man of high position from a prominent Alexandrian family. The family is asking questions and demanding reparations. Untie the story of Clematius' death,' he yanked the anchor thread off with a snap, 'and a dozen other truths may flutter loose into your hands as well. You need to release them all.'

The absent weft had freed a fringe that Apodemius picked apart with his knobby fingers.

'I want to know who's telling Constantius what and why, and only when we have separated every thread of this Clematius story from its neighboring thread, one by one, will I know how to advise the Emperor.'

'So the first thing I have to do is talk to Barbatio who sent in a report and see your friend Honoratus,' I said.

'No, Numidianus,' Apodemius said with a smile, 'The first thing you have to do in the court of Antiochia is not get yourself killed.'

CHAPTER 6, GOLD-PLATED DANGER

—THE *DOMUS* PICENUS—

The famous Greek philosopher Lucianos of Samosata wrote a diatribe against our great city of Roma in which one character quips, 'Romans only tell the truth once in their lives—when they write their wills.'

Clodius was about to hear the truth from Picenus now, only a few days before my scheduled departure for Antiochia.

I was goofing off at the barracks on one of my last afternoons, dicing with a few foolish recruits ready to lose their money. Verus had come to the Castra gates and summoned me by a thin note washed nearly blank with rain. It seemed Clodius wanted the whole household to trail after him the short distance to the ailing man's house.

Justina smiled to herself when she saw the motley Manlius train disgorge our drenched and disheveled selves at Picenus' front gate. Clodius' fine fringes and silks stuck to his back. My boots squeaked with water.

Inside the townhouse walls, the atmosphere was hushed and almost reverential. Only I dared to follow Clodius into the reception room where the burning candles and gagging incense would soon kill off Picenus, if his heart weren't failing already.

The seven witnesses required by law were standing in attendance, all of them *honestiores*, persons of status and property comporting themselves with great sobriety. This was a day of deep emotion for Picenus, who like most Romans of his class, would have been working on his testament for many months, if not years. It would be his last means of bestowing his supreme judgment on his friends, family, servants, and slaves.

The matron of the house had died nearly a decade before this. Picenus was disposing of estates and treasures from her side of the family as well as his own accretions. The legacy promised to be a sizable fortune.

'His wife bore him two sons, but one died suddenly of fever as a child,' Justina whispered as we assembled on stools and couches for the lengthy reading. 'The other was a tribune serving on the eastern front. He died in a skirmish with the Persians. Perhaps the old man has been dying slowly of a broken heart ever since.'

'No daughters?'

'No. Perhaps that's why he's so hospitable to a relative like myself,' she said.

I glanced down at her. The girl was innocent of any false modesty. Still in her early teens, Justina had no idea of her attractions—the perfect symmetry of her features, the grace in her lengthening limbs, and the pleasure of her attentive, keen-eyed observations.

But she did know the power of her thin connections to the Constantines. Married to Magnentius as a child, still carrying her toy doll in her arms, she'd attained both puberty and widowhood in the very next year. Even by Roman standards of the day, she'd stumbled all too soon on an inkling of her innate authority.

A few more guests dribbled in, despite the heavy downpour. Any retired senator's will was newsworthy to Romans. The tone and generosity of the bequests were the final highlights of any man's career. No one knew this more than the star of today's performance.

'You can proceed,' Picenus gasped from his couch. There was a clap of thunder outside and a self-conscious exchange of glances around the room.

The ceremony began at last, amidst sneezing and much blowing of noses. By divulging his will from his sickbed, Picenus was invoking an early Roman Republican custom, not to mention

74

ensuring that there would be no disputes among his legatees after his death.

The family's lawyer began with a careful apportioning of gifts to the old man's former supporters while in office. Sixty saccharine lines of *elogia* later, some thirty senior Romans all received exactly the same amount of money in revenues from Picenus' large fish farm in Neapolis.

Picenus had moved with the times and converted to the Arian Christianity favored by Constantius. However, the family valuables dated back for generations and spoke volumes about their pagan past. There was an ivory triptych with two women in Greek costumes carved in relief and a marriage casket covered in classical figures with the Christian dedication, *Proiecta and Secundus, May You Live in Christ* only recently carved around the circumference. There were seal rings and embroideries with Christian or pagan images, gold-glass marriage vessels, jewelry, ceremonial weaponry and a table groaning under the weight of the family's silver plate.

Clodius listened with ill-disguised boredom as these individual items were assigned to grateful *negotiatores* and other financial middlemen, estate managers, longstanding retainers, servants, and clerks—all of whom helped keep the family's affairs in order.

'The big stuff will come soon enough,' Clodius whispered behind his soggy sleeve into my ear. 'I know for a fact that there are Sicilian vineyards, *fabulous* oyster beds in Baiae, at least two estates in Gallia with cattle and lumberyards, not to mention silver workshops in North Africa.'

No witness wanted Clodius to hit it rich today more than myself. If he disappeared from our lives, I could apply to the courts as Leo's temporary guardian. Verus and I could sort out his education without interference until we located Kahina.

'Now for my library,' the Picenus whispered at the other end of the room.

'Oh, Jupiter,' Clodius muttered.

Slaves now lifted a long dust cloth to reveal piles of books and scrolls arranged across a banquet table. The scrolls sat in carefully labeled cases and heavy vellum and parchment codices had been positioned with their gold lettered spines upwards for bibliophiles to peruse. The old man's collection interested me, but not half as much as the reaction of today's recipients. As each first edition codex or treasured scroll was assigned to a member of the salon, there were smiles and eager thanks from those who knew their value and stiff acknowledgements from less lettered types.

Suddenly I heard *Parallel Lives* by Plutarch go to Clodius.

'What is that?' he whispered to me as he gathered up his layers of silk to accept his gift.

'Biographies of fifty Greeks and Romans and why they did what.'

Clodius' face turned bright red as he walked across the room to the table, received the hefty volume into his outstretched arms and stammered out his thanks.

'You're quite welcome, dear boy,' Picenus said with a wry smile. 'You're far too energetic and clever to waste your life hanging about invalids. Plutarch will assist your search for a true vocation.'

Clodius kept a fixed grimace plastered across his features. He clung to the possibility that Plutarch was just the beginning of his windfall. I fervently shared his hope.

The lawyer rested his throat for a moment. Picenus leaned back into the thick cushions of his couch. We were nearing the climax of his will and the lawyer summoned up his energy to close the proceedings with Picenus' final bequest.

'The remaining properties, listed here in order of their value in terms of revenue with the numbered deeds listed in a column here,' the lawyer held the lengthy appendix over his head for a moment for everyone in the room to see, 'are to go to *Domina* Justina, the illustrious daughter of Vettius Justus, former governor of Picenum, granddaughter of Julius Constantius by his first wife Galla, the son of Constantius Chlorus and half-brother of Constantine, our late Emperor.'

The room's occupants began to murmur in excitement.

'This lady of impeccable virtue has weathered many storms in her young life of obedient service to our clan. She has returned to our domestic altar unscathed in reputation and innocent of all bitterness. By this bequest I wish with all my heart to provide her with the security and social position she deserves and to reward her for the discretion, intelligence, and humor with which she has graced my final year of mortal life on earth. That is the end of the will.'

The show was over. There was polite applause as all eyes turned to the slim girl. Picenus grinned with satisfaction. He was sure that all the fashionable tables left in Roma would buzz tonight with his unexpected rout of the lounge lizards cluttering his salon.

Tears welling up in her eyes, Justina moved to the old man's side and without false reticence, embraced him. He was incredibly pleased with himself, but pretended he'd done nothing and just patted her elaborately braided hair with visible affection.

'It's all right, my dear, not such a great thing. I know I can count on you not to bet it all away on one of those glamor-boy gladiators.'

'Perhaps I'll take in the sights of Aquileia,' she parried. They both laughed at the absurdity of her ever wishing to visit Magnentius' favorite city again.

Clodius stormed out, pointedly leaving Plutarch on the edge of the garden fountain for the rain to ruin. He threw himself into his litter and pounded on the cushions in rage.

'A book! A *book*?' That's all I get for wasting more than a year with that senile fart?

We trudged in the downpour behind his litter in silence. The women servants huddled under an improvised canopy of leather over their heads but we stoic male escorts got drenched in a matter of minutes.

Clodius ordered me to attend him in the smaller of the salons while he changed into dry clothes.

'We're stuck with him now,' I warned Verus.

I loitered in the warm kitchen where I was offered a bowl of broth but I was sick to my stomach and had to beg off. For a bit of relief from the day's disappointment, I listened to the cook ridicule her master. After some ten minutes, I heard Clodius shuffling around in his house sandals. I followed him into a small alcove.

'I told you I planned to leave Roma with that money, didn't I?'

I nodded. 'What will you do?'

'My reputation is in shreds now. They'll be laughing at me all over the city. Something desperate is called for. Something that will bring a bit of luck back to this miserable, cursed household. I tell you, we've treaded on the toes of the gods, Marcus. Somehow we've turned the Fates against us.'

He slumped down on a low couch and ticked off the Manlius' calamities. 'My aunt Laetitia dies from illness. The Senator is murdered in an uprising right in his own study. The Commander dies for the wrong emperor on the battlefield. His new wife disappears under a cloud of treason. She has probably killed herself by now for the shame of it all.'

He lowered his voice to make sure the servants wouldn't overhear him. 'The Great Mother must be very displeased.'

The Great Mother Cybele. I rolled my eyes at the mention of this ancient cult. Other *agentes* at the Castra had told me that its arcane faith had caught on again among the panicked old houses of a few Roman clans.

'We must be cleansed of our past.' Clodius found a jug on a side table and helped himself to a generous goblet of wine. He didn't offer a drop to me. 'You agree, don't you?'

'I agree, absolutely, Clodius. You're not uneducated. And you're not lazy when you set your mind to it. In fact, whenever you wanted something badly enough, you worked fast to get it. The whole family pinned their hopes on you for years and your schoolmaster gave you high marks. You could start over and find work as a private secretary or get a job as a minor official—'

'A JOB?' Clodius burst out with a vicious laugh. For the second time since my return to Roma, I caught that glint of danger that lurked behind his eyes. I'd forgotten how when he was sent to a tutor and I to the Senator's study to read, he'd threatened out of jealousy to blind me. 'I talk about appeasing a deity and you tell me to get a *job*?'

'You said you wanted to make a clean start. What were you thinking of?'

'A ritual, of course.' He finished his drink and started to pace the little room. 'We can't afford a bull for a *taurobolium*. That would require money and I haven't the time or patience to raise funds. It will have to be a *criobolium*. We could get a ram arranged in a day or two.'

He rambled on. I hoped he wasn't serious.

Two evenings later, literally as I was finishing up my paperwork for transfer to Antiochia, Verus waited at the Castra Peregrina's Temple to Jupiter Redux while someone inside the barracks fetched me.

'The big bloodletting is fixed for tonight. It's against the law. You have to come and stop the idiot.'

'I've got a farewell party here at headquarters. Tell Clodius he can placate the Great Mother without me.'

Verus shook his head. 'The little lad's in danger. I can smell something brewing and I don't mean the cook's fish pie.'

'What do you mean?'

'Clodius keeps saying he's waiting for instructions or a sign.'

'You mean he's hoping for an oracle from some priest?'

Verus shook his head. 'All I know is he hopes that this ram bath he's planning will give him a vision. A meaningful dream.' Verus waggled his eyebrows.

'He can dream all he wants. I'll stop on my way out of town to say good-by to Leo.'

'It's serious, Marcus.' Verus grabbed me hard. 'Clodius has been talking to some pretty strange customers about the way they do things in the East. You better show up. I can keep my ears open, but I ain't got no strength in this old carcass if it comes to laying hands on my own employer. What with *Domina* Kahina nowheres about, he seems to think of Leo as . . . well, sort of *disposable*.'

It was my turn to grab Verus. 'Disposable? What do you mean by that?'

The trusty retainer shrugged. 'He says tonight the ram will reveal all.'

Verus told me the time and location of that night's ceremony. Clodius was dancing with danger. Only a few witnesses would be in on the secret.

Taurobolia and *criobolia* were not just nasty—they were indeed illegal. Pagan holidays in Constantius' Christian empire continued but the Arian priests complained to their sovereign that any blood sacrifice risked turning into a dangerous parody of Christ's sacrifice on the 'True Cross.' The new law against sacrifice was also a political message. Since the barbarian Magnentius had indulged in ritual sacrifice, down to the battlefield murder of a dazed village virgin before his troops, these gory ceremonies were, in short, crimes against the state.

I had the feeling that most Romans these days didn't mind giving up their primitive practices. Good society in modern Roma found the sight of a goat's throat gushing blood into a basin in simple bad taste.

Clodius had already proven himself a master of bad taste, but he wasn't an outright criminal. He must be desperate indeed. The ritual was to take place, as tradition dictated centuries ago, in a spot that now sat awkwardly close to Constantine's Christian basilica on the burial spot of Christ's apostle Peter.

We got there near midnight. A handful of Clodius' cohorts had shown up at his invitation, and at our arrival, they slunk forward from the shadows of the ancient city walls. They made their reluctance obvious, but despite themselves, they betrayed a grudging admiration for Clodius' defiant gesture. With their cloak hoods drawn low over their brows, it was hard to recognize any rivals from among the dandies at the reading of Picenus' will. However, judging by the surly mood, I suspected there were a few other souls who had turned up out of spite at Picenus' disappointing 'legacies.'

We waited in the dark under an uncomfortable drizzle. We were standing on land once used by Nero for his Circus. My mind took in the long history of ceremony and death surrounding us tonight. At least the weather kept all curious foot traffic to a minimum. Nonetheless, I was a government *agens* attending a forbidden rite. I kept my head down like the others and hung in the rear along with Verus and the male servants Clodius had coerced or paid to attend.

When it was obvious no one else was showing up, Clodius turned to the nervous pagan priest he'd hired for the ceremony.

'I suppose I'm ready.'

He took off his long rain cloak to reveal a second cloak and tunic bleached ivory for the occasion. When he lifted his hood, I saw that he'd trimmed and curled his hair. Wooden steps intended for the celebrant of a blood sacrifice had rotted away decades ago. Clodius had no choice but to slip and slide his way down into a foul and slimy trench assigned to this purpose centuries before.

The unlucky ram, its jaws tied shut and its legs tethered together, was rolled forward on the back of a wheelbarrow. Clodius' trench was covered with a roof of planks nailed together in loose, uneven rows.

After a few mumbled prayers to the Great Mother, the priest slit open the ram's throat. He jerked the animal's head down, directing the spurting blood through the slats to drip onto Clodius' face and shoulders waiting in the darkness below.

I imagined Clodius opening his mouth to receive the 'cleansing' offering. It was a steady trickle, nothing compared to the shower of hot blood a full-grown bull would have produced, but it was grotesque enough. Already I saw a couple of his witnesses, nervous at the possibility of being caught, slip away into the dark.

They had spotted some *aediles* on night duty heading along a boulevard some five hundred feet away from us. I tensed up, signaling the priest with a discreet hand to halt his prayers. We brought the ceremony to a standstill. The officers moved on. They seemed not to have noticed the bizarre behavior of a cluster of men watching an animal's death throes in the shadows of the basilica.

Finally, the goat gave up the last of its life's juice. The rain-slicked lid was lifted away. Verus helped Clodius back up the treacherous muddy slope. As Verus paid off the priest, Clodius grinned at us with a jaw dripping red and hair running with blood diluted by rivulets of rain. He turned his face toward the center of the city where the torchlights of the Forum glowed over the walls and shouted like a fool, 'I am *renatus in aeternum*, reborn for eternity!'

What he was, as Verus declared to me once his master was plunged into a hot bath back at the Manlius townhouse, was a 'gold-plated madman.'

'All the more reason to explain now, Verus. You said you're worried about Leo's safety. What did you mean by that?' I asked as we two dried ourselves us next to a brazier in the privacy of the servants' quarters.

'About a week ago, Clodius told me he had a dream—some vision of a tall man glowing with rays stickin' out of him, like the sun.' Verus spread his ten fingers wide around his ears. 'Sort of like that statue of ol' Constantine. You know the one.'

'Go on.'

'He told me he thought the vision represented the sun in the East and his golden future. That was before ol' Picenus did him the dirty.'

'Yes, but what did you mean, that he considered Leo as disposable?'

'I've put it together and here's what I think. He can't sell the boy because that's against the law. So how does he get him off his back *with honor* and without all of Roma's old families protesting? Make him a *gift*, right? Put him in imperial service, sort of. Make it clear that there ain't no more Manlius to inherit *and there won't ever be any.*'

'There won't ever be any? What did he mean? How could he know that?' My stomach was curdling. I wondered if Verus even imagined the implication of what he was repeating.

'He wouldn't get away with that here in the West. The old Commander has too many friends still, officials and military men, spread all over the place from Treverorum to Ravenna and Aquileia.'

'You're saying he intends to present the boy as a candidate for the eunuchs' order in Constantinopolis? But that's against the law, just as much as selling a citizen would be.' I could hardly utter the words.

'He asked me the other day if I ever found the key to the library. I said I'd give it another shot and asked, casual-like, why? He said he needed to check some law books, but then he said not to bother. He had a friend *from the East* whom he could consult. Then some man turns up, a stranger wearing the sort of getup you don't see off a theater stage, and they stay in the dining room until all hours, laughing and drinking.'

'It's all guesses, Verus.'

'Wait, you just hear. The next thing, that same night, Clodius rings for me to get Lavinia to get Leo out of bed and to present him all combed and dressed nice to introduce to this weird visitor.'

I'd heard too much to return to the Castra. I stayed the night, bunking down on an old pallet that had grown lumpy and stiff with years of disuse. At dawn I rose with ice in my heart for Clodius. Accosting him over his breakfast, I put it to him without any small talk.

'You're intending to offload the boy as a gift to the courtiers in Constantinopolis, aren't you? '

My question hardly fazed Clodius who was in too pure a mood after his pagan 'cleansing' to let a mere freedman irritate him.

'He's an orphan with a good name and a pretty face—but an orphan. I can't afford a fancy school and neither can you. You agree he needs a secure future. I hardly think the army has done this family any favors. The Senate is an empty shell. You don't expect me to spend the next decade listening to his verses in the hope he'll convert into a priest, do you?'

'Don't you know what they might do to him?'

'I couldn't care less and I don't intend to ask, as long as the price is right.'

'Price?'

'Well, perhaps nothing so vulgar as a registered exchange, just some sort of agreement between gentlemen.'

'And if he were disabled from fathering the next generation of the Manlius line, the estates would fall to you by default, wouldn't they?'

'Come to think of it, they would. That would be sad, but who could say?'

'It's a crime, Clodius.'

'There's no crime in offering a *gift* and receiving a little gratitude down the line.'

His heart was as cold as the sweat pouring down my temples. If I revealed to him that Leo was not only *not* an orphan but that *I*, a mere freedman, was his true father, I would have made it possible for Clodius to disinherit the boy on the spot. I could not leave Leo alone with Clodius for an hour now, much less a day or a month. But I had no legal authority to remove him from his ancestral home.

Like a cavalry rider trained to wheel his mount clear of a flying spear and then to advance straight back into the enemy's face, I changed my tack, softened my tone, and moved my stool closer to his couch.

'We go back a long way, Clodius. You should have confided in me. I can help you.'

Clodius lay back on his cheap pillows and shoved aside his dish of fruit. His eyes narrowed.

'How?'

'Done the wrong way, you cut the boy's value in half. Done the right way and at the right time, he's worth a fortune to the right people.'

'Good gods, what would you know about such things?'

And for the next half hour, I disgorged the gruesome details learnt at Einku's side—the potential for a high-flying career, for sexual congress, for a near-normal appearance, versus the risk of a disastrous mutilation sealing the boy's fate as a freak, a beggar, or worse.

Clodius' eyes widened as he learned how varied, secretive, and powerful was the world of imperial eunuchs.

'We were never friends, Marcus, but I must say, I may have misjudged you. You seem to realize, at long last, what a fix I'm in. You've been very supportive since you returned from your last mission. You went with me to Picenus' house and helped me out of that mucky hole last night. I wonder if I can afford to lose your counsel so soon, just when you're leaving for Antiochia.'

'I have no choice.' I produced a convincing sigh of regret. 'Just when we were getting to be friends. Who is left to see this awful situation through? Who shares memories of how it used it be, but you and I?'

'Well,' he brightened, 'what would you say to this idea? You and I take the boy and the three of us go to Antiochia together? You do whatever little chores you have to do, and in your spare time, you help me sort Leo out so that no one can say we didn't do the best for him with these eunuch powers-that-be?'

'Why, Clodius! Would you humble yourself to travel in my company all the way to the eastern edge of the Great Sea? We would be thrown together on the journey for weeks.'

'I'll do my best to suffer it for the boy's sake,' he mewed.

I returned through the dark and silent kitchen and vomited into the cook's rubbish barrel set along the back wall facing the alley outside. I felt dizzy.

Verus appeared in his tunic and bare feet. He carried an oil lamp and a wet towel in his hand.

I wiped off my face and burst out to him, 'He won't get away with it, Verus. He won't!'

'What can you do, Marcus?'

'That boy will not leave my protection if I can help it from now on, Verus, I swear. Pack up his clothes, even that blasted rabbit and his cage, and get him ready to travel. In the meantime, keep searching for those missing deeds, so we can get them examined by a lawyer.'

Unbeknownst to Clodius, Verus and I had discovered Matrona Laetitia's key to the deed box, wherever it lay hidden. That key now hung safely around my neck under my tunic, along with the three rings.

Verus nodded and then jerked his head in the direction of the dining room where years before as a slave waiter, I'd let the Commander's guests wipe fruit juice off their fingers in my curly hair as I lifted away their tables for the next course. Their laughing ghosts now watched the lonely Clodius scraping the last of some plum jam out of a bowl with his fingers.

'Am I coming too?' Verus asked and I realized that the wily old man had been eavesdropping on the whole conversation.

'No, you have to stay here and manage the estates as best you can.'

'Well, I was right about one thing, wasn't I, son?'

'What was that, Verus?'

'Gold-plated madman, right, Marcus?'

'Gold-plated, Verus.'

CHAPTER 7, THE BACK GATE TO HELL

—SELEUKIA PIERIA, ANTIOCHIA—

We caught the last eastbound ship leaving Ostia before the winter season made the journey intolerably rocky for all but the most intrepid of sailors. Centuries ago, the Great Sea had been closed to traffic during four months of winter, but Roma's enormous appetite could no longer do without regular shipments of grain, oil, and slaves to survive.

The dockyards teemed with porters unloading cargo necessary for the survival of Roma's welfare mobs. Overseers ran between offices and stalls, their pay sacks full of treasure and their fists bristling with dockets. Clodius' baggage rolled along behind us on a wheelbarrow as I led our little party of four to the pier where the towering ship tugged at its moorings.

The tide was pressing the captain and we had to hurry. Clodius went aboard ahead of us. Leo said goodbye to his beloved Lavinia with a brave and tearless dignity. Then we followed up the ramp.

Soon we were looking down on Lavinia. The weeping nurse looked so small, standing below on the quay next to empty Circus containers that had just delivered lions and crocodiles for Roma's entertainment. She waved us off as our great boat heaved itself away from the dock. Relieved of its tons of goods, the outbound vessel teetered high in the water. Already the distraught and loyal Lavinia looked very far away—even to me.

'Why can't she come with us?' Leo's imperious scowl, fixed since we first announced his departure from Roma, was worthy of his senatorial ancestors.

'She can't leave her own husband and children for the East,' I said. 'She's not our slave. There will be new nannies and maids in Antiochia. Anyway, aren't you getting too big for a nurse?'

'I'll have to make new friends,' he said. 'Will I ever see Roma again?'

'Of course. In the meantime, you have Festus for company.'

Indeed, in our uncomfortable corner of the enormous boat's chambers below—reeking of rancid olive oil and treacherous underfoot from broken pottery and splintered wood—Leo's furry pet Festus' red eyes blinked through the bars of his homemade cage. Already the rabbit had endeared himself to me. I'd noticed on the jostling wagon ride to Ostia that any time Clodius got too near his cage, the animal hopped wildly against the bars in protest.

It would take us about eighteen or nineteen days of lucky sailing on these gusty winds to reach Antiochia. That gave me more than two uninterrupted weeks to get to know my son. Clodius, green and puking, hovered over the edge of the ship's rail, or lay drained and faint on his bedroll down below. Leo showed no signs of missing his company.

This was an excellent start.

We sailed down the Italian western peninsula and then grabbed the wilder winds as we entered the imperial sea-lanes. Crouching together on deck, surrounded by the coarse conversation of sailors and buoyed by Lavinia's farewell snacks, Leo and I talked for hours on end. I could not stop looking at the boy. He had his Numidian mother's gentle grace and the Senator's proud expressions. Someday he might also have the Commander's tall bearing and possibly my quick ears and good memory.

But sometimes I was taken aback by a glimpse of my poor abandoned mother in the yearning expression with which the boy searched the far shores we passed. I even heard Leo upbraid Festus for messing his cage in a tone I imagine his noble Gallo-Roman great-grandmother might have used to reprimand a bath slave.

As we sat watching the sunbeams dance across the water, I described the late Commander and all his battlefield exploits, both before and after his terrible wounding at the hands of barbarian ambushers. I praised the learning and character of the venerable old Senator and I described my days as a child slave reading to the blind man in his library.

But I avoided talking about Kahina. I could never tell him of that desert night I held her in my arms to the thrumming of the drums pounded by religious fanatics preparing for martyrdom. How could I convince my son that I had made love to his mother never knowing she was promised to my own master, the Commander? How could I explain to him that he was better off without me as his father, a roving *agens* with no roots, no savings, and an uncertain future? How could any child understand being denied by his own father?

I certainly never had.

But Leo seemed to read my thoughts.

'Do you know my mother?' he asked after a few days out on the open sea.

'Yes, I do, Leo.'

'Is she very beautiful?'

'Yes, she is. Don't you remember her?'

'I remember how she smelled. Lavinia says it was the smell of lavender.'

'How does Lavinia smell?' I thought it better to change the subject.

'Like laundry.' He wrinkled his nose.

Leo had also inherited my mule-like streak of Numidian stubbornness.

'Do you know where my mother is right now?' he asked me the next day.

'No, I don't, Leo. I'm sure she's trying to come home as fast as she can.'

'A boy on our street said she would be killed if she came home.'

'Perhaps that's why she's waiting until it's safe.'

89

I suddenly saw that the spray on his face wasn't sea foam, but tears.

'But I shouldn't be going away then. If she comes home and I'm not there, how will she know where to find me?'

I held him tight and he broke into sobs. How worried he must have been all week, watching the waving hand of his nurse disappear from view as the Italian coast receded over the horizon.

'Verus, of course! Leo, *Verus* and our cook and Lavinia—they'll all be waiting for her. Verus knows where we're going. If anything changes, he knows the people in Roma who have sent me to Antiochia, and as soon as your mother comes home, he can send us a message.'

'That other boy said she's probably dead,' he wailed, burying his face in my tunic sleeve so the sailors wouldn't see him cry.

I reached down under my collar and pulled out the cord that hung around my neck. 'Do you see this ring, Leo?'

He nodded.

'After the war ended, your mother sent this ring to the house in Roma as a signal she was still alive. It belongs to you until she comes home. '

His eyes bulged with disbelief at the gold band with the blue stone.

'Why do *you* have it?'

'She meant it for you, but only for when you get bigger. I'm keeping it safe. Do you understand? It was her signal to us that she was alive. So don't believe stories from boys who don't know what they're talking about. You will see your mother again.'

'Do you promise, Marcus?' he snuffled into my tunic sleeve.

'I promise, of course, Marcus. You can always rely on old Verus and me.'

If he noticed that I omitted naming Clodius as a trustworthy guardian, the boy displayed the discretion of a Vestal Virgin.

In the evenings, I recited passages of the Iliad and Odyssey from memory to the boy. Clodius always flounced off in a huff of boredom and sarcasm. Each morning, I tutored Leo in simple Greek phrases he could use to make new friends or ask for what he needed once we reached Antiochia. After years of fighting, riding, training, and spying, my conversations with Leo brought back to me those simpler and more gracious years of my youth in a great house of Roma. At this wave of longing for the past, it was my turn to dissolve into tears one evening.

'Why are you crying?' Leo shouted over the flapping sails and the slosh of whitecaps against the wooden bow. A strong breeze sent threads of water streaking across my cheeks but he had guessed they were tears, not sea splash.

'Because I'm so happy being with you.'

'Because I'm such a good sailor?' He was learning how to tie knots from a kindly crewman who had children of his own back in Ostia.

'Yes, you're a good sailor.'

'Marcus, why do you talk in your sleep?'

'I'll have to stop doing that, won't I?'

Our ship was making progress. Leaving the Italian coast, we had seen massive cargo vessels arriving from Carthago, their decks groaning under hills of roped *amphorae* of oil and crates of redware pottery. As we moved past Greece, I held the child close and pointed out Rhodos, barely visible off in the distance, where an earthquake had destroyed the Colossus over three centuries ago.

'What's an earthquake?'

And so it went on, day by day, each answer prompting another question. It was a constant joy to me to observe Leo's eager mind, happy disposition, and open heart. He tended his rabbit on his own and gave no bother to the gruff men working on all sides of him. Living with Clodius had not tainted his soul. He had no memory of the Commander. His only heartache was the absence of his mother. I could only thank Lavinia for her affectionate nursing while Clodius and she hid him away in Ostia.

'I miss Lavinia,' he said after the early days' excitement had subsided into a calmer routine.

'Do you know why she's called Lavinia?' I tried to distract him from his loss. 'The original Lavinia was a very famous beauty. *Arma virumque cano, Troiae qui primus ab oris , Italiam fato profugus, Laviniaque venit.* "I sing of arms and the man, who came first from the shores of Troia to Italia and its Lavinian shores and was made an exile by fate." You see, Lavinia was the daughter of Latinus and engaged to marry the King of the Rutili. But she married the hero Aeneas instead—'

'Our Lavinia isn't very beautiful,' Leo interrupted.

'Yes,' I gave the boy a hug, 'but talking man to man as we are, I should tell you that a pretty face isn't everything, Leo. I suspect Aeneas appreciated her loving heart—and maybe her very soft and generous bottom?'

We were lucky with the weather and our seaborne idyll was over too soon. My spirits sank as the bustling shipyards of Antiochia's port, Seleukia Pieria, hove into view under a cloudless noon sun. Disembarking, I managed the luggage, including Festus and his cage tied fast with a red ribbon, while Clodius recovered his composure enough to commandeer us a wagon. We set off surrounded by Clodius' toppling boxes along the Orontes River Valley toward the ancient city without even stopping to get our land legs back.

Although it was hard jouncing for our joints on the rickety boards of the wagon, the ride gave us a chance to adjust to the dry breezes and scorching sun of an eastern November day. After a tedious morning of trundling through olive groves and irrigated fields, our wagon finally approached the city sitting on the eastern bank of the river and the imperial island on our left.

We clambered down from the wagon and boarded a skiff to avoid a tortured passage through the crowded city itself on our way to the palace. Slowly we passed the fortifications of Tiberius and the even older wall built by Alexander the Great's officer, the city's founder Seleucus.

The river forked ahead of us. The main stream hooked to the left of the island and out of sight. To our right a canal continued straight ahead to flow between the imperial island with its shining roofs and gleaming marble pillars facing the city on the opposite bank.

For decades, we Romans had heard tales of these 'rising' cities of the East, where the riches of trade routes and a favorable climate sprouted ornate buildings and brilliant societies that put the old capital's decay to shame. Antiochia was an ancient city, but from a distance promised modern luxury that Roma could no longer claim.

Sinking under the weight of half a dozen passengers, our little craft jerked into this right-hand channel under our boatman's expert oar. Now we navigated between Antiochia's stadium just on the toe of the imperial island and the city of half a million people in teeming neighborhoods rising on our right from a paved quay up into a gentle slope dotted with elegant villas and gardens. I counted at least four imperial bridges of solid Roman construction linking Antiochia to the island. All of these bridges streamed with foot and wagon traffic.

So this was the home of the very first 'Christians,' plus a large Jewish quarter in Kerateion and a significant Syrian quarter rubbing shoulders with Roman citizens of all kinds. Christians, pagans, Jews, silk merchants, spice traders, missionaries, messengers, society beauties—they were all too busy to notice yet more arrivals as we disembarked at last under a stone bridge that connected the island to the main avenue of the city. We wove our way through the pressing throngs toward the Imperial Palace.

Across the open parade ground fronting the Palace's inner walls, busy civil servants and other business people crisscrossed between the baths and the Circus, under an aqueduct, and into side alleys in every direction.

From the elaborate robes of many of the officials scurrying past us or loitering in the shade, I guessed immediately that Antiochia might turn out to be entirely to Clodius' taste for luxury, pretension, social glamor, and indolence.

Before leaving Roma, I'd read up on the city's ancient roots in the Castra's library. Julius Caesar had visited it. Tiberius had built two long colonnades to the south of the city. Agrippa had started to enlarge the theater and Trajan had finished it. Antoninus Pius had paved the great east-west artery with granite and King Herod had built a long public walkway or *stoa*, in the eastern part of the city.

Knowing all that, I could not at first explain two unexpected first impressions: first, that for all their finery, Antiochia's inhabitants seemed harried and unhappy-looking, and second that its facades were almost too new and modern. This hub of the thriving Eastern economy gave off an odd whiff of wet paint, like a newly erected theatrical set.

Of course...of course...the reason all this antiquity looked so fresh was that it was constantly under repair. Earthquakes flattened one quarter or another, over and over again. No wonder Antiochenes lived for the moment. More than one cripple we saw begging alongside the path of our cart might have lost that hand or leg to a collapsed building.

Everything here was old, but nothing was permanent, I thought to myself as we clambered out of the boat and up the shining marble dock steps.

Before I'd even begun my lessons with Einku, Apodemius had paved the way for my arrival with an express letter to Antiochia. None other than the towering Dacian, the former Lieutenant Barbatio and now the Master of the Palace Horse Guards, had kept himself busy at the Palace gates while keeping an eye out for my possible arrival today.

When Barbatio had served in Numidia as a lieutenant to Commander Gregorius, he had enjoyed mocking me, the eager slave. He never lost a chance to crack a clumsy joke at my expense in front of the younger officers seated around the council table in the *Legio III Augusta*'s meeting tent. To my relief, my rank and mission now impressed him enough to dispense with any offensive familiarities, though his rough humor remained.

'Marcus Gregorianus Numidianus, you're looking much older. Perhaps it's the heavy responsibility of such an important mission? What's with the kid and the tailor's dummy? Do you always travel with a rabbit?'

'Can you put them up?'

'If they're important, the Palace is huge.'

'Important only to me. Just a family problem I couldn't leave in Roma. The less said, the better.'

Leo and I now found ourselves in the heart of Constantine territory. For the moment, I didn't dare identify the boy as the heir of a leading rebel commander, even a dead one.

Barbatio shrugged. 'Brats aren't my department. Is that fancy man Roma's idea of a nurse?'

'Quite the contrary. Can the child be put in the safe care of a Palace lady? My travelling companion Clodius isn't talented when it comes to babysitting and I can't explain now, but this Leo's safety is of utmost importance. In fact, I don't want him to get near the boy again.'

Barbatio raised an eyebrow. 'I'll never understand the ways of your *schola*. There's a secluded nursery for the Caesar's two-year old daughter, Anastasia, and some of the other imperial toddlers deep within the family's wing. The maids are hand-picked for their reliability and gentleness, which makes up for our *Augusta*'s total indifference to motherhood.'

'The children are well-guarded?'

Barbatio looked at me for an instant. 'And you always treated me as the slow one, Numidianus.'

'Sorry. I'm sure you know your job.'

I led our trio behind Barbatio's heavy steps across the echoing polished floor of the Palace foyer. Clodius and Leo fell behind, admiring the mosaics and paintings that decorated every inch of wall, ceiling, and floor. As we moved through tall, heavy doors leading into the slightly smaller inner reception hall, Barbatio stopped short and turned around to face me, drawing up his massive armored shoulders.

'And I know yours.'

I shrugged off his challenging stance with disbelief. 'Come on, Barbatio,' I said in a low tone. 'Your messages called the highest levels of authority into question. You expected no cross-examination whatsoever? No scrutiny?'

He touched his sword in acknowledgement. I noticed that his *spatha* was no longer the battered weapon of North African days with its notched blade and secondhand grip. This was an unscratched beauty with a jeweled pommel so polished it caught a ray of sunlight glancing through the hall's floating dust motes.

'Of course, I expected someone to look into my reports. I hoped they would.'

'Actually, I'm only here to look into the conviction of a certain Clematius.'

'But you'll be keeping your ears open? Sounding out my reports?'

'I know your opinions have been received.' I was determined to be careful around Barbatio.

'I just didn't expect a jumped-up little freedman from provincial Africa would be given such a big job.'

'You're right. I'm a nobody. Sending me just shows how much they trust you. It's just a formality. Why would they waste a big shot?'

He relaxed his shoulders and nodded. The tactic of false modesty became me, so I wondered why I didn't employ it more often.

'Sure. Of course.'

'First I have to get the boy seen to.'

He gave me a sniff of condescension. 'I'll send someone to show you to the nursery. Then settle yourself in the room I've assigned and join me here in an hour. Let me host you at our famous *thermae*. Leave your fancy friend in pink to his own devices. Sooner or later, he'll find whatever he wants in town.'

Clodius had a letter of introduction himself to a contact in the Palace. He showed no interest in being seen at the public baths in my company.

So I alone was to be subjected to the sight of Barbatio's bare backside in a towel, a rump so hairy that his auxiliary fellows back in our army camp in Numidia Militaris had nicknamed him 'Rug Butt.'

But I could not have chosen a faster way of starting the investigation into Rug Butt's reports than a private conversation in the fuggy anonymity and noise of the public baths.

And I certainly needed a scrub.

⚚⚚⚚

A Palace guard wearing the insignia of the imperial *domestici* service, two winged angels, guarded the nursery door. He was reluctant to let me even trespass the corridor leading to the private residential wing. I found nothing more reassuring. Under the eyes of Barbatio's escort, I showed the sly-looking man my own insignia and papers. I was admitted only with my escort as far as the first door to the antechamber. After a minute or two, a wide-hipped crone in rustling red brocade robes encrusted with golden embroidery met me.

She looked Leo up and down and raised an eyebrow at Festus.

I explained to her that no one was to see Leo except myself, and that on no occasion or excuse was anyone else to remove him from her care. One look at the deep furrowed brow, the piercing black eyes, and heavy jaw and I relaxed. Clodius was unlikely to breach any maternal fortress overseen by such a Gorgon, almost more masculine than himself. I was proud of the way Leo let go of my hand to take hers and marched off carrying his little sack and rabbit cage to wage new battles of his own.

When I asked for directions to the baths, I was advised that every one of Antiochia's eighteen city wards had a bath, but that the Palace's baths were literally under my nose across the sun-bleached pavement of the procession yard.

I paid my fee and entered a *palaestra* thick with bronzed and naked young men, heaving their golden muscles at each other like a frieze running along a Greek temple roof. The clank of heavy weights falling on the floor and the slapping and shouting of wrestlers bounced off the walls.

I undressed and exchanged my things for a chit from a boy slave. I happily handed him my clumsy, dusty boots. As my bare feet touched the warm mosaic floor glinting cobalt, scarlet, gold, silver, black and green, I decided that my mission to Antiochia required a new pair of light sandals, at the very least.

I passed through a gaudy archway two stories high and scanned the main bathing hall bustling with more naked men. Every splash, slap, and salutation echoed between its marvelous marble walls and up to a domed roof of colored glass. A bright rainbow of dancing sunlight slanted down on the octagonal plunge pool. Its surface rippled with the kicking of lazy swimmers finishing up their day's ablutions.

Around the pool, a rectangular hall offered three cool, shaded alcoves on opposite sides. Slipper clad customers in towels settled on benches where they were tended by masseurs and bath boys carrying buckets, oil vials, and *strigiles*.

Barbatio was surely waiting for me in the cleansing steam of the *caldarium* beyond. I crossed the limp air of *tepidarium*, which sat relatively empty at this hour, and pushed open the double doors to the Hot Room. The sticky, smothering air offered me no refreshment, but I was here for the whisper of truth, not cooling breezes. Barbatio waited for me on a bench at the very back of the room.

'Nice baubles,' he said, eyeing the four valuables hanging on a cord around my neck, 'although this one's a bit rough.' He fingered the simple 'ring-key' *Matrona* Laetitia had worn which unlocked the Manlius family's missing deed box. I smiled but said nothing. Unassuming it might look, but that 'rough' ring might someday unlock far more wealth than Marcellinus' two jeweled and clunky gold bands.

I settled next to Barbatio's furry hulk. Hot jets of steam shot into the room through funnels only a few feet over our heads. I wasn't surprised to feel the bathhouse's great furnace room grumbling right on the other side of the wall against which I was leaning. The Master of the Horse Guards was ruby-faced already and not likely to spend more time in this oven than necessary.

'These rings aren't mine, just mementos that fell into my keeping. I'm hanging on to them to return to the rightful owners when I have a chance.'

I certainly didn't add that two of the rings had belonged to the *Magister Officiorum* of the usurper Magnentius and been rescued from the battlefield where Marcellinus lay butchered, nor that the blue stone belonged to the widow of Magnentius' former *Magister Militum*.

I hurried on to the business at hand.

'Tell me the story of Clematius, as you know it, Barbatio. Don't leave anything out.'

'Didn't you read my report?'

Was he getting nervous? I pressed, 'Tell me again.'

'All right. First you have to understand the set-up here.'

He glanced around the room to see that no one was listening through the steam.

'The Palace has many entrances, but there is one leading directly to the imperial suite of rooms accessed by a hidden gate along the outer back wall at the northernmost point of the island, here, where the Orontes circles around.'

He traced the island and the river encircling it with his finger on the oily film of sweat covering our bench. 'The city is on the far side, over here.'

'Yes, I see.'

'There is nothing overlooking this gate—not a house or hut, not even a donkey path, just olive groves and rubbish tips.'

'So this gate is a secret?'

'Not exactly. In fact, since last spring or so, it's become a well-known shortcut to the Caesar and *Augusta*, provided you know the password. Some months ago, this well-known society lady knocked on that door and asked to see the royal couple. She accused this Clematius, her son-in-law, of making incestuous advances toward her—of attempting rape.'

'Serious stuff. But why go to the Palace instead of a lawyer?'

'The imperial couple have encouraged anyone in Antiochia with a crime to report to bring the story directly to them for quick satisfaction.'

'Aren't the courts doing their job?'

Barbatio smiled a little through the mist. 'Note I said *satisfaction*, not justice. In my opinion, any honest court would have found Clematius innocent. We never heard any real evidence against the man except his mother-in-law's bitching. Look into it and I think you'll find that this respectable grandmother lusted after her daughter's husband but that time and again, he refused . . . to make her happy.'

'But would she soothe her pride at the cost of making her daughter a widow?' I shook my head. 'It's hard to believe, Barbatio. Are you sure you aren't risking your career on nothing more than hearsay?'

'I'm not sure his death was what she expected, but she was prepared to revenge herself, that's for sure. She went in through the Palace back gate wearing a fabulous diamond necklace and came out with her neck bare.'

I looked askance at such boldness but Barbatio pushed his thick finger into my chest for emphasis.

'Oh, I know my facts. The *Comes* of the *Domestici* answers to me, remember. Not one of the household troops has seen the necklace around that woman's throat again, even though she has visited many times since. Shortly after her complaint to the royal chambers, a death warrant that no one could overturn landed on the desk of Honoratus, the *Comes* of the East. Surprise, surprise, Clematius was found guilty of rape and promptly executed.'

'Why was there no appeal?'

'It all happened too fast. No one stopped to consider any political repercussions. Clematius wasn't from Antiochia, where people are keeping their heads down for a price these days. He came from Alexandrian nobility where I guess people still care more about the honor of their family name than fancy jewelry. His parents have been making it clear across three prefectures that they're not letting this go without a fight.'

I said nothing, but took silent note; the Honoratus who sent down the peremptory death sentence now under my scrutiny was the same Honoratus whom Apodemius expected to assist my inquiry. Was it likely that this man would find fault with his own actions? Or would he cooperate in the hope that an even higher authority would step in and take the responsibility off his troubled shoulders?

'Did it ever occur to you that Clematius might be guilty?' I asked Barbatio.

'No. This traffic into the Palace by the back gate has turned all of Antiochia's high society into a nest of tattletales, liars, spies, and eavesdroppers. One man even complained to me that it seemed his own bedroom had ears. I'd stake a year's pay he was innocent. Hades, I've staked my whole career by sending those reports.'

'But did you investigate the charge against Clematius yourself?'

'That's not my job. All I know is that the last year has seen one strange arrest after another, unexplained disappearances, and curious bankruptcies. City councilors and prominent businessmen sneak into the Palace every day to lay one accusation after another on each other. They're settling old scores and hoping that their rivals in jail won't come out. The whole city is crumbling under a wave of backstabbing and slander.'

'They looked calm enough this morning.'

Barbatio shook his head. 'Every accusation grows with the telling until it's dressed up and wagging its hips like a whore's dancing monkey. Turning in your rivals on a whim before they get you has become practically a municipal sport.'

Barbatio dried off his dripping face with a spare towel and jerked his head so I would glance across the room. Through the thick steam I saw a new customer seat himself safely apart from a second man on the long bench along the wall. A third man came in, but he too sat separate and silent. A fourth passed us as he appeared out of an adjacent steam room but he greeted no one on his way back to the main pool.

'You see that?' Barbatio ran his gaze along the men sitting around us, all in silence. 'No one says hello. No one chats but us. No one trusts anyone. Even the provincial administration is grinding to a halt for fear of accusations of corruption or rebellion—even *sorcery*.'

'Bad results can come from good intentions,' I argued. 'This Caesar Gallus knows nothing of government—even of this world. Remember, he lost his whole family when he was twelve, then the cousin who killed them all off suddenly recalls him out of house arrest in the fortress at Macellum, throws a purple cloak over him, marries him to the very cousin he himself widowed, and sends him off to rule the East. Maybe our young Caesar meant to start well by keeping his door open to all complaints?'

Barbatio scoffed. 'Didn't they warn you that this is all just a pantomime?'

I nodded as he continued to scoff: 'No one with a real job around here reports to Gallus. No one was ever intended to. The appointment was symbolic. Unfortunately, Gallus and Constantia are determined to throw their weight around and prove the Emperor wrong.'

'So the real wheels of administration turn in Constantinopolis?'

'There's worse. Gallus is sending so much grain to feed the legions on the front, food prices across the coast are shooting up. Merchants are hoarding against a further rise in prices. It's forcing a lot of people to sell off slaves just to eat. You haven't seen Antiochia up close yet. The really downtrodden are already going hungry.'

'But isn't Gallus just obeying Constantius' orders to keep the Persians at bay?'

I could see Barbatio wasn't convinced, so I pressed him. 'You know the Emperor subordinates everything in the Empire to border defense. He even let Magnentius take the Western Empire from his own brother while he battled for a truce with Shapur.'

'Oh, I get it, now.' Barbatio burst into a bitter chuckle and slapped his meaty thigh. 'I may be slow, Numidianus, but I'm not a complete cretin. You're here to *clear* Gallus and brand me a troublemaker? You're going to report back to his cousin on the Rhenus River that Gallus is a great little Caesar and that all this is just the Master of the Horse Guards making up lies?'

The other bathers looked up at Barbatio through the mist.

'Calm down, calm down. Could all this fear and these mysterious disappearances be Constantia's fault? We all know she's . . . unusual.'

Barbatio growled and fell silent, resting the back of his great ugly head against the dripping tiles. He'd hoped that his report had already earned him positive attention. Only someone as thick Barbatio could have imagined the Emperor relishing news that his trusted cousin was a disastrous politician.

Yet I could see that Barbatio was indeed surprised by my readiness to play advocate, like some naked Cicero in a flimsy towel tossing up one argument for the defense after another. And not just surprised but dangerously riled. This bull sitting next to me in a lake of his own sweat could be as fierce a fighter as any Persian. Since the days of suppressing Christian schismatics in Africa, he'd risen high in the world, faster than his brainpower alone would have indicated. That sword pommel spoke of new riches as well as higher authority.

Or was there something worse than mere indignation angering Barbatio? I recalled Apodemius' warning. Was Barbatio a tool in someone else's plot? If such conspirators thought I endangered their progress in discrediting Gallus in favor of General Ursicinus, I'd have to watch my back even in a steam room.

'I'm just here to get at the true situation,' I conceded. 'It's my first day in Antiochia. I come with an open mind.'

'Then why listen to me?' the gruff Dacian sneered. 'I'll mark you down for "Slum Shift" tonight. You'll be able to take the temperature of the underclass for yourself after dark. Although this city is so lit up with lanterns and lamps and bonfires every night, you'd think it was enjoying festival time year round.'

'I'd like that, thanks.'

'Maybe you will and maybe you won't.' He rose and yanking his towel tighter under his hairy belly, he led me out of the *caldarium* for a rubdown and a swim.

'The Caesar himself will be your tour guide.'

CHAPTER 8, PLAYMATES IN THE PALACE

—THE SECRETARIAT—

Barbatio had described constant traffic entering the Palace by the secret gate facing the blind northern banks of the Orontes. That night I would see for my own eyes that there was far more important traffic exiting the gate as well. As promised, he added me to a detail of palace guards that would accompany the disguised Caesar into the streets after midnight.

In the intervening hours, I hoped to squeeze in a meeting with the *Comes* of the East, Honoratus. News of my arrival seemed to have sped through the Palace. Honoratus was already expecting me. I was escorted up to the second floor of the Palace and along narrow labyrinthine corridors to a series of offices more spartan than the public reception rooms downstairs.

The antechamber of the office belonging to Honoratus was filled with scribes. I was adept at reading upside down and while I waited for the great man, I took note that his secretaries were all copying out notices and ordinances authorized, not in Antiochia, but in Constantinopolis. Barbatio was right. I was viewing a bureaucratic pantomime right here.

My snooping was interrupted when Honoratus signaled he was ready to receive me in his private office. The small room was lined with shelves tumbling over with dossiers and books but otherwise gave little clue to the character of this middle-aged man.

'My friend, Marcus Gregorianus Numidianus, welcome.'

He greeted me with unexpectedly hearty warmth. I was merely a freedman and an *agens*, so he didn't rise from his wide-armed chair, nor extend a hand. But he did gesture me to a padded stool positioned on the other side of his imposing desk.

Deep crevasses ran down on each side of his nose ending in sagging jowls. His tired eyes lay bedded in thick pouches. His clothes, though rich with the gaudy ornamentation popular in Constantinopolis and other eastern cities, were creased and far from fresh. I could assume he had seen military service, but those days were long gone and he might have been lucky to serve during years of peace safely distant from border dangers. Nonetheless, he looked like a man who had spent his life working hard.

He settled both hands across his paunchy stomach and leaned back from his desk. I detected the secret attitude of a man interrupted and harassed, disguising his impatience with an unconvincing bonhomie.

'How is my great friend Apodemius?'

'He is as well and nimble as his unlucky complaint allows.'

'He'll outlast us all with those liniments and ointments.'

There was a pregnant pause that was his to break how and when he pleased.

'It is a happy accident that our paths cross, Numidianus. I'm only passing through Antiochia on my way back to the main office in the New Roma.'

'A wondrous city, by all accounts. I haven't been fortunate enough to visit it yet. It's a much more senior posting in our *schola* than any I've earned so far.'

'Just two decades old and already it is a marvel! The architecture, the statuary, the religious relics, the gardens, not to mention the brilliance of its layout—all worthy of an empire uniting the entire world under the force and will of God. And even more wondrous, built on the site of Troy! What could be more fitting for the Empire, founded by Aeneas, to return to its ancient roots?'

I could not help raising a skeptical eyebrow, wondering not for the first time how the late Constantine had chanced upon the exact location of the lost city of Troy. But then his tireless mother

Helena, once a bar maid, had dug up the lost Cross of their Messiah. Perhaps Honoratus caught my cynical glance.

'Of course, the new Senate isn't anything like the Roman Senate of old Augustus' day, but still, the baths and the Hippodrome!'

'A pleasant place to be headquartered, then?'

He made an approving sound and waved a large hand covered in wiry hairs. 'The theaters are second to none. And of course, eastern dishes are fresher and more varied in spice than any dull winter fare in Gallia.'

'Indeed.'

'Of course, as *Comes* of the East, I've no time for pleasure.'

'Of course not.'

Comes was a title awarded to many men of various ranks as a reward for past service. Honoratus' current duties were far from clear to me. I saw that he had ample time to waste my appointment with this small talk. He was either a clever politician or a bore—probably both.

I'd had enough of the tourist talk. 'With such lofty matters to manage, I will take up little of your time with the minor case of Clematius the Alexandrian. My task is merely to check the details of the procedure and its outcome. It's more a political inquiry than a legal problem. Complaints from such a powerful family must be laid to rest.'

'Oh, things will die down. We have much more serious worries than the perverse sexual appetite of a young noble. Food shortages are spreading an atmosphere of . . .'

He waved his hand again, as if seeing off a troublesome insect, but he was anxious to get rid of *me*. From his study in faraway Roma, Apodemius trusted this senior official for some reason, but why? I trusted no one yet.

'May I ask, *Comes*, what exactly was your reaction when you received the death warrant?'

It was hardly a pointed question. Honoratus relaxed a bit.

'I was troubled by the speed of the process, I confess. Even if Clematius was guilty, the evidence was nothing more than the word of his mother-in-law against his protestations of innocence.

It was a flimsy case. His life might have been saved. We're not barbarians or *pagani*. We live in a modern age of Christian forgiveness. The boy should have been given more time and better counsel. He might have confessed, begged for forgiveness, made his contrition, and perhaps gotten away with exile.'

'Did you argue for this?'

Honoratus looked past me at his closed door. Was he worried someone was listening? He cleared his throat and lowered his voice. 'Tell Apodemius there was little I could do. I delayed the torture and execution for as long as I dared and sent an urgent note up the line to the Praetorian Prefect Thalassius. It was no use.'

'Was there no other action possible?'

'In the old days, I might have rallied the Senate of Antiochia to challenge the warrant and set up a proper public trial, but . . .' he waved his hand again in frustration.

'But?'

'There was no rallying the Senate. I arrived from Constantinopolis to discover that the politicians of this city have turned on each other like vipers in a pit. Antiochia is full of fear and impetuous vindictiveness. The example of Clematius has only fed the infectious idea that any accusation can put your competitor or rival into a dungeon without so much as a hearing.'

'I should like to speak to Prefect Thalassius.'

Honoratus said nothing, but wagged his head just enough for me to catch his hesitation. Perhaps in his opinion, Thalassius was not to be trusted.

'The Prefect is here in Antiochia?'

'Yes, yes,' Honoratus said. 'But I'd drop the matter. Tell Apodemius we'll settle with the relatives generously.'

'I cannot do that.'

'Then be careful. Thalassius is a proud and choleric man.'

'I have my task.'

'Really, it's just a family matter that went too far.'

'The involvement of the imperial couple did come up in Roma.'

'They listen to the people's grievances, for better or worse.'

Was it my job to tell Honoratus that this 'family matter' had inflated into an investigation into a Caesar's competence, or a possible case of treason at the state level, and that no less than the Emperor Constantius wanted the full picture?

I said nothing, but made no move to leave. Honoratus grew nervous.

'The boy is dead, Numidianus. The family in Alexandria will receive restitution, but not right away, not when the case is fresh. Later, when things have quieted down. We can't risk the appearance of a throne being blackmailed.'

'Of course not.'

I rose and thanked him, but the promise of restitution hung in the air. I paused before opening his door.

'So, *Comes*, you know Clematius was innocent.'

'I did not say that.'

'But—?'

'I repeat, I did not say that.'

'No restitution would be arranged for an incestuous rapist's clan.'

'I confess I remain troubled. You will not understand my meaning, *Agens*, but *a significant diamond necklace was never seen again* and I dare not say more than that.'

⚕⚕⚕

In one single day, two men had hinted to me that the blame for Clematius' execution might lie not with the Caesar but with his formidable *Augusta*, a cousin nearly a decade older in both years and political experience. I'd heard many doubtful hints about our new Caesar, but never that he wore ladies' necklaces. Roma's history left cross-dressing to the likes of the Emperor Elagabalus parading around the ancient Palatine in girdles and rouge.

I had hoped to avoid Constantia in this investigation. It was safer to leave her to those whips and handcuffs, silk pillows, and velvety, if aging, charms. To stand again within inches of those reddened lips, pointed white teeth, and determined black eyes sent me shivering in the opposite direction in search of a more attractive task.

I stopped to ask the notaries scribbling away in the outer office for the whereabouts of the Praetorian Prefect Thalassius. I was told to make a formal application for an audience. They looked up from their copying and the room fell silent as they watched me letter out my request. I worded it carefully, conscious that at least half a dozen hands would pass it around for the satisfaction of curious eyes before delivering it to Thalassius' private secretary.

They warned me I would have to wait a day, maybe more. The Prefect Thalassius was a very busy man.

I was about to finally take a rest myself. It was going to be a long night and I had risen on the boat at dawn to pack up our belongings and disembark. I was also slightly wrung out by the bath with Barbatio. Maybe I could nap right through the evening meal.

'*Agens* Numidianus? Marcus Gregorianus Numidianus?'

A graceful man as tall as myself, with curling black hair over a pale brow and wearing a spotless tunic with a salmon-and-gold embroidered hem blocked my passage. He took a deep bow from the waist. He was a slave as sleek as a racing hound, a soft-cheeked man whose sinuous hips and ingratiating lips were a clue to his nature, but he also spoke a curious Latin with the whiff of Armenia, north of our border, where castration was not prohibited.

He was a eunuch.

'Yes?'

'You are invited to attend the *Basilissa* in her quarters.' He used the Greek term for empress. Before I could say anything, he had slipped away down the spotless corridor, taken an abrupt turn into another corridor, and disappeared. When he realized I hadn't followed on his heels like a trained puppy, he took a few steps back and smiled at me again.

'You are *invited*,' he repeated. The smile dropped off his languid features.

I took a deep breath and followed him. We continued along the passageways lining the offices, each one smaller and quieter, until the cubicles finally petered out.

Then we climbed a short narrow set of stairs curving into a new wing of the sprawling Palace. We dodged through three or more curtained doors guarded by *domestici*. They nodded to my escort but said nothing to me nor asked for my *agens* papers. I was already lost in this warren. If I wanted that nap before midnight, I'd have to be nice enough to my hostess to guarantee myself a guide back out of this maze.

The last time I had seen Constantia, she had been sitting in a military camp chair in Pannonia producing an imperial diadem from her travelling sack. The diadem was her bribe to a key general, the ageing veteran Vetranio who commanded all the Danubian forces and thus controlled the geographic hinge between East and West. The diadem and the glory that went with such a gift from the Constantines was her lure to outbid and outwit a rival delegation sent from the usurper Emperor Magnentius.

I was an official escort for the barbarian opponent's team. Magnentius was trying to solidify a tentative alliance with this General Vetranio himself.

Constantia told Vetranio that day that the diadem came from the Emperor Constantius himself, but I kept silent at the back of the military meeting tent, knowing she lied. She wanted General Vetranio's support—not for Constantius—but for herself. She hated and feared her elder brother and despised the illiterate Vetranio.

And why shouldn't she hate our Emperor? After the great Constantine's death, the second-born Constantius had moved quickly to wipe out all contention for the empire. While the Lord Chamberlain, the eunuch Eusebius, held back Constantine's will, Constantius had roused the army to kill his own flesh and blood. He'd murdered Constantia's first husband, the noble General Hannibalianus, in this coldblooded family massacre that won

111

him the East. He eliminated all the adult Constantines except for his two brothers and two little cousins, Gallus and Julian and he put them under permanent and remote house arrest to be forgotten.

No wonder Constantius seemed to spend his life watching his back. He might have made a mistake not killing Constantia too. Or better yet, he should have given her a share of the Empire along with his two weaker brothers. Instead, Constantius ignored her pleas for safety, freedom, and some power of her own. But he'd done the next best thing—he had married her off to her little cousin Gallus and installed them in a symbolic court.

Surprisingly, I had not yet heard that this peculiar marriage was a failure. On the contrary, the incestuous pair had produced a two-year-old who was now entertaining my own son.

My eunuch guide slowed his serpentine progress. We had arrived at a set of grand double doors overladen with cedar carvings and bronze bolts. I smelled the suite of Constantia before my other senses caught up. Traces of amber and jasmine enveloped her chambers, braziers sent up beautifying steam against the dry Syrian climate, and incense burners competed for air in every corner of her rooms.

A tall, redheaded slave, possibly a Goth or Frank captured on one of the northern borders, admitted us through the next pair of engraved doors. He wore the soft robe of a eunuch, though his downcast gray eyes hinted that he hadn't been born one.

Constantia appeared soon enough at the sound of my boot steps.

I'm hardly an expert, but growing up in the Manlius salon, where *Matrona* Laetitia fought the signs of her illness with a formidable array of cosmetic weaponry, had taught me one thing. Money rarely hurts a woman's efforts to keep up appearances. Ambition, brains, beauty—the silky woman in this towering coiffure of dark braids and curls set off with jewels who stepped forward from her inner chamber to greet me had once had all three. But I was not surprised to see that these gifts, thwarted and abused by her brother's domination, had turned rancid—like perfume left uncorked or wine turned to vinegar.

The warning signs had been there all along.

'I am honored, *Augusta*.'

'Yes, it is you, although you are much changed. You served in Treverorum, *Agens*, before the civil war. You look tired. What happened to that boyish expression?'

'I am of no importance, *Augusta*, for you to concern yourself.'

'True, true, but you see, I am not too proud to welcome an old acquaintance to our court, no matter how illustrious my rank and how lowly yours. Abisak? Meroveus? Leave us alone.'

I bent one knee slightly in respect and nodded as the Armenian guide and the eunuch door guard departed.

'What's wrong with you, Numidianus? You look so drawn and troubled. Is your purpose here so weighty? I can hardly imagine anything in the East could account for those deep black circles that ring your eyes. What is your reason for coming to Antiochia? In Treverorum, you had just been promoted up from the riding circuit, I recall.'

'I was the Palace's postal officer, a *circitor* supervising the *equites* riders and their deliveries. You gave me a personal letter once for express delivery to the *Imperator*.'

She chuckled to herself. 'Come now, why so discreet? Weren't you also in Sirmium watching my negotiations with old Vetranio in the winter of 350?'

Foolish me, I had thought those piercing black eyes had overlooked me in such cold military tent crowded with heavily cloaked soldiers.

'Did you summon me here for any special reason, *Augusta*?'

She picked up a penknife by its ivory handle and toyed with its glistening edge. 'You were also at Mursa, weren't you?'

I bowed my head with respect.

'Did you sustain any wounds? Is that why you look so much older?'

'Only those of the spirit.'

'At least you survived. You obviously do your job well—or at least you know the right people.'

'I am now a *biarchus*.'

'Congratulations. But surely there's a special rank in your *schola* for a man like you, who is always in the wrong place at the wrong time?'

She tossed me that diamond-like smile. A daily brushing with a wooden stick, its flayed ends dipped in a paste of urine and emery, gave her the whitest teeth in the Empire.

'You *were* one of the Magnentius delegation to Sirmium, weren't you?'

'You have a good memory, *Augusta*.'

'For many things.'

She turned away suddenly and pitched the valuable letter opener across the room. Its point stuck into the wall just under a decorative hanging, a strange harness worked in delicate silver filigree. The wall also displayed a ceremonial whip of creamy white horsehair bound into a silver and turquoise handle, some gold ropes in heavy loops, and a pair of copper bracelets with snapping locks. I had not forgotten her reputation for bedroom creativity, although no one could actually interview or name a survivor of her private pastimes. I suppose her 'playmates' knew better than to boast.

I had rejected her intimate invitation once, well before her marriage. Now it seemed that anyone who rejected her advances angered her for life.

'You avoided my question. Why are you here? Have you come to the East to spy on me, *curiosus*?' The honey in her voice turned acidic.

'My business in Antiochia is too petty to trouble you. But I'm grateful for this chance to pay my respects and to congratulate you on your marriage and the arrival of a daughter.'

'You think I'm a complete fool, don't you?'

'On the contrary. You have risen to greater authority, responsibility, and independence than any other female in the entire Empire.'

She smiled and murmured, 'I'm not so certain the new Empress Eusebia would agree with you.'

She picked up a bronze mirror edged in Germanic cloisonné and stared at her reflection in its wavering reflection. 'Have I aged so very swiftly that my visitors now talk only of authority and responsibility?' she asked her image. 'But you never did cross the line, did you, you Numidian provincial? I'd forgotten how you were always . . . careful.'

I studied my dusty boots and waited to see which way this dangerous interview might swerve. We ex-slaves knew that silence was invariably the safest response.

She laughed a little more kindly now. 'You *do* think I'm a fool. Everyone does, because I settled for this plaster throne and paper marriage to a naive child. Keep up the good work, *Agens*. At least when you make *ducenarius* rank, you'll taste real power, whereas I could sit at the right hand of that blasted Christ up in the heavens, and I'd still be my older brother's puppet.'

'I must go now, to tedious duties far less appealing than your company.' I made to leave.

'Wait, Numidianus. I did ask you here for a reason.'

I had almost reached the very edge of her sitting room and almost freed myself of the suffocating air, but now I turned back. I waited, fearful she was merely tacking her skiff to another bank, but heading for the same awkward shore. This time I guessed wrong. She made no move to touch or trap me as before in Treverorum.

'We must protect the Caesar,' she whispered.

'From what?'

'From gossip, rumor, and complots. Numidianus, there are those who would obstruct my poor husband and discredit him. Many men would like to be Caesar.'

She walked toward me. All the sardonic insinuation had fallen away, leaving her eyes frank and wary. I had seen this woman by turns determined, seductive, frustrated, and disdainful. Now I saw that Constantia was genuinely afraid. She came up close to me and laid two thin hands covered with garnets, sapphires, and veined green stones on my shoulders. The thick tunnels of bracelets covering both her arms, which had always called to my mind a vulnerable woman's attempt to armor herself against her enemies, jangled and clattered down to her sharp elbows.

'People want Gallus to fail.'

'There are some unfavorable stories, *Augusta*,' I conceded.

'Of course there are. Gallus needs time, that's all. He wasn't trained for all this.'

She swayed all of a sudden, pulling me toward her. Despite my revulsion for the woman, I saw her own startled expression as she righted herself. I wondered if too much wine had made her unsteady on her feet.

'Time brings no guarantees. He needs wisdom, as all rulers do,' I said. 'You have experience to impart.'

'Yes, but over time things can go wrong.'

'Yes, things have gone wrong.'

'Is that why you're here?'

Now I judged she was ready for a real conversation and I seized the opening.

'May I ask you a question regarding a certain Antiochene who was offended by her Egyptian son-in-law?'

She slumped down on an upholstered stool and ran her hand through the coils of steam floating up out of tripod's brazier.

'That bastard Clematius? He was guilty.'

'How do you know, *Augusta*?'

'I heard the story with my own ears, every sordid detail, from the victim herself. There are things that I don't care to repeat or hear repeated. The woman had already suffered enough. Even I was shocked.'

It would take a lot to shock Constantia.

'Is that all you have to tell me, *Augusta*?'

'What else is there? These things must be reported to the appropriate authorities. I'm no judge.' Then her eyes lit up like an Alexandrian lighthouse with pleasure. 'But I watched his torture and death. He deserved every minute of it.'

'Is there anything else you could tell me?'

'The Caesar *wants* to know such things. He *asks* to know the truth, without a lot of bureaucrats and eunuchs keeping him in the dark, hiding things from him, and keeping all the power in their own hands. *He* wants to keep us powerless, but we'll show him.'

I didn't ask whom she meant by 'he.' She might have been referring to the Emperor, but I suspected I had stumbled on the Lord Chamberlain at last.

'Is "he" here now?'

'On his way back from Mediolanum via Constantinopolis. But whatever he advises, Gallus will keep at it, listening and learning. Every day my husband grows closer to his people.'

After midnight I would see just how close that was. I left the *Augusta* restless and preoccupied.

I checked in on Leo and found he was fighting off sleep until I came to say goodnight. Within seconds of seeing me, he had drifted off, exhausted but comfortable. The Gorgon told me that he had already made friends—or rather that the twitching, furry Festus had drawn new playmates instantly to his side. I repeated my instructions that his security was of utmost importance.

Well before midnight, I had finally eaten my fill of goose in coriander sauce and cauliflower in cumin downed with good wine and fresh water.

It was time to walk the streets with the Caesar of the East.

CHAPTER 9, PLAYMATES IN THE STREET

—THE BACK DOOR—

'You will accompany us tonight, *Agens*? Good. You will see our ears and eyes are open to every man or woman, senator, or fishwife. When you return to the West, you'll report that the Sovereign of the East misses *nothing*.'

The Caesar Flavius Claudius Constantius Gallus, son of Julius Constantius by his first wife Galla, pressed a manicured finger against my chest and pushed very, very slightly.

We were gathered in front of a large bolted door. Having returned with Barbatio through the same maze I travelled to visit Constantia this afternoon, I gauged it could not lie far from the lady's suite. This must be the notorious opening to the 'back gate' in the riverside wall.

Barbatio excused himself within a minute and hastened away to his nighttime duties. If the Master of the Horse Guards had travelled up in the world, the Dacian had also taken on more responsibility than his *Legio IIIA* tent mates would have ever tipped him for. I could see that in his plodding way, Barbatio was determined that not so much as a transgressing cockroach was going to blot his Palace dossier.

The Caesar was wearing the same cloak worn by other two men with him—sullen, heavily armed *domestici*—waiting for Barbatio to deliver me to them. But up close, even a generous woolen hood was not enough to disguise the Constantine ox-eyes, pale complexion, golden curls, perfect shave and spotless black leather shoes. His attendants certainly groomed him with finesse.

Gallus was my third Constantine ruler after Constans and Constantius II, or even my fourth, if you counted their distant cousin, the charming Justina. I didn't really count my brief glimpses of the Empress Eusebia and that strange and silent leftover sister, Helena.

I was concluding that, no matter how regal his bearing, a Constantine's family authority was not the same thing as the hearty naturalness of a Roman emperor in the traditional military mold. I assumed the patriarch Constantine had oozed a powerful air of command. A lifelong military commander, the usurper Magnentius had enjoyed it. Even old Vetranio of the Danubian legions had retained most of the necessary vigor to launch thousands of men into battle.

Constantius managed to fake it with success. Constans had lost it.

Gallus didn't have it and he never would.

Instead, we three trailed after him like sneaks rather than soldiers. We threaded like footpads down the island's curving shore of docks and warehouses until we reached the second to last bridge across the Orontes to the city.

We crossed the bridge and continued along an impressive boulevard shooting straight to the core of the city's three sectors. Under the blaze of hundreds of municipal lamps and lanterns shedding an overhead glow that turned night into day, we bustled toward the center of Antiochia. We were walking east, one guard explained to me. In ten minutes we would pass through the *Forum Valentis* to get to the busy commercial lanes around the *Theatrum Caesaris*.

I tried not to show I was nervous but the deceptive bustle of the daytime streets had given way to a ghoulish hush smothering this overly lit metropolis. A city that is too bright and too quiet is a strange combination, making each pedestrian as self-conscious as the last actor left standing on an empty stage. To the silent passersby who hurried past, we were hardly inconspicuous—a band of four expensively dressed men stalking as one toward the slummier quarters.

From time to time, Gallus stopped a stranger and asked him where we should eat or what was showing at the theater. We got few answers, some indifferent shrugs and once, at the mention of food, an angry shove that sent the Caesar slamming against a hard brick wall.

A guard reached for his sword, but Gallus restrained him. We moved on.

The paved clearing around the Forum stood quiet but was just as brightly lit as the boulevard. Tall marble columns cast long shadows like ephemeral swords of blackness across the paving stones. Sweepers and *aediles* on duty paced past us in wary silence.

Strange dark forms slipped and scurried under porticoes and behind columns lining the four margins of the vast space. I peered closer and saw we had an audience who did indeed notice us. There were dozens, maybe even a hundred wraiths wearing nothing more than rags and sores hiding away from the light cast by the giant torches. None of these people emerged from dark alcoves and caves of carved stone.

Suddenly, one of our guards cried out. I turned around, sword ready, and then relaxed. Someone had hurled a clot of excrement at his head. There was a scuffle as the hooligan rushed away to hide in some crevice or gutter beyond the public square. The guard brushed the turd off his shoulder. It spattered into flakes on the stones.

I waited to see if the Caesar would comment or decide on a reaction of some kind. He glanced back and shook his head in caution.

We kept on striding through the open Forum. As we reached the far corner, we passed a huddled group of a dozen or so souls watching a skinned cat rotate on a spit over a fire of burning street rubbish. I wondered how such a scrawny stray would possibly feed so many. I shuddered to think of what they might do with the rabbit Festus, fat and furry, sleeping next to Leo across the river.

Hulking over the rooftops to the southeast, the towering black outline of Mons Silpius mocked the bright city lights that glared down at us. Here and there in the distance, the campfire of some shepherd hut dotted the mountain's tree-covered hulk.

Gallus knew the way through the city as well as his guards. He dove down an artery that led us away from the Forum. With each block, the buildings sat closer and closer, constricting our route until we were in a one-cart lane. Gallus twisted off into an alley so narrow we could only follow him in single file.

Finally this stifling crevasse disgorged us into a busy side street. I found myself bumping shoulders and shins with the anonymous throng emerging after the night's performance into the warm night.

Gallus led us toward the rear of the theater building and said, 'We'll try them.'

In the vicinity of the shabby players' entrance, some eight or ten little wooden tables stood around a vendor's stall hawking beakers of wine and cheap snacks. A slight breeze carried the odor of fish balls, anchovy-stuffed eggs and mussels boiled with leeks and wine. After the sinister walk through the Forum, it was a relief to arrive at a place filled with life, no matter how rowdy. Girls as young as thirteen or fourteen bounced from one gaggle of customers to another. In their playful flirtations they kicked up the sawdust that collected discarded shells and spilt oil underfoot.

Lanterns in special *fornices*, or niches, studded the two-story back wall of the theater and cast their own artificial red glow to signal what the girls were about. With rouged cheeks and eyes lined with black Egyptian pencil, these females looked especially garish to my eyes. There was little an ex-slave like myself didn't know about women's boudoir tricks just from attending the great ladies of Roma but the white lead and paste rouge on these faces might have been applied with a farmer's trowel.

I was also struck by their rich, flimsy tunics and colorful *stolae*. Their fluttering sleeves and hems gave the impression of butterflies out too late after sunset. Then I saw that their finery consisted of hand-me-down costumes that were faded, torn, and stained with sweat and makeup from years of service on the stage.

There must be some Greek slang for these girls working the back of the theater district but Einku's language lessons hadn't got me that far. Anyway, I'd seen more than enough prostitutes in my time, first as an army slave and then as a circuit rider with the *agentes*. I knew that a society of women for hire boasted a protocol like any other community in the Empire. I knew that even girls who shagged for only a few *nummi* five times a day still divided up their humble world into a hierarchy no Byzantine eunuch would scorn for its complex snobbery.

There were whores called *alicariae* because they hung around grain mills waiting for clients, and whores called *prostibula* because they loitered in front of stables to service drivers and riders. Those of us who'd risen from the postal circuit knew that type of sturdy lady well.

I even knew four ex-slaves—clever girls—who had used their earnings as freedwomen to set up a business they ran without the interference of any man. I certainly counted them as friends.

So of course I waited for some kind of jocular explanation from our guards, the kind of jest or introduction to this world that men make to each other. Instead the Caesar's guards said nothing. They ignored the girls entirely.

I kept my head down. With my North African coloring, I blended in well as long as I kept my mouth shut. Not only did I not know any Antiochene jargon, I didn't know the local secrets. To joke with the scum of any town, you had to recognize the gangs who fixed the Hippodrome betting, the latest celebrity gladiator's name, and the best place to get your sandals fixed.

To my surprise, Gallus knew all this and more. As he bargained with the proprietor to free up a table for us, I realized the Caesar's Greek was astonishingly fluent for a boy locked up in a cushioned dungeon in Caesarea from the age of twelve. Then I realized that his keepers must have been Greek speakers.

'We'll have a round of your freshest grub,' Gallus said to the proprietor. He dropped a few coins into the man's greasy apron pocket and sat our party down next to a table of carousers who looked well into their cups.

The drinks were cool and the seafood fresh enough, but that's not why we were here. Our two bodyguards sat as stiff as the statues we'd passed in the Forum, but Gallus acted in his element. I watched the Caesar lean over to our neighbors to borrow their flask of *garum* sauce to season his fish balls. Within seconds, he was bantering back and forth across the gap between stools about the night's show, which had just ended. As they chatted, he toyed with a wide little knife set out for oyster customers. It reminded me of his sister's habit with letter openers.

One neighbor was garrulous enough. 'It was a comedy, taking the piss out of the high and mighty,' the man nearest to my back shouted to Gallus through the general roistering. 'Not all that tragic posturing,' he slung his fishy hands in the air mimicking a rhetorical pose. 'Just a rollicking good belly laugh. Go and see it.'

A scrawny beggar child came up to our tables. He held out a skeletal hand. I gave him a coin.

'Don't encourage them,' the playgoer barked. 'It's bad enough down in the Forum. Their parents train them to it.'

'The play's good?' Gallus asked.

'Well, it made fun of those squealers, you know, the ones who work for the Palace.'

'What squealers?'

The man threw himself back in mock disbelief and raised his eyebrows at me in appeal. 'Oh, c'mon, you must know. I mean the party crashers who smuggle their way into polite houses to listen to all the society tittle-tattle and then go rat for a big reward across the river to you-know-who.'

The man jerked his head in the direction of the Palace and winked at me. Under their hoods our two guards kept their eyes down and concentrated on sucking the garlicky olive oil off their mussels. They were making a great deal out of very little. My own serving was pitiably small. Someone knocked the rope supporting the vendor's lanterns and the sharp swing in the lights suddenly caught illuminated my companions' features. I got a jolt of surprise. My companions-at-arms were both beardless eunuchs. No wonder they showed no interest in the young women flaunting their wares around us.

'But my friend, why shouldn't people report injustice to the Palace? Isn't it good of the Caesar to open his doors to everyone?' Gallus pretended half-interest as he mopped up the juices on his plate with a scrap of flatbread.

'But he's so gullible, that's what's so funny in the play, don't you see? These two stoolpigeons named Fedor and Ilias make up wilder and wilder stories based on nothing of course but whatever nonsense they invent. No matter how ridiculous, the Caesar believes them and hands them sacks of gold *solidi*.'

'Hah!' Gallus laughed and shot me a look. I laughed on cue.

'Tell us more about this play,' Gallus said.

'Well, it gets so crazy that by Act III, Fedor and Ilias go to the back gate of the Palace with a wagon just to carry out all this gold the Caesar has promised them for *nothing*! They claim they needed advance payment for *expenses* and our stupid Caesar agreed!'

Our fellow diner began to laugh so hard, he had to stop for a moment to collect his breath. 'But then their slave loses control of the wagon brake and all their reward tumbles into the river and just then, the Caesar's wife comes out of the Palace gate and—oh, well, I can see you're not amused. I must have told it wrong. But I insist, you have to see it for yourself.'

The diner shook himself sick with laughing and then started choking on a piece of dry bread. One of his buddies pounded the victim's back and looked over at Gallus for sympathy. Then in an instant, the friend's eyes widened with alarm. His spine jerked straight up and he stopped pounding on the playgoer's back. He pulled on his laughing friend, trying to remove him safely away from our table.

'That's enough, Caduceus,' he murmured, 'It's time to get you to bed.'

'No, no, I haven't finished my wine,' Caduceus sputtered, still chortling and shaking off his friend's counseling hand.

Gallus smiled to himself and kept wiping up his plate. Our *domestici* tossed each other sly glances.

'You don't know who you might be talking to. This man might report *you*,' the friend whispered.

'What? Why? There was a whole audience in there that just saw the play, right? Is this man going to report a hundred people?'

'Keep your voice down. There's safety in numbers. Let the actors take the blame, not you.'

The drunken man lurched into Gallus' face and cajoled, 'You're going to report *me* for a bag of gold coins, my friend?'

Gallus smirked. 'Of course not. If we reported it, they might close the play before we got a chance to see it.'

'That's right. You see?'

The sober friend tossed Gallus a worried look. He pulled Caduceus up on his feet and dragged him away from the table. 'C'mon, come *on.*' He tossed a few coins on the table. The two men wove away between the outer ring of customers. They headed out of the little square and off down one of the myriad narrow alleys. We heard their hysterical laughter and cautions mingling and echoing off the brick walls.

'Get that man's full name from the owner,' Gallus muttered to his two eunuchs, 'and then make sure the route back to the bridge is clear. We want to talk to this *agens* alone.'

'You're sure, *Domine*?'

'Yes, of course. We'll be fine.'

The guards both gave me a warning look and then slipped back toward the narrow route to the Forum. Soon the other diners had turned away from the two strangers in cloaks. The clatter and conversation returned to the previous boisterous level.

I sipped the rest of my wine and waited. For many minutes Gallus just sat there, pensive and silent, watching the flitting girls and listening to the random banter of the quarter. I wondered if he had forgotten me, but then recalled that he had spent his entire imprisoned youth under the gaze of silent inferiors and minions.

I was left to my own thoughts, which revolved around the curious sensation of fear I felt in his company—fear of his weakness rather than any particular strength or talent I could detect. It was the irrational nervousness one might experience near the bedside of someone sick and contagious.

Suddenly, he leaned across the table and asked, 'Do you like eunuchs?'

'I haven't known many, Caesar.'

'Really? How extraordinary! Sometimes we get tired of being surrounded by eunuchs. All our life, they've been watching us . . . Do you like the Circus?'

I had trouble hearing him over the carousing going on all around our table. I leaned closer. 'Yes, of course, Caesar. Although I don't have very many leisure hours to attend the Games.'

'We like it when one of the boxers gets the better of his opponent and really starts pounding him down and the blood flows into the sand.' His fist clenched an almost empty beaker of wine. The fine knuckles of his hand became hard white knobs.

'I enjoy a good bet as much as the next man, Caesar.'

'We don't care about the betting. We just like to watch them fight it out. You know, the Circus is right opposite the Palace? If we slip out, nobody misses us. Some days we watch six or seven fights in a row. We can never get enough. You know why?'

'No, Caesar.'

'Because we feel so close then to life, we can forget who we are. We feel like we're the one doing the pounding, beating the man until his flesh breaks and his skull cracks.'

'Yes, I see.'

'Have you ever been on the battlefield, *Agens*?'

'Caesar—?'

'—or have you spent your whole life riding up and down the *Cursus Publicus* delivering letters from one end of the Empire to the other?'

I detected a complete contempt of bureaucrats in his tone.

'I was at Mursa, Caesar.'

It was none of his business that memories of Mursa woke me up in a cold sweat many a night. Again and again, I was carrying the bloodied Commander toward the medics' tents and each time, the nightmare let me down. We couldn't make it in time. He died again and again as I held him.

'Did the killing make your blood run hot the way the Circus makes ours?'

'I believe it does in some men, Caesar but not in myself.'

I only remembered the confusion, the pain, the exhaustion, the panic and the grief—but this would sound un-Roman. So I said 'Homer wrote of bloodlust, so I know it exists.'

'Yes.' he smiled to himself. 'Is it true we lost fifty-four thousand men in one day?'

'I believe we lost enough more, but no one could count. The fighting started late in the day and continued through the night. When the sun rose, it was impossible to tell where one body ended and another began, the limbs and guts of men were so intermingled.'

Gallus leaned away from the table and nodded to himself with a strange sort of satisfaction. 'None of them were eunuchs, that's for certain. We wish we'd been there.' He gave an envious sigh that turned my stomach, as if I'd said he'd just missed a particularly exciting chariot race.

I wanted to change the subject. 'Are the servings in Antiochia always so stingy?' I pointed to the pathetic hill of mussel shells left in each of our bowls.

'Times are difficult,' Gallus shrugged. 'If you're hungry you can eat your fill back at the Palace. We come here for information, not food.'

'The people who do come here for food won't be leaving with satisfied bellies.'

'If they're going hungry, it's hardly our fault,' he said, tossing me an angry glance that put me in my place.

I had had enough Constantines for one day but of course it was up to the Caesar to decide when to leave. He tried to make conversation again with one or another of the diners nearby, but the hour was late. The portions were meager and the bad wine was going to their heads. Their state of drunkenness or fatigue was too advanced for the Caesar's pointed games.

I suspected we were about to leave when the man who had dragged his friend Caduceus away from the tables suddenly re-appeared in a pool of lantern light behind Gallus' shoulder.

Underneath his short cloak, his weapon hand was crooked around something at his waist. He approached the Caesar from behind before I could intervene and put his lips to Gallus' ear. He said in a low voice:

'I trust we're not going to have a trouble about that conversation a while ago, my friend. You dress like someone who doesn't need any more gold than he already has.'

Gallus shrugged but he didn't turn around or let the lanterns overhead shine onto his telltale features. New coins had just been minted that bore his profile, with its high-bridged nose and pursing mouth. The man leaning over our table might be carrying the Caesar's image in his coin purse at this very minute.

'We don't want any more trouble than you do, Citizen,' I said, rising to my feet and inserting myself between the seated ruler and his accoster.

'You speak Greek with the accent of a westerner, Stranger. You may not understand the ways of Antiochia well enough to stick your nose into this little conversation,' he warned me.

The laughing around the other tables fell to a murmur. Stools scraped back through the sawdust as the lingering diners backed away. Some of them scuttled out of sight through the players' door at the back of the theater.

Then out of the far shadows at the other end of the square slunk a dozen other men headed right for our table. They held out naked blades, already extended to take me on. Their eyes were gaunt and hollow. Their arm muscles were slack but sinewy. They might have been living on mussels and anchovies—and little else—for a long time. The rest of their faces were hidden under threadbare rags tied over their noses.

Whatever they planned to do, it wasn't eating fish balls.

'*Domine*, prepare to run for the bridge.'

Gallus rose to his full height, turned and whispered straight into the first man's face, 'We have no intention of running. It will only excite his friends more, like curs chasing a hare. In fact, we'll watch your fight with pleasure.'

It was chilling, the way his voice rose with excitement, as if he were signaling combat from the safety of his imperial box set high above my head in the arena. With an elegant palm, he suddenly shoved the whisperer hard and back against the row of defenders. They quickly swallowed him up and closed ranks.

Now a much taller man emerged from the pack with the stance of a trained fighter. Gallus took a few steps back.

There was a risk that if I concentrated on this larger attacker and made the first move, the others might circle round us and, like catch dogs on a hunt, trap and finish us off.

Or they might take fright. The Caesar was showing no inclination to make his escape. It was a gamble I had to take.

I pulled my *spatha* from its scabbard and advanced on their champion. I had no shield, so I yanked a light wooden stool up by a leg. Using that, I moved on him with short thrusts to test his speed and eye.

I had startled him with my confidence, yet he recovered fast enough. He moved on me, bringing his sword from up high down toward my left shoulder but of course, I had foreseen his preparation. I dodged, letting the stool take the blow and holding it well up in front of my face, I swung low at his unprotected calves. He sidestepped but wasn't ready for an army trick I'd learned as Commander Gregorius' *volo* bodyguard—to feint a broad leftward swing but without warning stop short, twist, reverse and then carve my blade back through the air to the right.

It took a lot of strength and expert timing but I was lucky. My blade caught his calf and he cried out. I seized my opportunity and with a simultaneous forward thrust of my left arm, I smashed the stool seat into his lowered head. Although the stool had none of the impact of a shield boss, I heard a satisfying crack of bone as he fell back into the arms of his fellows.

I pulled back to be ready for the next comer and gauged the remaining opposition. One man took a few steps forward but hesitated. I tossed the stool aside and grabbed his tunic front with my free hand. I spit into his face. In a low voice I murmured, 'Take me on, if you must, but your *Caesar* would hate to see a good citizen die.'

Even under the garish glow of those dancing lanterns, I saw the blood drain from his brow. He stared past me, hard at Gallus in his hooded cloak, standing not far away with his arms crossed over his chest and eager eyes flashing with anticipation at the next bout. I may have leaked the truth of Gallus' underhanded recreation, but that indiscretion tossed the dice my way.

The man turned, shouted something in Greek too quick for me to catch. The whole gang took to its heels down that murky alley opposite.

I paid the cafe proprietor for our mussels, fishballs, and wine and hurried the sovereign ruler of the East back toward the bridge and his waiting escorts.

It was late when I finally found my assigned room and could wash away the evening's sweat. I fell on my mattress that night and for once was not haunted by the phantoms of Mursa.

Instead I found my mind returning over and over again to two very different but equally grotesque images imprinted on my memory of a first day in Antiochia. I couldn't forget the starving people in the windblown Forum standing huddled in a circle while they waited for their roasted cat to be ready for the sharing.

Worse, I remembered the flushing joy on Gallus' face as I hurried him through the fetid back alleys of the theater district back to the comfort and luxury of his imperial retreat.

'I must reward you,' Gallus had panted as the sentries at the bridge stopped us long enough to recognize their supreme officer. 'Name the amount.'

'It was my duty, Caesar.' All I wanted was a clean bed at last.

'All right then, not now, but later. I will not forget this evening. When you think of a reward, I will grant it. Oh, that was fun!'

Chapter 10, The Hall of Mirrors

—THE CAESAR'S PALACE—

The Praetorian Prefect *Praesens* Thalassius summoned me to his ground-floor meeting chamber early the next morning. Before I kept the appointment, I passed by the imperial nursery.

'Someone came for the boy,' the Gorgon whispered in a husky voice. 'His cousin is named Clodius?'

'He is the very man I feared. No, he is no blood relation. He wants to do the boy grievous injury. You didn't let him in?'

'No,' she said, but despite this reassurance, she looked troubled. Clodius must have worked hard at gaining entry.

I paid her and the nursery guards very well as a token of my thanks and found my way out of the imperial wing. After a few false turns, I trotted down a lengthy corridor. It was lined with tall windows of painted glass that reflected my hurrying form as I searched for the way to the bureaucratic wing of the Palace where Thalassius worked. As I hurried along, I took mental note that at the Eastern Empire's inflated rates, the Gorgon's pay was going to be double Lavinia's wages back in Roma.

I needn't have rushed. The Prefect's expressionless *domestici* kept me cooling off in a marble-pillared anteroom the size of a small gymnasium for ten minutes. Finally they ushered me into an interior room made cheerful by sunlight pouring down from a high window onto a dozen heads conferring around a long marble table.

As I was announced, Thalassius looked up at me from the head of his council. He made no effort to disguise his irritation at my interruption and that annoyance was reflected on the expressions of his grim-faced officials.

'Gentlemen, this is one Marcus Gregorianus Numidianus. Declare your business, *Agens*.'

I now faced one of the most powerful officials at Gallus' court, an old man somewhat over fifty with no time to waste. Compared to the colorful tunics and embroidered Eastern robes worn by the other councilors, his own garb was old-fashioned— almost ridiculously classic in its simplicity. He wore no jewelry or insignia, no decorative trim on his immaculate cream tunic or fringe on the unbleached woolen toga draped over one shoulder. His sparse white hair was trimmed tight to his scalp.

'I've been sent to check procedures in the case of Clematius the Alexandrian executed for incestuous rape.' A secretary recorded my words in shorthand almost more quickly that I got them past my lips.

'At whose request?'

'The *Magister* of my *schola*.'

His impatience rose. 'Your *schola* answers to the *Magister Officiorum* who reports directly to the Emperor. Do these orders come from Roma or Arelate?'

'My instructions come from Roma.'

'I see. The case of Clematius. Is that all?'

'Yes, Prefect.' The Castra masters taught us that the shortest lies worked best.

'Make all the files available to him,' he told a secretary. He waved me off and turned back to the senators. 'Who has the latest figures on wheat stocks arriving by land?'

I did not depart.

'Prefect, I beg a moment. I have questions to put to you. Perhaps we could speak in private?'

'Have you read the archive reports?'

'Not yet.'

'Then why would you have questions for me? I acknowledge the legal right of the *agentes* to investigate any matter, but before even reading the reports? Waste no more of our time.'

I had calculated badly. He was an accomplished manipulator. His secretaries were already flipping through their records for the wheat figures. A grain merchant was announced from the outer hall. Carrying a bundle of receipts, the merchant walked past me to the vicinity of the council table. A eunuch attendant took my arm to escort me to the archives room for study.

'*Agens*, wait!'

I turned as Thalassius examined me more carefully.

'Are you a Christian, *Agens*?'

'No, I am not a convert to that sect, Prefect.'

'It is the religion of our Emperor. Then you do not know what I mean by the Trinity?'

Thalassius made the Sign of the Cross and all his councilors did the same.

I was flummoxed. 'I know that the nature of Trinity is the subject of important theological disputes about the nature of Christ that have divided the Christian world, Prefect. They are too subtle for a pagan's comprehension. I know that the Emperor follows the teachings of Arius and has banished the Christian leader Athanassius from Alexandria for his insistence that Christ is—'

'The Trinity is something you should study,' he said, and with that cryptic jibe, waved me off.

I had been dismissed. As a slave child attending the old Gregorius, I'd seen hecklers removed from a Roman Senate meeting with more courtesy. There was nothing I could do for the moment.

I was retreating with my escort to a side door when the astonishing sight of the Caesar Gallus brushed right past me, ran up to the table, lifted Thalassius by his tunic and screamed, 'We told you to lower the grain prices. You and your hellhounds have raised prices!'

Thalassius' deputies peeled the Caesar off the Prefect. Thalassius shook himself and he turned his face to the wall as he took deep breaths to recover from the shock. My escort dropped my arm and ran back across the mosaic floor to assist Thalassius.

Gallus composed himself and in a scarcely less hysterical voice, asked, 'Why weren't we informed of this meeting?'

'Senate affairs are far beneath your station, Caesar,' Thalassius replied.

'You mean above our understanding, you supercilious, insolent paper-pusher.'

'The economic affairs of Syria are complicated,' Thalassius said. 'It's not only a question of the marketplace, but of production and demand. The harvest was weak this year and a weak harvest pushes prices up across the whole province—'

'Don't you talk down to us!' Gallus shook his fists at Thalassius with frustration. 'It's hoarding that is pushing up prices.'

'We have no time to chat with you at all. If this morning we can manage to assess the size of overall grain stocks between the Constantinopolis market down to south of Antiochia, we can adjust prices upwards to draw shipments to us faster.'

'Stop making excuses. Fill my markets with bread immediately!'

The nervous senators looked across at Thalassius. He seemed unfazed that his patient rebuttals were only driving Gallus into a frenzy. In a gesture of further disdain for the Caesar's presence, the Prefect sat back down in his chair and surveyed his deputies.

'Let us proceed. Mayor Luscus?'

A round-shouldered grayhead rose to his feet and was careful to look to Gallus before he read from his notes.

'Gracious Caesar, as you know the army's demand for wheat at the disputed border, particularly the *Legio X Fretensis*, has put a premium on tighter stocks this year and that in turn has triggered hoarding. In reaction, we have *raised* prices both to prevent any more hoarding and to encourage faster importation from producers farther afield into the Antiochia area,' the senator Luscus explained. 'The figures are here, Excellency.'

With a trembling arm, Luscus extended his sheaf of accounts to the young sovereign.

'Our people are starving! They're eating rats and rotting fish!' Gallus shouted at them.

'Our welfare stocks are used up, Caesar. Lower prices are useless if there is nothing left to price,' another senator said.

'There is famine out there on the streets! You are the hoarders! You're—! You're all—!'

Gallus sputtered with fury, then burst out at the guards posted around the edge of the room, 'Arrest this Senate! Arrest them! Arrest every single one of these greedy bastards! *GUARDS!*'

Barbatio burst into the room at the head of some two dozen *domestici*. He must have been standing, armed and ready, in the anteroom waiting for Gallus' command.

I sheltered against the doorway connecting to the archive rooms next door and watched as a dozen men in ornate finery were dragged, shoved, and prodded away from the table and into the main reception hall beyond. Mayor Luscus ran after them, protesting. Barbatio's face was a mix of nerves, efficiency, and brutality. I wondered how the arrest of the municipal senate was going to be portrayed in one of his clumsy, misspelt reports back to the West.

But Barbatio had left Thalassius untouched. The whole confrontation had taken less than two minutes. The Prefect sat alone now, facing the length of an empty marble table scattered with papers.

As a visitor to Antiochia, I had witnessed a terrible scene. I hardly dared breathe or move for fear of causing the Prefect more humiliation.

Slowly, Thalassius stood up and leaned both his hands on the table. His head hung low with discouragement perhaps, but then he lifted his face to survey the vacant room and discovered it was not quite empty.

Pride flickered in his fearless eyes. Thalassius did not feel humiliated by the Caesar's outburst at all—quite the contrary.

'Read the reports, Numidianus, *all of them*,' he said, his voice thick with anger. 'Then come back to me.'

꙳꙳꙳

The archive on the Clematius case turned out to be more interesting than I would have guessed. Perhaps Thalassius wasn't just trying to forestall a private interview. I copied out the name of the mother-in-law accusing Clematius of the crime. I confirmed that no other formal testimony had been taken before his arrest and conviction, and that his protests even under torture had included numerous counter-accusations of jealousy, seduction attempts, and cruelty by the mother-in-law to her daughter, his wife.

Attached to the main report were post-execution appendices, many of them brief notes about his character and background. Clematius had been about thirty years old, of sterling reputation, a good employer, and a man on the rise in local financial circles. Having formed a partnership with a brother who remained behind in Egypt, Clematius was quick enough to have nearly cornered the Antiochene market in quality cotton imports.

Someone who rose so quickly might well have made enemies. Now Clematius was gone for good and no doubt the competition to dominate the local cotton market had picked up after his demise. If his case had been handled correctly, then more of the larger story might have emerged. But the case hadn't been handled right at all. There had been no one to defend him even *pro forma* and even the follow-up reports looked sloppy, hasty, and in certain bits, even self-contradictory. If Thalassius and his friends were in a conspiracy to discredit the Caesar, they could start by tearing this dossier apart.

I flipped through the brief records again. That was it. Thalassius had admonished me to read *all* the reports.

'Is there any more on this Clematius conviction?' I asked the bent and bony registrar curating the judicial archives. He was as dusty as his files and I imagined I could have actually traced a path through the flakes of dried scroll and leather that coated his white eyebrows. The little man peered up at me as if years of reading had strained his sight.

'Nothing more on him.'

I pondered this as I tied up the file with its golden string and handed it back to him.

'Were there any other cases similar to this one?'

'How many years you want to go back?'

'The reign of the current Caesar, for the moment.'

'That's about three years. You got much time, young fellow?'

He walked up and down the shelves where stacks of dossiers sat piled behind us. He disappeared from sight for many minutes and I heard him humming along to the thud of record books and files. Soon he returned, trundling a little cart ahead of him. It was filled with more than a dozen heavy files bound in that same gold string.

'Start wherever you like,' he shrugged. 'I guess you *agentes* are as nosy as they say.'

I asked for a beaker of fresh water, found a table and stool and dug back in.

Not many of these cases had gone to court, but dozens of charges—for arson, rape, fraud, robbery, and murder—had been laid under the reign of the current Caesar. They all resulted in sudden convictions by imperial fiat. What trials had been conducted had been comically swift, lasting only an hour or two. Defense witnesses had been rejected on flimsy grounds. Families had appealed and lost and then appealed again, complaining that legal fees due to unjust incarcerations had left them bankrupt without anything left to pay their lawyers.

Some cases petered out in bailiffs' reports that defendants reduced to bankruptcy had escaped Antiochia without warning by night and could not be traced. Sadder files ended with the stomach-churning details of torture as reported by humorless jailors in the featureless handwriting of a professional clerk. 'Satisfactory confessions' had been obtained after the removal of so many fingers, so much skin, so many eyes or ears, the flaying of so much skin or the burning of nipples and genitals.

Paul the Chain was the only man I knew who could have read the whole table's worth of gore with any relish. Halfway through, I took a break and reviewed my notes. I finished off my beaker of water warming in the sunlight pouring through the window. Something odd struck my mind. I went back to check the files again. I looked at the index of documents starting each file, and then I riffled through the first complete dossier, then the second and then a third, a fourth, and a fifth.

Each dossier was missing one numbered document. Exactly one, never more, but without a title for the missing entry, how could I guess what it was? Some final document authorizing execution? A letter of appeal from below or a protest from above? When there was so much shameful left here to read, what could be so sensitive that it couldn't be included? Who had filleted all the files by just one single page? And where had those pages gone?

'There are pages missing from each of these,' I told the archivist. 'The index says there should be a page here, and here and . . . here.'

He glanced at the indexes and said, 'I'll have to look into it.'

He waited and then glanced up at me with a strange and expectant expression on his face. Was there something else I should say, and if so, what?

I heard an angry scuffle in the small walkway between the council meeting room and the door to the archives.

'Is he in there?'

Clodius came roaring up to me and pounded his fist on the archivist's counter, sending up a cloud of dust.

'How dare you, you greasy Numidian, how dare you deny me access to my own family!'

'Clodius, come with me. Let's discuss this out in the gardens. This is a sensitive matter where things can be overheard and misunderstood.'

Clodius swallowed his torrent of abuse long enough for me to get him through the public reception rooms and outside into the imperial outdoor enclosures. This gave me many valuable seconds to gather my wits. We found the Palace gardens laced with walkways, fountains, and bare fruit trees basking in the midday heat. No one in their right mind wanted to be outside in this heat and I wanted our conversation out of the earshot of those obliging eunuchs who seemed as ubiquitous as flyswatters indoors.

'Leo is safe for the moment. He's learning the ways of the court. I thought you wanted to make a gift of him. What good is a gift that can't speak Greek and makes a fool of himself?'

Clodius stared at me in disbelief and then burst into cold laughter. 'You idiot, with all your books and quotations! No one here cares if a pretty child can speak Greek—or speak anything else for that matter! While you've been wasting time on one of your tiresome errands, I've already announced my gift and negotiated my "thank you." Now it would be decent of you to allow me to deliver what I just promised! That crone in the nursery won't let me even see the brat, much less remove him.'

I had been a fool to think that Clodius had been spending the last twenty-four hours enjoying himself in the baths or theater. As I had credited him back in Roma that night we dined together, when Clodius wanted something, he was determined and crafty. He had no preoccupation in this troubled city but offloading the boy to the highest bidder. I had learned that evil sniffs out evil quick enough. He'd already found his buyer.

'I have to be brutally candid with you, Clodius. I've been looking into it and whatever your friends in Roma told you, it's just as illegal in the Eastern Empire as it is in the West to take a healthy child and hand him over to be castrated. You risk prosecution. It could mean execution for you.'

Clodius pushed me down on a garden bench and leaned right into my face. 'I've talked all that through. Are you blind, Marcus? Has the midday heat gone to your head? Haven't you noticed? This place is crawling with eunuchs. And do you know why?'

'The Emperor is famous for having hundreds of cooks and eunuchs in his courts?'

'Because that Palace right there is *run* by eunuchs. I know you think I'm a bit of a fop but even I couldn't wear that much perfume without being laughed out of town. As it is, I can't show my face in Roma because of Picenus and his bloody will. Now I've just been promised enough money to pay back all my debts and set myself up in one of the western courts, like we said. Treverorum, maybe, or even Mediolanum.'

'No five-year-old could bring that much.'

'You're pretty smart for a slave. You're right. The Manlius estate's revenues are worth even more, once the debts are paid off.'

I was confused, possibly by the sun, the buzzing of insects, and the shimmering garden vista, which for a few seconds wavered like heat off the desert in front of my eyes. For an instant I felt as if the pavement under my feet had turned to water. I gripped the stone bench with both hands. Was I sick? Had I been poisoned?

'Clodius? I'm not feeling well. I think I need some food. I haven't had much sleep. What were you saying?'

Clodius looked a little dazed by the noon sun as well. He was leaning on a tree for support. 'I was trying to explain to you that control of the Manlius portfolio, which I admit is temporarily suffering from over-borrowing and missing documents, is worth more long-term to a rich investor than a mere boy.'

Now I had full comprehension of the 'deal' Clodius was trying to strike.

'You can't sell the Manlius properties without the deeds, and there's always the Imperial Land Registry to deal with—'

'I've solved that problem and if you help me, I'm willing to give you a cut. Someone acting as the boy's regent, someone with bottomless pockets, can revive the estate properties and supervise the Manlius income for Leo, just as I have. Providing Leo sires no heirs, and soon enough that is going to be very unlikely, that certain someone could expect to transfer those rights to any executor they choose. I've just met the perfect recipient for my gift—an expert on wills, on property, and on eunuchs. A man who doesn't care about the law whatsoever.'

'Who is he?'

'He is so powerful that he can arrange a little "accident" that might befall the brat, with no questions asked. It's a little secret between us, but as soon as Leo is in his care, I can leave for home.'

'Who is it?' I felt my panic overriding common sense. It couldn't be *him*.

'Nah, uh, uh. You give me Leo and I'll tell you who it is.'

I begged off his insistence that I let the Gorgon release Leo into his care so soon after arriving after such a long trip. I promised to deal with the matter tomorrow at the latest. Meanwhile my mind raced with the implications of what Clodius had worked out and how I could better ensure Leo stayed secure from his cousin's clutches.

There was only one person I could think of that met Clodius' awestruck description, yet that man wasn't in Antiochia. He was still on his way here from Mediolanum via Constantinopolis.

Or was he?

☙☙☙

I left Clodius in the gardens and found Barbatio in the imperial stables behind the guardhouse on the opposite side of the immense Palace complex. The main building for the horses was so vast and elaborate a structure, it could have happily housed a Roman clan of thirty. Barbatio was supervising a couple of assistant guards carrying out an inventory of equipment. Somewhere in the rear of the building, I heard the stomping and snorting of horses in their paddocks, the splashing of buckets and the swish of brooms on hay. The usual smell of horse sweat and turds floated through the warm breeze. I gawped at dozens of ceremonial harnesses, banners, processional masks, and saddles laid out like Midas' treasure on the tack tables in front of us.

'Barbatio, is the Lord Chamberlain in Antiochia?'

With a look of distaste, Barbatio gave me just the answer I most feared.

'I hear he arrived late last night by express carriage and started business at dawn without losing a moment, which is just as well, because he had a pile of correspondence waiting for him.'

'Has he presented his respects to the Caesar or the *Augusta*?'

Barbatio shrugged. 'Why should he? He's too busy to bother with them until the pressure dies down.'

He turned from his inventory lists and flexed his barrel chest at me. 'You investigated my story?'

'Your account about Clematius is corroborated in writing, all except the diamond necklace. That remains hearsay. I still have to talk to the mother-in-law. But first I have to see Eusebius. Where is the *Clarissimus*?'

Barbatio walked me out of the stables and into the glare of the unshaded parade ground. I was struck yet again by his expensive getup—the polish and spit of his sword belt and armor, the fine woolen tunic, and the expensive polished boots. He turned me by the shoulders to face the broad Palace facade stretching from the walls overlooking the baths on our left to the walls facing Gallus' beloved Circus on the right.

'That is the administrative wing,' he pointed to the left side, 'and that is the private wing,' he pointed to the upper windows on the right, 'and Eusebius' office is buried deep in the belly between the two, like the center of a web where the spider sits and pulls all his little threads.'

'Can you take me to him?'

'Not now, Numidianus. Can't you see I'm busy? If you're in a hurry, ask one of the *domestici* to escort you through. If they give you trouble, say you carry a message from me.'

It was not hard to find a eunuch. It would have been harder not to trip over one, but I thought it would be easier to deal with one who'd witnessed my authority as an official visitor with a commission over the last twenty-four hours.

My worries were unfounded. I accosted two of the silent types swishing past in lavender silk robes and silver-tasseled damask slippers carrying towels and refreshments to the administrative wing. I asked for a guide to the Lord Chamberlain's rooms.

'Certainly,' one said without a moment's hesitation. He gave his pile of towels to his companion and stretched out his hand. 'This way, *Agens* Numidianus.'

I concluded that there wasn't a single member of the 'third sex' in the entire building who didn't already know my name, rank and at least some of my purpose in Antiochia.

I trailed after him in silence, working out how to destroy any idea that Clodius might have planted in Eusebius' mind regarding the Manlius estates. Soon we two were gliding along the long corridor of polished glass when something caught my eye. I stopped and realized I was trembling. I'd seen a mirage. It was the reflection of a long woman's dress in a mirror, but not just any dress—a dress I recognized.

The dress was sewn from fine silk dyed a clear and noble blue and hemmed with a red and gold embroidered trim that floated and danced around the wearer's legs. I had never forgotten that dress. How many such dresses were there in the Empire? Hundreds? Dozens? I had admired only one.

It was Kahina's dress. I was sure of it. Fashions had changed since the war and I could have sworn women weren't wearing that drape or cut these days. Clodius, damn him, was an expert on women's fashions, but I wasn't waiting for his opinion. It was Kahina's dress, the very same dress she'd worn during the long Aquileian summer in the court of Magnentius. It had been a stifling summer—the dead and pregnant calm before the storm that broke over our heads.

It had to be the same dress. It went with that girdle of woven gold and red that matched the hem and was in that distinctive blue that Roman tunic vendors called 'Phoenician.'

I ignored the summoning gesture of my mystified guide. Without any explanation, I sprinted off in the direction of the dress, chasing faster and faster, unsure whether I'd seen the original or just a reflection bouncing off the polished glass panes along the walls and even multiplying their images between each other at all these corners, angles, and curves of corridor.

I glimpsed her again now, just a fleeting silhouette, a narrow slice of blue, slipping away down the narrowing arteries into the private imperial wing. I continued to trot after her, finally losing the bewildered eunuch before I reached the end of the corridor. I stopped for a moment to figure out where she had turned next.

Another *domesticus* spotted me now. He hailed me in a languid way, but I was already safely past him, turning and panting a bit in the heat, but there she was again, just within my sights. This time she wasn't getting away.

'Kahina?' I shouted. I dashed toward her but she didn't turn because just then one of the imperial maids had come up and distracted her. They were exchanging some words at the end of a very long and unfamiliar passage.

'Kahina!'

She didn't answer my echoing cry. Her back was still turned to me as she conversed with the other woman. For a moment I remembered my dashed hopes last October back in Arelate that Kahina would be in the last convoy of prisoners. I recalled that wave of crushing disappointment all over again. But that woman hadn't been wearing *her* dress, hadn't covered her hair with the matching *palla* Kahina always wore with it, and hadn't wrapped her waist in Kahina's favorite red and gold girdle.

I ran up to her and took her by the shoulders.

'Kahina!'

She turned abruptly and lit up, saying, 'Oh, Marcus, I can't believe my eyes. Is it you? You survived Mursa after all.'

I couldn't believe my eyes either. The woman smiling up at me with shining eyes sprouting with tears was not Kahina, but *Roxana*. She was a girl I'd trained with, a fellow *agens* I'd bedded, and in the end, a traitor I'd cursed for riding off with the same General Silvanus who had betrayed everyone in Magnentius' doomed court.

As beautiful and impetuous as ever, Roxana threw her arms around my neck and kissed me passionately.

Chapter 11, Friends in Low Places

—The Imperial Wing, Antiochia Palace—

'Why are you wearing *Domina* Kahina's dress?' I threw off Roxana's suffocating embrace and glared down into her eyes.

'Oh, Marcus, don't look at me like that. To find you here in Antiochia, of all places!'

'You stole it all—the dress, the girdle?'

'No! *No!* It was Kahina's gift to me after that terrible row in Aquileia. It was her peace offering and I gave her an inlaid cosmetics box in return. Don't you remember how we fought over something silly?'

Roxana lowered her eyes because the real trigger of their vicious wrestling match on the floor of Empress Justina's private suite had been jealousy—jealousy over me.

I didn't flatter myself that I was any kind of lady-killer—I leave that to other men. There are tireless 'swordsmen' like my *Ioviani* friend Cornelius. He managed to keep a dozen girls satisfied on the basis of a kind word, a generous purse, and sympathy for their lowly plight. At the other end of the social scale, there are celebrity gladiators who attract the exclusive ladies of polite salons. Between arena victories, they were more than ready to gratify their fans' voracious lusts. The more notorious of these famous lovers were so pressingly endowed that their bosses had to thread their penises with clamps before a match to restrain their vital energies.

There was no such requirement with me. I was half Cornelius' age and got half his salary. And while no one complained of my skills in bed, I suspected I could have learned a lot from a skilled gladiator. But just this once in my life, two women had pulled each other's hair out over an amulet that belonged to me. The amulet was merely an excuse. They had realized that at one point or another, I had made love to each of them.

A young man making his way alone through life doesn't easily forget such scenes but there were other things on my mind right now.

'I must see the Lord Chamberlain.'

'Oh.' Roxana's happy expression faltered and with it went my initial impression of exotic beauty untouched by the upheavals and betrayals of recent years. She had changed since Mursa. We all had.

'He's hardly been here a day. I haven't seen him myself.'

I wondered if she was still spying for Eusebius. She had fled to him for both promotion and security, quitting our service in haste and silence. To my knowledge, she was the only female Apodemius had ever recruited for full-time training as an *agens*. It seemed for a time that Roxana had blossomed into one of the *schola*'s star agents. She had excelled in every task our instructors set. Her secret successes during and after training had earned my admiration and envy.

In the end, however, Roxana betrayed our service—not because she'd failed to meet Apodemius' requirements—but out of frustrated ambition. She felt unrewarded for her bravery and brains by a male hierarchy that used her primarily as a honeyed means of trapping powerful men.

Back at the Castra, Apodemius had written her off as 'his failed experiment'.

'Don't scowl, Marcus. I know Eusebius will want to see you,' she drew back at my cool tone.

'Where will I find you later?'

'Ask for me at the entrance of the corridor leading to the nursery wing. I work there as one of the ladies attending the poor princess Anastasia.'

'You answer to that crone who bars the door to all men trying to enter?'

'That "crone" knows her job. So do I. The question is, what is yours? What are you doing here so far east?'

'I can't explain now, Roxana and certainly not to you. You betrayed the service.'

'So you are here on a job? I had hoped . . . will you come to me tonight, Marcus? Ask the crone where to find me.'

I agreed to that much. I would ask Roxana later who she really worked for. Her old 'target,' the traitorous General Claudius Silvanus, was far away defending the troubled Rhenus River border. Perhaps she was her own woman now. More likely, she still spied for Eusebius. If so, she could help me in protecting Leo. In any event, Apodemius would be interested to know I had discovered her here.

As Barbatio had warned me, Eusebius' offices sat buried deep in a windowless set of rooms, devoid of the elegant luxury he enjoyed in more permanent rooms. Within twenty feet of his door, I could have finished my search just following my nose. He had not changed his heavy use of scent, a mix of amber and sandalwood.

'Bring him to me,' I heard the eunuch's voice answer his secretary behind a carved cedar door.

Eusebius had survived the civil war by staying at a safe distance from the conflict. His smooth cheeks carried no trace of the years of division and destruction. His lifeless fawn-colored hair was the same. The hem of his wide maroon robes stood out on either side of him, stiff with heavy gold embroidery swishing across the floor as he greeted me.

The only noticeable change was an increase in the bulging of his eyes. They gave his bloated face the look of someone close to bursting. I was sure the man would have oozed beads of pus or bile, not blood or sweat, if someone dared to prick him.

His thick lips and soft white hands repelled me as much as ever. I had not thought Barbatio's description surprising. I often thought of him myself as a fat, pale spider, a dominating head full of greedy secrets attached to an oversized abdomen stuffed with confiscated riches. He was always stretching out his tentacles to acquire more. Indifferent to morality, he cared nothing for the Empire itself and was happy to divide and conquer its interests for his personal benefit.

Apodemius' reports with false information to Eusebius in my name must have worked well. The eunuch still thought I was his man. He was wrong, of course, but I needed his help too much to disabuse his warm welcome.

'Lord Chamberlain. I'm glad to see you looking so well.'

He was not alone. My appearance in the doorway interrupted his intimate conference with a guest. The tall, elegant visitor with a high-nosed profile rose from a wide-armed chair. With fingers hampered by iron seal rings around his knuckles, he arranged his official's cloak around him and readied to leave.

'Governor Theophilus, please don't go. This impetuous *agens* will only take up a minute.'

'Our business is done for the moment. I've told you all I can. You've told me what you can do and what you can't. I'm going to rely on your influence with the Caesar nonetheless. Good-day, Lord Chamberlain.'

I bent a knee as this haughty Theophilus swooshed past me on his exit from our company. I wasn't surprised when Eusebius sighed and confided to me, 'Theophilus stands on too much ceremony, like so many in the East. Our business hadn't even really started but he took offense when I admitted a *curiosus* into the room without his permission.'

I ignored the deprecating *curiosus*.

'I can retire and wait outside, *Clarissimus*.'

'Not at all, Numidianus, it does such men good to insult them from time to time so they know where they really stand.'

'He is . . .?'

'Of course, how could you know? That was the Governor *Consularis* of Syria, Theophilus.'

Eusebius settled himself back down behind his capacious desk. The surface was polished to a shine. There were no papers in sight.

I recalled the bent and timorous Luscus discussing the diminished grain supplies with Thalassius just before Gallus' imperious interruption.

'Does Theophilus want to raise grain prices, like Mayor Luscus?'

Eusebius stared at me, clearly startled that I was so up to date on the grain debate.

'The Governor Consularis would like people to think he has been an imperial consul proper, but of course he's merely pretending. He has no real power, even less than poor Mayor Luscus.'

'But he would agree with Luscus that prices should be made more attractive?'

'Yes, but in the meantime, he wants to import an emergency supply and distribute it free as welfare, which would suit the Caesar. I don't know where the money for that would come from. Either way these things work themselves out. Poor Luscus remains shut up in prison along with the senators.'

Eusebius had wasted no time himself in catching up with events. Before I could ask how the Senate might be rescued, he hastened to change the subject.

'I had no idea you were in the East, Numidianus. This gives me a chance to thank you for your dispatches.'

His eyes bulged out suggestively.

'I hope my information proved useful. I've never forgotten your timely protection in Sirmium. I owe you my life. Paulus Catena has not forgiven my escape, thanks to your hiding me away in that brothel.'

Eusebius took out a silk handkerchief and patted down his moist forehead. 'Oh, I enjoy frustrating Catena's amusements.'

'Lucky for me.'

'I have no sympathy for that kind of thing. If I want a man dead, he dies. I don't need to watch him eaten by insects in a vat of honey and shit. That Hispaniard's provincial desires are so crude, he bores me.'

'Your desires, Lord Chamberlain, are mine, I'm sure.'

Eusebius gestured to a wide glass-covered dish sitting on his desk. He lifted the cover to reveal an exquisite silver-handled fruit knife next to a selection of glistening plums.

'Delights from Damascus?'

'I've been feeling unsteady since my arrival, so no thanks. Perhaps I'm not used to the food. In any event I prefer honeyed figs.'

There was a telltale pause as his lashless eyelids flickered. Then he resumed, 'If you're not visiting the East for the spices, why are you here, *Agens* Numidianus?'

'To clear the judicial case of an Alexandrian, one Clematius, off the complaints books.'

'That doesn't concern me, surely?'

'No. I seek your help, Lord Chamberlain, on a private matter.'

He smiled, his suspicions of intrigue confirmed. His teeth were discolored and rotting, as if the poison of his character mixed with his sweet diet like a corroding *acetum*. 'Good. Private affairs are always more interesting than local grain prices or old court cases. Tell me more.'

'I'm afraid it interferes with your *own* private affairs.'

His smile turned to a grimace. 'What could you possibly know of those?'

'It concerns a gift to you of a small child concluded as soon as you arrived?'

'I spend little time in Antiochia and when a pile of correspondence waits on my desk and the benefactor haunts my doorstep, I accept any tribute or contribution to the court with grateful speed.'

'Surely your duties to the Emperor mean you don't have time to waste on a child?'

'I am a devoted follower of the presbyter Arius. Any orphan needing sanctuary will always find charity in my Christian heart.'

I could make Leo out to be more important than he was and scare Eusebius with the law but I now hesitated about the threat mere law held for the man over whom even Constantius II was said to have only *some* influence. And in the last two days I'd seen how Roman law meant nothing when the Antiochene jails groaned under our feet with people imprisoned on a Caesar's whim.

I could take the opposite path. I could claim that Leo had nothing to do with the Manlius estates and that he was a nameless street urchin dressed up by Clodius to dupe the eunuch.

What I couldn't do was tell that truth—that I was Leo's natural father and that I held the key to the deeds to his fortune, even if their whereabouts remained a mystery. I couldn't say to the world's most powerful eunuch that the thought of what might happen to my own son in his care made me nauseous with terror.

But an *agens* is trained to hew as close to the truth as possible when he lies, as close as he can get to that narrow sliver between success and failure. First, I had to know exactly what Clodius had told Eusebius. I let an uncomfortable silence compete with the heavy incense fugging up Eusebius' office and discouraging even fruit flies from trying his questionable plums. I wanted to prompt the vain eunuch into a further explanation.

Finally, Eusebius shrugged with a little impatience. 'A somewhat déclassé Roman nobleman says the boy is an orphan of the civil war on whom a large aristocratic estate is entailed. Obviously he needs a guardian worthy of his lineage. This Clodius can no longer shoulder the burden and I am happy to make the boy my ward.'

'Clodius is lying to you.'

'How could you know that?'

'You disappoint me, Lord Chamberlain. I thought you had a file on everyone. I know that family better than any other. I grew up as their slave and earned my manumission as a *volontarius* in the *vexillatio* commanded by Leo's father.'

There was a long pause. I was pleased I'd set him back on his soft, fat feet in their hand-embroidered slippers, so different from the goatskin shoes Apodemius wore.

'I see. That's why you were so well-informed in your letters to me on the doings of that traitorous Commander Gregorius?'

'Precisely. There are no Manlius estates left,' I bluffed now. 'The boy is not only an orphan, he's a pauper, impoverished by that very same Clodius who now makes you a present of his heavy debts. The estates are beyond recovery, deeply mismanaged, and by all accounts, overgrown with weeds and ruin.'

Eusebius' egg-yolk eyes widened. I saw his spider-like brain tugging at his mental web, this way and that, to calculate his next move.

'So why do you interfere?' he asked at last.

He had me for a moment.

'Let me have the child. Eventually I'll put him in the army. He'll have to work off the family debts, but at least they won't be yours. I'm sure Clodius has woven you a fine tapestry of dockyards in Ostia, vineyards and herds in Sicily, oyster beds along the western coast—'

'—and more, much more, *Agens*.'

The eunuch's breath quickened. I could see that to Eusebius, property was as stimulating as a naked barmaid was to my tavern pal Cornelius.

'Oh, the fortune was there, in the days of old Senator Manlius, but the deeds are irretrievably lost. The whole estate has been frittered away. A hundred debt collectors will be thrilled to learn that the wealthy and powerful Lord Chamberlain's pockets are now theirs to raid. Becoming the guardian and sponsor of the childless scion of a dying Roman clan is only going to bring you headaches in the long-run.'

He smiled to himself.

I waited.

'I'm told he is a beautiful boy. If I didn't know you better, I would suspect you wanted him for yourself.'

I said nothing to this. Did he hope to sell Leo on, along with the problems that I'd outlined?

Then he said, 'If you had wanted to spare him the knife for continuing the Manlius family tree, you could have simply reminded me that castration is illegal in the Empire.'

'I haven't been long in Antiochia, Lord Chamberlain, but already I see that the law here bends like grass in the wind before authority, majesty, religion, and fear.'

'How beautifully phrased. You tactfully left out "the power of avarice." You could have impressed poor Gallus with all your rhetoric, but then, the *Augusta* manages her little play-Caesar and I manage her, so what would be the point of making speeches to him?'

I could see from his smug expression how the current arrangement suited the Lord Chamberlain just fine. I made a note for Apodemius; we could discount Eusebius as a conspirator plotting to overthrow Gallus in favor of General Ursicinus or any other robust contender for the Eastern throne. As far as he was concerned, Gallus was the perfect puppet.

'Numidianus, if I give you the boy, I expect something in return.'

'Anything you ask, Lord Chamberlain.'

'I want Apodemius. I know his agent network stretches from Londinium to Alexandria. I want him to work with me, not against me.'

'You know that's not within my power to deliver.'

'Pity.'

Eusebius took up the fruit knife and began to dice a plum into little squares of juicy pulp.

'As *praepositus sacri cubiculi*, the man in the "sacred chamber" itself, I sit closer to the Emperor than any man in the Empire. Next year I'll even be the intermediary for a meeting between Constantius and Pope Liberius, so you might say I sit even higher—next to the Divine Himself. I also run rings around the rest of the family but,' he chuckled to himself, 'who couldn't? Still, I sense opposition from a city that has otherwise become irrelevant and resentful—old Roma.'

He chopped the fruit pieces as he continued. 'You cheated me, Numidianus.'

'Surely not, *Clarissimus*.'

'Your promised dispatches turned out to be useless. They always arrived too late, full of grandiose descriptions and slightly inaccurate troop numbers that kept the Eastern army at bay for months on end.'

The fruit pulp began to drip and he slid it along with the pits into a polished copper basin. 'Your reports were carefully drafted rubbish intended to mislead the court of Constantius.'

'I had no intention of—'

'So why should I trust you now? I must assume everything you say is false and that this pretty, defenseless boy is worth a fortune to anyone who has the keeping of him.'

'Lord Chamberlain, you've misunderstood completely!'

'I think not. In fact, I am going to accept my gift and what's more, tomorrow I will put in motion the arrangements for a certain accident to happen to him—who can say when or why? The Fates only know. After his period of nursing and recuperation, this child's entry into our ranks in the Palace will guarantee him an education among friends, a lifelong brotherhood of powerful mentors, and a guarantee that he'll never, ever be bothered with the tedious concerns of family or their hangers-on such as freedmen like yourself.'

I stood there, stunned.

'I've finished toying with you, Numidianus. Unless you can deliver Apodemius to me, unless the crippled old fool agrees to a truce and lets me run the whole shop with no further interference, you and I have nothing more to say. We have no deal but I'm so very grateful you alerted me to the true value of my little present.'

⚜⚜⚜

Eusebius didn't know I had bought the Gorgon's favors. I hoped that gave me crucial minutes to get myself to the private wing of the Palace and remove Leo from his reach.

Roxana was waiting for me. I couldn't fully trust her, but I had no time to test her loyalties yet again. If she had duped me by changing her loyalties from Apodemius to Eusebius, I felt no qualms taking her in my arms and kissing her without hesitation. One good deception deserved another.

'Oh, Marcus, I didn't expect you so soon.'

'Roxana, I need your help, *now*.'

'Yes, yes, what is it?'

'I have to take a child out of the nursery. I couldn't leave him in Roma, so I brought him with me to protect him from sale and castration, but he's not safe here any longer. Eusebius has just accepted the boy as a "gift" to the Empire.'

'Poor thing.'

'The Lord Chamberlain plans to adopt him as a ward of the eunuchs, but we can't let him do that. You said you made peace with *Domina* Kahina. This is her son by the Commander Gregorius. In their memory will you save him now?'

'Their son? With us here in Antiochia?'

'Yes. Can you bring him to me out of the nursery? His name is Leo and he has a pet rabbit. You've got to help me hide him in the city somewhere and you must not betray him or me to Eusebius' so-called men.'

I was taking an enormous chance on her loyalties. But I also remembered Roxana as the bravest, strongest and cleverest *agens* in our training year.

She hesitated, knowing better than I the punishments within the eunuch's power. Then she glanced down the corridor behind me and back over her own shoulders. She whispered, 'Of course. I know a place. Come with me.'

I had paid dearly for the Gorgon's silence but now I found the price of her cooperation a downright bargain. While I waited, she let Roxana pass through a room of napping youngsters beyond which she found Leo playing with Festus outside. The nursery doors gave on to a high-walled patch of garden overlooked by numerous Palace windows. Any one of those windows might belong to a member of the imperial household. I prayed that the heat of midday kept all curious heads safely within as we collected the confused Leo and bundled up Festus, his cage, and the boy's meager belongings. I wanted to leave no trace of my child in that nursery.

Roxana covered her elegant blue dress with a *palla* of nondescript light gray wool. Drawing the shawl over her hair, she led us down more of those narrow corridors perfumed with ladies' scents, spicy meals, and the cedar wood of the East.

I pulled Leo along behind me as Roxana led the way with the rabbit cage in her arms. After a few twists and turns, I realized where we three were heading—out that very back door into which so much evil slid in, with slanders and lies tumbling over themselves in a rush to flood imperial ears.

Roxana muttered a few Greek words to a *domesticus* guarding the exit. He unbolted the heavy door. We found ourselves now blasted by the bright noon sun. No one else stood outside the Palace wall along the riverbank. We set off down a well-trodden footpath strewn with rotting weeds. On the opposite side of the water, a few farmers rested in the shade of their wagons under trees stripped of fruit.

I held Leo's hand tight, as we slipped along the high wall of the Palace compound. At our back were the various sounds of the Circus workers preparing for the late afternoon Games—grunts of exercising men, trainers' calls to hungry and irritable animals, and the wheels of the mechanical floors grinding back and forth in rehearsal for scene changes and different kinds of fighting.

'Where are we going? Where's Cousin Clodius?' Leo asked.

'I don't know. Just follow Roxana.'

When we reached the southern end of the imperial island, we hired a skiff. Roxana told the boatman to work us quickly past the watchtowers overlooking the water. Finally, seated in the bottom of the boat, I waited with Leo for Roxana to answer the question that hung between us.

'We're going to a small hideout I keep for when I need to be alone.'

We were sure that no one had followed us but we were conspicuous out on the water, exposed to the view of both banks. We disembarked at the city's southernmost bridge over the river.

It connected to the main state road that linked Antiochia to the neighboring town of Seleuciam. We plunged into a busy quarter housing more public baths and shops. Sticking to side streets filled with sewage and tottering apartment buildings, we distanced ourselves farther and farther away from the fine public spaces around the Forum, the racy theater district, the Forum and the more expensive baths.

I had little time to take in the atmosphere of the streets at this end of the city, but I know we fought off clusters of beggars and avoided tripping over vendors' stalls and faded traders' placards until we stumbled back out onto Antiochia's main south-north throughway at the point where it passed an open *agora*.

Here, there were fewer starving wraiths but the small leafy park teemed with drivers arguing their way around impatient pedestrians. A mood of anger and volatility colored the faces of passers-by.

None of this distracted Roxana. She led us as fast as she could down the crowded street for a few more blocks lined with pretentious but crumbling facades of secondary civic buildings and faded mansions fronted by gardens walled off from the poor.

Leo was tiring fast. I hoisted him onto my back, hoping that he wouldn't be spotted in the midst of these clamoring, unhappy people.

'That was the *Agora*,' Roxana said, 'and beyond there, the *Ampitheatrum*.'

The boulevard now squeezed itself between two stone barriers of crumbling fortification. These were the old Walls of Tiberius that had once barricaded Antiochia but were now missing the original gates that had greeted arrivals from the south.

On the outside of these walls we continued into a low-rise shantytown of hovels linked by unpaved lanes strewn with refuse.

The foothills overlooking the city lay nearby. We finally arrived at a house so small it was hardly more than a shed. It was built right into a curve of the ancient stone walls and nestling in the lap of a steep slope of brush hanging above us. Perched safely above the slums where we hid was an elegant district of tree-shaded villas, winding lanes, and walled gardens.

Roxana nodded. 'That's the *Epiphania* district for the old families and officials who want to live as far from the Palace as possible,' she said.

'In the name of the gods, what is this neighborhood?' I panted.

'The district where no one asks questions.'

Inside Roxana's hideaway, there was a comfortable chair, a bed piled with clean, folded covers, a small woodstove equipped with a metal pan and spoon. She had stored a couple of trunks here as well.

Roxana didn't pause for breath. She disappeared back out into the blinding sunlight to get supplies from her neighbor. The cool darkness inside was already a relief. I bathed Leo's forehead with a rag dipped in the basin she provided.

We three sat at her rough-hewn table and ate goat milk curds with bread and honey. After that I wanted Leo to lie down on the bed to nap, but he refused to leave Festus' cage.

'Then you can keep him company here,' Roxana said. She put the cage into a small alcove at the back of the shack where the floor was covered with straw. She laid down a soft rug. Within a few minutes, both the boy and his caged pet were curled up together, sound asleep.

'Where are we, Roxana?'

'Many months ago,' she whispered, 'I realized that Eusebius no longer trusted me as completely as when I first arrived during the heat of the civil war. So I found this place to get away from him when I had to, to think and to keep my something of my life private from the Palace.'

'Why did you ever trust him?'

'He had said he could use my skills. He promised me a good chance of promotion and regular pay. Then he scoured me clean like a common clay cooking pot of everything I knew about Apodemius, our *schola*, my knowledge of Silvanus, and the court of Magnentius.'

'Didn't you see he was untrustworthy?'

'Not at first. He sent me on a few assignments and I did well. I did jobs in Constantinopolis, Damascus, and Palaestina. He was pleased and even paid me bonuses. But once Constantius won the war, Eusebius seemed to have less and less use for me.'

'But you got the highest scores of all of us. With your Castra training, surely even he—'

'Not Eusebius,' she sighed, rinsing the street grime off her face in a little basin. 'Yes, he's clever, but he's weakened by greed and by his own nature. In the end, he trusts only his own kind. His knowledge of women seems limited to females of Constantia's sort. He despises her, but he plays on her desires and disappointments and especially her fear of Constantius.'

'You're nothing like Constantia. Even Eusebius could see that.'

She shook her head. 'In both of us, Eusebius found frustrated women.'

She wrapped one arm around my waist and together we sat side by side on the edge of her bed. I felt her loneliness.

'They train us to serve the Empire, but who . . .?'

I pulled her hand away and sighed with the pain of memories filling the little room.

'Roxana, you betrayed the service.'

'I should have betrayed Silvanus, but I was weak.'

'Was he just an assignment to you? Or did you love him?'

'At times he seemed almost as close as a husband. Oh, I know now I made a mistake. I suspected he was wavering. He talked too much about the troop strength gathering on the other side. Then Eusebius found out about me—I don't know how— and wrote to me in Aquileia. He wanted to know as much as he could about what Constantius was facing, how they should weigh Magnentius' forces against them, and whether Constantius should offer a compromise again. Why didn't Magnentius take his offer and settle for the West? Why did he want more?'

'Eusebius knew that Silvanus was your particular assignment?'

'I told him myself. Apodemius had always known Claudius was the last to join the rebels. He was always likely to be a critical link, but I ended up too close to him. In the end I couldn't betray him. So when he defected to the other side, I had to face the truth. I'd failed in my mission. I thought there was nothing left for me to but to turn to Eusebius.'

My silence must have felt like disapproval to her.

'Silvanus was good to me, Marcus. He was a noble man.'

'I thought him so until I saw him riding off with the cavalry under his command that dawn. But if Silvanus hadn't defected, if someone had prevented him in time, the balance in forces might have held. A negotiation would have been the only solution. Don't you realize how many lives could have been saved?'

'The signs were there—but defection? I delayed sending up the alert until it was too late. I couldn't bring myself to accuse him of treason to Magnentius. I'd been a failure as an *agens*. That last night . . . I panicked.'

'So you fled to Eusebius here in the East.' I stroked her hair. She seemed suddenly as lost as a little girl in a marketplace who'd lost sight of her mother.

'I admit, I was also angry with Apodemius. He had employed me like a whore, not an *agens*. Eusebius guessed that was my weakness—my professional pride—and he turned me against the *schola*, bit by bit, letter by letter.'

She was sitting there, defiant and ashamed at the same time. I had seen these two sides of her nature before—the skilled lover slipping into my bed in the Castra or straddling me with furtive passion in the grand corridors of Aquileia's court for a midnight tryst I'd been too startled to resist—and this other girl, still clever and brave, but so alone and friendless.

'Can you forgive me, Marcus?'

'So many men died, Roxana. I was *there*. Hades swallowed us up that day. It only spit a few of us back alive.'

'You can't lay the dead at my feet. I didn't turn Silvanus away from Magnentius.'

'I thought you did on someone's orders. I just didn't know whose.'

'It was the sacrifice of that peasant girl that turned Silvanus' stomach, then his loyalty.'

This public and savage ritual murder had stunned all the barbarian emperor's nobler followers.

There was a sudden rustling noise. I straightened up and checked my sword. Leo was fast asleep. It was just Festus scratching his claws into the straw through the twigged bars of his cage. I rose and peered over at him. I hadn't seen him this agitated since Clodius last tried to pet him.

I went to the door to check the street. Two women sat across the alley with their eyes shaded by colorful shawls as they worked shuttles of wool around in circles.

Not for the first time since arriving in Antiochia, I experienced a moment of dizziness in my head and unsteadiness on my feet. I sat down again on the bed next to Roxana and laid my head in my hands to collect my wits. I had only just arrived in Antiochia. Who could be poisoning me? Who wanted me dead?

'Roxana, I'm not feeling well. Time and again I get dizzy.'

'Oh, Marcus, that's just this city. It shudders underfoot all the time. A few days ago, the Palace laundry workers told me that snakes had come out of their shelters in the fields beyond the city and that mating frogs were gathering in clumps along the riverbanks.'

So that explained Constantia's momentary swaying and my episode of dizziness in the Palace gardens.

The shantytown outside was still, except for a clatter of dishes somewhere outside. At least Leo wasn't disturbed. The race away from the island had exhausted and confused the child.

'I need to rest,' I said.

'Go to sleep,' she said. 'I'll watch over the boy.'

'Just rest. I won't sleep. Sleep brings back memories of Mursa that wake me up again.'

I laid myself out and closed my eyes. She stretched out next to me with that blue silken dress hardly concealing the lovely body I had found so fascinating years before. She smelled clean and yet womanly, of bath powder and hair unguents that dressed the heavy brown coil that hung down to her girdle. She was taller than Kahina, so from beneath the gold and red embroidered hem, two graceful ankles twisted around my shins. She laid her head on my chest. I felt her warm breath brushing my neck.

I closed my eyes and sank into the peace of the little room but within a few minutes, Mursa rushed back to me, despite all my efforts to forget—the masses of tents, the clattering horsemen, the snapping banners and the blaring horns. On that fateful day Roxana had escaped off alone, without a word, at first light. I had stayed and fought through one whole afternoon and an entire night among tens of thousands of doomed men.

Was it fair that her battles would always be the struggles of a woman while mine were that of a man, no matter our shared Castra training? I felt awash with tenderness for her and this carefully tended little shack, her only real home. Desire and pity for her flooded me like a cooling wave of the Great Sea. She sensed my exhilaration at holding her close.

'Marcus,' she whispered.

I rolled over and kissed her. She had changed in ways less visible to the eye. The youthful windstorm of her animal lovemaking was gone. After the first few minutes of tender caresses, she extricated herself gently from my arms and hung a tattered tablecloth on hooks across the doorway blinding off the alcove where Leo still slept.

She returned to my side and lifted her outer dress—Kahina's dress—to lie down again in her undertunic of translucent ivory silk. She had matured from the quicksilver sylph I'd once watched swimming alone at night into an enveloping, curvaceous woman but there was a new vulnerability to her maturity.

I remembered her as a fierce conqueress of men, both wary and yet keen to direct my pleasure. Now I knew she was giving herself up to me as never before. Her smooth arms trembled as I felt myself inside her again and knowing her hips could give dangerous delights, I stilled her movement and slowed her down to reassure her that there was time, if only precious little, for her to feel less alone in the world.

I used my lips, my fingers, and my body to give her as much comfort as these isolated months had denied her. With a last convulsion, her sighs died down and I released all my soul's tensions with my last energy.

But to my confusion, her shudders continued and the bed shook under us.

Festus rattled and banged against his cage which was shifting in the straw until it had tumbled right over. He scrambled out the opened door and started squeaking and hopping out from behind the tablecloth. I chased him under a table and finally grabbed him, pushing him back into the cage, and fastening his red ribbon with a firm knot.

Leo didn't stir. I heard deep rumbling outside the shack, as if the nearby mountains were walking toward the river. The earth started shaking visibly underneath the table and chair, which started to inch forward on its legs.

I flew across the room and wrenched the cloth off the alcove doorway. Leo woke up and stared at me in confusion. I reached for the rabbit cage and saw that even back in the security of his cage, Festus was wilder than ever with terror.

Always have friends in low places, Apodemius had said. The escaping snakes . . . the clustering frogs . . . and now Festus.

The rabbit was warning me of danger but it wasn't only the earth's shaking that alarmed me as I looked up from the alcove into the room.

Roxana had risen from the mattress and was staring past me at two eunuchs in Palace cloaks breaking down her door.

Chapter 12, The End of the World

—THE ANTIOCHENE SLUMS—

'Marcus!' she screamed at me, her eyes still staring across the room. Confused and afraid, Leo looked up at the intruders.

Pushing the sleepy boy deep into the straw at the back of the niche, I drew my *spatha*. I was confident I could take them on and steadied myself for a quick rout. Since that evening stroll with Gallus, I knew these Palace fixtures for the cowards they were. But for good measure, I gripped my *pugio* in my left hand.

They backed off for a moment. Then the taller one pulled back his sword and surprised me with an expert move to catch me in a feint and knock the dagger from my hand. I parried it and thrust at his loins. He dodged back.

The other man looked avid to gang up on me, but he hadn't gauged their female opponent very well. Hair wild and undertunic askew, Roxana had grabbed a kitchen knife and moved in on him from the side. Without a word, she rammed the blade between his ribs. He gasped in surprise and slumped against the side of the narrow doorway, trying to take in the speed of this nearly naked woman's victory.

The first man now had both of us going for him. He was backing away toward the door. I hoped that at any minute, he'd trip backwards and fall over his partner's twitching corpse.

A thunderbolt startled us all, but the rumbling came not from the sky above, but again up from the ground. I felt the earth roll beneath my feet. The roar grew louder and I felt myself heaved up a little. A whole shelf of Roxana's humble pottery dishes teetered and then fell onto the table, shattering into painted sherds. At the same time, I was jerked sharply to my right and almost thrown off my balance. I grabbed the alcove doorframe to catch myself but almost lost my grip on my sword.

Leo ran right under my arm toward Roxana who had been thrown sprawling backwards on her low bed.

Our opponent had slammed into a wall but at least stayed upright. I saw him staring at us wondering how to make the most of his advantage while we all fumbled for our balance. The sensible move would have been to make his retreat while we were all in the grip of the quake, but I saw his eyes light on Leo and I saw he wasn't leaving without the boy.

'Run, Leo,' Roxana gasped. 'Get outside!'

'Festus!' Leo turned back toward the alcove.

'Forget Festus,' I shouted.

I kept my eyes fixed on the eunuch who was setting himself up in fighting stance again. I was circling around the shack now, trying to gauge his long reach.

But Leo was too stubborn and loyal to abandon his rabbit. Before Roxana could manage her way to him through the subsiding shaking, he had scrambled past me and taken the rabbit cage into his arms.

For a moment, the earth settled. The remaining eunuch and I parried with my sword, trying to find an opening for my dagger to make a swift and lethal plunge.

Roxana tried to get the boy outside, but her tunic hem had got itself pinned to the ground by one of the shifting bed legs. I heard her cursing, but kept my eyes on our enemy.

I held off the attacker for as long as it took Roxana to rip her hem free but the attacker was making his move on me now. Our swords clashed and I saw he was better than I'd thought, not wasting his strength on a move that didn't nearly fool me each time. I lost ground to him, but Roxana saw that, while his back was exposed to her, she had her chance—if only she could recover the knife sticking out of the other eunuch's body.

Bewildered, Leo stood for an instant with the rabbit cage in his arms. He was trapped on the other side of the shack between the eunuch and the table.

'Get OUT, Leo!' Roxana screamed but a sudden roar from the earth drowned her cry.

Then the world seemed to fold in on itself, and the shack was like a small boat caught in the crush of a massive wave and I saw the alcove strut I had been holding a moment before splinter into two pieces as it snapped down on itself.

The shaking grew wilder and wilder and I felt myself flung away from the others. I thought I saw Leo still clutching his beloved pet as he scampered around the fallen eunuch and out the door but I couldn't be sure because just then something slammed into my head from behind.

I sank into darkness.

⚡⚡⚡

'Marcus?'

I opened my eyes. Roxana was dressed again and leaning over me, shaking my shoulders and crying, 'Marcus! Marcus!'

'Where's Leo?'

She was panting, 'He obeyed you, Marcus. He made it outside to safety before I could reach him.'

I looked up and saw clear blue sky. I was covered with dust and rubble from the broken walls, but apart from a sizeable lump on my head, unharmed. Roxana's face and dress were blanketed with the ashen brown dust that covered everything around us. Her anxious tears left streaks running down her face but true to her steely soul, she stopped crying as soon as she saw I was conscious.

The room began to shudder again. I reached up to her and held her tightly, wrapping my arms over her head. After a terrible minute, the shaking subsided. I now saw over her shoulder that the second eunuch lay on the floor, stabbed dead in the back and fallen near his partner.

She followed my glance. 'I finished him off when he made after Leo but then part of the roof came down on us.'

Roxana had used her Castra training well.

'Eusebius put them on our trail.'

'No, I'm sure we weren't followed.'

'Roxana, they were watching for us here all along. Eusebius must have known of this place and sent after us. Go get Leo and I'll deal with these bodies.'

We heard screaming and high-pitched wailing that made me dread the scenes that awaited her outside, but I had other work to do first. I hastily buried the two men in the debris.

By the time I got out into the lane, Roxana had circled the immediate quarter and come up empty-handed. We started to search the blocks of her slum farther along the lane. The more I saw, the more fear surged up in my breast. There were many other small children, crying or just stunned and left wandering along through the dust-clogged alleys. All around us people pulled and dug at the ruins with their bare hands in utter panic at mounds of featureless rubble and grit still powdering the sunny sky with clouds of dirt.

I let Roxana lead the way. Without her sense of direction in that confusion, I would have been lost my bearings and revisited the same ruins over and over again. We called Leo's name until we were hoarse. I realized with mounting panic that if we hadn't found him in the first half hour, then the first hour, and now as the afternoon waned and the bodies began to appear laid out in rows of pulped flesh, that Leo might be lost to me forever.

'Someone must have grabbed him outside and taken him straight back to the Palace,' I said.

'No, if there had been a third attacker, he would have been with them in shack to make even quicker work of us.'

'There has to have been a third man. Or who took Leo?'

Roxana kept me calm. We returned to what was left of her home and searched for the two spinners I'd seen sitting in view of her door. When we finally located one of the old women, she said no third man had been lurking outside Roxana's shack. She had seen the other two attackers approach the house.

'There was no third man,' she said.

Roxana told everyone about a boy carrying a rabbit, wearing good clothes and knowing no one—this boy would bring a reward that would change a man's fortunes.

But people were too frantic to listen to us, there was no one in charge, and no help at hand. The breeze picked up a little as the afternoon wore on, lifting the smell of blood and emptied bowels to our horrified nostrils.

I cursed my foolishness. At least in the Palace Leo would have been safe from the quake. I should have done something else, anything else, to thwart Eusebius. Hiding him here among these strangers had triggered the Fates' irony.

'A small boy with a rabbit,' Roxana kept saying.

'A cage in his arms?'

We stopped at a man's call. He was sitting just where the old Tiberian gates gave passage to the city proper.

'Yes, yes! Did you see him?'

The man said nothing more and examined us both. He was wearing a simple worker's tunic, wrapped tight around his loins for agility and he gestured us to him with a calloused hand.

'Did you see my boy?'

'I might have. The kid had a rabbit.'

'Dressed in good clothes, with light brown hair, clean face.'

'A well-tended child, yes, with a rabbit.'

'Who took him?'

'A woman.'

'A woman?' Roxana's voice rose with impatience.

'He wasn't hurt.'

'Who was she?'

'Where did they go?' I tried to control my anxiety, happy to hear this witness saying Leo wasn't dead and buried under some ruin.

The man waited. I blocked out the turmoil around us and concentrated on this one man. 'I asked you, where did they go?'

'That way.' He pointed through the ruined gates in the direction of the Agora.

'Did you recognize her?'

'I might have.'

He clammed up. I took out my purse and offered him a fair price for the information. As I reached over, he spotted something more enticing—the rings on my neck cord.

'What was this woman's name?' Roxana seemed unaware of the thoughts running through this villain's mind.

'I can't remember. The quake shook up my memory, I guess.'

'Will this jog it any?'

I held out my coins.

'What do you want?' Roxana screamed at him.

'I want nothing. It is you who wants something,' he said.

'Do you know the woman who took him?' We were now bargaining, not asking.

'I guess so.'

I untied the cord around my neck and unthreaded one of the precious two rings I had sworn I would return to the widow of the slain Marcellinus. Titus Gerontius Severus had refused it that night in Arelate as he lay dying, but now I saw the Fates had known its true use.

'Here, is this worth your breath?'

The man took the heavy ring from me and slipped it on his finger. It fit him only too well. He looked at Roxana's dust-streaked face and said quietly, 'It was Zeva, the wife of the tunic-bleacher Khristos. She led the boy straight through the old gates here and up the main road toward the Agora. His shop faces opposite.'

'Does she live here?'

The stranger looked around him, at the devastation that had befallen the entire slum and said simply, 'She used to.'

'If you see her again, you will get word to me at the palace. My name is Roxana.'

'Or you'll lose the hand that wears that ring,' I added.

At least we knew Leo had survived the earthquake. But we still had to find this laundryman's Zeva. They must have been on their way to the shop.

We moved north pushing through hysterical crowds and accosting everyone with questions, asking for Zeva to no avail.

We were not alone in our terror. Other names shrieked through the dusty air and other wails pierced the noise and panic.

As we progressed from the shantytown, we zigzagged northward along each residential street, from the river and back to the main boulevard and back to the river. The construction of the houses grew more solid and with each street, proved themselves to have been more resilient to Nature's anger.

We found the bleach shop, now a mass of shredded tunics, and vats of urine spilling into the gutter, emptied of customers and staff.

'Who has seen Zeva or Khristos?' we shouted to everyone passing the shop. My throat constricted as I saw a man's bent figure leaning over a woman in the alleyway covered in broken stones.

'Khristos? Are you Khristos?' Roxana shouted, running up to the man.

He turned to us, tear streaming down his face and nodded. Before I could form the words, for fear of what we had discovered, Roxana had barked out the question on my lips.'

'Where is your wife Zeva? Where is our boy?'

'This is my wife,' he sobbed, pointing to the woman stretched out before us. 'Her brains are smashed out. Some loose rock struck her down.'

We had reached a dead end. Khristos knew nothing of a boy, nor did any of his companions, leading the grieving man away as they wrapped his wife's corpse into a canvas.

If Leo were wandering here alone, surely he would be within view but he was nowhere to be found. Had he been taken in by another kind stranger or seized by an opportunist recognizing a ransom might be had for a boy wearing such good clothes?

The sun was setting. We had now spoken to hundreds upon hundreds of people. A rabbit in a cage. A small boy who couldn't speak Greek. Some listened closely, with sympathy in their haggard eyes, while others brushed us away with impatience. There was less damage to buildings in the center of the city and so we came across fewer grieving families. But everywhere

Antiochenes continued to survey the damage by lantern light and to organize themselves one way or another.

Roxana and I finally reached the Forum. Its elegant statues and marble paving were submerged in a sea of desperate people clamoring for the municipal officials to provide water and food. There was no way we could penetrate this wall of people. If Leo were somewhere among these crowds, he might easily be trampled underfoot.

'The food stocks are empty! The market is destroyed. Go home! There is nothing!' someone cried at them.

'I must return to the Palace before dark,' Roxana said. 'I will have to deny whatever Eusebius accuses me of, and pray the Gorgon did not betray us.'

'Eusebius is a dangerous opponent, Roxana. He sent those men to wait for us. He knows we had Leo. We're lucky this Zeva dragged him away from those creeps.'

'But Eusebius knows I carry some of his secrets, too,' she said. 'He'll hesitate to act until he knows whether or not I've shared them with you.'

'Then I will go back to the slums and keep hunting for Leo without you.'

We said good-bye along a side street cutting between the Forum and the river canal facing the island. In the distance, the Palace and Circus stood unharmed and the indifferent sun washed the sturdy imperial walls in a pink glow.

My ears were deafened by the roars of the city's population gathering by the thousands in front of the great basilica at one end of the Forum. I watched Roxana's receding figure in a ragged, grimy blue dress that had once fluttered like a stream through the corridors of Magnentius' court in Aquileia. I saw everything in the tatters of that dress—the leftovers of so many dreams of reviving the old order, of living with dignity as free men and women, and of defending the Empire. Was this the Empire for which we'd trained—where eunuchs hunted down little boys, welfare supplies stayed hoarded away, and a courageous woman reached the top of her class only to end up a nursemaid to pampered toddlers?

I collapsed there on the street and tried to hang on to my wits. If I had broken down, who would have noticed amid all the pandemonium and death? I was only one of thousands in distress. There was too much lost now, too much buried, for me to hold my emotions in any longer. My duties to Apodemius called me toward the Palace on its isolated island and my duties to everyone whom I loved demanded I find Leo.

Only Roxana understood, and even she remained ignorant of that final truth—that Kahina's son was actually mine as well, and that only I remained to protect him and his legacy from oblivion.

I remembered the joy on the Commander's face as he told me of Kahina's motherhood and the happiness of listening to the Senator praise the child's quick mind. I heard again the devotion of Verus guarding over him and the tears streaming down Lavinia's face on the Ostia quay. Most of all, I counted my days on board the ship with Leo as the happiest days of my entire life.

I returned to the shantytown that huddled in chaotic darkness relieved only by the occasional torch flame. I found Roxana's little corner of the quarter near the old Walls subdued in the grim business of digging out what could be saved and finding what little nourishment could be salvaged from the rubble of cooking pots and grain containers. Roxana's demolished shack sat ignored by everyone. Broken roof beams barricaded her front door and the collapsed walls slumped into shapeless slopes of rubble. But I examined very nook and space there in the hope that Leo had somehow returned.

I gave up and returned north through the Tiberian Walls again. There were so many turns he could have taken retracing his steps from the Agora. People had lit bonfires to illuminate the work of digging and uncovering, but I looked up at the comfortable homes still perched on the slopes above and realized that Leo might have climbed into the foliage of the foothills or even penetrated a villa garden protected by their low walls.

It all depended on what had happened after Zeva was struck down.

After three or four hours of fruitless searching, the moon hung high over the mourning streets. I saw now that only by using the Palace could I locate my son. I had to get more manpower from someone. I could no longer waste my time wandering these unfamiliar streets alone and unaided. Barbatio! Surely he could send out a search party.

I was starving and exhausted. It took me more than half an hour to get back to the island. I found a way into the Palace by way of the kitchens to beg some scrap of a meal. I thought no one would notice my return.

I was wrong. Honoratus was still here with us in Antiochia, but transformed from the complacent gabbling official regaling the wonders of Constantinopolis. The garrulous *Comes* had no time for small talk now. He came rushing down the corridor after me as I sought out the modest chamber I'd been assigned. I intended to wash myself and eat quickly before returning to the streets with Barbatio's men in the hunt for Leo.

'Marcus Numidianus Gregorianus! Thank the gods you're safe! The Prefect Thalassius is demanding to see you.'

I remembered that early this morning Thalassius had been far from keen to see me, and had rushed me off to the archives the way he might dismiss a boy to do his Latin grammar homework.

Honoratus was panting with alarm. 'He's in grave danger and his family is with him. But he wants to see *you*, he says, in your official capacity.'

'That makes no sense. If his life is in danger, he needs a doctor, not an *agens*.'

'Come, no more arguments,' Honoratus gasped.

He gathered up his stiff robes to speed me to the Prefect's private chambers. 'He said, bring me the *agens* from the Western court.'

I found Thalassius lying in a darkened bedroom, his windows' heavy drapes muffling the calamitous sounds of the city in upheaval across the river. His bedside was crowded with secretaries and family members. Two Greek doctors stood by. One was taking the patient's pulse.

176

'It's his heart,' the other murmured in response to my questioning look. 'Must you disturb him?'

'I am Marcus Gregorianus Numidianus. The Prefect has asked for me.'

The impatient man I had seen only this morning in council trying to alleviate the city's hunger pains now fought against his own agony. At my name, he opened his eyes and gestured for me to bend close to his lips. He wanted no one to overhear us.

'Did you read the files?' he whispered.

'Yes, I combed a year's worth of cases. I saw disturbing patterns in the miscarriage of justice, Prefect.'

'Yes, yes, of course. Anything else?'

'I'm sorry to say that according to the registrar's index, a page has been removed from each dossier.'

'I removed them.' He gestured for water. I waited while a sponge was laid to his parched lips.

'Ask for another file,' he whispered. 'Tell your *schola* I fulfilled my duty to the Empire.' He started to choke and needed the sponge again. 'There are three honest and independent witnesses, a trinity.'

Thalassius lifted three fingers of his pale hand just a little off the heavy brocade coverlet. 'A *trinity*. Do you understand?'

'I think so, Prefect.'

I straightened up and moved away from his bed.

'Let him go now.'

Honoratus hustled me out of the room and shut the door behind me. I was standing alone in the corridor of the residential officials' apartments, one story above the public reception rooms. I knew that whatever Thalassius' precautions, we might have been overheard in that room crowded with sycophants, clerks, and guards.

The whole Palace was in turmoil because of the earthquake and there was no better time to return to the archives for the hidden file. If I intended to do anything without the prying eyes of Eusebius' ubiquitous eunuchs watching from every corner, now was the best time.

I knew the Palace better now and needed no smooth-cheeked *domesticus* to show me back to the official council room or the moonlit little passageway to the archivist's desk. He usually slept on a cot in a side room with his keys to the valuable stacks of ancient scrolls and books, dossiers and certificates hanging off his belt. I could see the empty cot from the counter. How could anyone sleep during this horrible night? I heard him in the back of his library maze, checking the shelves for disorder.

'Come here, man!' I ordered. There were occasions when the fear of our *schola* and the universal dislike of the *curiosi* were tools we used without hesitation.

I leaned over to him and stared into eyes blinking up at me with fear, like Leo's twitching rabbit.

'I need a file,' I said.

'Yes, but it's late and I'm—'

'One more file,' I said, grabbing him by his stiff silk collar. 'It's marked, "*Trinity*".'

'Oh, yes, yes, of course,' he said, nodding with obvious relief. 'I know where to find that one right away.'

He shuffled away into the shadows. While I waited, I looked back through the narrow window-lined corridor at the night sky outside. Above the Palace walls, coils of thick smoke swirled across the face of the moon.

The city was on fire. My heart clutched again, thinking of Leo and my pressing need to get to Barbatio and back across the river with some trustworthy men.

I was determined that whatever Thalassius had wanted me to discover, I wouldn't let him down, but my heart said Leo came first. And I was troubled by the look on Thalassius' face—of resignation as much as deathly illness. The doctors had said it was his heart that had failed in the shock of the earthquake, but I had also seen next to his bed a plate of half-eaten Damascus plums.

I clutched at the 'Trinity' file and over the archivist's protests, thrust it under my tunic and sword belt for safekeeping and fled the archive room in search of the Master of the Horse Guards.

I found Barbatio and his men, mounted and guarding the Palace perimeter along the parade ground in a phalanx six deep stretching between the Circus entrance and the Palace baths.

'I need men,' I shouted to him, over a clamor of crowds on the other side of the river. 'I need a search party!'

'I can't spare anyone. Look at that!' Barbatio shouted, pointing across the narrow strait where the skiffs tugged at ropes tied to the dock. 'They've set fire to the house of Eubulus, a city councilor. They're saying they'll burn the whole city down if we don't release more grain supplies.'

Across the water, a hundred dancing torches waved above the sweating, reddened faces of quake survivors.

'Give them what you have!' I shouted up to him.

'It's all gone! The Caesar made no preparations for emergencies. *She* spent all the funds on finery for her women and bribes for her spies!'

'Can you hold them back?'

'You see what we have? This is it. The eunuchs are hopeless in a crisis. We need real men now! All the eunuchs know how to do is destroy men, not to protect them!'

I looked back up at the Palace, ablaze with lanterns shining out of the windows of the residential wing on one side and the officials' wing on the other. I knew that the one place where preparations might have been made for an emergency had no windows lit at all.

Where was Eusebius?

'It's a lucky thing for those senators that they're in jail. At least they're safe from this horde.' Barbatio muttered. His horse bucked underneath him and he yanked hard to discipline it. He could not allow this situation to get out of hand or his career was finished.

'Caesar! Caesar!' the crowd chanted. A few small boats managed to load up with angry Antiochenes and force their oarsmen across the river but Barbatio's men forced them away from the imperial quay.

The standoff threatened to last all night. I could not get even half a dozen men from Barbatio to look for Leo. The angry multitude on the opposite shore had grown from a few souls to many hundreds in less than half an hour.

'Caesar! Caesar!' Once the chant had started, it echoed behind them. Then suddenly it died down.

The ranks of cavalry blocking the bridge parted to allow the Caesar himself to advance from behind where Barbatio and I watched. Gallus braced his shoulders and loosened his purple cloak, sending it flowing behind the heels of his polished boots in the evening breeze.

From the far end of the bridge, he faced that screaming mob-animal with its hundreds of gaunt faces and hungry hands pawing and clutching at him through the air.

Gallus was not alone. The stiff-collared Syrian Governor Theophilus, the *Comes* Honoratus, and a third man followed him with less confidence. They fell back a few steps when the Caesar proceeded across the bridge.

'Who's he?' I asked Barbatio, indicating the slender, hollow-eyed official who inched forward behind Honoratus.

'The legal expert, the *Quaestor* Montius,' Barbatio said, 'but no laws will help them over there.'

The gold and purple stripes that shot down from their imperial collars to the hems of their elaborate robes glinted in the light of the flames. A dozen armed eunuchs advanced behind the officials, so even Montius was forced forward with the other three. They almost created the impression of a procession of calm officialdom.

The crowd made a semi-circle for Gallus and his companions at the far end of the bridge. The Constantine smiled, as though all his secret night trawling had been worth the trouble, if only to meet tonight's crisis with mastery.

'We look after our people, we know their hearts and—'

'Do you know our hunger?' a man interrupted from the back of the crowd. Jeers and catcalls flew at the young Caesar who shouted back:

'Our horse guards will clear the city tomorrow morning of all foreigners, flushing out all the filth—the Persian refugees who eat your food, the secretive Jews in their exclusive quarter who hoard and lend for a price, and the disputatious Egyptians who prey on good Roman Christians of this city with their cheap merchandise and counterfeit coins,' he shouted.

'We need food now!' a woman cried.

'And you will have it once we've cleared out all the city's hangers-on and freeloaders. The dancing girls, the beggars, the parasite merchants and their pandering pickpocket slaves—all those useless mouths and stomachs must leave at dawn tomorrow at the point of our swords!'

Some of the screaming died down as the mob's leaders began to listen with ears pricked for something more than words to fill their stomachs.

Gallus, however, seemed satisfied with his performance. With a salute of farewell, he turned his purple and gold back on them to return across the bridge to safety. The unhappy people heckled his retreating figure.

'We need food now, tonight, Caesar!'

'Caesar! Come back! What food we had left today is buried beyond our reach.'

'There is nothing left in the imperial silos,' Gallus shouted back from the end of the bridge. 'You have eaten it all. And it is your senators who have let this happen to you.'

'Punish them!'

'Yes, yes, the people's voice must be answered.' Gallus turned to Barbatio and shouted, 'Bring the senators here to the bridge, now.'

I saw Honoratus' face at that moment and knew in the next why Apodemius had advised me to trust him. His honor as a Roman official would not permit an atrocity to happen.

He held his hand out to stay the completion of Gallus' command.

'Bring the senators across the bridge! They must be executed here and now!' Gallus disregarded Honoratus and shook his fist over his head. I saw with revulsion that he was smiling at the crowd.

A roar of approval went up, a savage cry from bellies that hung slack and heads drunk with resentment.

Honoratus walked past Gallus standing at the far end of the bridge and lifted his hands to still the crowd. He dared to challenge Gallus with outstretched palms in appeal. 'As custodians of these people, we must countermand your order, Caesar. We will not break the law of the Empire. Our senators have labored for weeks to prevent famine. They have been convicted of no crime.'

There was a wail of disbelief from the mob.

Honoratus raised his hands even higher to calm the sea of rising tempers. 'Any accusations that they have been derelict in their duty must be referred to a higher authority.'

Mounted in front of his watchful riders at our end of the bridge, Barbatio surveyed the drama across the water. He was holding his men in check and waiting to see how Honoratus' defiance of the sovereign played out.

The *domestici* inside the palace were useless and the army garrisons Gallus commanded in theory were sound asleep up and down the seacoast. The true muscle of the Eastern Empire was employed against the Empire's foreign enemies. The *Legio X Fretensis* was camped in the sands of Ayla on the Red Sea protecting the spice traffic coming to the Empire from India. The *II Flavia* and its auxiliary forces were far to the east facing the Persian front.

Only Barbatio and his few hundred horsemen were on hand tonight, armed and ready to deal with violent citizens.

'Ain't the Caesar himself the highest authority on hand?' taunted an anonymous mobster.

'The Senate cannot answer tonight. They are all in prison awaiting trial.'

'I said, execute them here and now!' Gallus screamed back at Honoratus.

At that, an arm jerked out from the center of the mob and something flew through the air. Honoratus was hit with excrement but he held his ground, with both his hands still held high in mute defense. More foul clumps flew up from the mob and spattered his long robe.

Gallus sputtered with rage at the *Comes* of the East. By the flickering glow of the lanterns, lamps and torches, I saw the Caesar's face turning as violet as the gorgeous borders of his tunic. It was one thing to ridicule a Caesar as inexperienced and impotent as Gallus in the privacy of the council chamber. It was quite another thing to disgrace him in front of the city he claimed to rule.

A brute in rags emerged from the crowd and stood facing Gallus on the edge of the stone quay. He was a leader brave enough to challenge the imperial house.

He waved his clenched fist and its reflection joined the images of a hundred torches rippling and reflecting off the dark waters. 'Order us food from the neighboring provinces if there is nothing left for us!'

'Ask the Governor of Syria himself what I should do,' Gallus replied. A smile of irony crossed his lips. 'Here he is, Theophilus himself, standing by my side. For if Honoratus, the *Comes* of the East, disregards my command and answers to an even *higher* authority, then surely it must be you, Theophilus.'

Gallus even bowed his head in a nod to Theophilus. He played his theatrical moment with unexpectedly vicious expertise. The crowd hungered for satisfaction. As it was not to be wagonloads of bread, oil and meat rolling now through the streets of rubble and dying, then it would be death itself.

Gallus stretched his head of soft blond curls toward the mob and shouted, 'No one could possibly go without food in Antiochia if the Governor of Syria had not willed it so. Isn't that correct, Theophilus?'

Gallus stepped smartly back and extended both his arms in the direction of the rigid Governor. He could not have given the crowd permission more clearly than if he had trussed and basted Theophilus in front of them with his own hands.

The mob broke into a riot and rushed at the Governor. The arrogant, noble head of Theophilus suddenly jerked this way and that as he fell prey to their hysteria. Those elegant hands I had seen bidding Eusebius farewell this morning, still weighed down with the iron seal rings of his high office, reached up and flailed in the air to no avail. The stunned governor appealed for help over the braying rabble carrying him away from the bridge and into the city. We could hear his screams through the mob's triumphant cries.

Barbatio spurred a charge of horsemen down the narrow bridge to rescue the Governor but almost immediately his passage was blunted by the fuming Caesar marching in the other direction along the bridge to the island followed by Honoratus, Montius, and a party of eunuchs closing their tail and fending off attackers with their spears. Precious seconds were lost as Barbatio's proud horse hesitated so that the remaining officials could follow Gallus to the island end of the bridge and safety behind the Guards' lines.

I had already drawn my own sword and was waiting for Barbatio to decide where to attack. Though I was on foot, I had assumed we could force the herd off Thalassius in time to save his life. But whenever I had faced lines of soldiers before, I had at least known that the bloodlust filling their breasts was fed by the same sense of honor that filled my own.

Tonight the opponent at the end of the bridge held no rank and saluted no code of loyalty to the Empire. It was a vicious human Hydra that knew nothing beyond animal rage. It howled with empty mouths and busied itself with a coiling frenzy that swallowed the Governor of Syria into its maw.

In the next minute, I saw someone waving Theophilus' ring-covered hand up in the air, a hand connected to a bloody arm with its shoulder bone and sinews exposed to the ghostly glow of the Caesar's garish city. Theophilus was no longer the sum of his parts. Still famished, the crowd would do what they liked with his remains. I refused to imagine the worst.

Barbatio had already taken action to save the rest of the court. His guards held the bridge while an escort rushed the Caesar, Honoratus, Montius, and the others into the imperial compound.

The Palace forces retreated to the last man behind the huge outer gates. As they were bolted against the city, Barbatio dismounted and organized a cohort that would slip across the bridge to rescue what remained of Theophilus for burial. He ordered the rest of his shocked and demoralized troops to rest and ready themselves for the action ordered by Gallus for the next day. All foreigners would be driven into exodus. But after the murder of Theophilus, what had looked like a quick cleansing of some token numbers of the foreign population now threatened to become a fight against mass riots.

'I don't like fighting Romans of any kind, citizens or rug traders from Arabia. It's wrong,' he said to his second-in-command. He turned and saw me. 'Numidianus, why were you crying for my help?'

'You served Commander Gregorius well in Numidia,' I said. 'Now you must help me save his son.'

CHAPTER 13, FLUSHING OUT FILTH

—THE PALACE OF ANTIOCHIA—

'Tomorrow I'll have to save many lives, not just one child,' Barbatio said. 'A purge of foreigners means hooligans looting empty houses and abandoned possessions, resistance and fighting, and just more killing.'

We entered the Palace Guards' precinct together. The stables were frenetic with preparations for the next day. Barbatio may have had his orders to, 'Flush the filth out of Antiochia,' but first troops and horses needed rest and sustenance. Slave grooms curried the over-excited horses and tossed fresh hay into the stalls. At least the horses still had enough to eat. The men supped on thin soup and flatbread from the Palace's dwindling stocks.

The Master of the Guards unbuckled his sword belt and heaved out the day's tension from his enormous chest.

'I warned you in the baths, Numidianus. The Caesar listens to spies and tattletales, but he's deaf to the truth. Couldn't he see in their faces tonight that he was flirting with violence?'

'What can you learn of people if you spend your whole childhood isolated with eunuchs under lock and key?'

'Well, I could have taught him more than any eunuch,' Barbatio said.

'Anyway, how can your few hundred guardsmen drive these communities out of a city of half a million?' I asked. 'Can you simply weed out moneylenders and dancing girls and drive them out through the gates?'

'We'll make a show of concentrating on certain quarters, bash a few dozen heads, and round up the more flagrant rascals. The others will get the message and take to the roads.'

'They'll only come back in a few weeks. Antiochia is the oldest and richest city this far east.'

Barbatio shrugged. 'There's no point in defying Gallus' command but you're right, it'll do no good. For all his sneaking through the back streets, our golden-haired Caesar doesn't see what makes Antiochia's heart beat.'

'Where will they go?'

'They'll just head north and south. In less than a week, the streets of Myriandros and Seleuciam will be jammed with begging refugees.'

'What will happen to them?'

'The famine has hit all the towns around us. You saw what happened to Theophilus. Gallus is a danger to us all.'

Smoke from the city's fires billowed over the island and ran its dark fingers across the face of the moon. In the depths of the stricken neighborhoods, the *vigiles* were putting out fires and the *aediles* were trying to restore public order. The deadly night was subsiding into that deepest sleep that comes before first light. Under the stark torchlight in the emptied street at the end of the Palace's bridge to the mainland, what couldn't be recovered from the gruesome remains of Theophilus had been left on the paving stones and were already feeding ravenous rats.

My boy was out there somewhere. I had to head back.

'Barbatio, in a few hours you're going to visit every corner of the city. Your guards are my only hope. I've spent every hour until sundown hunting for this boy.'

'This is *Gregorius'* child?'

'The child of *Domina* Kahina and the Commander, yes, out there somewhere, taken during the quake,' I said.

'Who took him?'

'We were in the slums built up below the Tiberian Walls. I lost consciousness during the quake and the boy ran off. He was led away by some laundryman's wife, but we found her dead near the Agora and no trace of him.'

'The city's full of waifs,' he said, wiping his brow with a dirty tack rag. 'How would we know this one?'

'You met him on the quay when we arrived. His name is Leo. He doesn't speak any Greek, only Latin. With any luck, he's still carrying that rabbit.'

'With any luck, the rabbit has been eaten and not the kid,' Barbatio answered. 'What in the name of the gods is he doing in Antiochia with you?'

'That Clodius is an evil man, Barbatio. He planned to give the boy, along with his inheritance, as a fly for the Lord Chamberlain's spider web, a delicious morsel for *cutting* and devouring.'

I made a sharp and unmistakable gesture across my groin.

'I wanted to keep Leo as close to me as possible, to keep him from harm. I snuck him away from the Palace yesterday when I realized Clodius had struck a deal with Eusebius as soon as we landed.'

Barbatio winced. 'Nature cheats some men of virility when their nuts stay glued up in their loins. And I've seen one or two lose their manhood in battle. But no innocent boy should fall into the Lord Chamberlain's hands.'

He squinted at me by the stable's dim lamplight and rubbed the black stubble covering his wide chin. Reaching into a rough niche gouged out of the stable's granite pillar, he pulled out a hidden goatskin and offered me a swig. I tried one swallow and spit it out onto the straw-colored floor.

'Strong, huh? They brew it out on the border from dates. Anyway, what's the boy to you? The war changed the fortunes of tens of thousands, but you and I have come a long way from the *Legio IIIA*.' He took another swig. 'I aim to go even farther.'

'You recall my devotion as a slave to the Commander?'

He scoffed as he removed his shoulder pads and breast armor. 'That's good! Really good! I was there, in that tent, the day you came back with the information they needed on those ratbag Circumcellions. What *I* remember is you fighting the Commander for your freedom even after you completed your mission. He all but broke his promise. He wouldn't have freed you if it hadn't been for that slave medic Ari quoting the rulebook to his face in front of witnesses, me included.'

'Find the child, Barbatio. He's everything to me.'

He patted my shoulder and shook his head. 'You owe the Manlius clan *nothing*.'

'Find the child, Barbatio. Just find him. I'll pay anything you ask.'

'Zeus! Anything I ask? All right, one of those rings.'

He drew my neck cord out of my shirt and after considering Kahina's jewel, examined the gaudier one of Marcellinus. It glittered red and green in the light. Its gold band was worn but still heavy rolling between the Dacia's thick fingers. I'd tried to bring Kahina back to life by offering a ring, to no avail. Now one of these treasures might save my son.

'I've already lost one ring—for very little in exchange. I'll give you a ring only if you bring me back the boy, alive and well.'

'Don't start hunting yourself until dawn or you'll get yourself killed out there. I'll tell my men to keep an eye out. But if we find him,' Barbatio sighed with relief as he loosened his boots for a short rest. 'I can suggest much better ways to make use of him than whatever Eusebius had in mind.'

'I'll take him home to Roma, of course.'

Barbatio peeled off his stiff woolen socks and winked up at me from his squeaking stool set amidst all the harnesses, banners and saddles that reeked of sweat and leather.

'With nobody in that dead corpse of a city to care whether the boy lives or dies? Think about it, Numidianus. Some of us add to our pensions, *Agens*, when Fate tosses unwanted souls our way.'

⚔⚔⚔

'There are three witnesses,' Thalassius had whispered.

Dawn was still an hour away. I hurried to read the 'trinity' file secreted under my shirt, but where was I safe?

I could hardly trust the seclusion of my assigned room any longer now. Eusebius knew I had robbed him of his 'gift.' The

190

eunuchs' attack in the slum was proof enough. What's more, events had emptied the Palace of sensible minds who recognized the status and privileges of an *agens* carrying an investigating mandate from his *schola*. No man was safe in Antiochia tonight, not even a state agent on official business.

Thalassius was dead, but whether from a heart attack or poison, I had yet to discover. Honoratus had locked himself into a possibly fatal confrontation with the Caesar. Theophilus lay in gory pieces, dismembered by jackals already selling off his expensive robes. The senators languished in chains beneath the paving stones.

Only Eusebius seemed impervious to the crisis sweeping the city. He'd stayed secreted away, untouched by all the nightmares outside.

And the Caesar's wife? She, too, remained an invisible shadow over the events of the last twenty-four hours.

As for Clodius, I must admit, I gave him not even a glancing thought. Like vermin safe under the floorboards, Clodius would always survive turmoil overhead, even an earthquake.

I re-entered the Palace with its gloomy halls of marble, corridors of glazed windows, and elaborate carved doors. As if gliding along the threads of their own silken netherworld, Eusebius' eunuchs shuffled and slid along on their business through the maze of corridors. Especially slippery were the *silentiarii*, courtiers assigned to muffle the noise of the real world outside from the imperial dwellers. They seemed to be doing their job very well tonight.

Skulking down the labyrinth of basement passages, I discovered the Palace kitchens at last. A complex of low-ceilinged rooms that led off in different directions, they were as busy as a town square on festival day. Clearly, the occupants of the Palace continued to eat, even if the rest of the city starved.

The walls bristled with hooks and chains from which hung huge meat forks, graters, tongs, jugs, molds and all kinds of pots and pans. Through an archway I could see the great row of *furni*, a wall of brick ovens topped with domes. They blasted heat out of great mouths into which the slaves tossed new loaves and out of which they swept heaps of ashes.

I plunged into the smoky black air and stopped a slave reeking with sweat.

'Is there any chance for some soup and bread and a corner where I won't be any trouble?' I shouted over the racket.

'Take your meal with the postal riders, why don't you?' yelled a swarthy cook-boss whose former fat rolls now hung like empty coils off his chest under a apron covered in stains.

'I'm not up to their gossiping,' I said.

The boss raised a disbelieving eyebrow, so I shrugged and added, 'And I owe them a week's salary in gambling losses.'

The postal cubicle at the front gates of any imperial court was a convivial respite even in troubled times—but also the most public lookout point for any suspecting member of the imperial staff.

The cook took pity on me. Wiping his greasy hands on his thigh, he slopped some watery lentils into an unglazed bowl ready for the discard pile and topped it with a piece of stale bread.

'If you soak it into the broth, it might be edible,' he said.

Crouching in a grubby corner, I opened the file onto my knees and there, numbered exactly as I had expected, were the letters penned by the Prefect of the Palace to the Emperor Constantius II in Mediolanum.

I compared Thalassius' accounts with Barbatio's version. If Barbatio was an honest witness, he was also a blundering, florid and openly ambitious one. The Prefect Thalassius on paper was a witness of a much higher and more impartial caliber. He had been no striver—he already enjoyed as much authority as he could exert around the foolish Gallus. His cool analysis of the situation in Antiochia must have shaken the Emperor far more than a screed from a Dacian in charge of the Palace Guards. Thalassius stuck to terse reports of justice delayed, ignored, or countermanded:

An Antiochene gold merchant faced charges of using false weights and phony amalgams. He'd been arrested and executed on the basis of testimony from a single Palestinian who then disappeared from Antiochia a week later and was never seen again.

A prominent engineer named Epigones, enriched by decades of construction work repairing official buildings and monuments, had been accused of falsifying work reports and inflating estimates. His company had been confiscated, reparations made to his 'victims,' and Epigones forced into bankruptcy and exile with his family. Too late, his accusers turned out to have used false identities. An independent engineer had assessed his work and business practices as 'sound.'

I fingered through Thalassius' neat summaries of more than a dozen such cases, all in the last year. I read for half an hour before I rested my eyes. No account was so salacious or bestial, even distilled by Thalassius' dry tone, as the incest and rape charges against the Alexandrian Clematius. The paper removed from his dossier was perhaps the saddest because the case in question gave off the whiff of desperation, as if the youth Clematius had been so prominent and reputable only the most outrageous and offensive allegations could dent his social standing.

His tortures were also the most stomach-curdling to read. Broken legs, disemboweling, the savage use of torch and chain—these were all employed against the innocents of Antiochia but Clematius' agonies had been prolonged on purpose. The memory of Constantia's glee at viewing the young husband's torments made me swallow hard.

His prosperous business, like all the others, had been confiscated.

I paged through the accounts, back and forth, but found no reference to the last member of the trinity of witnesses. There was no third man here to corroborate the impartiality and implications of Thalassius' messages to the throne.

Of course, these three men would make every effort to avoid appearing like a cabal of conspirators. Barbatio had never mentioned Thalassius, perhaps for the same reason.

I gulped down the last of my bread and lentil soup, knowing that the slaves who brought me my meal might be as hungry as anyone during these difficult days. I lingered also because crouched there behind the cooks lording it over their sweating assistants, I found safety in numbers.

Food and drink also helped to calm my racing thoughts. I fought off the panic about Leo and tried to concentrate on my job. Case by case, I read, the accusations had been delivered through that back door of the Palace directly to the imperial suite. Orders had been carried out of it—orders to arrest, torture, and bankrupt the accused.

And suddenly I realized that, whatever haphazard lies and bribes the Caesar and his imperial partner solicited in their frustrated desire to impose their authority through fear and suspicion, they were only half the story—because this was no *spontaneous* traffic of informers and spies carrying tales of offenses to the 'back door' for mediation or punishment. Perhaps Gallus and Constantia had become the butt of a playwright's jokes, but someone had seen them as a useful route to revenge or acquisition.

I saw it clearly, all of a sudden, when I reviewed the telltale ending to every single case.

In every instance, the victims' *wealth* disappeared into the Palace where there were no windows to let in the daylight . . .

The more I read Thalassius' file, the more I saw that whatever the protective insignia on my tunic, I was no longer safe in Antiochia—if I had ever been safe at all. I had robbed Eusebius of his 'gift,' but more important, I had finally detected his concrete purpose in keeping the Caesar Gallus 'in power.'

Property, construction companies, and trade monopolies stretching far across the Eastern provinces—the Lord Chamberlain was amassing all of these into a vast illegal fortune while the boy Caesar and his vicious wife played at 'open' rule.

I sat there, my beaker of wine drained and my flatbread gone, the pottery bowl scraped and licked clean. I rubbed my weary eyes and asked for a hot cloth to wipe my grimy face clean of earthquake dust and ash.

I considered my position.

The Emperor Constantius II was hoping to hear from me that the East was stable in his cousin Gallus' hands. If there was a conspiracy to overthrow him, then I was to name the plotters and watch as they were executed.

If I knew what was good for my career, I'd report that Gallus was learning under the tutelage of Constantia and Eusebius as fast as could be expected. Then I'd find Leo and race for Roma, leaving the East to its lawless hellishness.

But better men than I, plus the ambitious Barbatio, had decided that the reign of Gallus and his vicious cousin-spouse could no longer be tolerated. Was Eusebius and his shadow empire of eunuchs their true target?

I needed to complete my report to Apodemius in the hours of night remaining and get it into the safe hands of a rider leaving for Constantinopolis at dawn. If Eusebius thought I had died along with his eunuchs in the southern shantytown, then I had earned myself a few hours' head start.

And I was counting on Apodemius' Persian operation having detained him still in the New Roma. I tallied on my fingers the days and the express horse relay stations required for my report to reach him by the surest route... Antiochia, Myriandros, Tarsus, Caesarea Mazaca, Ankyra, Constantinopolis. If he had already returned to the Castra Peregrina, I was out of luck... Philippi, Heraklea, Dyrrachium, Appolonia, Capua, Roma... He would get my message in fourteen days instead of the six a horse relay could cover.

Scrounging for scraps of kitchen paper from the cook's supply office, I wrote my report to Apodemius in code. I knew he would be unhappy to read it. It was not what the Emperor wanted to hear and one question stuck in my mind as I coded. If Constantius already had three independent witnesses telling him the unpalatable truth, why did he need my investigation? Perhaps the reports of the third man had been intercepted.

What's more, without pre-judging the motivation of the third witness in the trinity, how could Apodemius or I assure the nervous Emperor that these informants weren't profiting by

Gallus' insanities to install their own man, such as General Ursicinus?

All I could say was that the material beneficiary of the so-called 'crimes' putting dozens of Antiochenes in prison or worse was a man we all knew only too well—and the man Constantius trusted more than any other in the Empire.

I needed that third witness' name but I was in too much danger to wait.

I finished my report and folded the single sheet of coarse paper flat, sealing it with candle wax from the kitchen. Apodemius wanted his information delivered short and to the point and if any man could have broken the code as easily as my clumsy seal, I was already a dead man.

I darted through the abandoned official corridors and was heading across the empty parade ground for the postal riders' cubicle at the Palace gates when—just before I entrusted my report into the hands of that most junior of *agentes*, the nightshift rider—I stopped and thought of Honoratus.

Was *he* the crucial voice that would persuade Constantius beyond a doubt? Had his reports been intercepted?

I had to risk it. Moving softly back along the reception halls to the stairs I had mounted for Thalassius' suite, I hunted for Honoratus' office. If he was the third man, I could amend my report and give Apodemius more ammunition when he delivered the bad news.

'*Agens* Numidianus?' A firm hand clutched my upper arm from behind.

I turned in the shadows to see Montius, the Palace's legal authority, staring at me with those hollow, haunted eyes.

He was the last man I wanted to start questioning me. '*Quaestor*, it's late and surely after what you saw tonight, you want rest as much as I do.'

'Your room is not in this wing, I believe.'

'I seek Honoratus on business.'

'Too bad. Honoratus took the risk of going to his home in the Epiphania, *Agens*, like so many others, to check on the safety of his family members and property. Even the sturdiest homes may be slipping from their foundations tonight.'

'Can you get someone to guide me to his house?'

'No'

'Can you give me his address?'

'I cannot. Anyone wearing Palace insignia is in danger on those streets tonight.'

'Yet Honoratus braved the streets.'

Montius shot a mistrustful glance down the corridor. 'Whatever your business, I doubt it's worth the risk. In any event, the *Comes* Honoratus may be too preoccupied with his own problems to trouble himself with yours. He acquitted himself honorably this evening, but I fear he'll pay a high price for saving the senators.'

'Perhaps valor must take the place of justice in Antiochia, *Quaestor*.'

He sniffed. His fingers fiddled with the ends of the thick felt belt pulled tight around his empty belly.

'I'm not stupid, *Agens*. You're here to investigate the legality of the case against that Egyptian boy who raped his mother-in-law. You intend to report that I've failed in my legal duties. I should regard you as my enemy.'

'From my brief research, I find that justice was denied in dozens of cases. Aren't you the lawyers' lawyer of Antiochia?'

'I advised caution and justice every single time, I assure you, but my legal knowledge went unheeded. The Prefect Thalassius was noble, but too formal and slow in his work habits. He was a man of the old school too overtaken by the audacity of events to act on my advice in time. He could have told you of the number of times I begged for support. I saw him taking notes. I know he made records that may have escaped your eye. Now he is dead.'

'A death no man deserves.'

Montius seemed unruffled. 'We will soon have a new prefect—a stronger, more decisive man.'

'You have someone in mind, don't you?'

Since Montius seemed ahead of everyone else, I wondered now if he, not Honoratus, was my third honest witness in the trinity. He had guessed that Thalassius recorded the anomalies and injustices, but he did not know the 'trinity' file was hidden on my person even as we spoke.

With a scrawny arm, Montius pulled me behind a wide marble pillar and stepped on his toes to whisper in my ear.

'There is one on his way—one Domitianus, a former state treasurer of *spectabilus* rank and now a prefect in Constantinopolis. I sent for his help many weeks ago when I saw Thalassius was out-maneuvered.'

'Where is Domitianus now?'

'He will arrive tomorrow, unless the flow of refugees fleeing the earthquake clogs up the *Cursus Publicus*.'

'Is the Caesar informed of this man's appointment?'

'The Caesar will try to prevent the installation of any new prefect in Antiochia. He thinks every official is an obstacle to his rule. I am now the highest official remaining, *quaestor sacri palatii*, although not the most powerful.'

Montius did not have to name the Grand Chamberlain.

'Is Eusebius informed?'

Montius shook his head. 'No, I am summoning Domitianus on my own legal authority before it is too late for all of us.'

I took the scraggy lawyer by his bent shoulders and whispered back into his sallow face.

'I must ask you a very important question, *Quaestor*. This is an official question in my capacity as an investigating *agens*. Have you reported the deterioration of the situation here to the *Imperator* himself? Have you written to Constantius of these affairs?'

Montius stared at me, his eyes white orbs in the blackness. 'What? Did the Emperor not entrust the East to his own flesh and blood? You might well ask, have I ordained my own death? Do you think I want to end up like those senators down below, praying for a quick death?'

'No, or you would have spoken up long before this when you saw justice trodden underfoot.'

'You . . . you must speak to Domitianus when he arrives,' Montius said. 'You must tell him everything.'

'If I'm still here,' I said.

He nodded with relief.

'And if you're still here,' I said to his ghost-like figure racing away from me down the long corridor.

CHAPTER 14, THE PREFECT'S FATAL STEP

—DAWN IN ANTIOCHIA—

I had to get out of the office wing before it filled up with agitated secretaries and lurking eunuchs not seconded to deal with earthquake emergencies. So I asked a female laundry slave rolling a nightshift wagon laden with fresh bed linens to show me Roxana's private chamber. I knew she would help me search again for Leo.

It turned out to be a very small room on the humble edge of the imperial residential wing. But for a few sad flimsy tunics on a hook, combs and a nearly empty scent bottle, the space stood vacant. Her bed hadn't been slept in.

Of course, Roxana hadn't promised to wait for me there, but I worried nonetheless. Now where could she go? How could she return to work in the nursery with Eusebius' eunuchs hunting us down for Leo? Her tiny hideout was a pile of timber and stones. Where was she? To whom could she turn for protection?

Barricading her door as best I could with a rickety chair, I lay down on the bed to wait until it was time to go back out with Barbatio's men into the city.

I dozed off despite myself and soon the horrors of Mursa were reaching for me all over again amidst the screams and the blast of horns. The blaring noise terrified me. It was more real than ever. I woke up in a cold sweat. The horns were still there. I realized I was hearing the summons of a *cornicen* signaling his fellow Guards.

The dawn had not yet broken the ashen sky. Roxana was still gone. It was time for me to get going without her.

Barbatio wanted to be in full occupation of the city before sunrise. He refused to lend me a horse to ride through the streets with his men.

'My men and I know what to look for and you'll only be in our way,' he said. The evacuation of the streets was sure to be a brutal business. I tried to change his mind again, but he pushed right past me, followed by a groom carrying his saddle. He couldn't make more time even for me, a veteran of Mursa's blood-soaked plains.

'Don't worry. I'll have that ring off you by nightfall,' he promised. It was too little for me to cling to. I would have to resume the search on my own.

Sullen *domestici* guarded all the entrances set in the Palace walls as Barbatio led his men riding out four by four through the mist covering the bridge to drum all the 'filth' of foreigners past the city's perimeters.

In the wake of their clopping hooves, a chill silence descended the imperial island. The night torches had burnt low. There would be no entertainments at the Circus today and no gambling at the lean-to stalls barnacling the stadium walls. A few intrepid young men crossed the empty pavement to use the *thermae* and found the doors barred. Beyond the bridge, a city of half a million hunkered down in the ruins to wait for relief from hunger and homelessness.

The sky was still dark gray when the *Quaestor* Montius stopped my preparations to leave.

'Honoratus will see you now, *Agens* Numidianus.'

'Later. I'm going out to the city to hunt for someone.'

'Last night you said you had to see the *Comes*. I informed him of the urgency. Do not play with the court of Antiochia,' Montius admonished me.

I would borrow crucial minutes to corner Honoratus, but no more. I retraced those same corridors I had covered before, only now with a better sense of direction. It seemed a long time ago when the argument in favor of the Caesar Gallus had been a matter of checking a slander or two and confirming the procedure used to convict an incestuous Egyptian upstart.

The outer office desks that had been manned by curious notaries and scribes sat abandoned. I stepped right into the private room to find Honoratus sitting behind his desk as before, safely returned from his villa on the hill.

He had slept even less than I. His deep jowls drooped down either side of his face as before, but the tired eyes had turned bloodshot. All attempts at bonhomie were gone. The gaudy official robe stained during the evening by the shit of disgruntled rioters had been traded for a simple tunic in bleached wool cinched in with a wide leather belt with iron struts.

As soon as I shut the door behind me, I said, '*Quaestor* Montius informed me last night that Prefect Domitianus will arrive soon from Constantinopolis.'

Honoratus waved a weary hand. 'I've just had to break the news to the *Quaestor* that Domitianus has been in the immediate area for days on end already. He has been billeted by General Ursicinus with auxiliary troops to the southeast of here.'

Before I could express my surprise, he shook his head.

'Yes, *Agens*, don't you waste your breath—it's true. The Prefect Domitianus holds this imperial court in so much disdain that he passed Antiochia without so much as paying his respects to the Caesar of the East or his Senate.'

'That cannot be merely a social misjudgment.'

'Take that stool, there. You must be as weary as all of us.'

'Does Gallus know this?'

'He had just found out when the earthquake struck. This morning he sent a rider east with an order that the Prefect present himself without further delay.'

He put his face in his hands. I wondered if he'd even slept the night before this last. And with his reference to riders, I remembered the sealed and coded report for Apodemius still folded tight between my sock and boot cuff and Thalassius' thick file wrapped around my *spatha* blade, well hidden inside my scabbard.

'Surely Domitianus will comply? Isn't this what Montius hoped? Isn't it what you hoped when you sent those secret reports to Constantius?'

It was worth a shot, but my dart missed its target. Honoratus looked stricken.

'What reports to Constantius? What secret reports?'

'Haven't you sent reports to the Emperor describing events under this Caesar's reign?'

'You think I'm mad enough to provoke the Emperor? He slaughtered half his family for less. Who would suggest such a thing? Surely that's not in your coming report? Whoever suggested that is a liar!'

I spoke as softly as possible. 'Thalassius told me, *Comes*.'

I would not have betrayed the Prefect's deathbed confidence in life, but death left me no time to waste.

I pressed on: 'Thalassius said three independent witnesses had communicated to the Emperor that Gallus was both incompetent and dangerous. Thalassius himself was one, a credible authority but alone not enough to depose a Caesar. I know the name of the second, a rougher, military-minded witness, but Constantius knows that man's crude and emotional accounts must be offset against his ambition to rise to tribune under a Caesar Ursicinus.'

'I know nothing of this, nothing at all. Thalassius could not have named me because I am not the man you seek. I flatly deny any correspondence with the Emperor.' The blood drained from his knuckles as he gripped the arms of his chair.

'No, he did not actually name you, Honoratus. But Thalassius said there was yet a third witness in a "trinity" of witnesses, and I believe him. I also have my own theory about this "trinity".'

'Leave me out of all this. I insist.'

'If that third voice had successfully reached the ears of the *Imperator,* then even Constantius would have been convinced that Gallus must go, despite himself. Apodemius would not have sent me here at the *Imperator*'s most confidential request. I am guessing now that the third man's reports never reached the Emperor safely—but that this witness doesn't *realize* his messages were intercepted.'

'And you still insist I was this third traitor to the Caesar?' Honoratus burst out.

'Who stopped your letters?'

'I have nothing to do with this conspiracy! What makes you think me even capable?'

He rose to his feet and I thought that with a weapon in his hand, I would have had to fight him right there in his office. Even in late middle age, he now showed the inner mettle that had won him the title of *Comes* so many years ago.

I tried not to show I was shaken. 'Why not capable? I saw you defy Gallus last night, only seconds before he tossed Governor Theophilus to the wolves out there.'

Honoratus trembled with anger. 'I knew you were trouble when Apodemius asked me to help you. I tried to steer you right. You came asking me about Clematius and I suggested that—'

'—that the *Augusta* Constantia took a diamond necklace as a bribe for pressing charges against Clematius and sending a warrant through her husband for his immediate torture and execution. But there's much more behind this trail of convictions and ruinations that has led this city into Hades. I think you know much, much more.'

'And I think it's time you went back to Roma to file your report,' he said. 'If you know what's good for you, you'll let Apodemius handle things from here. He should never have sent a man ranked *biarchus* to handle such a delicate affair. It should begin and end with Clematius.'

'Perhaps first I'll share my findings with the Prefect when he arrives.'

I left Honoratus standing there behind his desk, where so recently he had sat comfortably touting the glories of Constantinopolis. As the morning light struggled to penetrate the pall of smoke billowing over the city, Honoratus seemed frightened by his own recent actions and the Caesar's inevitable retribution to come. He had defended the Senate bravely out on that bridge, but now he and I both saw the limits of his courage. Something told me that over the next days and weeks *moderate* courage was going to be worth less than hot tips on yesterday's chariot race.

But the old man had convinced me of one thing. I was still short one crucial witness.

♛♛♛

I wanted to stay on the island not one more minute. By now a simple question from Eusebius to any of his eunuchs could have confirmed my survival of the earthquake and the death of his two unnatural hounds. I had to disappear back into the bowels of the city and stay there until I found my boy.

Dawn was breaking over Mons Silpius. I resigned myself to sending my report to Apodemius as incomplete as it was. I added a line of code saying the new prefect Domitianus would arrive any hour now at the invitation of the *quaestor* Montius.

I slipped out past the Horse Guards' barracks to the postal riders' cubicle. After the production of my *schola* papers, I passed my report to the first northbound *eques* carrying dispatches for Constantinopolis. As the more senior *agens*, I was free to inspect his nearly empty mailbag and the registration book. No official documents had been dispatched since before the earthquake. Antiochia stood in flames and rubble, but possibly the Western Empire did not yet know.

A sudden rumble from beneath the parade ground pavement triggered shrieks from within the Palace.

The earthquake was returning.

Wails echoed across the parade ground, reverberating between the high walls of the Palace, baths, and Circus. The tremors below mounted into undulating waves turning stone to liquid beneath my very boots.

The rider and I threw ourselves across the barracks and embraced a granite pillar that stretched wider than our arms' circumference in the corner of the vast stables. He was a young Greek, no doubt recruited west of Constantinopolis. I detected fear in his eyes, though he was wearing the *petanus*, a soft riding helmet, while my own head was bare. I kept my eyes wide open, ready to dodge loose tiles flying down on us from the roof.

After a couple of minutes, the tremors subsided. The screeches of panicked women lingered through the windows of the imperial wing. The young rider took a deep breath, recovered his horse with a calming word, and mounted.

'Get going, fast. The road up to Myriandros should be clear for now,' I said.

'I want to get out ahead of the refugees. Nerves are raw and people who have just lost their homes are sensitive to uniforms of any kind.'

'You're carrying something equally sensitive,' I warned him. 'Another earthquake could bring down this whole imperial complex. It's essential you escape with that satchel without any more delay.'

I imagined even worse tumult rising up in the city. By now Barbatio's guards had thousands upon thousands of people packing their belongings under sword point. All five bridges leading to the imperial island had been sealed off under the Master of the Horse Guard's command. Barbatio wasn't taking any chances with the Caesar's personal security.

I knew he had sent a request for backup troops well before dawn by fire signal towers linking Antiochia across the sandy eastern reaches to none other than his mentor General Ursicinus closer to the Persian front.

But the more minutes I lost in the barracks' backrooms trying to find a spare horse, the more I realized that no signal of reinforcements had come back.

I could stand it no longer, horse or no horse. I headed on foot for the central bridge to demand permission to cross the river canal and go back into Antiochia. Just then I saw a familiar figure had spotted me and was fleeing in the opposite direction.

I gave chase, rounding the side of the Palace that faced the facade of the *thermae* and dodging down a narrow lane that separated the men's from the women's entrances, and then twisting right again down the rear of the baths facing the outside leg of the Orontes.

My quarry turned right along the rear Palace wall facing the steep riverbank. I thought I'd lost the chase, but then to my astonishment, the flying silks reappeared and then vanished again. I ran along the entire length of the high stone facing until I'd reached the northern tip of the island where the end of the Circus nearly reached the river. I continued around the wall until I saw the river main channel rejoin the river canal off in the distance to the north.

I retraced my steps, this time using some of my wits to look for telltale footprints in the wet earth leading down to the river or damage to the lush band of weeds that rooted along the back of the wall. Following some fresh prints I found myself stopped short.

I looked up at the Palace wall.

Clodius had escaped me by going through the back entrance to the imperial apartments. So now I knew he'd survived the earthquake. Neither the Fates nor I had finished with him yet.

I pounded on the heavy door for a full five minutes until a grim-faced *domesticus* opened a small grate to await my word. He stared at me blankly, even when I showed him my insignia and told him my name and rank. At last he admitted me into the Palace passageway.

'Another man just came in. Which way did he go?' I panted at him.

'I am instructed to say no one passssed,' he lisped, staring over my head. I heard his words, but my nose picked up another's trail, the sweet amber scent of a man far more powerful and evil than Clodius.

'This is an emergency! You see my papers? Answer me! Surely you saw a man in colored silk tunics come through this door only a few minutes ago! Eusebius must have been waiting for him here.'

The *domesticus* smiled as much to himself as to me and hissed, 'You missssunderstand me, *Agensss*. I am inssssstructed to say that no one *ever* comessss through this door, and therefore no one ever doessss.'

It was only then that I realized that this eunuch was possibly the most discreet doorman in the Eastern Empire, a man incapable of identifying anyone passing through this back gate to hell.

The eunuch was blind.

⚠⚠⚠

It seemed that the Fates did not want me to cross that bridge to look for my son. They were conspiring to distract, obstruct, and frustrate me at every turn. I gave up the search for Clodius and forced my way past a pair of surly guards manning one of the lesser bridges. I headed back into the city just as the red-orange rim of the sun crested the peak of Mons Silpius.

The situation was even worse than Barbatio had warned. Some entire streets had been evacuated by the *aediles* and *vigiles* so that looting and raiding would stop and fire blocks could be set up to save the central municipal buildings.

The authorities had driven thousands upon thousands of hungry people to the north and south. In the mayhem, many had lost contact with their family members and trusted friends and were left to wander and argue with strangers on all sides.

Worse, the bloodthirsty mob that had torn Theophilus apart had its counterpart in every district I explored in vain. After some half dozen skirmishes fought to keep possession of my sword and even my life, I soon realized that whatever my weapons and skills, my insignia made me an object of envy and anger.

I fought hard for more than an hour to cover little more than five or six blocks. I struggled into half-collapsed houses and under the teetering rubble of dozens of office buildings. Not only did I not find Leo, I realized how thoroughly whole neighborhoods had been emptied of every soul in an effort to save Antiochia from complete destruction.

I knew I might have better luck if I could only get half a mile farther to the south—closer to Khristos' laundry facing the Agora with its green spaces where a child might well take shelter in the bushes from all the chaos around him. I'd been searching for hours when I heard my name.

'You there! Are you Marcus Gregorianus Numidianus?'

It was one of the Horse Guards working his way carefully up a street riven with deep and dangerous crevices. One false step could break a horse's leg.

'Yes, do you have news of the boy Leo?' I cried.

'No, everyone is to head back immediately to the Palace at the command of the Caesar himself.'

Fifteen minutes later, I arrived back on the imperial island and stood in attendance with the assembled court, but as dusty and sweaty as any of the civil emergency workers still out on the streets. We were waiting for Domitianus to arrive.

Gallus waited on his gold gilt *cathedra* on a dais in the center of his main reception hall surrounded by his personal entourage. Some ten minutes passed before Constantia joined her Caesar in full regalia, followed by her own attendants, both female and otherwise. The tallest of them was that redheaded guard. I looked up to discover his gray eyes locked on my wary face.

The courtiers were dressed for the occasion in defiance of the debacle that had reduced Antiochia to ruin They were dazzling with the weight of gold sleeves, jeweled rings and neckpieces, high, embroidered collars and ornate belts. Only Honoratus seemed to know what was happening beyond the bridges. The *Comes* was still dressed in his plain robes, just as I had found him in his office.

But Honoratus had not stood passively by, either. For someone who protested his impotence and innocence to me just before dawn, the *Comes* had wrangled a second minor victory over the Caesar Gallus' temper—he had won the release of the senators in time to greet the incoming Prefect.

I hid at the back of an anonymous chorus of courtiers, in case Eusebius made some tardy entrance. We had been waiting in uncomfortable silence for more than half an hour when horns blared out beyond the Palace wall.

Domitianus galloped through the gates at the head of a squadron of thirty light cavalry supplied by General Ursicinus.

Perhaps Honoratus had argued that the Caesar should try to impress his new official with this full court reception, the Senate included, especially during these hours when Antiochia was *in extremis*.

In my opinion, any such gambit was bound to fail.

The Antiochia 'government' Domitianus met as he strode into the imperial reception hall was a blatant confession of municipal disarray. The senators were a particular embarrassment. They had been rousted out of their cells without time to shave, bathe, or eat properly since their incarceration. They were a pathetic sight, just a gaggle of bones and filthy finery, huddling together in the far corner of the hall. More than one wrist or ankle glistened with raw flesh where the fetters had just come off in time for the meeting.

I hung back behind the tallest sentries, anxious that Eusebius not spot me. I cautiously scanned the rest of the audience, all of them no doubt commanded to attend as peremptorily as myself. The *Magister Officiorum* had mustered hundreds of notaries, secretaries, and representatives of leading families on less than an hour's notice.

Eusebius and his senior eunuchs had stayed away.

Roxana was nowhere to be seen among the ladies of the court. Their white face powder and cheek rouge couldn't mask the ravages of panicked tears over the earthquake tremors.

Gallus waited for Domitianus to approach and kiss the hem of his purple cloak. Instead Domitianus paced the width of the great hall, back and forth, back and forth, to survey the miserable imperial assembly. He pretended he could not tell which young man with blond curls, gold diadem, and furious expression might possibly be the Caesar.

'Why are you insulting us?' Gallus shouted down from his dais. 'Why have you not presented your credentials to our court before today?'

Even Honoratus was taken aback. The senators kept their eyes fixed on the mosaics under their feet.

'I wasn't feeling very . . . well.' Domitianus gave Gallus the smile of one who enjoyed the rudest good health before continuing:

'I come today simply to extend an invitation. Depart Antiochia, Caesar, and return to your *imperator*-cousin's side. Know that if you delay, I shall at once order your emergency supplies cut off and the troops of your palace to be withdrawn.'

'How dare you?' Gallus shrieked.

'I have the authority to do this.'

Domitianus then turned his back on us and exited the Palace, followed by his well-armed soldiers. He was halfway to remounting his waiting horse in the parade ground before Gallus realized what had happened.

'Arrest that man! Kill him!' Gallus screamed.

Montius stepped forward. 'An arrest would be unseemly, illegal, and hardly expedient. Why Caesar, when you're not empowered to appoint even a sanitation officer or aqueduct manager for this city, how then can you venture to kill the Prefect of the Praetorium?'

Ignoring his sputtering sovereign, the *Quaestor* then turned in appeal to the quaking audience. 'If we have so little respect for authority that we go around arresting the prefects from Constantinopolis, then we might as well go out into the streets and pull down statues of the Emperor Constantius himself.'

Hearing this, the Caesar flew off his chair and yelled for his *domestici* to seize Montius as well.

Within seconds, as they held down the protesting *quaestor*, Gallus seems to find his normal speech at last.

'Stand by us, men, brave men, that's right, that's right, because you're all in as much danger as we are. This *quaestor*,' he sneered, 'has just accused us of being rebels resisting the majesty of the *Augustus*, our own cousin and brother-in-law. Just because we ordered an insolent *prefect*, a *prefect* who comes here and pretends he doesn't know what proper court etiquette demands, to be arrested?'

Gallus shrugged and with a lighter tone added, 'We only meant to frighten Domitianus, that's all. That hardly makes us a rebel.'

Montius looked up at the cowed imperial onlookers and read his own doom in their stunned expressions. Sprawled across the mosaics, he began flailing for his life but it was already too late.

The Palace sentries bound his hand and legs with ropes and were dragging him outside already, where we saw other men following Gallus' orders had done the same to Domitianus. At Gallus' next instruction, they connected the two men by these ropes to the saddles of imperial horses, preparing to drag them through the churned-up streets of Antiochia.

The shocked Prefect's face turned white as he saw his court slippers removed to allow the ropes a better grip on his ankles. His once-fastidious posture gave way to a frantic clawing at the faces of his assailants who returned his blows without mercy.

Gallus gave a signal for his Palace guards to encircle Domitianus' escort squadron. The hundreds of toadies under the Caesar's authority easily outnumbered General Ursicinus' auxiliaries. As the two horses dragging the prisoners started up, Montius' arm joints gave a loud crack. I knew that before they'd even crossed into the city, his two limbs would be torn off or at best, rendered as limp as a rag doll's.

To my disgust, the mayor Luscus, just released from jail himself, starting screaming encouragement. Like some foreman bawling out dock slaves dragging their feet as they loaded containers, he urged his fellow senators to do the same.

'Release me,' Domitianus screamed at his military escorts, but the Caesar had already marched up to their senior officer's horse. Facing the breast of a magnificent stallion dressed in full livery, Gallus held up both imperial hands to hold them back.

It was a sad irony to see Gallus capable of real command at last, if only to ensure the savage atrocity we were about to witness.

The Palace riders set off across the bridge and into the city dragging their gruesome train. Gallus ordered the horrified squadron to return to General Ursicinus' camp. He gave them

Domitianus' cloak and helmet with the 'compliments of the House of Constantine.'

The horror of the scene had silenced all but Luscus who could not shut up in his haste to curry favor with Gallus. The others drew away from the mayor and shunned him.

Honoratus and the remaining senior officials returned to the Palace in silence.

Only the *Augusta* Constantia still stood there on the parade ground as hundreds of onlookers drifted back into the Palace in revulsion and shock.

Her eyes were afire. Her breath heaved up and down beneath a *stola* and matching dress of garnet silk. Its neckline glistened with small rubies stitched down with silver thread. Against her black hair—freshly coiled, curled, oiled and set with gold beads— her costume glowed as deep red as the pools of blood scattered around the paving stones underfoot.

Her eyes fell on me, watching her. She smiled, a sly and willful show of those sharp teeth, even as I fell back in wariness at her approach.

'It's all right now, *Agens*,' she said. 'It's all going to be all right from now on. Constantius will understand at last who's in charge. You'll see, Numidianus, I have my own ways of fighting insolence. Tell them that in your next dispatch.'

With this enigmatic message, she nodded to me as if we shared new secrets between us and glided off on small toes bound with filigreed gold rings and soft goatskin sandals.

⚜⚜⚜

I ate with a few of the Horse Guards left behind in the sickroom and saw that when fare was needed to keep the Palace defenses strong, there was ample grub to be had. I hadn't had such a meal since leaving Roma. After the boat's dried rations and the madness of days on end avoiding Eusebius' possible recipes for my last supper, I resolved to eat with no one else until my departure.

With Leo—I swore—only with Leo would I be leaving this hellish metropolis. I mounted the ramparts along the Palace wall and watched for a glimpse of returning Guards. They returned, but without my son in their arms.

Barbatio rode in last. He was hungry, angry and marked by skirmishing with ejected city dwellers. Some of his men were carried in, wincing with burns or limping. Some were injured by falling roof tiles or timbers, and some brutally maimed by the 'filth' they were forcing from their homes.

'We were lucky not to lose a man, but it isn't over. Tomorrow we finish with District IV around the foothills. With any luck, Gallus will have forgotten his order within a week and they can all drift back to reclaim most of what they lost.'

'The Senate is out of prison and Honoratus is still in place, but—'

'Is that all we missed?' he chuckled.

'Hardly.'

I gave a quick account of the fate of the Prefect Domitianus and *Quaestor* Montius. Then I rounded on Barbatio with frustration.

'Who was the third man reporting these abominations? If you know, tell me now, and I'll send a report to my superiors that will have you confirmed as *Magister Equitum* of the Western Empire within a month.'

It was a promise I had no authority to make, but Barbatio exuded ambition far beyond his capacity and I thought it might drag the truth out of him.

Instead he polished off his watered wine and asked, 'Who says I want to leave the East?'

'It's easy enough to assume. You don't belong here, Barbatio, working side by side with these half-men. The West needs soldiers like you in command of real fighters to push back the Alemanni. Or go to the Persian front to serve Ursicinus. Antiochia is nothing more than a foul crib in the care of imperial babysitters.'

'But the money's here, Numidianus, right here. If I want to move up in command, I need to save up. You know as well as I do that the right position and powerful contacts cost money.'

His stubbly face was covered in ash and sweat. He stank of the city's erupted sewers and battered corpses. He hardly seemed a man on the rise after a morning spent driving innocent Jews and Egyptians out of their homes.

'Look at yourself! What money is there in all this?'

'Didn't I say that there were ways of helping yourself to the war booty passing through your hands? Antiochia's still an important market for certain things.'

He patted the magnificent belt that strained to hold in his belly and pointed to the sword pommel inset with topaz stones picked out by gold cloisonné.

'What kind of booty?'

His black eyes turned sly. 'Any kind.'

'Weapons?'

'Certainly.'

'Medicines?'

'Oh, no, the Greeks have that market cornered and always will.'

I waited and Barbatio heard someone call his name. I recalled the despair on Titus' face as he refused the ring I'd offered in exchange for information on Kahina's fate in the hands of a middleman working with someone in the East—'*a soldier.*'

'Prisoners?' My voice was almost too faint for Barbatio to pick up through the clatter of guards dismounting, disrobing, and washing.

'What did you say?' He looked back to me, already worried about the next foray back into the city. 'Oh, don't worry. When we find that kid, I won't let him fall into the wrong hands.'

Which told me that my old acquaintance Barbatio knew exactly who the wrong hands were. But before I could press him for details, he had trotted off answering the call of one of his lieutenants.

CHAPTER 15, THE SECOND RING

—ANTIOCHIA BURNING—

My report to Apodemius was safely out of my hands and travelling north. For the moment, I abandoned hope of finding the crucial third witness. I'd more than done my duty to the Empire. Now I was free to relieve my personal agony by searching again for Leo.

On two forays through the ruins, my eyes and legs had failed me. I had to start using my brains. I had assumed some kind stranger had led Leo to safety once that laundrywoman Zeva was killed by the falling debris, but perhaps his escort had not been so much a stranger as an enemy.

The Gorgon might know more and I'd paid her enough by now to tell me.

It wasn't easy to move through the Palace undetected, what with slipper-footed *domestici* monitoring the private imperial wing at regular corners. Even the echoing main reception rooms were milling with minor officials delivering hourly reports on the earthquake's turmoil sent in by municipal emergency workers.

But there was one possible way to avoid notice. I slipped outside and down the alley between the Palace and the baths once more. Again, the blind eunuch opened the grate and demanded my name, but this time I whispered, 'Clodius.'

He smiled warmly and swung the cedar door open to admit me, but something told the man with his heightened sense of smell flaring his nostrils that I wasn't the perfumed dandy I claimed. He reached out to catch my sleeve and question me further, but I wrenched free and slipped past him into the corridor.

He was more conscientious than I expected. I dodged his long, sinuous reach and padded away as noiselessly as I could but over my shoulder I saw him hunker down low in his official cloak, like a bloodhound trying to catch the scent of an escaping fox. Then he whistled long and low. He was summoning more of his brethren, sighted ones, to arrest me before I could hide.

The nursery wasn't far from where I slid along the polished walls, but it was in one of the wider, well-lit corridors lined with wide marble pillars. Sheltering behind these pillars one by one, I hid from the pack of hunting eunuchs now crisscrossing the maze of access routes to the private suites of the imperial family. I had two advantages over them, sheer strength and desperate courage, but I hoped I wouldn't have to take on a lethal fight in the heart of the Palace itself.

By the end of the corridor, I knew I had lost them for a minute or two. I could hear their Greek whispers echoing down a neighboring antechamber as they searched for me behind screens and curtains. I found a small door and going through it, discovered myself in an undecorated servants' passage, a narrow shortcut to avoid meeting the imperial family in the grand ornate corridors.

I paused to catch my breath. The passage was dark and worn but in regular use—clean of any cobwebs or dust. It was only a matter of minutes before some bath attendant or laundry girl discovered me lurking there. I moved along the passage, testing the doors and keeping my nostrils and ears wide open for clues as to which way to chance my escape from the eunuchs.

There was one place they would never expect to find me, a place conveniently close to my destination. I darted back out into the imperial wing with renewed determination to risk everything. Moving with stealth from one alcove to another I searched for that forbidding entrance festooned with those orange brocade curtains as best I could remember it.

The occupant wasn't my ally, but her last words to me were enough to suggest she wasn't anyone else's, either.

I tapped lightly. I heard the bronze bolts slide back one by one. The cedar door cracked open a few inches. A pair of light grey eyes scrutinized me. Then the door swung wide. I faced the castrated prisoner-of-war with his perfumed red curls. My appearance in reeking garments and filthy face startled him.

'Forgive my appearance. I seek the *Augusta*.'

'She's in her bath now attended by her ladies.'

'She must see me. Tell her the *Agens* Numidianus seeks urgent sanctuary from her.'

'I will pass your message.'

'Wait!' I slipped into the room on his heels and grabbed his sword arm. He misunderstood my gesture and with a skilled twist of his leg, tried to hook my left leg out from under me. I threw my left arm around his neck and with my right, pushed his jaw toward the ceiling.

I switched into Latin.

'Careful, my friend,' I whispered. 'I've done the same military training as you, plus lots more you can't even guess at. You're not from the East, are you?'

'No.'

I removed his weapons and let go my tight stranglehold around his neck. He moved away and dropped his gaze to the polished floor.

'Where are you from?'

'Gallia Belgica.' His Latin betrayed the tinge of the northern provinces.

'Name?'

'Meroveus.'

'You're no Gallo-Roman.'

'I'm a Toxandrian Frank. Five years ago, I fell into the wrong hands.'

'You happy here?'

He wouldn't meet my eyes.

Who owns you?'

'I'm not even sure. If I try to leave, they'll kill me.'

'You've actually tried?'

He couldn't meet my gaze. 'No. How could I face my family again? I'm no longer . . .'

'You didn't try.'

'Who would want me like this?'

'Tens of thousands of us in the West long to see beloved faces again, however damaged by war. You're hardly unique.'

I gave him back his weapons and nodded for him to go ahead and plead with the *Augusta*. As he disappeared into the inner rooms, I wondered where my comforting words had come from. I must have been thinking of Kahina. True, I wished her alive and home again to mother our Leo, but until now, I'd nurtured an impossible illusion of a woman untouched by civil war.

Was I prepared for whatever came home?

Half-lurking behind the folds of flaming silk drapes, I scanned Constantia's outer chamber as I waited for Meroveus' return. Her walls bristled as ever with the jeweled handcuffs, silken ropes, and gaudy harnesses of her intimate 'games'. But the ornate belt displayed not far from my nose had collected a layer of thick dust. Her toys and decorations had become tokens of discarded indiscretions.

I kept examining her chamber from my hiding place. Was there a balcony exit or a skylight? No, all her windows were tightly barred against intruders. This might be an imperial suite, but it gave off all the allure of a glamorous jail cell.

The braziers burned moist steam into the dry air. The incense masked a fug of female bodies closeted too close together. The cloying scents of amber and jasmine that Constantia used in her hair mingled with the perfumes of her lady attendants and slaves. The air smelled like stale garden flowers left too long in their vase. The clouds of smoke and dust outside the sealed windows seemed honest by contrast.

Through an archway to the inner chamber, her bed looked readied to sleep in.

It wasn't the first time I had the impression that the Augusta napped during the day and lived for the night. She avoided the unflattering harsh daylight with its prying eyes and tiresome obligations. On the other hand, the midnight's shadows obscured her fading looks and protected the identities of her gossiping 'visitors.'

The Frankish eunuch returned and granted me a wan smile. 'She will hear you.'

I followed him through her bedroom and down a short, narrow corridor to the ladies' baths. With a bow, he left me at the door.

'Come in, *Agens*.'

The *Augusta* had dismissed her female attendants. I stood a few feet from a square marble pool sunk into the center of the floor. The Emperor's sister lay stark naked in the warm water, cloaked only by the shimmer of oil droplets floating across its surface. Whether it was arrogance, madness, or a habit acquired around the indifference of eunuchs that left her exposed to my male scrutiny, I couldn't say.

I averted my eyes from the bobbing white breasts and strands of black hair floating in the water.

She gave me that smile of unnatural white.

'*Agens*, you seek my help? I recall it was you who promised to help us.'

'I did my best, *Augusta*.'

She nodded. 'My husband said you saved his life, which is more than we count on from his usual escorts.'

I turned away, embarrassed by her pale limbs looking so vulnerable now that they were shorn of their usual layers of jewelry. She was like a soldier robbed of his breastplate and insignia.

'What do you want of us now? You look like you yourself need a bath. Take off that filthy shirt.'

'I'm hunted down by eunuchs out there. I need to ask the mistress of the nursery who exactly sent the men who followed me when I withdrew the Roman child I left in her care. I need to know who my enemies are.'

She lifted her pointed chin clear of the water and gazed up at a gaudy ceiling painted with hairy satyrs rutting rosy nymphs.

'The nursery? Suddenly so many people avoid the nursery. Ask my daughter's nurse.'

She rang a small bell sitting among her towels and unguents. A veiled woman entered from another small door, carrying a grotesque little girl. I stared despite myself.

The *Augusta* tossed me a sardonic laugh.

'Yes, Numidianus. That is my daughter, Anastasia. The future of the Constantine imperial house! The best that two cousins could produce!'

Disgust was my first reaction, then revulsion and pity. The child had a very tiny head covered with thick black hair that hung over a low brow. Her distorted little mouth dominated a chin too small to warrant the description. Her legs hung over her nurse's arms like two bowed sticks, as if the bones were too weak and deformed to bear the weight of her stunted body. She must have been somewhere around two years old, well into the happy age when most children are discovering the thrill of skipping away from their nurses.

'Direct this man to the mistress of the nursery,' Constantia ordered.

'I need a private route,' I said.

The veiled nurse nodded and turned away.

'Yes, this girl will show you . . . wait, *Agens*.'

'Yes?'

'You heard that bastard Domitianus tell my husband to depart. On whose authority did he say that, and where did he expect the Caesar to go?'

'He would not have said it on his own authority, *Augusta*. The Caesar might be well advised to pay a visit to your brother to clarify matters.'

'Yes, I see,' she said and waved me off with an oily hand.

I followed the unhappy imperial child and her silent nurse through the small door and found myself in a corridor even narrower than the one leading to the bath chamber. It might have been devised to allow the mother private access to her firstborn without the interference of courtiers or slaves.

However, as the door closed on the sight of the Caesar's wife, the child's large eyes stared back with desperation at her mother. Her wagging arms reached back for an embrace. Her distended

222

lips tried to form words and failed. I realized that her young mind was as impaired as her body.

Constantia had showed not a glimmer of interest in her Anastasia.

The corridor was almost pitch black. I followed the nurse with her drooling burden under a wall sconce shedding the feeble glow of a single oil lamp.

Perhaps now I would get the answer I was seeking—or perhaps I was walking into the final trap in this nightmare maze clouded with incense and doubt.

Then, as when a nightmare changes the chariot in your mind into a boat and a stranger's face in a dream turns into a friend's, I was caught by complete surprise.

We three had just turned a sharp corner and arrived at another door, equally small and discreetly recessed. We entered a tiny chamber with a high window casting a bit of thin sunlight onto the stone floor.

The nurse deposited the little girl on a bed surrounded with a high metal grille that caged her in from the world. Then she lifted her veil and turned to speak to me.

'This is Anastasia's sleeping chamber. You see how tightly the door can be bolted to prevent her from crawling back to her mother's rooms?'

I was staring into Roxana's eyes. Her face shined with blue bruises and cuts from the collapse of timbers in her small house.

'You risked returning here?'

'I have not yet set foot in the nursery but I've confirmed that Leo is not there. I had no choice but to come straight to the *Augusta*. I know too many of her dirtiest secrets not to rely on her discretion and protection. I move only between these two sets of rooms until I can escape Eusebius' network of spies. Antiochia is no longer safe for me, Marcus, and since we robbed him of that boy, it's no longer safe for you, either.'

'But you are taking me to the nursery?' I saw that Anastasia's tiny cell led onwards via yet another bolted door.

'That way there leads you to the room where the other children of the court study and play. Why did you want to go there? The boy is lost.'

'Wait here, while I—'

'Marcus! Stop! Are you out of your mind?'

'I'm going to ask that old woman to name the man who paid her to betray us.'

'We agreed that they were waiting for us. Eusebius must have known of my hideaway for months.'

'I'll ask the old woman.'

'What old woman?'

'Why, the headmistress of the nursery, of course, the one I nicknamed the Gorgon. I paid her well to watch over Leo and keep Clodius from getting to him.'

Roxana threw her head back with a harsh laugh.

'Marcus, that is no old woman! That is a man, or one of Eusebius' half-men, reporting to him each morning and night.'

'Then why did you trust him when we left with Leo?'

'Because I had no idea that Eusebius already knew where my little house was or would send them ahead to lay in wait for us there. He must have had me tracked long ago, when he sensed I'd grown distant and less loyal to him. Now there's no place in Antiochia where I'm safe. I was deluded to believe there was anywhere in the East hidden from his penetration.'

'Doesn't Eusebius know you're hiding in here?'

'No. I never lift my veil. I have to entrust my life to Meroveus, the Frank who guards the *Augusta*'s door from the world outside. He hates Eusebius as much as I do. If I can rely on anyone in this madhouse, it's that poor soul. He hasn't forgotten what it is to be a man.'

'So there's no useful information for me in the nursery?'

'Only more lies and danger. You're not safe anywhere in the Palace. You must leave when I give the signal that Constantia has gone to dine with Gallus.'

And so together, we waited in silence, sitting on the floor at the bedside of the neglected and miserable granddaughter of the great Constantine.

'Most Romans expose such children to prevent a life of suffering,' I said. 'That's what *Matrona* Laetitia told me in Roma when I was a young slave.'

'They paid so little attention to her from the moment of her birth, they didn't notice her deficiencies until it was too late, I was told.'

'Perhaps it is their Christian God's way of punishing them for the wrongs they do others,' I said.

'Why do you care so much about this boy, Marcus? He's lost, like the Commander Gregorius and his mother, and like so . . . so many other good people.'

'Because he is *my* son.'

There, I had blurted it out. I had trusted Roxana with a dangerous secret that could deny Leo even the sourest grape or last rotting oyster of his vast legacy. We could not find the Senator's will among the lost deeds and the Commander had died intestate. Roman law assumed inheritance by the legal son or next of kin, not a cuckoo slipped into his nest by a pregnant wife and his ex-freedman.

'I see.' Roxana avoided my eyes. I heard the quaver in her voice as she asked, 'Was it before the marriage of the Commander or during it?'

'Before, of course, before. Before I even knew Kahina was promised to him. Our love was brief and innocent. Leo was better off—'

She sighed and sank her face into her hands. 'There was always something, something that escaped even me, and I thought myself the best of spies. I wondered . . . and now I understand everything.'

'Not everything,' I said, 'but enough.'

For the other dark secret—that I was also the Commander's bastard slave child—might be too much. And I had no paper proving that I was the Commander's rightful son, only his dying confession.

'You'll always love Kahina's memory, won't you?'

I nodded. 'I must save our child. And can you deny, Roxana, that you will always cherish the memory of your days in the arms of General Silvanus?'

She turned to look at me at last and suddenly kissed me on my cheek, for once without any of the professional lust of her Castra Peregrina training.

'You are my only friend, Marcus and perhaps more than that. You've told me your secret, so I will tell you mine. There is not a single night since I left Claudius in that camp field of Mursa that I have not prayed to the gods for one more chance to see him again and to know he is safe from harm.'

'In Arelate, I heard he was about to be named *Magister Militum per Gallias*. What better assurance that he is not only well, but thriving in his career?'

'I cared for him as a man, not a commander.'

'Perhaps he still feels for you, Roxana.'

I said that only to comfort her, for I recalled the way Silvanus had spoken of Roxana in the aftermath of the massacre, as if the young woman was out of his life forever. He had wished her well, but no more.

'Perhaps,' she whispered.

We sat there listening to the imperial child whimpering in her crib. We were trapped and frightened, both of us indulging in the comfort of happier memories and longings. I had never felt closer to Roxana than that moment when we were at our most defeated and alone.

'Listen!' she whispered. 'That's the *Augusta* getting dressed.' I heard the chink of jewelry and tapping feet of her lady's maids beyond our narrow corridor. Roxana pulled down her veil and left me waiting with Anastasia, who cooed at me as I rose to my feet and gave her a final wincing glance.

The suite was empty. The Palace inmates were gorging on their final stockpiles of food. I seized my chance and escaped to return to the search.

⚔⚔⚔

My eyes itched in the city's dampened light, so thick with dust and fire. I longed for sleep. I needed sleep—real sleep, deep sleep—without the roar of battle and clash of swords ringing in my dreams until I bolted upright in my bed. But I couldn't sleep. I wouldn't ever sleep again, for knowing Leo was out there somewhere, with only the gods knew whom, or worse.

I doubted any of Barbatio's men would venture out with me now—they had a second difficult day ahead of them tomorrow. They wouldn't sacrifice a meal or their rest to embark on the private quest of a lone *curiosus*.

For a moment, the maddened idea of inviting the Caesar himself to go on one of his exploratory tours to see the true suffering of the city in a crisis crossed my bleary mind. Of course, he wouldn't have survived five minutes among 'his people' today.

The bridgehead where Theophilus had died was heavily guarded, so I loped for a few minutes southward down the island. Only a few men manned the last bridge at the island's squared-off tip. It was a route that fed into a crowded mess of swampy land dotted with hovels, derelict warehouses, and locked-up merchants' offices. It fed directly into a main street cutting across the city to join the boulevard that ran through Antiochia to Myriandros in the north and Laeodicea to the south.

I showed the sentries my insignia and lied, saying official business required that I pass their cordon thrown around the Palace district.

I plunged into the chaos of District I, checking both my weapons before I zigzagged the ten or so streets Roxana and I had scoured before.

Down here the streets were jammed with more people in distress. The few municipal officials I saw were frantic under the strain. The *vigiles* were collaring any able-bodied men to fight spot fires and the *aediles* were arresting looters and troublemakers. I kept my head low and worked my way toward the Agora. I kept my bearings through the ashen sky by making sure that the dying glow of the sun behind Mons Silpius was on my left.

The neighborhoods had fallen into worse condition since the first hours after the earthquake. A main aqueduct had cracked and was threatening to engulf the whole city in water. Already broken sewage pipes had flooded street after street with clots of excrement. Foul pools drowned foundations on all sides. Many a tottering apartment block threatened anyone testing the narrow walkway beneath.

'Look out over there!' The smoky-faced brute yelling at me to clear out of the way had both arms braced to control a mule team in harness. Under his whip, the poor animals strained at long ropes hooked to a three-story building about to collapse. Another team had commandeered a military *ballista* to launch prongs over the parapets of ruined buildings in time to pull them down before they caught the draught of flames.

They were going to destroy a whole block of houses in the hope that a firewall would protect the *Theatrum Caesaris*. The mussel seller, the dancing whores, and the gang of theater fans had vanished in a sea of cracked paving and jutting pillars.

'I'm hungry,' a young woman said at my side. She clawed at my sleeve and pointed to her baby, made of nothing but eyes, jaw, forehead and stick limbs covered with the thinnest flesh. I knew that no earthquake had done that overnight. Other frightened women clutched at me as I passed, all of them starving. There was no market in sight—not even a basket of rotting fruit to steal.

My own clothes were covered with grit and sweat. I hid my insignia and hoped I might well pass for an Antiochene soldier as long as I kept my lips sealed. There was nothing I could do for any of them. I kept up my pace, searching darkened doorways under falling roofs, exploring trenches where the earth had opened a crevasse and climbed stairwells open to the sky. There were a thousand places a small child might shelter. A school of scrawny toughs ran ahead and behind my footsteps, taunting me like small fish swimming alongside a large one. A few threw chunks of rubble to get my attention. I tossed a few coins in their direction.

People had slept out in the streets in the clothes on their backs. Where Roxana and I had moved quickly through the stunned, immobilized city the day before, now campsites for hundreds of desperate people blocked my path over and over as I wound from one lane to another. Some people were weeping, both men and women, for lost family and friends. Others scratched and gouged with their bare hands or twisted kitchen tools at buildings that tilted treacherously overhead.

Some simply sat in a mound of broken plaster and stone. They gazed at me with empty eyes when I talked to them.

I made sure to ask any child within reach if he or she had seen Leo. The Castra instructors had often said that your average child saw and heard more than most pre-occupied adults—that the young are natural spies.

But these hardened youngsters only laughed in my face— whether at my lousy street Greek or my preposterous search for a single boy in an ocean of want—I didn't linger to ask. I scrutinized the women with especial care. Another woman, perhaps even a friend of the unlucky Zeva, might have taken pity on Leo and fed and sheltered him, whether out of pity or greed for a ransom hardly mattered.

Dusk finally closed in around the city. I rounded into the main boulevard near the Agora. The blind eyes of empty windows along an entire city block overlooked no light other than a few torches and bonfires. The *vigiles* were hard at it, seconding any spare man to work a bucket brigade. I looked up over their brawny shoulders to see what was so urgent.

Fire had eaten halfway down the great oval walls of the Amphitheater. The ruins were smoldering, their blackened timbers sticking into the moonlit sky like decayed teeth from a skeleton's mouth and sending up the occasional spray of red sparks.

'Make yourself useful, Citizen!' a district boss shouted to me. He slammed an empty wooden bucket into my stomach and pointed to a fountain that was still functioning somehow. So many hands were pitching and dipping into the water, only a few inches remained at the stony bottom of its basin.

'I'm looking for a little boy!' I shouted as I dipped and traded buckets, again and again. The word went down the line, but all I got were looks of compassion from bereaved parents and their neighbors.

After a quarter of an hour, I saw these poor people could offer no clue to Leo's fate. I peeled away and clambered over rubble and around ruins, working my way always farther and farther south hoping to hit the main road where it pierced the remains of those Tiberian Walls.

Breathless, a woman in a homespun tunic and torn shawl covered with blood came running after me. She caught my sleeve.

'Were you looking for a child, did you say?'

Her Greek was thick to my ears. For a moment I looked at her blankly, then found my tongue.

'Yes, a boy named Leo, led through the gap in what was left of the Tiberian Walls after the earthquake. He was with a laundryman's wife named Zeva but she died.'

'They've been trying to dig out a child, over there.' She pointed into the darkness slashed through here and there with moving torch flames.

'My boy's name is Leo. Is he Leo?'

'Yes, yes, something like that, perhaps.' She pushed me off in the direction of yet another team still working by lantern light some five hundred feet away from the Agora.

'Is a child in there, a boy named Leo?' I cried.

Two burly men straightened up from their labors as I ran up to them. Too exhausted by hours of digging to answer, one thrust his shovel into my hand and asked an urchin nearby to run for water. I went at it, along with a half dozen others, all of us digging at the hill of timber, plaster and rock.

'How do you know he's in there?'

'He was crying for a long time, but he's gone quiet now.'

'Whose house was this?'

The man next to me said, 'Not a house, just a public water trough for horses and mules passing up the main road from out of town.'

He pointed to a layer of broken tiles along the top of the hill of rubble. 'There was a small apartment overhead for the water worker's family. They got out okay, but the boy might have been trying to get a drink from the pipe.'

'Are you sure he's alive?'

'Who knows? We just want to uncover the trough and get the water flowing again.'

A third man came up the line. 'We've got to quit soon, call it a night, and get some rest.'

'But you can't quit!'

He shook his head. 'We've been digging straight since yesterday, friend. We're the second team that's worked on this collapse.'

'But my—'

'I've lost my wife and her sister.'

He patted me on the shoulder. 'Everybody's been at it now without a break since the earthquake struck.'

'Listen,' I turned to the few men left. They were standing around with sagging shoulders and blistered, bleeding hands. 'I can pay you with this.' I untied the cord around my neck, and pulled out Kahina's ring. My heart gave a wrench as I held the last tie with her in my open palm but if it saved her child, it was worth it.

'It's worth a year's wages for at least three men.'

They looked at me with sad eyes, until one of them reached out and took the ring from my hand.

'All right,' their leader said.

At that moment, I knew that any one of them could disappear with her circle of gold and blue into the night and I would only be the poorer. I'd seen thugs threaten Gallus and a hungry mob pull Governor Theophilus to pieces. I'd seen them cheer as horses drew Prefect Domitianus apart. There I was, my tunic hiding the insignia of the *agentes in rebus*, and I was begging them, even bribing them, for their last measure of strength and time. After the venality and slaughter that filled Antiochia from its Palace to the poorest hovel, I knew I shouldn't be surprised or angry with them or myself if they took the treasure from my grasp and laughed as they turned their backs on me.

Yet as I scanned their sooty faces creased with lines of sweat and tears, I had to believe that for all the evil I'd seen since I arrived in Antiochia, the Roman Empire still bred good men and women of honor and compassion.

At that moment, I put my faith in the decency of complete strangers.

We went back to work.

The collapsed building was unstable, sending a sudden river of loose earth shifting down onto the gravel at our feet. One of the men standing halfway up the ruin lost his footing on some tiles and slid down to the bottom, sending us choking on clouds of plaster dust.

After an hour, four of them begged off, relinquishing claim on the ring and wishing us well. They drifted off into the arms of mourners, wives and sisters offering them water and scraps of food.

Their leader and I kept on digging, hoping to break through to an opening inside letting in air and hope, but one of the timbers leaning slantwise started to wobble, threatening to crash down on the remains of the roof still visible at the far end of where I'd started.

Any wrong move and Leo might be killed.

'Is there any opening he could crawl out of?'

'We got one started on the other side, but he doesn't answer anymore. I think he must have got trapped under fallen debris.'

'So we've got to crawl in and pull him out.'

'We need to uncover the entire ruin to get the water going, Friend.'

'That will take another day. He can't last that long. We've got to pull him out right now, if there's any hole going in.'

'You won't get anyone to do that. There are people all around here with crushed legs and arms—if they were still alive when the quake hit, now they're just dying where they're stuck. I'm not going to crawl in there and join 'em.'

For hours, we had tried and failed. Lanterns were burning low. The wind was picking up a little, making firefighting more difficult for the men who still had an ounce of energy left.

I dug on slowly and carefully, learning that working from above was safer than weakening the foundation and triggering another collapse. But I couldn't find any spot that didn't shift and spill more plaster dust and broken wood.

Then I saw a dark space between some timbers. I reached in. I felt nothing but open space. It might lead to the innards of the collapse. I laid down my shovel and brushed with both hands at the opening, working it wider and wider without knocking the timber leaning overhead. I worked at it until the space was as wide as my shoulders. I grabbed a torch and held it as close as I dared to shed light into the hole. Some two feet through the thick wreckage, there was a black and open space. The torchlight illuminated the side of a large, long stone trough nearly covered with chunks of roofing planks.

A small white foot peeked out from behind the trough.

'I see him! I'm going in,' I shouted to the last man next to me. 'Give me as much light as you can.'

I unbuckled my sword belt, with its precious secret papers of Thalassius still curled tight around the blade of my weapon in its scabbard. I entrusted it to a youth of about twelve watching me with huge eyes. Then I thrust my head and shoulders through the hole again. I felt people easing me from behind past the thick debris and as my body blocked out the light, I moved ahead face first into the pitch black. I sucked in my stomach, trying to make myself smaller and wriggle my hips through without dislodging anything.

I heard some of the team returning and yelling outside for more hands to help me. Finally, I felt my head and shoulders drop forward. I was inside the remains of the low-roofed structure. I pulled my torso forward until my legs were inside as well and crouched into a ball between a fallen floor of wooden planks and rubble beneath my boots.

The men outside handed me a small pottery oil lamp on a long stick. I eased it ahead of me. Fallen beams and the wooden frame of a collapsed window blocked my way to the trough. I kept my eye on that small foot, lying motionless a few feet away from my reach. It was impossible to lift the roof crushing down on us, so I pushed my head underneath and worked my body forward like a snake pulling and stretching, closing the gap by inches.

'Take it slow,' shouted one of the men.

'Hand me a trowel or something!'

I felt them poking some tool tied to a stick at my hips. I reached back and got it into my grip. I scraped away bits of plaster and shards of cooking pots and torn bedding and felt my way forward, pulling myself closer and closer. At last, my hand clasped the small heel.

It was still warm. I could feel the pulse of his blood coursing through his ankle.

I tugged until I caught hold of both tiny legs and dragged the boy after me as I worked myself backwards, minute by minute and inch by inch. Plaster drifted into my nostrils and clogged my throat. The broken flagstones gouged their sharp corners into my outstretched arms and legs. My shirt caught on an iron nail and ripped in two as I moved backwards.

I pulled the boy toward me in the blackness. As I made some progress back toward the exit in the ruins, I rolled over to my side and embraced him against my breast and then passing his small head, still breathing, down to my waist, working him past me so that he could be pulled out first.

Every second counted.

I could hear weeping and shouts outside, rising to a wail of hope as someone reached past my knees and got hold of the little ankles, pulling and easing him out until they were sticking out into the open night air.

Then I stopped as I felt them extracting him with care, past the wobbling shafts of broken wood and tumbling stones.

He was out.

I heard a woman cry out, 'Leon! Leon!'

A cheer went up and there was pushing and shoving outside as a mob crushed around to resuscitate the rescued boy—who was not my Leo.

I cried out with grief. Yet there I was, waiting to be extracted myself. I knew the excited crowd was forgetting me as the joyful mother kissed her unconscious little boy and people begged water to rouse him.

Then some fool pushed against the ruin from outside. I felt the apartment floor that pressed down on my back suddenly shift like a lever on a pivot and push at the wall of rocks that supported the hole I'd entered. There was a rumble and I felt the wide plank come sinking down with its full weight on my back. The lantern flame went out.

Now I couldn't see a thing or move.

I couldn't even feel my legs.

The sounds outside were very faint now, muffled by a new collapse around the hole. I tried to breathe. Little traces of air still moved in and out of my nose, but I was pinned down, unable to help myself or even to raise my arms.

I was sure they'd rescue me, yet minutes passed as I waited for any sensation of shifting earth or light at my feet. I shouted but knew how faint my voice might be. I shouted again and there was no response.

Nothing. The air felt close and I wondered if it would last.

Terror seized me as I thought of the thousands of others pinned down tonight like me, their limbs trapped and crushed as they bled to death. What had happened out there? Were they leaving me to die while they revived the child?

I waited and waited. I heard nothing now, nothing at all. I couldn't move, couldn't see, and soon perhaps wouldn't breathe. I had been buried alive. I knew how high this hill of rubble and wood stood—two stories' worth of heavy shoveling and scraping.

So, this was it. My thoughts drifted away from wondering how long it would take for the air to run out on me, or to where Leo might be, or whether he was even alive.

I was afraid to move or even try to breath too deeply. I kept my eyes closed and thought of my coded report travelling now through the night by relay rider to reach Apodemius soon. If I didn't live to see that day, at least Apodemius would realize I had died as nobly as any *agens* in my class.

I choked hard as another intake of breath drew a whiff of something rotten into my nostrils—a filthy chamber pot spilling into the debris or a piece of kitchen refuse drawing maggots. I felt my insides were shutting down with the weight of the ruins on my back. Each time I exhaled the stones pressed deeper down on my lungs. It was harder to get breath back in.

Soon, I would be dead like my beloved Leo, his mother, the old Senator who had tried to give me the legacy of words and honor, and the Commander who had tested me for courage and independence. And I hoped that all these deaths had not been in vain and that if there was some great spirit or invisible history of the Empire's anonymous millions, it would not find the House of Manlius wanting in nobility or courage.

It was no good despairing. I concentrated on my report. It should have been more convincing. I had done my best, but if I had found the third witness promised by Thalassius, Constantius could not have disregarded the debacle that had befallen Antiochia. And then, to fight off my panic and anger at dying smothered in a distant Eastern city, I concentrated hard on who that person could have been.

It was probably someone who was more loyal to the West than to the East and someone who trusted his message would be read with a modicum of respect, if not immediate belief.

It had to be someone like the proud Thalassius who could separate his self-interest from the foul state of Antiochia's affairs and someone like Barbatio who, for all his ambition and petty greed, knew in his belly that his fellow soldiers died for a Roma that was better than anything Gallus represented.

It had to be someone literate, free-minded, even bloody-minded, with a streak of daring or defiance in his personality. It was someone willing to risk being accused of rebellious conspiracy if his messages landed on the wrong desk.

I forced myself back to consider who in the Palace matched this description. It didn't describe the vacillating Honoratus or the trembling senators with their downcast eyes and quaking limbs led by the hysterical, loquacious Mayor Luscus.

It couldn't possibly be a eunuch caught in Eusebius' sticky net. It would have to have been a very special kind of man.

But I had not met such a person in the entire Court of Flavius Claudius Constantius Gallus. And I knew that if I had met such a man, willing to confront the Emperor with the worst news he could possibly hear, that I would salute him as worthy of our ancestors who built the Empire out of courage and laws.

I closed my eyes and prayed to the gods to give me a swifter death. I would not be able to endure many more hours of this. The air would be gone and I would pass out, but until then, the urge to scream was overpowering me. Only fear of choking to death on dust kept me silent.

Then I recalled one such person. It was too late, but I knew who was the third witness. I smiled to myself with the irony of it all. If I had got out of this burial alive, we could have worked doubly hard to save Antiochia together. But we had come to trust and forgive each other too late for that.

The pain in my lungs was replaced by a sudden and sharper pain cutting into my left shin. I was happy to feel anything at all below my waist but fearful that a dangerous beam might be slicing into my leg.

The pain jabbed harder again and again. It was the edge of a shovel cutting into my flesh. I screamed as hard as I could just at the moment a rough hand got tight hold of my boot and began to tug.

Chapter 16, A Second Invitation

—THE CALLIOPE TAVERN—

The diggers carried my bruised body to the nearby lower slopes of the Epiphania District below the elegant villas overlooking the grassy knoll of the Agora. The mother of the boy I had saved told me that her precious Leon had opened his eyes and recognized her. The boy would live. In gratitude, she and her companions bathed my cuts with vinegar and brought me hot broth flecked with a few sad lentils and some dry crusts to dip into it.

After eating under their approving smiles and thanking them, I'd closed my eyes and turned away to hide my bitter disappointment in the face of this mother's happiness. I had given up Kahina's precious ring and for what? I had got nothing in return and yet . . . perhaps if I had not persisted, the small Leon would have stopped breathing by now under that treacherous roof.

I roused myself just as the torches across the city had burnt through the small hours of the morning. As a cool pink light crested the slope at my back, I gazed down on the blackened ridge of the remains of the Amphitheater, still smoking into the sky. All the red sparks had died at last. Most of the other fires had been quenched. People were hungrier than ever, but from where I rested, I saw the trail of foreigners forced out of their homes by Barbatio's horsemen crisscrossing with the small outlines of a few wagons trundling toward Antiochia from the south. The wagons carried sacks of grain to relieve a bit of the starvation—no doubt at a price.

I reached down to make sure I still had my sword belt and the cord around my neck with Marcellinus' remaining ring and the ring-key of *Matrona* Laetitia.

I was too weak to continue the search on my own. I needed help.

I couldn't re-enter the Palace without a trusted escort at my side. Even the authority of Honoratus might not be enough, since he'd infuriated Gallus by defending the lives of the Senators. If the only thing that weighed now in a man's favor was the force of arms, then the Master of the Guards was the only man left to rely on.

I stumbled back northwards through the subdued city until I came to a ramshackle tavern barely upright on the boulevard leading to the main bridge where Theophilus had died. Breakfast business was quiet and the daily menu a sad statement of affairs. Across the painted board, I could see the dishes that had been crossed out, one by one, as supplies dwindled. I bought a beaker of diluted drink—more water than wine—and a few dried apricots and wrote Barbatio a message to meet me as soon as he could at the Calliope Tavern.

Several beakers later, the Dacian loomed in the tavern's low doorway. He hadn't shaved or washed, and with his armor clanking over the hubbub of the sullen customers, he drew suspicious, ugly glances his way.

He sat on a stool opposite me with an air of a man who has no time to waste. He looked me up and down and reared back from me with a scowl.

'You look like something coming off the casualty lists.'

'I got trapped under a collapsed roof pulling out a child.'

'The one—? No? Well, I've seen worse already this morning. You're lucky to be alive.'

'So your men found no trace of him either.'

He shook his head, 'Sorry.'

I looked across the crowd, feigning more composure than I felt. For a minute, the gruff soldier was silent, observing that his news was hard for me to bear.

I took a deep breath. 'You were right. Domitianus was right. Thalassius was right. Gallus has to go to the *Imperator* in the West and leave someone else in charge of the Eastern prefectures.'

'Ursicinus.' Barbatio grinned through his stubble. He was picturing his advancement to *magister equitum* or even higher. There would be ample time to shave once he had reached the top tents.

'If your general is the best man, so be it. I have no chariot in this race, but that's not for you or me to decide,' I said. 'How much did you discuss the content of your reports to the West with Thalassius? And who instigated these reports, you or him?'

'He did. He persuaded me that it was in my interest. I was to keep my reports completely independent of his. I was willing to do it because I trusted he intended to lend the weight of his position to the bad news.'

'And he never told you if there were others reporting on Gallus?'

'He assured me that we weren't alone but he wouldn't give me names and he promised not to name me to anyone else. If everyone sent in his own report in his own words, it looked less like a conspiracy. So I was angry, all right, and damned scared the other day in the baths when you suggested I was out on a limb by myself.'

'You did what was required. Thalassius had a third witness. But that person's reports have been intercepted, I'm sure of it.'

'By whom?'

'By the person who likes the *status quo*. The man who profits from all the scandals and bankruptcies. The person who spends his appropriated profits on thick perfume and silken slippers.'

Barbatio leaned back and drained his cup with one thirsty gulp. 'He's a dangerous enemy.'

'For the boss of my *schola*, he's the *only* enemy in the end. What's more, I believe Constantia knows it somewhere in her fevered brain and Gallus knows it because he's been surrounded by eunuchs since boyhood. Honoratus knows it, which is why he prevaricates, and Roxana, one of the nursery attendants, knows it because she spied on the *agentes* for him and now lives to regret it.'

Barbatio sighed. 'I'm short on time. You called me here for something.'

'Yes, to tell you I've sent a full report—as full as I could make it—to my boss who should still be in Constantinopolis running an undercover Persian operation. I expect instructions in return and I'll need your men to back up any action.'

'You can count on me, and probably on the legions of the East to move at the right time.'

'That's not what I mean. We can't be seen to be violently overthrowing a Constantine, even if Constantius himself wants Gallus out.'

Barbatio took a deep breath. 'Gallus isn't going to just hand over his diadem.'

'If the *Augusta* isn't exactly a polished politician, she's certainly a survivor. Yesterday's triumph over Domitianus wasn't enough. She realizes her boy caesar is becoming a liability.'

Barbatio shrugged and waited for me to go on.

'This is not something you do publicly. It has to be handled right. If anything, you'll probably get an order to do nothing or even withdraw. Do you think you can handle that on the military side?'

'I think so. I'm not sure. I'm not in charge of anything more than the Palace Horse Guards.'

'I also want something else.'

I pulled out my neck cord and twisted the chunky ring I'd promised him for the return of Leo.

'You remember this? It belonged to the late *magister officiorum* to the Emperor Magnentius himself. I was going to return it to his widow, but other lives are at stake and I think she'd approve. You know this is worth a year's wages to you. Not to mention how great it'll look with that fine belt buckle.'

'Maybe.'

His black eyes widened despite himself as he saw the ring afresh, reflecting the feeble rays of the morning sun. 'But I told you, we didn't find the kid and I don't think we ever will. You're offering me that ring just for trying?' He let out a chortle of disbelief.

'No, I'm changing the terms. I think you know how to find his mother.'

Barbatio stared at me with a dull expression. 'The Commander's widow is dead.'

'She was *reported* dead. That's how certain people make sure there aren't any more questions. I think you know she's still alive.'

He stood up from our table, adjusted his sword belt, and tossed a contemptuous fistful of coins on the table.

'This should cover your breakfast, but lay off that wine. It's going to your head.'

I reached across the table, grabbed his sword belt and yanked him hard back down on the stool.

'I don't need to make another enemy, Barbatio, but I heard things in Arelate from Catena's last prisoner convoy. If you're part of any slave traffic that took the Commander's wife, you'd better make good on her return or—'

'Or what?'

'Slave traders don't make good aides to top generals. You're no better than a pimp, a flesh vendor, and a disgrace to the army. Ursicinus will want to start his reign with a clean slate of irreproachable officers.'

Barbatio slammed his fist on the table in frustration. 'How did you get into the *agentes*? Is that how they train you to write your reports? You've got no evidence, no proof of anything, just a wild accusation. I wouldn't take that insinuation from a citizen and you're nothing more than a freedman. Why, I've attended banquets where the roast piglet was dressed up as a freedman just for laughs.'

But for all his bluffing, Barbatio stayed on that stool. He was afraid of something or someone.

I leaned over the table again.

'Here in the East, Barbatio, I think you've noticed that the Caesar is regarded as something just less than a god by many people. And our Caesar, whatever his mistakes, can have a

Domitianus torn up between two horse teams for not paying his respects.'

'I'm in good with the Caesar,' Barbatio boasted.

I parried with a confident nod. 'And I'm in better. I saved his life out there, during that night of touring the theater scumlife. He promised to do me one favor, *whatever and whenever I asked.*'

The huge soldier shifted on his seat. I could see he was torn between his loyalty to the old *Legio* IIIA and the memory of Commander Gregorius versus some new 'friends' who promised to make him rich for funneling 'rebels' through Antiochia to slave markets across the border. He had hinted he could make better use of Leo than putting him in army service and now I guessed what he meant.

'All right,' he said after a heavy pause.

'When did you last see her?'

'I never saw her myself. The trail is dead. Most of those shipments have dried up.'

'How can you talk of the wife of the Manlius patriarch as a *shipment*! You were always a thug, Barbatio, but at least in Africa you were a Roman soldier. I see you've reverted to full barbarian brute. Did your mother wade across the Danuvius at night to bed with the Goths?'

'For gods' sakes, don't you realize that times are changing? All those old books you were raised on and their phony ideals died out centuries ago.'

Clodius had told me the same thing, but I didn't believe either of them.

'But you know the men who sold her? And they know the man who bought her?'

'Give it up and get off my back. If she's still alive, and I'm not at all sure she is, she might be anywhere by now—Egypt, Constantinopolis, even Persia.'

He heaved an impatient gust of anger across the table. 'You don't understand, Numidianus, this isn't the West or even Roman Africa. You can't just call up a list of prisoners' names like you would with a registry of retired veterans or a class of *agentes*.'

'You're going to find her through your contacts.'

'Take it from me, the less people ask, the better.'

'Except when it comes to you. The more you ask, the faster you'll get the answers that are going to save your reputation and career. Or I demand that favor of Gallus and squeal to Ursicinus that you traffic in Roman citizens.'

'It'll take money.'

'Yours. You'll pay up front and get it back out of the sale of that ring, but only once I see this woman's face. Now get started, and I'll let you know as soon as I get orders from Constantinopolis. Tell the postal riders I'm waiting here and tell no one else or you'll regret it.'

He might have wondered why I played so tough, but I'd already worried about Barbatio's plans for Gallus. I realized that he might broker a deal between General Ursicinus and Eusebius. If he did that, I was an easy obstacle to remove from their path to consolidating power with Gallus still in place as puppet. My hope was that General Ursicinus found the Lord Chamberlain's wily machinations as repellant as I did. In any event, holding a threat or two over Barbatio couldn't hurt.

I hired the Calliope's whore for the afternoon. She was at least twenty-five years old and missing half her teeth.

It hurt my purse and hurt her feelings more when I said I only wanted to borrow her room with its basin, soiled mattress, and rickety toilet table as my temporary office.

Nonetheless, she was grateful for a customer of any kind, because earthquakes and starvation don't make for lusty men with time and pocket money to squander. The only clients seeking her skills this week would be those few grain merchants I spotted heading into town and a handful of *vigiles* captains come payday.

'What's your name?'

She sheltered her thin bare arms in a threadbare shawl a million miles from the elegant silks and heavy embroidered damask brocades that adorned even the maids in the Palace less than a quarter of a mile away.

'Calliope.'

'My Greek is that lousy? I asked your name. That's the name of the tavern.'

'No, *Agens*, I understood you fine. That's what the owner says I should call myself. Makes it easier on everyone.'

'What name were you given?'

She hesitated as if to even utter her true name out loud might bring down a punishment from the proprietor.

'Athena.'

I thought of the Tavern of the Seven Sages back in Roma where the cheerful Delicia had praised Cornelius for remembering her name. I remembered being a slave myself and felt gratitude all over again that even in slavery, I'd been loved, educated, and protected. But then, even as a slave, I'd been their flesh and blood.

Athena was grateful in the end to have the afternoon off her back, and I settled in to wait for the last postal riders of the day to gallop into town. People came and went from the tavern, had no more than a glass, and caught up with whatever news had passed over the counter during the hours before. Like all drinking holes, it was the hub of both bad news and good, of messages that some people had died while luckier ones survived. Some acquaintances had been drummed out of the city while others were hiding until the Caesar's fury against foreigners and lowlife petered out.

It was better than any 'tour' with Gallus dressed up in an actor's idea of street garb. Listening through Athena's open archway to the traffic in the public room gave me an indelible impression of Antiochenes as a childlike, pleasure-loving, and emotional people. They were more passionate than industrious with their energies. With ample food and drink to ease their days in good weather both winter and summer, they normally led an easy life compared to us in the West. But now they were enduring dark weeks of hunger and death for which they seemed unprepared. They needed a strong Caesar who led them well, not one who goaded them into irrational murder.

Toward dusk, I left the confines of Athena's graffiti-covered room, having done little but finish more notes on the 'three witnesses.' I threaded my way between the unwashed diggers and tired repairmen pitching up to quench a long day's thirst. Positioning myself near the doorway under an awning that sank over to one side on poles that had lost their hold in the cracked paving, I kept watch.

At last I saw a clean-shaven youngster trotting across the bridge from the imperial island.

He was scanning the street and as he approached, I spied the insignia of our *schola* on his tunic. He was about eighteen. I hailed him with a particular gesture we devised at the Castra half in fun but always in secret. For once, the signal saved us both time.

'Name?'

'Probitus.'

'Rank?'

'*Equites*, second class.'

'Home *mansio*?'

'Tarsus. You're Numidianus?'

I nodded. 'Tarsus is two hundred miles from here. Have a drink on me.'

I took a packet from his hands and smiled with relief. The outer wrapping was innocuous, just crudely pressed paper that working class people used to keep accounts and tally gambling scores if they didn't have a wax tablet handy. Inside was a second envelope and this one was sealed with wax impressed with the image of a small mouse. I have rarely been so happy to see vermin.

It contained a letter written on finely woven cream-colored paper with an even texture and a customized golden border around its artistically torn edges.

While Probitus enjoyed his drink, I decoded the familiar writing at the little toilet table in Athena's alcove of peeling plaster and scattered cosmetic jars.

Its message could not have startled me more.

'*Honoratus, Lord Chamberlain, and you to accompany Caesar and Augusta to Constantinopolis without delay.*'

I decoded it again to see if I'd missed anything. How could Apodemius be coordinating the movements of Eusebius?

I examined the paper with the heat of a lantern for secret writing. There was none. I checked the surface for indentations of the real contents, using the black residue of a lantern with a gentle finger. Nothing. I went back to the main room where the hard-riding Probitus was searching the menu tablets for something—anything—left in the kitchen to fill his empty stomach.

'Did you carry any other messages?'

'One for the Master of the Guards.'

'From whom?'

'His wife, Assyria.'

'I had no idea the brute was married.'

'Oh, he gets lots of letters from her and this one was particularly thick. There was one other letter, for the Lord—you know.'

'For the *Praepositus Sacri Cubiculi*?'

'Delivered it into his chubby little paw, man to *man*.'

'Show some respect, Probitus. Not a lot, but some. Any other deliveries?'

'Still got one for the *Comes* of the East but I'm starving.'

'Leave that one with me.'

He shook his head in despair at the posted menu and for the sake of his stomach, I pointed to an item at the bottom of the list. 'Avoid anything that looks like a small rat or cat,' I said.

'I'll go with the lentil *puls*,' he told the bar man.

'When you're finished with your soup, I'm sending you to the Palace front entrance back on the island with this note. It's an invitation to the *Comes* of the East, Honoratus, to meet me here to collect his letter.'

I handed Probitus my cursory translation into plain Latin of Apodemius' unexpectedly conciliatory plan. 'Tell him I'm waiting here no longer than another half hour.'

Honoratus arrived within twenty minutes. Probitus had guided him and now stood talking outside with the tavern proprietor about earthquake damage to the road leading south.

Honoratus took the letter from my hand and read it while I waited.

'What's the meaning of this, Numidianus?'

'Do you still deny you've sent messages to the West?'

'Why would I condemn the poor ignorant boy? Time will work its own miracles. Gallus and Constantia couldn't seriously reign over a cockerel match, much less a capital city, but while I'll stand up to them to keep the Senate alive, I'm not going to plot their downfall.'

'I know,' I answered. 'But did you bend the other way and send messages of *praise* and *reassurance* just to please Constantius?'

'How dare you question my word yet again?'

'And yet, it seems, we can expect to hear that the Caesar has decided to go to Constantinopolis. Why? Things are starting to move, but I can't understand this order. Explain it to me.'

'I have no idea. I have heard nothing of this. And why does Apodemius suggest the Lord Chamberlain should accompany the Caesar? Are they working together? Surely your *magister* and the Lord Chamberlain are fixed enemies. Apodemius has trusted me enough with that sentiment.'

'It would be very bad news to learn that Apodemius is cooperating with Eusebius.' I admitted. 'If Apodemius doesn't have any other plan, it might mean that the West has lost its independence of the East.'

Honoratus sighed. 'Since the elder Constantine, all signs have gone in that direction. Without the support of the East, the West *is* lost.'

'Keep our meeting secret.'

'Yes, of course. I must go back to the Palace to make preparations before I am missed.'

'Lie low and act ignorant. You don't know anything about it yet. You'll wait for Gallus to announce this visit to Constantinopolis. You'll prevaricate, as is your style, babble something about how impossible it all is without more notice, gabble about how glad you are to be returning to that fine city, and generally make sure nobody suspects you had advance notice. I'll play dumb as well until I'm notified.'

Honoratus stood and gathered up his robes to leave.

I grabbed his sleeve. 'And one more thing, *Comes*. Please make sure the *Augusta* includes the Frankish attendant Meroveus in her travelling guard.'

'Meroveus?'

'Yes. He's the only one I can imagine not trying to stab me in the back.'

Honoratus scurried off, lifting his tunic over upturned paving stones and scattered rubbish as he headed back to the relative safety of the Palace.

All around me, cartloads of rubble—marble chunks, sacks of plaster dust, rocks, and broken furnishings—were rolling toward the river to be loaded onto barges. I strolled to the end of the quarter from where I could see the activity on the Orontes current flowing between city and Palace.

Other passing barges sat low in the water under the weight of dozens of decaying bodies. Boatmen wore scarves across their faces to ward off the stench. They were headed downriver to deliver the dead to mass municipal pyres already sending smoke furls into the afternoon breeze beyond the end of the island.

Some of the barges bore less dramatic loads—the daily offtake of rubbish and kitchen trimmings in barrels headed for waste dumps outside the city walls to the south of the main road. A wide flat vessel, so deep in the water that the brownish ripples lapped like a tongue at the turnip shavings and fowl carcasses slipping out of their hessian bags.

Then something familiar caught my eye.

'Boatman,' I shrieked. 'You're practically drowning out there! Who loaded you up to your balls?'

He laughed back as he worked at his oars. Where do you think?'

'The Palace?'

'They're never short of imperial shit to dump on us, but I tell you, stranger, it stinks like any other.' He pointed straight to the imperial dock.

sI dogged his barge, running along the city quay and peering hard at his load before he dropped out of sight in the fading sun of the wintry afternoon. I had to convince myself that what I'd spotted hadn't been my own wishful thinking.

For dropped between two patched sacks filled to the brim with rotting entrails, feathers, and fruit pulp, a little animal cage floated past me. It could have been anything discarded by an impatient cook lining up fowls to roast, except for one thing.

A familiar red string tied to the cage door drifted loose overboard and trailed in the silty brown water—floated away and out of sight.

CHAPTER 17, A CAESAR'S LAST DECREE

—THE PALACE KITCHENS—

I hid out at the Calliope Tavern until the sun had set but not a second longer.

It was time for me to move. And my weathered friend Athena had been on her feet all day, serving customers. She actually *wanted* to lie down—a novel sensation that meant she needed her mattress back. The last favor she granted me was not what many men would have asked, but merely a good scrubdown using a borrowed *strigil* and razor plus a basin full of warm water from the bar.

I was certain now that Leo was still alive, but that he was in great danger, wherever he was inside the Palace.

I knew Clodius had survived the earthquake and re-entered the Palace at least once since Leo's disappearance—the blind doorman's hissing recognition of his name told me that. But the doorman wouldn't be fooled yet again and they weren't all blind. I couldn't risk trying to get through that back door into the Palace a third time.

Though nothing could stop me from hunting Clodius down in the back corridors and more lowly chambers of the rest of the Palace, there were dozens upon dozens of rooms. I could waste precious hours searching door by door. Clodius *must* be somewhere within—I could never imagine him lasting an hour in the streets of the devastated city. Flitting among Antiochia's poor and hungry in his flamboyant orange silks and royal blue fringes, he'd stand out like a sauced peacock on a golden platter.

So how was he surviving?

Of course he had to eat. Possibly he'd pilfered or begged off the kitchen staff the same way I had got myself a miserable bowl of soup. What's more, the kitchen doors might be the safest way for me to re-enter the imperial halls.

Just before the torches lining the bridge leading to the island were lit by wary palace attendants, I slipped across. Barbatio was nowhere to be seen in the Guards' barracks. It was full to the brim with his horsemen and any one of them might have been bribed to look out for me.

I sought the anonymity of the imperial vehicle stalls nearby. I crouched low, behind the serried wheels of carriages, procession chariots, and delivery wagons embossed with the Constantinian Christian logo, 'Chi Rho'.

The smell of worn leather, horseshit, and axle grease were strange comforts as I watched dusk sink these relics of more glorious days into blessed obscurity. There was little illumination along the far alley between the Palace and the now empty Circus ground. I would slip along to the northern tip of the island and vault the wall into the Palace vegetable garden, over-picked and parched, and then get into the Palace by way of the suppliers' entrance.

I finally found the humble entry. I slipped into what smelled like the laundry rooms. I froze as I came face to face in the dark with an entire troop of *domestici* standing to attention with arms stretched out wide and stiff to snatch me.

It was a full minute as I waited for them to say something or make a move on me. My heart had stopped pumping before I realized I'd stumbled into the drying room. These were no sentries. Dozens of tunics were hanging to dry in the dark next to piles of folded towels and bed linens.

It reminded me that these tunics belonged to dozens of live men in uniform beyond those doors and that all of them were ready to earn a bonus by apprehending me on Eusebius' order.

I braved the bustling, smoky chaos of the kitchen once again. The kitchen staff took little notice of me until I stole a sausage from a pile and got my wrist slapped by the same boss who'd seen to my nourishment only the night before.

'What are you doing back again?' he asked. 'Still dodging your gambling debts?'

He wasn't going to buy the same excuse twice.

'I'm looking for a hungry guest, a hanger-on.'

'Aren't they all hangers-on?'

'This one's a true Roman, a really *fashionable* Roman.'

'Oh, gods, I know the one.'

The cook twisted his lower lip with distaste. 'He'll be down here soon enough, begging for a scrap. I don't know whom he's afraid of, but he's one jittery fellow. Says he's trying to leave town, but what with the earthquake, the roads are jammed with starving refugees ready to rob a—'

'I have to talk to him. Where can I wait?'

'In the oven room, over there. We've finished baking for the night. Supplies are too low for pastries, but hey—those ovens are still hot! Watch out for the sparks.'

It seemed that, with the sight of the trailing red ribbon, my luck might have changed.

Beyond the busy kitchens, in their own alcove through a great stone arch, sat the giant ovens blackened by decades of smoke. Tonight their red embers glowed softly through gaping mouths set against a low-ceilinged brick wall.

I crouched in the darkest corner, away from the hellish glow of orange light pooling across the stone floor. On the other side of the archway, the bright kitchen's powerful torches shed light on the butchers still working away. They were dismembering roasted pigs for the hundreds of hungry Palace clerks and sentries upstairs. The flames of their open fires licked at pots standing on iron tripods. Cooking slaves tended red and green peppers charring on heavy grills. Other slaves hauled huge *pultarii* for stewing up humble chickpeas and winter vegetables for the slaves cleaning toilets, laundry, and bedchambers.

Any rabbit would have been skinned and marinated by now.

More than an hour passed. Now and then a wordless slave skirted past me to toss some kindling into the ovens to keep them smoldering low until they were needed again. A bundle of cooking spits, lethally sharp but covered in animal grease, stood propped in the corner waiting to be cleaned. There were a few iron bread paddles and a pile of cracked pots ready for breaking into pieces to line the garden walks.

I heard voices in the kitchen and looked up.

'Here he is,' the cook said. With a disdainful shove, he pushed Clodius through the archway.

'Where's Leo, Clodius?'

He was startled to see me and backed away, dropping the roasted crackling he'd cajoled from the slaves. I rounded on him and cut off his exit to the kitchen. He moved deeper into the alcove.

'How should I know, you double-crossing slave? You've caused me a lot of trouble.'

'You know very well. That nursery hag or whatever he is alerted Eusebius or you and he sent two henchmen to wait for us in the slums. Eusebius guessed we'd turn up there.'

'I don't know what you're talking about.'

'Where were you hiding?'

'You can't get him now.'

'Where were you? Hiding behind the walls? Did you follow that poor woman who was trying to rescue him?'

He backed off some more, but didn't deny anything.

'Did she refuse to hand Leo over to you? Did Leo hang back? Was he reluctant to go with you?'

'That child was mine, not yours!'

'What did Leo say when he saw you?'

'That stupid woman didn't understand a word of Latin. She didn't believe I was his cousin!'

'Clodius! That woman Zeva was taking Leo to safety!'

'That creature, stinking of urine bleach and stew? She saw his good shoes and nice tunic. She wanted *money*, of course. And I don't have any left!'

'And so you killed her? Smashed in her brains?'

'The city was catching fire, for gods' sake! *I was in a hurry!*'

'Where's Leo now?'

'It's too late!'

Clodius tried to sail past me through the archway but I blocked him again.

'Tell me where he is.'

I drew my *pugio* and reached for him, but he dodged me and grabbed a greasy cooking spit. It was longer than my dagger and sharp enough to take out my eye if he got lucky. He jabbed at me, trying to push me away so he could make a run for it through the kitchens. I pulled my *spatha* and with both weapons extended, began to test him with a thrust from my right and a jab from my left. I knew Clodius was no fighter.

'Where's the boy?'

'I don't know.'

'Did you give him back to Eusebius?

'You'll never get him back *now*. You won't even want him back after his "accident".'

'I'll have you convicted in Roma for this.'

Clodius threw his chin into the air with a defiant, 'Well, wasn't that our plan all along? Didn't I explain it to you from the beginning? And didn't you play along, with all your expert explanations?'

'You bastard.'

'Oh, no, no, no, Marcus, I think it's *you* who's the bastard. Or did you think I hadn't guessed after all these years? You think I don't look into your features and see the Commander, all stubbornness and pride? Isn't that why you're so concerned? Isn't the little brat your half-brother?'

'Indeed he is *not*.'

I said it with such conviction that Clodius had to believe me. For a moment my honesty confused him. Then his eyes widened with disbelief. He threw back his head and hooted with laughter, his flame-colored silks and blue fringe wafting around him as he doubled up with laughter.

'Oh, no, that would be too rich, too good, too fabulous. You and that jumped-up housemaid Kahina? Parading around the townhouse as the virtuous Manlius matron? Locking *me* out of the wine cellar and the library?'

'Clodius!'

'Is it possible? That every one of the blood descendants of the respectable House of Manlius is not who he seems?'

His insinuations, coming too close to the mark, terrified me.

'You're raving.'

'Well, perhaps you're right.' His laughter died down and he gripped his greasy stake tighter. 'That would be too much to ask of the gods as a reward for my great ritual sacrifice. Because the Commander never acknowledged you, did he? So I'm still Leo's rightful guardian and this is my solution to his future.'

I lowered my weapon, feigning resignation, 'Yes, I suppose you have that right.'

As soon as I saw him relax a jot, I swung my sword and knocked the spit out of his hand. Now I lunged to encircle his throat with my left arm, but he dodged me again, dancing away on those flimsy slippers he wore. He was dangerously close to the ovens as his fine silks brushed the glowing wall of brick.

I reached again to get hold of him, but he screamed before I'd even got at his throat because his blue fringe had got caught in the low-burning embers. The thin silk began to twist and tighten, turning into black threads as he shrieked. Then the gossamer tunic fabric flowered into a tiny flame that he flailed and batted at with his palms. But this only fed the fire and sent a long flame licking up his arm. With seconds, the over-tunic was burning a trail right up his back, its delicate weave as flimsy as a scorched butterfly wing.

'Water!' he screamed. 'Water! I'm burning!'

Despite my fear, I reached into the flames trying to get hold of his tunic and rip it off, but my hand came up with nothing but floating ashes. His orange under-tunic had caught fire now. He was trying to pull this mess of igniting silk up over his head. But he only made his plight worse as the woven braid on his collar caught on the clasp of his gold necklaces.

There was a sudden splashing wave as shouting slaves came through the archway pitching an enormous *pultarius* of dirty dishwater over Clodius. Seconds later, another pair of slaves rushed in with a heavy maroon travelling cloak. They threw it over Clodius' head. Pushing him to the ground, we all rolled him in the cloak together, muffling his shrieks of pain.

Finally the uproar subsided. We waited over his thrashing body until all the flames had been smothered. Finally the wet and ashy cocoon went limp.

'That was my best cloak and I expect him to replace it,' said a familiar, silky voice from behind me.

I rose and turned to see the round and sweating figure of the Lord Chamberlain, his heaving black silhouette blocking the light of the kitchen beyond.

'Take what remains of him to the slaves' infirmary.'

'But *Praepositus*,' said the cook looking on in horror, 'this man told us he was your guest and that we were to feed him. He never said he was a slave.'

'My guest?' Eusebius chuckled. 'This unfortunate person was nothing more than a . . . tradesman . . . offering samples.'

Half a dozen slaves bore Clodius off in a winding sheet. He was trembling and whimpering with shock, close to fainting. Through his burnt-off clothes and hair, I saw white papery boils lifting the skin off his face and arms in great patches. He made no further protest as he was carried away.

I was left alone with the Lord Chamberlain. Charred scraps of Clodius' finery still floated in the hot air rising off the burning stoves.

'Where is the boy, Eusebius?'

'I've received a very strange notification, Numidianus. It seems that the Caesar is expected in Constantinopolis to appear before the Senate there.'

'Where is the boy?'

I still had my weapons at hand, but they were useless against the most powerful man in the Eastern Empire surrounded by kitchen cooks and slaves.

'The Senators of Constantinopolis wish to pose some questions about the fate of their Prefect Domitianus, I suppose.'

'Where is the boy?'

'I've advised our Caesar to decline this invitation.'

'Where is the child?'

259

Eusebius took a few steps toward me, 'You see, I smell the hand of your arthritic old Apodemius in this. Luckily I've persuaded Gallus to ignore this invitation. He's safer here at home, earthquake or no earthquake.'

'*Where is the boy? What have you done with him?*'

'I wish you would stop going on about that child. You were the one who told me that he was worthless, that his legacy was depleted, and that I was only assuming onerous debts by taking him on as a protégé.'

'Give him back to me.'

'Even if I had the little boy, which I don't, I would hardly entrust him to a *rebel*. I'm escorting you now to the Caesar. Your troublemaking has come to an end, Numidianus, but only Gallus can actually decide on your punishment. He's still the Caesar, after all—just.'

He held out his pudgy arm to escort me out of the kitchens. I stayed where I was.

'Yes,' I said, 'Only the Caesar Gallus can decide my fate, just as he decided so much in the past, like the case of the gold merchant with the false weights or the construction engineer with the inflated estimates. Yes it was Gallus who had the final word, but only one word, *just.*'

It was a fatal error.

'So *you* have the documents missing from the archive records,' Eusebius rounded on me, his yellowish-brown eyes glittering with satisfaction. I now carefully re-inserted my sword into its scabbard.

'Take him to the Caesar now,' he commanded in a loud voice. Four *domestici*, tall but beardless men flexing bare arms of oiled white fat, appeared in the archway and seized me.

It was a long march from the kitchens to the main imperial reception room where Gallus sat conferring with his re-assembled court. We interrupted his interrogation from the dais of the municipal reconstruction teams.

'What is this, Lord Chamberlain?' Gallus looked over, startled and tense, at the confident entrance of his Lord Chamberlain. 'We've barely got things underway. Important staff members are still missing, and there are emergencies everywhere. We'll be working late into the night. Our people need us.'

'Caesar, this is another player in the determined conspiracy I've been warning you about—another ally of the General Ursicinus.'

'I've never met the man,' I protested. 'My business here is straightforward—to confirm the judicial process regarding the Egyptian cotton merchant, Clematius. I have completed my assignment. I am ready to return to Roma.'

'We've told you before, Lord Chamberlain, we won't hear any more of these accusations against General Ursicinus. Whatever makes you think he conspires against us?'

'He would take your diadem from you, Caesar.'

Gallus laughed. 'General Ursicinus is far too busy to plot against us. He suppressed the Jewish revolt and burned their cities to the ground. We ordered him to finish them off, kill them all, even the ones too young to shave. He obeyed us to the letter. Now the towns of Tiberias, Diospolis, and Diocaesarea are no more, just smoking ruins, thanks to Ursicinus. Is this not loyalty? Stop bothering us with these groundless rumors.'

'I have arrested this man standing here for conspiring with the Master of the Guards in sending unfavorable reports of this court to the *Imperator* Constantius. I tell you, their purpose is to promote Ursicinus at your expense.'

'I have never met or spoken to this Ursicinus!' I protested.

Gallus peered at me. He himself had lost sleep since the earthquake, but whether from overwork or simple terror, I couldn't tell. He recognized me as the *agens* Barbatio sent to escort his night stalking. He had expected my attendance to witness the reception for the Prefect Domitianus. He had demonstrated that he wanted me to carry favorable reports of his leadership back to the West. I held out hope he would resist Eusebius' accusations.

'You have proof of this, Lord Chamberlain?'

'Why do you think you were summoned to the Senate in Constantinopolis, Caesar? The Master of the Horse Guards has sent them lies.'

261

Gallus turned to me. 'Do you deny meeting with the Master of the Horse Guards?"

'Of course not, Caesar. Barbatio is an old *contubernalis* from our service with the *Legio III Augusta* in Numidia Militaris.'

'You see, Lord Chamberlain. What could be more natural? They are old comrades-in-arms.'

Eusebius heaved with eagerness to take over the interrogation. His chubby hands twisted with frustration. He couldn't wait any longer for Gallus' ingenuous questioning to reach the nub of his allegations.

'So you do have ties that stretch back and run deep into the military?' Eusebius asked me.

'I don't deny it, *Praepositus*. Why should I?'

'Do you deny serving under Commander Gregorius when he was the *magister militum* for the rebel usurper Magnentius?'

'Yes, I deny *that* with the greatest vigor. You should know your government protocol better than that, *Praepositus*. I took my orders from the *schola* of the *Agentes in Rebus* in Roma. I was posted to duties supervising the imperial communications for that court in Aquileia.'

'But you resumed your connection with Barbatio when you arrived here? You talked in secret about plans to remove our Caesar and install the General Ursicinus in his place? You were seen in the baths together as soon as you arrived. There are Horse Guards who saw you in the barracks and will testify that you offered Barbatio a ring as part of your plotting.'

Eusebius heaved with the excitement of revealing the breadth of his spy network.

'This was no conspiracy.' I turned to face Gallus and continued, 'Barbatio and I discussed the welfare of a boy I brought with me here to Antiochia, whose safety I still seek. I believe the boy is in the custody of the Lord Chamberlain's staff right now, hidden somewhere in this vast building. The boy is a citizen of Roma whose welfare I hold dearest to my honor. He is in grievous danger of bodily harm of the most atrocious, irreversible, and vicious variety any male can suffer.'

Gallus blinked and leaned forward in his chair with curiosity.

'We are confused. This is a completely different story from your tale, Lord Chamberlain.'

Eusebius stepped up to the *cathedra* and leaned close to the Caesar's ear, but I could still make out his words: 'I possess copies of treasonous messages between this Barbatio and General Ursicinus.'

I shouted across the polished floor, 'That's nothing more than proof, Caesar, that your Lord Chamberlain tampers and adulterates the imperial mail services, an offense that carries a heavy fine. I'll bet he reads and corrupts your most private communications.'

It was a safe gamble to take. By now I suspected none other than Eusebius of intercepting the messages from Thalassius' third witness to the West, but I didn't dare mention that now.

Eusebius spat out his fury. 'You're a fine one to accuse others of tampering with imperial records and communications. You've removed official reports from the case histories in the Palace archives. There are pages numbered in the index which have gone missing.'

I watched Eusebius' bulging eyes. I had hit a nerve with my accusation that he read Gallus' mail. I gambled that the insecure Gallus couldn't leave his audience with the impression that all the power lay in the grand eunuch's hands down to the last written memo.

Eusebius was risking a lot now to regain the upper hand. No doubt he'd long suspected the Prefect of the Palace of sabotaging his fortune-building and he'd checked the files on his arrival in Antiochia, just as I had. He knew pages were missing, but he lacked the password 'trinity.' That blinking mole of a shuffling archivist had flummoxed even the Lord Chamberlain's supremacy. Now Eusebius feared that even poisoning Thalassius hadn't stopped up the leaks.

Gallus looked from his secretaries and counselors to his guards and slaves. 'Missing papers? Robbing the archives? The record of our glorious reign must not be adulterated. This is a serious charge.'

'Then *he* must be stopped,' smiled Eusebius.

'Search him for official papers,' Gallus commanded. 'If he's a thief, he'll be condemned.'

I wondered if they would search my weapons as thoroughly as they stripped me of my garments. Within a minute, I was standing nearly naked before the entire court's scrutiny. There was a moment's confusion when the *domestici* found hidden in the high cuff of my boot a small multi-purpose knife on which razor-sharp blades, spoon, paper cutter and tiny pick were concealed. It was a clever, versatile weapon issued so far only to trusted *agentes*.

'Search his scabbard,' Eusebius said with an authority that told me someone in the kitchen had seen me the night before roll up the precious report and wrap it around the long blade of my sword. More proof, if his sudden appearance to save Clodius wasn't already enough, that I had never been as safe in the kitchens as I'd hoped.

My sword was pulled from its scabbard. Probing fingers and instruments were scraped around inside.

'Nothing, Lord Chamberlain.'

Eusebius rushed over with impatience. 'Give it to me.'

One of the *domestici* handed my sword belt to Eusebius' outstretched hand.

The Lord Chamberlain pushed his pudgy white fingers as deep into the recesses of both the scabbard and *pugio* sheath as he could. His flabby arms joggled as he poked and snorted. He found nothing inside. Only I knew where Thalassius' files were secreted away now. It was not a place that Eusebius was likely to frequent.

Gallus glanced self-consciously at the municipal officers standing to the side and waiting to resume reparation plans.

'We've always taken your advice on such matters before, Lord Chamberlain. Listening to good counsel has kept us on the throne so far. But we like this African. He is the first man we've ever met from Numidia Militaris. He strikes us as a robust and virile example of provincial Roman manhood, which is more than we can say for most of the people we've met since we took up the diadem here. You were not with us at the time, Lord Eusebius, but out on the streets of Antiochia, this man saved the life of a Constantine.'

It was perhaps my last scrap of luck and I seized it now.

'For that, Caesar, you promised me one favor, whatever I should ask.'

Gallus looked relieved. 'Why that's right! Eusebius, we are still in this man's debt and we can't see how a man who fought off a gang of ruthless thugs could have been planning our destruction at the same time. Why, all he had to do that night was to let them cut us down and send a letter to General Ursicinus the next morning that this golden throne was his.'

He smiled at the gathering around his feet and got a nervous titter of laughter for his clever deduction.

'I assure you he is planning your downfall,' Eusebius said, looking straight into my eyes. 'Yes, he reports to his *schola*, to a *magister* who has no ambition but to see your cousin return to the East so that he can install his own puppet as co-ruler in the West. There is a growing sympathy, or shall we say, pathetic weakness in the West for promoting rough and unlettered barbarians into positions of power. Has the House of Constantine not learned its lesson already from the crippling losses at Mursa under the audacious assault of that tyrant Magnentius? Even now, haven't they left the defense of the northern Rhenus to a Frank, the ambitious General Silvanus, who fought under Magnentius until the last second of the last hour?'

Gallus hesitated. Finally he said, 'The court must know that our word is our word. You have one favor of us, *Agens*, and even should you demand your release from these capital charges, we would be forced to grant it. Give the man back his weapons and clothes.'

Slowly I redressed and armed myself, playing for time while I considered my desperate position. I could see Eusebius' troubled scowl as he weighed the danger of seeing me freed to dig deeper into his avaricious schemes. I also saw the set expression on the young Caesar, for once determined to dominate the Lord Chamberlain by making good on his promise to grant any single request I made.

It was late. The impatient courtiers waited for me to stay my torture and execution by articulating my 'favor.' Suddenly I felt myself back in the old Senator's library, a child on that special low reading bench he'd built for me, my knobby knees supporting his heavy book of myths.

I remembered reading the story of Zeus' fatal promise to grant his earthly lover Semele one and only one wish. Her desire was to see her lover by daylight in his true form. Sadly, Zeus had to grant her wish, though he knew the divine brightness of his godly form would incinerate his mortal beloved.

Semele got her wish—but burned to death.

Now I had one last wish, only one favor of the man who played at life and death as if he too were a god. It was my only chance.

'Then this is the favor I ask, to be granted in full and for good, in exchange for the honor of saving your life, Caesar.'

'Yes, yes, you're free to go and these charges will not be revived,' Gallus said, brushing his jeweled fingers through his thick curls with brio. He had shown the court that no ruler could better anticipate a subject's desire faster then he.

'Caesar, with respect, that is *not* the favor I ask of you and I accept that with this request, I have no choice but to die under torture answering the unjust charge of treason.'

CHAPTER 18, THE FINAL INVITATION

—THE PALACE COUNCIL HALL—

A murmur swept the court.

'I don't understand, *Agens*. Don't you want to live?'

Gallus grabbed the wide arms of his *cathedra* and leaned down toward me in disbelief. 'Do you have any idea of what they do to rebels and troublemakers down there in the dark? Do you know how hard the *silentiarii* work to muffle their shrieks? We can't bear it, but the *Basilissa* tells us of such horrors that we beg her to stop.'

I approached the foot of his dais. 'Caesar, my request is that the Lord Chamberlain present the boy Leontus Manlius Gregorius to this audience, immediately and unharmed, and that he make no further attempt on this child's welfare or property.'

Gallus put his hand to his forehead. 'This child? The *agens* is back on that child again, Eusebius. What are we talking about?'

'I haven't the slightest idea. I'm hardly in a position to be a family man.'

His joke drew loud and cynical guffaws from the court. Eusebius' bulging spider eyes were shining now as he bluffed his sovereign. No doubt he rejoiced that in trying to save Leo, I had just condemned myself. His secrets were safe. I was already trapped and spinning in his silky threads of greed, soon to be swinging half dead in his sticky web.

Gallus scanned his court. 'Does anyone know what this *agens* is talking about? What child? Someone go to the nursery and fetch us any child named Leontus.'

A quartet of eunuchs hurried off for the residential wing. Watching them go, Eusebius smiled with a terrifying confidence. He smoothed the colorless wisps he called hair flat down on his scalp. I was sure that Roxana had been right when she warned me away from the nursery door. Leo had never returned to the Gorgon's supervision after the earthquake.

Gallus waited with fingers tapping on the gilt arm of his chair but the Lord Chamberlain relaxed and murmured to an assistant as if bored watching a wrestling bout from the imperial Circus bleachers across the street.

After ten minutes' excruciating wait, the eunuchs returned empty handed. 'There's no one named Leontus there, Caesar,' said one.

Eusebius sighed. 'This glorified messenger boy, a lowly freedman, is wasting the Caesar's valuable time while Antiochia starves.'

'You're right, Lord Chamberlain. We have more important business. You have one last chance to propose a different favor, *curiosus*,' Gallus said, deepening my despair with that off-kilter sympathy he had worn in the theater slums of his midnight city.

'I will not change my request.'

'Don't you see?' Eusebius slapped his white palm on the marble pillar next to him. 'By making an impossible demand, this rebel is stalling for time! This child will never be found because he doesn't exist! He has fooled you, Caesar, and for that alone, he must be punished.'

'Yes, we see,' Gallus answered with little enthusiasm. 'But we still owe him the one favor. You must ask another, *Agens*.'

'I ask no other.'

'But the child can't be found.'

'That is my favor. The honor of the House of Constantine stands or falls on it.'

Another horrified murmur swept the hall. To question Gallus' imperial credibility was to aim for his Achilles Heel. Mayor Luscus had been dragged by horses to his death for less. I'd had the last throw of my dice and they'd landed right at Gallus' spotless red satin slippers.

I'd gone too far.

'The Lord Chamberlain is right,' Gallus said, giving Eusebius his hard-won victory. 'This child Leontus Manlius Gregorius does not exist.'

'Oh, but he does exist, Caesar. Here he is,' a woman called out in a firm, brave voice. 'He was hidden away, a prisoner in the Lord Chamberlain's private suite.'

And there between two pillars leading away into one of the endless shadowy corridors, stood a veiled woman in a familiar blue dress with red trim. She led Leo by the hand past the councilors and sentries to the foot of Gallus' dais. My boy cried out with happiness when he spotted me. He tried to break free from Roxana's grip to run into my arms. She smiled at me through her thin veil, but it was the smile of sad resignation.

From her sanctuary with the poor Anastasia, she must have witnessed or overheard the eunuchs entering the nursery in their search for Leo. And she had gambled that the coast was clear to satisfy the last chance of rescue. She'd risked her life to search for Leo in the Lord Chamberlain's most private quarters. With her success, Roxana stood exposed to Eusebius' waiting vengeance for all her betrayals.

Once his counterspy, she now revealed herself before the whole court to be his enemy. I watched her with fresh eyes, since her daring confirmed my belief that only *she* had the courage to be my third witness. Hers were the honest eyes whose reports to the West had been thwarted by the wily eunuch. Her independent spirit was the reason he had kept her under his surveillance all the way to her little shack.

Roxana longed to come home to the West. The only possible way she could rehabilitate herself was to file reliable warnings about Gallus' disastrous reign and hope to be believed.

But as the months went by, Apodemius had never responded. She had kept silent about her growing fears. She must have realized sooner or later that her reports had fallen into the wrong hands. Her attempt at restoration in the eyes of her old sponsor back in Roma had failed.

So today Leo was saved. But the only two people who could guarantee his continued security were utterly condemned.

Certainly Gallus realized it.

'So, here is the wretched child. Come closer, boy. Don't be afraid. Well, he appears to be in one piece. We hope that satisfies your expectation of our imperial word and certainly Eusebius will foreswear any further meddling in his affairs. Although we don't see how we can return him to you for more than a brief farewell, because we cannot help you now, *Agens*. You stand charged with rebellion and will be subjected to interrogation in the dungeons below.'

'Give me a proper trial where I can clear myself of any crime,' I insisted. 'All *agentes* are protected against prosecution under the laws of the Empire.'

'Oh, I know the rules, but rules . . . rules.' Gallus shook his head as if law books were of no more of use to the Eastern Empire these days than sheep entrails and Vestal Virgins.

'We used to have trials, but they seemed such a waste of our time, since they always ended with a guilty verdict,' he shrugged. 'This city is in a state of emergency. We have no time for political theater when the entire city cries out for our attention. Why, on the advice of the Lord Chamberlain, we've even turned down an invitation from the Senate in Constantinopolis so we can attend to the emergencies here. We're sorry for you, *Agens*, but glad to see this matter of the child resolved.'

Gallus had lost interest. He scanned the cowed faces around him, soliciting a bid to end the audience. 'Read out the charges against this man, quickly, quickly.'

And at the Lord Chamberlain's signal, one of his eunuch scribes took out his writing tools and began to scribble as Eusebius dictated an accusation that I fomented rebellion against the Caesar Flavius Claudius Constantius Gallus.

The scribe asked for the spelling of my name and rank. It seemed the only thing I was going to be allowed to say: '*Schola, Agentes in Rebus, biarchus* first class, freedman Marcus Gregorianus Numidianus.'

270

My hands and ankles were then shackled. Roxana, Leo, and the rank and file of the Antiochia court watched with varying degrees of compassion. Bewildered at everything that had happened to him, Leo started wailing with disappointment. Roxana's face turned paler than ever underneath her veil. She would be joining me soon, she knew.

'We will deal with the Master of the Guards tomorrow. Is all this tiresome business finished?' Gallus sighed.

I felt eunuch hands with long, thin fingers snap an iron collar around my neck and link it to a chain. I was yanked like a dog across the broad expanse of spotless mosaic toward a door I had never noticed. It led to a corridor I guessed enjoyed very little return traffic.

Behind me, I heard an attendant announce the next order of business and turned my head to say good-bye to Leo, but was slapped and yanked so hard I stumbled and fell down onto my knees.

I was struggling back to my feet just as my fellow *agens* Probitus entered the reception hall and handed a message to one of the *domestici* for delivery to the Caesar. There was an exchange of sharp words as I saw Probitus do what any *agens* with an message of imperial importance is trained to do—insist on seeing it reach the hands of the ruler himself.

Gallus opened the letter as I watched.

'Why Eusebius!' he cried out. 'You've misled us yet again! This is a letter from our own dear cousin, the Emperor Constantius. We're not invited to a Senate hearing in Constantinopolis about the death of Prefect Domitianus. Constantinopolis is just a stopover. We are to continue on to Mediolanum where the Emperor proposes *elevating us*.'

The councilors burst into obedient applause. Gallus beamed at the assembly. 'Wait, wait, we are to travel under the protection of the tribune Scudilo of the *Scutarii, et cetera et cetera*, with the *Basilissa* and all our attendants. *To be elevated!* Oh, someone tell her immediately! It says... the Imperial Escort in charge of Route, Logistics, and Clearance of the *Cursus Publicus* is named as...' the Caesar read on and then looked up with a startled expression to stare at my collar and shackles, '*Agens* Marcus Gregorianus Numidianus.'

⚚⚚⚚

Probitus was halfway along the *Cursus Publicus* back to his *agentes* base in Tarsus before the court of Caesar Gallus had collected itself for the triumphant journey to Constantinopolis and parts west.

Roxana and Leo remained under the protective wing of the sharp-toothed Constantia. In saner times this would have seemed an appalling proposition, but as the imperial party prepared to travel, the fickle eye of the giddy Caesar made me nervous. The rest of the party—including Honoratus and the military protection seconded from the legions posted to the east—would have no time for a tiny boy.

To my great relief, the Lord Chamberlain was not invited by the Caesar to accompany our party. He suffered his exclusion by retreating to his rooms inside the depths of the Palace without protest or comment.

My job was almost overwhelming me already and even on the eve of departure, I was still mapping out logistics for food, stopovers, and possible dangers *en route* in time to discuss with the officer Scudilo arriving at the head of his cohort that evening.

Clodius had survived his accident. I visited him in the slaves' infirmary—little more than a row of pallets and lamps laid out near the laundry rooms—out of a sense of obligation to my former mistress, *Matrona* Laetitia. His aunt had loved him despite his sour character. And despite my bastard birth by her mending slave woman, Laetitia had always treated me with kindness.

For her sake, I now made sure Clodius was decently treated. I felt no further loyalty to a man who had destroyed so much. I'd spent my childhood being abused by him, but with that furious, jealous outburst of his, the unspoken truth had exploded between us like a *ballista*'s firebomb landing on a siege tower.

Clodius had suspected for some time that I was more Manlius than he—with or without adoption papers. Perhaps he had always eyed that crude *bulla*, the old Senator's sentimental gift to the slave boy, with distrust. More than once, in a childish wrestling bout, he'd tried to pull the cord with its clumsy amulet right off my neck out of jealousy.

But it wasn't just my hours spent reading to the blind Senator that curdled his spirit. And it couldn't be just the casual but tender way the Commander ruffled my hair and cuffed me around the ears when I carried the little dining tables to and from the *triclinium* when he hosted his military guests.

No, Clodius was simply fruit off a different vine and as any farmer will tell you, grafts don't always take. It seemed that every vestige of loyalty and honor that the Manlius men had tried to instill in their proposed heir Clodius had failed to take root.

Now he lay on a filthy, unsheltered mattress, the last male of *Matrona* Laetitia's venerable Roman line. On either side lay two Palace slaves injured in the quake. I could see his hair was only singed down to the scalp—he'd always been very careful with the cut and curl of his hair—but his face was horribly burned. Medical slaves still overwhelmed with quake victims had haphazardly bandaged his wounds. He dozed, groaning with pain every few minutes, through the stupor of the Greeks' powerful drugs.

'How long will it take him to heal?' I asked.

'The pain will subside, but the wounds will be terrible to bear,' said an old slave with a grave expression.

'Try to keep him out of pain,' I said.

'The lower half of his body suffered the worst.'

'Will he be able to have children?'

The medical slave shook his head, as if to say it was unlikely. 'Such injuries shouldn't happen to a good man.'

I held my tongue and acknowledged the man's professional bedside platitude with a polite nod. I gave him a gold *solidus* to cover Clodius' expenses.

Barbatio waited inside the Horse Guards' barracks to say good-bye to me with a sullen and proud expression. He was shifting horse tack alone with a distracted air. I wasn't fooled.

'You know you're lucky I silenced those treason allegations against you in time,' I said.

'Lucky? With you still holding a sword over my head, like that Greek bastard—?'

'Damocles. Call it the sword of justice, nothing more.'

'Well, at least you've used up your precious favor with the Caesar.'

'But I still have his ear and there are always the suspicions of Eusebius to feed.'

'You won't find me left alone here at Eusebius' mercy, that's for certain,' he said.

'Once you find the lady, your career and reputation will have nothing more to worry about from me, I promise.'

He started to protest, 'You have no idea how many people—'

'I have the child back and he needs his mother.'

'I have new orders of my own. I'm too busy to help you find her.'

'I don't care where you go. But wherever you are, you will keep looking until you find *Domina* Kahina.'

He started to bluster again but without warning, I laid the point of my *pugio* against his throat before he could drop the pair of saddlebags in his arms. I flicked a tiny bit of mole off his throat, and shook my head.

'Barbatio, why do you always look like you need a shave?'

⚔⚔⚔

'Why would our *Imperator* Constantius, divinely inspired though he is, hoist his cousin up even higher toward the heavens?' the *Comes* Honoratus asked me. 'What could possibly be next? Co-Emperor of the East?

'Gallus is already a danger to anyone within his reach of his whims,' I said.

274

'As an emperor, he'll be a monster,' the old man muttered.

We were riding through the vassal state of Cappadocia and were only a half-day's progress away from a night's stopover in Antoniana colonia Tyana. This was a city famous for its exceptionally long aqueduct and, more basically, for its sheer survival—it had been spared from vengeful destruction by the self-proclaimed 'master and god' Emperor Aurelian during his war with the Palmyrene rebel, the Queen Zenobia—spared at the request of the ghost of Apollonius, the philosopher of Tyana, who appeared to Aurelian in a dream.

Or so I was told by an auxiliary soldier from around these parts. He helped us negotiate replacements for some of the horses exhausted by our crossing through the passes of the Taurus Mountains.

As I gazed westward across the broad plains ahead, I looked forward to some fresh water and hot food. I also wished that the helpful ghost of Apollonius would appear to me in a dream. He might explain how all the efforts of so many good and sensible Romans to rein in the destructive vanities of the Caesar Gallus had failed.

The starving city of Antiochia sat four days' travel behind us to the southeast now while its ruler rode toward his 'elevation' to only the gods knew what. Wasn't the shattered city, still burying its dead and festering in its corruption, proof enough of Gallus' unsuitability for the ultimate honor? That's what I would have asked the ghost of Apollonius. Instead my dreams rang out with the screams of ghosts sinking into the muck of Mursa.

Honoratus and I rode together near the head of the procession, sandwiched between ranks of military horsemen provided by General Ursicinus.

Some thirty carriages bearing imperial logos carried the Constantines and their personal attendants a hundred feet behind us on the state road.

Leo and Roxana were hidden away in a carriage with other ladies of the *Augusta*'s court, trundling behind Constantia's enormous gilt and black enameled imperial vehicle. The grey-eyed Meroveus rode alongside them, straight-backed in his saddle and ever vigilant. I noticed him watching me whenever we gathered our company for a rest or change of horses.

Out of professional duty I should have tried to eavesdrop on the privileged conversations between the Caesar and his own courtiers, but I preferred the rigor and impartial discipline of the Roman army trotting on either side of my own horse.

It was a cool and clear morning. If the vehicles held up and the weather stayed fair, we'd make Ancyra in five more days, then Nicomedia and Constantinopolis in a little over another week.

It would be my first sight of the New Roma and my last chance to enjoy it before the new Caesar took charge. The idea that I was also going to witness its degradation under Gallus, even temporarily, sickened and frightened me.

'I wasn't posing a rhetorical question, Numidianus!'

Honoratus reclaimed my attention. Lost in my thoughts, I had let the *Comes'* explosion of bewilderment at Gallus' imminent promotion hang unanswered.

I smiled in apology to him but I had no explanation to offer.

For a man of his age, Honoratus displayed a 'good seat' in the saddle. Not for the first time, I surmised that his honorary title had come to him by way of military exploits rendered years ago under an eagle standard. His age, his bearing, and his pride all spoke of service to the great Constantine.

'As Co-Emperor he will be monstrous, I agree,' I replied. 'Have you realized, *Comes*, that Gallus' promotion is a step toward putting him in command of the fight against the Persians?'

Privately, I couldn't see believe it myself. Long ago, Gallus' beautiful young cousin Constans had battled well, then fallen into dissolution and brought shame on his command. Constantine II, the eldest son of the family patriarch, had died quickly in the battle with Constans over territory.

Only Constantius II had inherited the stuff of military conquerors. Pitting his blond play-caesar cousin, a boy of no education, no military training, and no life experience whatsoever, against the formidable Shapur II would be the stuff of Greek comedy—or tragedy.

It made no sense. I felt despair in the pit of my stomach that Apodemius had agreed to this farce.

I argued with myself, trying to be fair to my superior. And I debated with Honoratus as we covered mile after mile.

Did Constantius have any choice? The Persian enemy was ever-present. Shapur had pinned Constantius down here in the East for far too long. That had left a vacuum in the West where the barbarian usurper Magnentius romped to power on military disaffection.

Finally Constantius had reclaimed the mandate of his family name and subdued Magnentius, but the civil war left him with such a diminished fighting force, he couldn't push back the Alemanni descending from the Alps and at the same time manage a war in the East.

And there were rumbles that a fresh Persian assault was visible on the horizon.

The ninth King of the Sassanid Empire was now in his mid-forties—experienced, determined, and proud—and why not? Shapur II may have been the only king in history to be crowned before he was even born. The crown had been placed upon his mother's belly. He was certainly more confident about the support of his own deity than any Christian Roman, whether born to the purple or stealing it off another man's back.

The only reason Constantius enjoyed any breathing space now was that Shapur was busy repelling attacks from the northeast by Scythian Massagetae and other Central Asian tribes. A hasty truce was necessary with the Roman Empire and it was holding—for the moment.

The most able and persistent of Shapur's opponents along that border was Grumbates, ruler of a people called the 'Xions,' but no one knew where these ferocious nomads had come from. They weren't the old familiar foes of the Persians, the Hephthalites.

Not long ago, Apodemius had shrugged these Xions off as pests that wouldn't come to bother the Empire, but perhaps he was wrong. The Xions seemed to be something entirely new and nasty. They had short limbs and eyes recessed into flat faces under elongated, conical heads they molded in infancy with special wrappings while the skull was soft. No one knew the purpose of this hideous mutilation.

The most worrying rumor was that Shapur was negotiating through intermediaries to recruit these savage 'Xions' into his own ranks. Absorbing their hostility meant he might once again turn his face to the West and, stronger than ever, cast his tigerlike smile at the vulnerable Roman cities of Syria.

As Honoratus and I discussed Constantius' political considerations, I saw some confusion on the official's face, perhaps because I didn't share all these pieces of military intelligence. For now they were little more than the gossip of low-ranked *agentes* resting from their rides. But it was precisely such a banquet of tidbits that informed Apodemius' great map scattered with roving colored pins.

I didn't need Apodemius' hundreds of secret memos and debriefings to know that the Empire was not ready to fight another foreign war. We did not have an army fit to face the Persians. I knew because I had seen that army commit suicide in one day and leave over fifty thousand good men lying in the mud.

How could I now explain to an official of the East that the great Roman Army of the West, that legendary machine that made foreign hearts quake with fear, was on its last legs? Men like Honoratus trusted in its strength, its history, and its future. They thought there was always more time . . . time for Gallus to learn how to rule, time for wrongs to be righted, time for moderation and equivocation, and time for playing both sides of the fence.

'You lied to me, Honoratus,' I said to him suddenly as Tyana's walls and mile-long aqueduct hove into view.

His head shot up but his glance dodged mine.

'I almost believed your denials. But *somebody* wrote a report to Constantius that his cousin needed more time to mature. Somebody saw what was happening but that "somebody" blamed the wife for her corruption and avarice. He even tipped me off to a diamond necklace bribe because that somebody was still faithful to the memory of the old man. He couldn't bear to see the heirs of Constantine destroy themselves. Give them a chance, somebody thought, and things may come right in the end. And who's to say he was right or wrong?'

I reached over and patted Honoratus' sun-spotted hand gripping his reins. He looked over at me with sagging eyes full of appeal.

We rode on in silence until we had reached the gates of Tyana.

Suddenly Honoratus said, 'And even though many good men died while this somebody watched an insane child lose control of a whole city, who's to say the misguided old fool, too loyal to his late Commander Constantine, didn't mean well?'

Chapter 19, Constantia Rides Solo

—ANCYRA, GALATIA—

'When did his outbursts begin?'

'After we left Archelais,' Meroveus whispered to me after supper. It was not the first time he had confided to me that there was trouble brewing in the imperial cortège. Although at first I worried that Meroveus was passing information to me only to ingratiate himself, I now took his warnings at face value.

Back at the Castra, Einku had taught me to judge a eunuch as I would any other man. I was discovering that Meroveus was a trustworthy and observant travelling companion. Roxana had been right to seek sanctuary from Eusebius in Constantia's suite under the discreet guard of the Frankish prisoner-of-war.

I had already noticed during our journey that the Caesar and his consort weren't at ease. Only a few hours before, the city of Ancyra had greeted Gallus' massive train of carriages and troops with impressive pomp and expense, including a procession of overdressed municipal elders and underdressed dancing girls. One would think that when surrounded by the deafening clamor Gallus would feel his power at last. But he seemed no happier in Ancyra than in any of the other towns on our route that had drenched him with honors and entertainments.

The two cousins didn't seem prepared to enjoy their sudden celebrity free of Eusebius' interference and the constant surveillance of his eunuch force. That should not have surprised me. They were a couple that had always preferred the protection of night to the exposure of day.

Once I caught sight of them squinting over the ranks of polished armor and ceremonially masked cavalry trotting past us to the blare of horns in the bright sun. They reminded me of two animals suddenly discovered under a rock and left blinking and immobilized by the blinding sun.

Surely this was the public adoration that Constantia had always dreamt of—the mass adulation she'd been denied for so long by her domineering brother! Yet she looked unsteady as her carriage crossed the river that parted Ancyra into two. She shrank back from the thousands of subjects lining the street to admire her.

'What are they shouting? I cannot understand them, Numidianus,' she complained through her window as I rode alongside her black and gold carriage.

'The Ancyrans are Celts, *Augusta*. They are speaking Galatian.' And indeed, it sounded to my ears similar to the tribal dialect I'd heard three years before in the imperial capital up on the northeastern Rhenus, Treverorum.

Constantia emerged to general cheers, but she looked more than uncomfortable, almost unwell, as she graced the city at her feet with that eerie smile of pointed pearls. Her Caesar looked even paler than the *Augusta* in the bright daylight. He could not produce more than a frozen grimace.

The imperial party rested overnight in a suburban estate lent by a local grandee while our cavalry escort camped beyond the town walls, as usual. At dusk that night, Meroveus found me eating with some of the soldiers and listening to their gossip. It didn't hurt for an *agens* to pick up the soldiers' idle chitchat about a rising commander like the General Ursicinus. I also wanted to show Leo what a camp layout looked like. Whenever he got the chance now, the boy chose to ride at my back, clinging to my sword belt, feeling the open breeze on his face. I said a prayer of deep thanks to the gods every time those tiny arms wrapped themselves tight around my waist.

It was odd now to look up from my meal to discover the wary Meroveus hovering around the army campfire for a private word with me about rows between Gallus and Constantia.

'What are you doing here? Why tell me about outbursts? They're none of my concern,' I told the Toxandrian.

'I need help and I don't trust those other courtiers.'

'All right, all right, what's so troubling?'

'Things are more than troubling. The *Augusta* is *terrified*. She asks that I sleep at the door of their chamber each night.'

'How violent are these outbursts?'

'Unpredictable and more dangerous with every night. The Caesar goes to sleep as normal and sometimes he even takes a sleeping potion. For a while, all is quiet. Then in the middle of the night, he wakes up screaming and battling with phantoms of his imagination. Without really seeing, his eyes are open. He takes his wife by the throat so hard I have to pull him off her, finger by finger.'

'What is he screaming?'

'Names, only names.'

'Whose names?'

'I don't know most of them, but once I made out the name of Montius the *quaestor*.'

'They slept in separate quarters in Antiochia. Can't she find a different sleeping chamber?'

'She worries about his safety in these unfamiliar towns. She orders us all to keep close guard around the clock.'

'Does Gallus wish the *Augusta* harm?'

'No, not at all. During the day, he is horrified to hear what he has done while asleep. A few nights ago, he nearly pulled out half her hair before we finally brought him to his senses. He said he was trying to "kill the snakes" and "stop the bleeding." He kept jabbing with his other hand at her eyes. He might have blinded her.'

'Eat something, Meroveus.'

'No, thank you. I must get back before they miss me. What do you think? Is someone poisoning the Caesar's mind?'

'Something else comes to my mind. Did you have The Furies up there in Gallia Belgica?'

'No, *Agens*.'

'Lucky you. You see, Gallus dreams that Constantia is one of the Furies, the three Goddesses of Vengeance, also known as the Daughters of the Night. They have snakes for hair and blood dripping from their eyes. It's their job to punish all crimes against society when the law or the state fails to intervene. They punish the criminal who has escaped human justice by driving him mad.'

Until now Meroveus had shown me suitable respect, but his skeptical reaction told me he was not a religious man.

'Do *you* believe in these Furies, *Agens*?'

'I didn't until now.'

I'd lost my appetite and pushed the bowl of unfinished lamb hash away with disgust. 'What do you want of me, Meroveus?'

'I can't guarantee the *Augusta*'s safety on my own. You have to talk to Scudilo. He must station his soldiers closer.'

'I'll speak to the tribune, but it's not appropriate they serve as praetorians. We're only an escort, not an imperial staff.'

'I'm loyal to my duties, despite everything. But I can't go another full night without sleep and guarantee her safety.'

'I'll join your guard tonight. Thank you, Meroveus.'

I didn't say anything more to the slave. It was not his business to know that I too woke up during the night in a cold and terrified panic at the horrors that visited me without warning. I fled from one ghostly blade only to encounter another and another, all of them poised to draw out my entrails.

Would I never, never escape Mursa?

⚸⚸⚸

It was the Caesar himself who summoned me at nightfall by way of his Ancyran host's favorite slave. Gaining entry to the borrowed villa with a show of my papers and insignia, I found Gallus surrounded by elaborate roasts, stews, and pickles that looked hardly touched—but no companions. He was nibbling at a small plate of fruit.

'I am startled to see you dining alone, *Domine*.'

'We sent them all away. We're tired of eating with strangers every night. Half the business they bring to our attention strikes us as some sort of sham. It feels more like they're cross-examining *us* to find out what our secret plans are. We have no secret plans.'

He threw a date pit across the room, 'We have no plans *at all!*'

'Surely the *Augusta* is excellent company on the road.'

There was a long pause between us as he spat out seeds. I glanced around the room, curious to see if anyone was listening, or lying in wait, or lurking somewhere behind a screen or in an alcove. I circled the room, trusting my nose more than my eyes but detected no eavesdroppers.

Gallus was going mad, perhaps, but he wasn't blind.

'Stop that pacing. Yes, we're alone. We don't like eating with a gaggle of castrated ninnies any more than we like eating with a bunch of small-town big shots. We spent time enough surrounded by eunuchs as a child.'

It was not for me to ask why I was standing in the center of the room watching him pick at his food so I waited until he remembered I was in the room.

'*Agens* Numidianus, we need to ask you a favor.'

'Certainly, Caesar. I will never forget the great favor you granted me.'

'Is it going against any specific orders from your *schola* if you speed ahead and escort the *Basilissa* to Mediolanum before the rest of our main party?'

'We could not make much better time than our current speed, Caesar. At this rate, our whole carriage train will reach Constantinopolis via Nicomedia in less than a week. Surely you wish to enter Nova Roma with your future Empress at your side?'

'No, we don't. We don't at all. In fact, we like Ancyra. We're going to rest here for a few days. But the *Basilissa* should ride ahead and spend some private time with her brother, don't you think?'

He avoided my startled expression.

'Some who love the *Augusta* have worried that she is wearied by our travel. May I suggest she might also enjoy a rest in Ancyra?'

'No, you may not suggest anything, Numidianus. Your job is to escort and we want you to escort the *Basilissa* to Mediolanum.'

'Stop balking, Numidianus. It's my idea,' said a familiar voice from the doorway.

Constantia entered the *triclinium* and walked over to Gallus' couch. She was still garbed in a fortune of silk tunics, brocade robes, and jewels rattling their golden song around her wrists and ankles. She laid a perfect white hand on his shoulder. Her pungent perfume floated off a towering confection of black curls pinned down with jewels. There were black circles under her dark eyes to match.

She was dressed for the eyes of her public, more lacquered and stiff than ever. Yet we three were alone. I detected a nervous desperation shared between the two cousins.

'We think it best if I consult first with the *Imperator* on various matters of state. It's important we discuss the honors for the Caesar's promotion in advance.'

Was this Constantia's subtle means of escaping her husband's sleepwalking assaults? Or was there more political than personal fear behind those brilliant black eyes? Did I detect a canny suspicion of the brother-emperor, a more permanent distrust that had sunk its teeth into her mind the night he murdered her beloved Hannibalianus?

'Then we shall leave Ancyra in the morning, *Augusta*. Are we splitting the cavalry escort?'

She smiled. 'We leave the military protection for the Caesar. I don't wish to upset our hosts by taking away the military glory of his presence here. We leave two hours before dawn.'

꠹꠹꠹

So Leo, Roxana and I rode free of the Caesar's volatile scrutiny at last. We were now a tiny party of only three carriages and a few spare horses. We set off rumbling without any fanfare northwest along the *Cursus Publicus* before the sun's rays had even bounced off the gentle current of the Ancyra River.

It was as if I'd broken through the grip of a terrible nightmare peopled with nothing but beardless men with wide hips, elongated limbs, and lisping voices. The walls of Ancyra receded from view well before we stopped for breakfast at a rough state *mansio*. Roxana fetched wine and bread for the veiled imperial traveler who would not leave her carriage. The rest of us dined simply at a wooden table under an awning outdoors.

'The *Domina* should get some fresh air while she has the chance,' Meroveus joked. 'I hear that the smells of the great Constantinopolis match old Roma in the high heat of midday.'

'A capital city that's only twenty years old and smells as bad as Roma shows tremendous potential,' Roxana winked.

'Her breath smells bad, too,' Leo chirped.

We adults stared down at the child nestled on the bench between Roxana and a hairdressing slave.

'Who do you mean, Leo?' Roxana prodded him.

'When she leans over to talk to me, she smells ugly.'

His innocence protected him from nothing worse than our inquiring glances.

Later, after she'd laid Leo to rest on the cushions in her carriage and went to fill a basin of water for the *Augusta*, Roxana took me aside.

'The child was telling the truth. Constantia is very unwell. Her breath is short, she's running a fever, and her tongue is coated with a foulness that all her brushing cannot cure.'

'I thought it was the press and roar of the crowds that made her unsteady.'

'I thought it was lack of sleep. But she is sick.'

'We should stop and get her a medical examination.'

'She refuses every kind of help, insisting that she has to reach Constantius in time.'

'In time for what?'

'In time to find out what this so-called "elevation" consists of.'

It was, in a way, my first glimmer of hope. My faith in Apodemius and all the systems put in place to check the insanity of Gallus' reign would be restored if there were an alternative to promotion for him in the works. Perhaps there was some parallel fate in store for Gallus that made out of our imperial tour a more purposeful charade.

'I wonder what she knows or expects.'

I didn't need to add the obvious to a trained *agens* like Roxana. If Caesar Gallus became Emperor of the East, Constantia might be Empress, but the Lord Chamberlain's power would be multiplied beyond any eunuch's wildest dreams. But Eusebius had been caught out back in Antiochia. He had discouraged Gallus from this imperial journey and, in a show of independence, Gallus had dropped Eusebius' name from the travelling convoy.

'Luckily for us, we're clear of that man's plots and poisons, at least for now,' Roxana whispered.

As usual, we set off again before dawn with the *Augusta* insisting on keeping up the 'express pace' of a trained military cohort hastening to the battlefield. This meant risking her carriage wheels on some parts of neglected state road and skipping *mansio* after *mansio* where we might have stopped for refreshment and a change of teams.

Finally I countermanded her imperial frenzy on the strength of my authority as the official *agens*-in-escort, for the sake of our depleted stomachs and frothing horses.

We had crossed the border from Galatia into Bithynia and were well on our way to Nicomedia, when Meroveus signaled a sudden halt from his position next to the *Augusta*'s carriage.

'When's the next station?' he called to me from his saddle.

'My papers list a small stopover called Caeni Gallicani. Why?'

'Will they have any medical help? She's burning up and going delirious.'

'I doubt it. But we can hope. I'm officially responsible for her safe arrival in the West and if I can't even get her safely to Constantinopolis—'

'I wouldn't want to be in your boots, *Agens*.'

We now drove ourselves even harder, the carriages jouncing on the paving stones as we made for the next town. Caeni Gallicani was only a very minor station with limited horse stock, few rooms, and nothing in the way of amenities for a Constantine.

Constantia looked disheveled and wild-eyed as her ladies assisted her down the steep steps of her gilded vehicle. For a second, she clung for support to the gold eagle pommels to balance herself. Her maids took her arms and carried their burden into the only clean room available. They laid her down on a simple bare mattress next to a nightstand set with a rough pottery basin and two crudely finished goblets.

Already the stationmaster's wife was stammering with nerves at the sight of such an imperious party thundering into her yard. She hardly guessed the half of our situation. To announce our passenger was the *Augusta* herself would have only frightened the poor woman into paralysis. I needed her collected and competent if we were going to get Constantia through the night alive.

'All we can hope is that the fever breaks. Bring us as much cool water as you have, clean cloths, and weak wine. And if there is any medical person within reach, get him.'

Roxana and her ladies bustled to make Constantia more comfortable. They peeled off her heavy ceremonial robes now covered with dust and sweat, layer by layer, to change her into a light tunic of soft bleached wool. I sent the stationmaster's wife to fetch more water and pillows.

For the first time since that day Constantia received me while soaking in her luxurious bath, I saw her thin white arms denuded of the piles of bracelets and heavy metal cuffs she always wore. Her trendsetting coiffure had become hopelessly tangled, with strands of hair crusted against her temples by salty perspiration. Her mouth reeked of sickness. It seemed she could keep nothing down.

'Do you suspect poison?' I asked Roxana.

'She has a taster, that girl Melissa.'

I glanced over at the well in the courtyard, where the now-familiar silhouette of the hefty Melissa was cranking up a bucket of fresh water. If anything, she looked healthier than all of us put together.

Meroveus entertained Leo at a safe distance. We were all worried about contagion.

'If she's being poisoned, it isn't in her meals,' Roxana concluded. 'I'll check her cosmetics and hair ointments.'

I recalled Roxana's expertise back in training at the Castra when she had shown up the rest of us in Poisons Class with a deadly *fibula*. But I'd passed the same courses and knew my poisons. There were some that acted quickly—poisons for murdering a foe so fast he had no time to name you—or so slow he would never catch you at the act. And we all carried a deadly dose for when there was nothing left to an *agens* but torture or dishonor, as well as a small supply of rue, a famous all-purpose antidote.

Constantia's illness seemed both slow and inexorable, like an evil shade that had been settling on her for weeks. I recalled her too-bright eyes and frightened pallor at each demanding procession into city after city on our route—no matter what she ate or with whom she chatted.

I had taken her strange comportment as the symptoms of the sudden weight of power and acclaim poured on the heads of the imperial couple. But perhaps Constantia had been racing against an invisible timekeeper inside her twisted soul. Could it be that in this maelstrom of murder and violent accident, the most bloodthirsty of all the Constantines was in danger of a *natural* death?

'The *Augusta*'s asking for you,' a lady's maid said to me after we'd rested in Caeni Gallicani for half a day.

'Is she any better?'

'Her thoughts seem clearer.'

I heaved a sigh of relief. If the fever had subsided, she was out of danger and, as her senior escort, so was I.

'Numidianus, I haven't been well for some days.'

'Perhaps for weeks, *Domina*.'

'I always felt I could rely on you, from the day in Treverorum when I entrusted you with a letter to my brother.'

'Yes, I remember that day, *Augusta*.'

'And you did save poor Gallus from the scum in Antiochia that night.'

'It was my duty, of course.'

'Does anyone ever serve our family for any reason other than duty?' she asked, closing her eyes and fighting for a painful breath. 'Sometimes I think Roxana shows some heart in her, something beyond mere duty. She feels some pity for my Anastasia. I could never love the poor child, but Roxana treats her as if she is a . . . person.'

'Roxana is unique among women, *Augusta*. I have known her to be independent of mind from the very first day we met.'

'Then you two have that in common.'

'You protected Roxana from Eusebius. She will always repay your kindness.'

'Always?' Constantia gave a wry hollow chuckle. She started coughing and choking. A maid hurried into the room, lifted her up, and tried to get some sips of water into her mouth.

Constantia's fit died down and she shoved the poor girl aside. 'Over there, Numidianus, in that chest near the window, yes, open it.'

I unlatched the heavy clasp and raised the domed lid of her travelling case with its *Chi Rho* insignia embossed on its bronze bands and hinges.

'Inside that toilet box there, you'll find a green silk bag.'

I opened her carved toilet box. I could not see a silk bag in that jumble of stoppered vials, eyebrow tweezers, ear picks, combs, and tunic pins, many set in tortoiseshell or embossed with an ivory 'C.'

'Now, lift the tray on top and search until you find the green bag.'

Her box had a false bottom. I lifted the tray and pushed aside one drawstring bag after another, until I found a green silk sack.

'Give that to Roxana . . . when this is over,' Constantia panted. I could hardly hear her faint words.

I tucked the heavy bag safe into my tunic under my sword belt and told her, 'You must rest now—for all our sakes. If you were to slip away, the Caesar would be cruel in his grief and vengeance. So now that the fever is down, please try to rest.'

Her colorless lips, parched and flaky, formed words that failed to come. Her maid put a sponge soaked in clean water to her mouth.

'No, no, give me my medicine,' Constantia got out with effort. A second maid standing at the foot of her bed hurried to mix some syrup with wine into a cup.

'How long have you been taking this medicine, *Augusta*?' I asked.

'For some weeks now, after the breathing problems started. It helps the fever go down a little.'

That simple statement triggered more coughing, thick and hard. My alarm resurged twofold. Quickly, the maid darted for the basin already stained with dried bits of blood as the *Augusta* brought up a gagging flow. A torrent of bile-colored mucous clots dotted with blood erupted from her mouth, spraying the bowl, the maid, and myself.

'She's been like this for about a hour or so,' the girl murmured as she left the room to rinse out the basin.

I took the vial of medicine in my hand and turned it over and over, and wondered to myself.

'The blood of the Constantines draining away,' Constantia sighed. Her head dropped back on the coarse hemp pillow.

'Who has been treating you for this dreadful condition?'

'I had a doctor in Antiochia,' she whispered, 'but he didn't want to leave his other patients.'

'A Greek, of course.'

'No, not Greek. He was . . . Egyptian, I think.'

'An Egyptian? From Alexandria?'

'Yes, perhaps. It's not important.'

Constantia died as the sun was setting over the hills beyond the humble village. I left her to the care of her weeping ladies and went outside to the well and drew a fresh bucket of water. Pulling off my tunic, I washed myself from head to toe, scrubbing off the stench of vomit, blood, perfume, sweat, diarrhea, ambition, frustration, and corruption.

I handed the green silk sack to Roxana when I'd finished purging Constantia from my being. I had no appetite or thirst. I wanted to take a walk into the rolling hills through a herd of goats grazing beyond to rid myself of this clinging confusion and disgust.

We would have to wait now for the imperial party to catch up with us. I would have to confirm to the Caesar Gallus that his wife had died on my watch. I gathered my thoughts and, as I briefed the rider who would carry the bad news back to the main imperial convoy, I decided to cherish these few days of peace in Caeni Gallicani—for I was sure they wouldn't last.

I finally returned from my walk in the hills to find the others had finished their evening meal in silence. Leo was once again asleep and safe.

'Are you sure that green sack was meant for me?' Roxana asked me when the others had retired for the night.

'Yes, why? What bauble did that creature favor you with?'

There was no longer any reason to hide my contempt for the imperial family.

Solemnly, Roxana took my arm and led me fifty feet beyond the fence bordering the relay station.

'Look, Marcus, and tell me what I should do.'

She reached into the sack and pulled out a necklace of stones set in a triangular bib shape that would cover a woman's entire upper chest. Dozens of diamonds with a slight sheen of rose glittered in a setting of finely worked gold wire. There it was, the blood price for the death of an innocent young Egyptian from Alexandria. Its market value was more than Roxana could have earned in decades—even at top rank if she'd stayed with the *agentes in rebus*—but as a mere nursery maid? Not even in a lifetime.

'They look flawless, but I never saw her wear them. I wonder why?' Roxana said.

293

'You *will* wear them, and beautifully,' I said, kissing her cheek, 'but only after we have had the initial "C" engraved on the clasp.'

'In memory of Constantia?'

'No, in memory of a noble man named Clematius.'

Chapter 20, A Day at the Races

—CONSTANTINOPOLIS—

Four days later, our apprehensive advance party saw the line of the imperial cortège stretched across the eastern horizon. Shortly afterwards, it reached our rendezvous point at Constantine's abandoned palace in Nicomedia and our somber convoy set off, reunited again, for the New Roma.

The *Augusta* Constantia's cleansed, perfumed, and swaddled corpse travelled in the rearmost wagon while her bereaved husband rode at the head of the train. As before, Honoratus and I rode with some of the *scutarii* some hundreds of feet ahead of the convoy to secure the road. I still trembled in my saddle from the ordeal of informing the Caesar the details of her death, but to my surprise and relief, he had not arrested me for dereliction of duty. He said he blamed himself for letting her travel without him.

I wondered what Eusebius' reaction at the news would be when it reached him in Antiochia. Constantia had been a poisonous thorn that resisted his control and surveillance over the family dynasty. Yet Constantia had cautioned and counseled the young Caesar in ways Eusebius no doubt found opportune.

The ruler of the East was now beyond anyone's calming influence.

Over our clopping hooves and rumbling wheels, we all heard Gallus wailing for hours on end in the isolation of his fine-wrought gilded carriage. Constantia may have been the spouse of a normal man's nightmares, but she was the only trustworthy friend Gallus had ever known—always greater in ambition, cruelty, and bitter experience than he and yet always protective, prudent, and half-resigned to their impotence.

Whatever else they had in common, they had both lost their families to the cold-eyed ambition of Constantius II. Now Gallus travelled westward to place his life in that very killer's hands.

I made sure Leo stayed with Roxana and the mourning maids far to the rear where the boy was well out of earshot of the Caesar's hysteria.

For my part, it was paramount I stay as close to Gallus as possible for the sake of security. But I didn't get more than a few glimpses of him until we reached the shore of the elongated bay facing Constantinopolis to the west.

We halted in a district the Constantinopolis residents called the Peran en Sykais—the 'Fig Field on the Other Side.' The days of fig orchards were long gone. Despite the richness and length of our train, our arrival went unheralded as we passed through bustling suburbs and factories. Then we came upon a teeming open fish market flanked on all sides by warehouses and docks.

We halted along the eastern shoreline of the Vosporus.

From where I rode between the ranks of legionaries, I stretched over my saddle and shielded my eyes against the brilliant sky and the water's reflection to get a better view. Here was the old Constantine's wealthy new city, fattened on Egyptian grain diverted from Roma, greased by East-West trade, and adorned with statues and mosaics stolen from Roma and her ancient little sisters strung across the Empire.

A couple of hundred yards away from where our horses rested, dozens of ferries and barges crisscrossed the gleaming water that separated these suburbs and their mindless throng of businessmen, sailors, and dock managers from the self-important new imperial jewel.

The Great Palace also waited for us across the water, sitting on a slope overlooking the high walls of a vast new hippodrome and the Baths of Zeuxippus, already famous. But to a child of Roma—even this transplanted Numidian slave boy— Constantinopolis seemed as two-dimensional as a stage set. I could even make out the scaffolding still buttressing Constantius' ongoing repairs to his father's so-called 'Magna Ecclesia,' a church of such Herculean scale and shoddy design that it had already collapsed on itself.

A gilded man hovered in the air above the Palace and an endless sea of roofs that stretched from the promontory poking into the sea on my left hand to the right. I knew there was a boulevard that led out from the city proper to Constantine's walls that cut north to south across the peninsula from the Vosporus down to the Sea of Marmara.

A flying man? As I shook my head in bewilderment at the dark figure silhouetted against the sky, a local guide explained. This was a statue of Constantine himself sculpted as Helios, the Sun God. The bright sunlight had obscured his marble pillar from my sight.

Under a halo of seven rays, this Emperor of Gold gazed eastward toward the enemy land of Persia. All that was missing from the sculpture was the chariot that the legendary Helios drove daily around the earth. I imagined that any such chariot would have hardly resembled the battered vehicle from which Constantine's grieving nephew now staggered out.

Gallus surveyed his brash new capital across the water.

'Is there no one here to greet their future emperor?' he shrieked at a blue sky marred only here and there by the smoke of cooking fires and puffs of dust kicked up along the roads.

'We sent messages ahead,' I said, looking at Honoratus.

'I'm sure the proconsul will come, Caesar,' the *Comes* nodded.

The truth was that I was certain of nothing. The city had only been consecrated seventeen years ago. I knew from the banter around the Castra back in Roma that this upstart town had only just risen on the back of Constantine's massive land handouts to favorites and aspiring householders.

As an imperial 'capital' to replace Roma, it seemed a joke to us. As yet it had no permanent *praetors*, tribunes, or *quaestors* to keep order. It had no experienced administrators to curb corruption in food distribution to its exploding population. It had no urban regulators to supervise its feverish public works programs. Sewers, aqueducts, statues, baths, villas, roads, and churches—they had sprouted up like mushrooms after a spring rain.

A capital city run entirely by construction bosses and antiques salesmen—that was the Constantinopolis now clamoring for our attention. More officials would no doubt come with time—Honoratus had set his sights on rising in Constantinopolis after a long career elsewhere—but who cared about a mere Caesar when you had to keep a building crew on deadline?

'We won't wander in like some barefoot priest on a pilgrimage to Jerusalem,' Gallus muttered. 'Go across the water and get someone,' he ordered a decurion dismounting from his horse.

'That would be my responsibility,' I interrupted, 'as your official *Cursus* escort.'

'No, you stay with us, Numidianus,' he said, switching to Latin. 'You saved our life once and you may have to do it again. Send a soldier.'

'Get who?' the decurion asked.

'Someone! Anyone! Give him some names, *Comes!*' Gallus screeched with a voice hoarse from weeping, 'or we'll tie you up in chains and toss you to the bottom of that bay.'

Honoratus scribbled out a few names of important officials.

A contingent of a dozen soldiers commandeered a small boat. After some twenty minutes, we made out their gleaming figures disembarking onto the opposite shore like specks of mica crossing the sand. They disappeared through gates in the walls.

Roxana found me among the waiting riders. As always, she led Leo by the hand. Even with Eusebius left behind in Antiochia, we rarely let the boy out of our sight. He was carrying a toy wagon she had constructed out of woven twigs and soft reeds twisted into wheels. I felt a wave of gratitude and trust, but even more respect when she spoke next. Her years wasted on babysitting had robbed her of none of her *agens* skills.

She pointed a finger with an innocent expression at the two slopes marking the central points of Constantinopolis, as if we were merely two gawking tourists. But she murmured under her breath, 'The soldiers garrisoned in the towns we passed as we followed in your trail were always in the middle of decamping.'

'Always?'

'I believe they are being repositioned on purpose.'

'Why?'

Two of Gallus' slaves strolled past us. We greeted them with an innocent nod. Roxana made sure they were well out of earshot before resuming:

'To prevent Gallus from strengthening his defenses by adding extra troops to our imperial train. I shared a drink with one of the centurions on the road. General Ursicinus had ordered this man's contingent to move south and assume command over Antiochia and parts east.'

'That's not so strange. Someone has to take charge there.'

'But as they passed us, these troops made *no salute* to Caesar Gallus. Even the most senior officers kept their eyes averted. They simply ignored our banners.'

I turned away from the bright city in the distance and stared down into Roxana's subtle brown eyes.

'They made no acknowledgement *whatsoever?*'

'Not one. Such disrespect could be no oversight, Marcus. And there's worse. One of the courtiers told me that when Gallus was halfway to Nicomedia, a Roman politician named Taurus— ever heard of him?—passed through the same station where they were refreshing the horses. He was on his way to his new post as *quaestor* in Armenia. He moved on after a full night's stay without presenting himself to Gallus or even sending a salutation.'

'An odd way to behave with his new supreme sovereign. Did Gallus notice these things?'

'If he did, he didn't admit it. He's so habituated to insults and obstructions from the Lord Chamberlain and those officials in Antiochia, perhaps he doesn't realize what ill omens these are for his "elevated" reign.'

'Did your centurion mention the whereabouts of General Ursicinus? Do you think he might be staging a rebellion?'

A legionary broke into our whispered speculations with a summons from the Caesar.

Roxana laid her hand on my arm. 'It's not over yet, Marcus. Be careful. If he's angry, he'll be looking for someone to blame for her death. Even in a good mood, he enjoys bloodletting. As his power increases, so will his cruelty.'

I found Gallus resting inside his lonely carriage. The interior of gold and silver brocade drapes and carved cedar wood stank of food, wine, and sweat-soaked grief. Unshaven and unwashed, he lounged on a bank of gaudy pillows. His slaves hung back from his carriage steps, waiting for the moment he would readmit them to his presence. I envied them their banishment and hoped a swift and abject apology would set me free from his dangerous company.

'I apologize again, Caesar, for this delay. Our forward message should have produced a reception party for you. I'm sure the city means no impertinence.'

He looked up at me through swollen eyes bloodshot from weeping.

'We suffer bad dreams, *Agens*. Night after night, we see horrible things.'

'Dreams are only phantoms to be swept aside with daylight.'

He grabbed my wrist and twisted it to hold my attention. It hurt but I wouldn't let him see me wince. It was the suffering in others that gave him pleasure.

'Listen! They return each night, dragging their entrails along the pavement outside the Palace back home, or holding their own dismembered arms between the ragged stumps of their shoulders, like Theophilus.'

'Memories of the riots in Antiochia will grow fainter. The earthquake shook all our nerves and now you've suffered an even greater shock.'

'In the dreams, some of them are hungry. When we try to listen to their problems, when we promise them grain, they aren't grateful at all. They try to eat *us* alive. We force ourself to wake up to count our fingers and toes in time.'

He tried a feeble smile as he released me and stretched his ten fingers in front of his bleeding eyes.

'The *quaestor* Montius, he—'

'These dreams will disappear in time, Caesar. Constantinopolis is a fresh start.'

'She visits us every night.' He looked up from his fingers and stared at me. 'You let her die, didn't you?'

'There was nothing one could do. The *Augusta* lies in her carriage, ready for burial. She will find peace in the New Roma.'

'We still need her . . . we fear her, *Agens*. Now she wants her death avenged.'

'These dreams will disappear.'

I was lying through my face to a haunted soul. I knew full well such dreams didn't fade.

It was an ironic blessing that our Caesar Gallus suffered from no education to speak of. The great Plutarch wrote that dreams, particularly immediately before the death of a man, are the most accurate and meaningful of all. Was Plutarch right? What meaning did my own ghouls hold out for me? Was my own death at hand?

'Perhaps once we're elevated, we'll sleep easier,' He rubbed his greasy face in his hands.

'And the pleasures of life will return,' I said out loud. I was only trying to reassure myself and I failed.

'We always enjoyed the Games and races. They made us forget the years locked up behind the walls of Marcellum,' he said, gazing at the city beckoning outside his carriage window.

'So you mentioned that night in Antiochia.'

I kept to myself his obvious delight in their gore and cruelty.

'Perhaps you would like to call your slaves to prepare you for your subjects?'

He nodded. I used the excuse to escape him while his slaves got to work on his febrile body.

Our soldiers returned at last with a senator of Constantinopolis, a mere *clarus* in rank but still a senator in name.

Gallus emerged from his carriage, clean-shaven and combed. He faced a quaking, decrepit man three sizes too small for his fabulous blue and gold robes.

'Where are the elders of this city? Tomorrow you will have cleared our route for a procession leading to the Great Palace. We expect the whole city turned out to hail our arrival. There will be chariot races to acclaim our accession to *imperator* at noon. How many will be there?'

The senator said nothing. He seemed dazed to find himself in front of a living Constantine. Gallus stepped forward and slapped him hard with a speed that startled all of us.

'We asked you, Cretin, how many people will we see lining the boulevard?'

'Some eighty th—th—thousand will cheer you, Caesar,' the old man said.

'Whip this man for failing to address us as *Imperator*!' Gallus ordered Meroveus. The Toxandrian stood in attendance, looming tall and somber-faced over the impromptu audience.

'But Caesar, such good news has not yet travelled so far,' the old senator protested. 'Are you already *Imperator Designatus*?'

'Flog him for the insult he pays us. Haven't we just told you, donkey turd, that we are Co-Emperor *now*?'

The old man suffered the further indignity of losing control of his bowels out of fear. Meroveus dragged the senator away by his collar. The Toxandrian glanced back at me. I returned his look with the slightest shake of my head. I knew without a word exchanged that Meroveus would make sure the old senator got safely home with his hide, if not his undergarments, intact.

We retired uncomfortably for the night in a camp well upwind of the fish district. Our imperial and military banners hung limp and dust-coated from the journey. Our carriages spread out toward the outskirts of the district as our bonfires were lit.

I sat up with some of the legionaries, tossing dice and learning some bawdy Greek songs and jokes. I didn't want to sleep. I was more fearful of my dreams than of the coming days of

Gallus' vicious whims. As the other men slipped away, I settled down outside the carriage where Roxana and Leo slept.

I realized now that Leo was all the home I had. Although the intensity of my fierce negotiations with Barbatio hadn't faded, the *idea* of Kahina had become more vivid than any memory of her face or voice. Perhaps I was letting her go. Finally I dozed off. The dead of Mursa were merciful for once and left me alone.

I felt someone poke me with something sharp. I reached for my *pugio* before I was fully awake.

'Are you the *Agens* Marcus Gregorianus Numidianus?' a woman whispered out of the shadows behind the carriage wheels. She was jabbing me with a crude fishing pole.

'Try the soldiers, woman, I'm too tired,' I muttered, then sat up, fully awake.

'Who knows my name?'

I lurched under the carriage in time to catch a handful of unbleached wool. I dragged the woman back toward the dying fire nearby. Grabbing her by the chin, I turned her features to the light. She was a Greek, but no common fishwife. Her face and hair were clean, her teeth good, and her eyes more amused than frightened.

'This is for you, Numidianus.'

She pressed a note into my palm. Then, still bent low, she scurried off into the shadows before I could ask her name.

I opened the note and saw only a nonsense message of jumbled letters and numbers. Only when my glance had hit the sketch of a small mouse at the bottom of the rough fish wrapping paper, did I decode its two words with a practiced eye.

'*Cavete aranearum.*'

Beware spiders.

⚜⚜⚜

It seemed incredible, but I knew better than to dismiss a warning like that. Apodemius had worked hard to build up a reliable chain of communications. He didn't waste it on idle speculations. I would be looking for the rotund shadow of the Lord Chamberlain or a sinuous trace of an imperial eunuch wherever I went today.

But his mystifying caution seemed irrelevant because, even if he had followed us this far, Eusebius had nowhere to hide.

A few hours later, the streets of Constantinopolis were dead empty as we rode in state, four horses abreast, between the colonnades lining the grand Mese Boulevard. We passed through the empty Forum Bovis and then the deserted Forum Tauri, and then under the great pillar supporting Helios Constantine still basking his face in the sun with stony indifference to his nephew's arrival.

We passed the silent Law Courts on a hill and then descended to start up an even higher slope leading to the Augustaeum Square. The shop fronts were closed and the traffic so desultory that a few boys played ball in a street that should have been filled with shoppers and hawkers.

Where was the populace of Constantinopolis? There were no cheering subjects lining the streets—not even eight or eighty, much less eighty thousand.

Gallus carried his helmet in the crook of his arm, letting his blond curls bounce in the breeze. He was trusting, as so often before, that his innocent good looks would beguile his subjects. But his handsome features turned threatening as he led us forward under the wavering shadow of our eagle standard and we crossed one empty junction after another.

I felt sure that blood would flow on this day. All I hoped was that it wasn't the blood of anyone I cared about and that it stayed on the sand of the hippodrome's field. As we trotted up the final paved slope, our backs erect and banners snapping, we heard a sudden cheer echoing from marble wall to wall above us on the summit.

Gallus smiled with relief and signaled with a limp hand for us to step up our pace.

So his people were waiting for their new emperor at the very center point of Eastern power. No doubt we would find them assembled around the Milion, the famous new monument from which all distances were measured across the entire Eastern Roman Empire. Every trainee *agens* knew this when he memorized the routes and station *mansiones* he might have to travel if assigned courier duty in the East.

But no, I was wrong.

The beautiful square, with its burgled statues, fresh mosaics, and gilded roofs stood as empty as the streets. On our left was the imposing entrance to Constantine's Palace fronted by a towering gate called the Chalke after its dazzling bronze roof and portals.

Directly ahead of us was the entrance to the *thermae* attached to the enormous residence. On our right stood the entrance to the new, elongated hippodrome.

But there wasn't even a stray cur in sight. Gallus turned and stared me at with a loathing that chilled my blood.

The cavalry officers lowered their gaze, fearful that the Caesar might take out his wrath on one of them. I could almost see Gallus' infuriated confusion distorted in the bronze sheen of the Chalke.

This catastrophic insult would be laid at my feet. Meroveus hung back with the ladies' carriages. At this moment I could have used his backup in any physical showdown. He might be a eunuch, but I detected a northern fighter in him still.

An officer wearing the insignia of a praetorian marched across the empty square from the direction of the hippodrome.

'Welcome, Flavius Claudius Constantius Gallus.' He gave the curtest of nods. 'The people of Constantinopolis invite you to take your place in the imperial box within. The Great Thorax is about to race for the Blues.'

'The Great Thorax?' Gallus sputtered. 'The Great *Thorax*?'

'Surely this is meant as an honor,' I murmured. 'It may need a little time to learn the sentiments of this great city, Caesar.'

We dismounted and walked through the arched tunnel of the hippodrome's imperial entrance, leaving the bulk of our mounted escort outside under the titular command of Honoratus. The *Comes* gave me no explanation for hanging back.

His enigmatic expression as he bid me farewell put me on my guard.

Gallus entered the imperial box, followed by myself, half a dozen of his personal retainers, and a gaggle of trembling pages that he'd dragged along from Antiochia.

With stern expressions and stiff backs, we flanked the Caesar on all sides. He settled down on the thick cushions of the imperial marble *cathedra* carved right into the stone box suspended over the finish line.

The crowd's chattering dropped off to a hush. Gallus was used to the half million ravaged peasants of Antiochia, feverish with thirst and hunger. Famine had not touched the privileged new elites of Constantinopolis. If Gallus allowed himself a small sneer as he surveyed their proud faces, they offered little adoration in return.

I thought the silence would never break until at last, some Greek in the upper bleachers shouted, 'Hail, *Imperator!*'

The cry was taken up, with almost criminal hesitation, from level to level. Finally, the many thousands rose to their feet and waved whatever they had to hand—fans, stoles, programs—but I heard a trace of mockery in their cheers.

Did Gallus detect it?

The acclaim subsided far too soon. Gallus knew it. Suddenly, from another part of the upper bleachers, another voice pierced the hum of the crowd as it settled, 'Hail, the Constantines!'

And then I felt a chill come over me. I *knew* that voice. I recognized it even as my thoughts drowned under a tumult of thousands of obedient Roman citizens echoing the call in waves of tempered enthusiasm. More than a few changed the words to, 'Hail, Constantius!'

I searched the crowd for a familiar face, but even the general location of that loyal heckler was impossible to pinpoint among all those thousands upon thousands.

We had only arrived in time for the final race of two dozen listed for that day. Some among the sporting crowd were already gathering up their pillows and cloaks to escape the inevitable crush at the exits. Perhaps they had lost all their money or were simply tired of seeing Thorax always win.

One fool of a vendor penetrated the imperial box to try to sell Gallus a fancy glass jug engraved with Thorax's brutish features.

With a casual authority to convey his impatient contempt, Gallus held the *mappa* aloft. The crowd quieted down a bit and the final betting closed.

Below us, the Blues' champion *essedarius*, the promised Thorax, thundered into view. The roar that erupted from the stadium hit the imperial box like a powerful gust off the Alps. Thorax was a muscle-bound *hordearius*, bulked up on barley and beans. He was the only driver not wearing a helmet and his shaved scalp glistened in the sun.

He positioned his team alongside the other competitors and wrapped the harness reins tight around his waist, slowly, so that the crowd had time to admire his bravado. This was an often-fatal Roman style of driving. The more cautious Greeks gripped the leather straps loosely in their hands in case of a crash.

A coterie of society ladies leaned down from their perches and tossed Thorax cries of adulation as he fixed his chariot into the starting position. He reined in his *quadriga* along a line of horse bucking behind the bars of their *carceres*. They waited for Gallus to drop the cloth and signal the spring-loaded gates to release the racers.

Gallus let the *mappa* flutter to his feet. The teams took off and thundered around the *spina*, the central barricade, for three full turns. I saw no reason to cheer Thorax or any of the other drivers as they jockeyed to the right and left, fighting always for the inner track, but never gaining a clear distance from the pack. The spectators shoved and keened for a better view once it was clear that the Blues and Greens had pulled ahead. Anyone who'd laid his week's earnings down on a surprise from the Reds or Whites was once again a poor man.

Gallus rose to leave. He had been insulted and now he was bored. There were only two more laps to go. Suddenly Thorax wrenched his team to the right and sent one of the Greens smashing into the *spina*. An outsized marble dolphin tottered from its stand along the upper edge and came crashing down on one of the Red chariots. The crowd screamed in horror as the Red driver fell on to the sand. A lagging White chariot stampeded right over the fallen man, turning his upper arm and torso to pulp before our eyes.

Gallus sank back into his chair and leaned forward. He was suddenly transfixed with pleasure. I saw the flush of excitement filling his pallid cheeks and a smile spreading across his perfect lips.

He was no longer bored.

'*Naufragia!*' he cried, using the Latin for shipwreck to share his glee with me in particular.

Gallus turned his hungry eyes back to the crash, eating up the sight of the poor driver's flailing agonies as the teams roared toward the far turning point, the *meta*. The Caesar was twenty-nine years old, but he looked like a child released from a tedious lesson in time to watch a fistfight outside his classroom. Yet the hungry smile he had bestowed on me was fed by demonic wiles, not childish whims.

His obvious lust for mutilation repelled me—and there was something more. I wished he hadn't singled me out for the rapacious smile beaming up on me. That grin shot a bolt of alarm right through me, the rush up my spine of someone about to go into battle.

More riders fell on the fourth turn at the far end. It seemed that Thorax had been dawdling for his own amusement at the end of a long and profitable day, only to close his accounts with a bang. The final turn brought a near fatal crash between his chariot and a Green pulling up alongside him with a leer from the rival that only drew a laugh from the champion.

Thorax drove his team flat against the side of the other man's lead horse and sent the rival chariot flipping into the path of the oncoming laggards.

Thorax crossed the finish line. His horses, frothing and shining with sweat, drew him up to the imperial box. Gallus reached for the laurel crown and descended to the rails. He laid it on the winner's slippery dome. Thorax lifted the wreath off his head and waved it in the air as he took a victory lap around the entire course to the admiration of his city.

Then Thorax tossed Gallus' laurel wreath onto the oozing mound of flesh that marked his first victim's resting place. Galloping away to the approval of the mob, the insolent champion disappeared through the riders' archway.

Gallus stood in shock, staring at the entrails in the sand below crowned with his own wreath. The crowd ignored their Caesar and milled out of their seats to collect their winnings or get their dinner.

'*Imperator*, we should go now.'

I nudged him as gently as I could.

'They should wait for us to leave first.'

'They're unaccustomed to having an emperor in their midst.'

'Then they will have to learn. And so will you, Numidianus.'

More than anything it was the tone of his voice that signaled danger closing in on me. I had dismissed the clue in his blazing eyes ten minutes before, but I'd already witnessed how he had vented his lethal temper on Thalassius, Honoratus, Domitianus and Montius. And now that voice told me that my turn had come.

'You accepted blame for this insulting reception. We're holding you to it,' he said, facing me with the venom of his soul coloring his eyes. 'We've kept you at our side because Eusebius warned us not to trust you. He predicted you would show your hand during this journey ... and now you have. You let our consort die in that miserable town. Her tormented soul begs us for satisfaction. Now you've made sure we were humiliated on our first visit to our new capital.'

'But they hailed you with all their hearts, *Imperator!*'

'They followed some idiot fool, some single voice who hadn't been bribed to keep silent,' he shouted in my face.

He leaned toward me to whisper, 'We decided your fate the morning we arrived to find no delegation here to greet us. You were in charge of escorting us here! You were sent ahead to lay the ground for a triumph! Instead they toss our imperial laurels on a corpse for the entire world to laugh at!'

'We could not have foreseen this—'

'You're trapped, *Agens*. We've told our troops to cut you down the minute we leave this stadium. Constantinopolis needs to be taught a lesson. Your *schola* needs to be taught a lesson. Your execution is our first imperial act in this city. What better place than the hippodrome square? By the time your masters hear you've died, it will be too late.'

He now moved in a rush to get out of the imperial box, pushing me ahead of him. I was surrounded by his vicious little pages, all of them producing *pugiones* from under their tunics and setting us running to keep up with the purple cloak of their sovereign leaving the hippodrome through the exclusive imperial passage. There were too many of his minions, testing my sides with their sharpened points, for me to use my sword. The tunnel was too narrow and dark for me to make my escape.

I braced myself to face the officer in charge of my assassination. I knew the troops would obey Gallus. After all, I had seen these soldiers hang back and let the Prefect Domitianus be dragged to his death from the back of a horse. Why would they hesitate at killing a lone *curiosus*?

Any second now we would emerge into the Augustaeum Square where Scudilo's cavalry waited to arrest me. We found the exit still jammed with spectators. Gallus slunk back into the shelter of the imperial exit, pressing himself against the curving stone arch like a fearful rat in a sewer.

'They mustn't see us crowded among them, like a common peanut seller,' he said.

He wanted to hold our party back until the Square was clear enough for the army to make their move. So I broke free and lurched forward into the sunlight, shoving the startled pages out of my way as I plunged into the anonymous crowd.

'Where are you going, *Agens*? Come back here! We command you!'

I lost them for a minute, as I plummeted forward, shoving my way through matrons, children, and gangs of squabbling

Blues and Greens fans, running on my toes in a swelter of punters to peer over their indifferent shoulders.

I pushed through the clusters of lingering gamblers. I forced families and lovers asunder to gain distance between stabbing pages and myself. I looked up over indifferent shoulders and searched for Gallus' troops standing positioned out of sight beyond the perimeter of the Square.

I had to avoid those soldiers. I prayed to the gods that if I saw a ghost from my past in the next few seconds, it wasn't an elusive specter of my overwrought imagination, but for once merely the face of someone who could save me. I had to find that heckler from the top of the stadium. He was my only hope.

I kept on dodging, diving, and scuttling. The crowds were thinning out dangerously. I looked up and beyond them I saw a familiar figure, but it turned out to be only that vacillating Honoratus lying in wait for me.

My panic deepened. Had the *Comes* stayed behind with the squadron only to supervise my death? He had authored letters of praise for Gallus—he'd as much admitted that to me on the journey. Did his loyalty to the Constantine dynasty run even deeper than that? Was he now covering his tracks by eliminating me?

However when I dared to emerge again from a cluster of departing spectators, Honoratus stood at the far end of the Square next to only one other companion, not a raft of military men.

The crowd took no notice of this stranger, but with a wave of relief, I did. Why should they notice the Roman master of disguise now striding toward me with a reassuring smile on his face?

Only by his boots did I recognize him.

He was dressed like any other gentleman of Constantinopolis in the colorful robes of Eastern fashion set off with slightly too much jewelry. A barber had dyed his white hair black and arranged it in wispy curls over his wrinkled forehead. Only those worn goatskin boots, protecting his gnarled, painful toes, remained unchanged.

I threw myself on the two old men with a cry, 'Honoratus, where is the legionary escort? They have orders from Gallus to kill me.'

'Dismissed and breaking camp as we speak. Their job is done. From this point on, we use only soldiers chosen by the Emperor himself.'

I turned to Apodemius.

'You got my report?'

'Yes, Numidianus. Very interesting reading indeed.'

'And that was *you* crying out in the crowd?'

Apodemius smiled, 'Playing for time to keep the Caesar safely in his seat. I hoped to make the crowd roar loud enough to drown out the march of his legionaries retreating from the Square.'

He preened a little for Honoratus. 'I've always had a soft spot for the theater. Did you like my Greek accent? I think I played my part rather well today.'

'Was it acting? The Caesar sleeps with a letter promising promotion next to his breast.'

Apodemius nodded and smiled, 'You've played your part well, too, Numidianus, but it's not safe to expect too much thespian talent from an *agens* of *biarchus* rank.'

'Wait,' I said, placing a hand on his age-spotted arm. Roxana is travelling with us. She has learned a hard lesson. She wants to come back to the *agentes*.'

'Roxana, my star recruit.' Apodemius twisted one of the braided tassels hanging off his belt. 'As I recall, she always learned her lessons better than any of the boys in your year. She was my failed experiment in exploiting feminine wiles, Honoratus. Of course, Eusebius would have spotted her. I should have known he would. That was my mistake.'

'Why Eusebius and not others?' Honoratus asked.

A thousand sports lovers milling around us were impatient to get home. They pushed us this way and that as we inched away from the Square, riding the tide of jabbering locals.

'Because Eusebius isn't susceptible to her sexual charms or blinded by the veil of womanly weakness that lowers the defenses of us healthy men.'

He glanced at me with indulgence and perhaps a tiny flicker of vanity in his own fading virility. 'She was a costly error,' he admitted, running his knotted fingers through hair shining with hair oil.

'Please, give her another chance, *Magister*. I found out too late that she was Thalassius' third witness.'

Honoratus was listening with relief and fascination to my disclosure.

'She took enormous risks in reporting to Roma, but how could you know that at the Castra? All her messages were intercepted by Eusebius.'

'Well, perhaps,' Apodemius said. 'The idea of turning her around again is an old man's challenge. I might not be able to resist it once this job is over. Tell her to see me back in Roma. Now, where is our over-excitable sovereign?'

Through the separating multitudes, we could dimly make out the frantic Caesar across the Square. He was still exhorting his darting pages to hunt me down.

Apodemius leaned on my shoulder for a moment to ease his knees. 'But you and I must hurry, Numidianus. Our charade is reaching its final act at last.

'Why did you warn me by note about Eusebius?'

'Because the Lord Chamberlain is tracking you, exactly as I hoped. But as with all chariot races, it's important that he not catch up with us too soon, not before we reach the climactic final turn in the game.'

Ahead of us we heard a panicked command, 'Bring us our troops!' turn into a heartfelt howl, '*Where did all the soldiers go?*'

Apodemius took a deep breath and withdrew a packet of imperial documents from his satchel.

'Have your weapons to hand, Numidianus. It's time to share Constantius' latest orders with his cousin.'

Chapter 21, A Home for Caesars

—ON THE ROAD TO POLA, ISTRIA—

Apodemius wanted time alone with Gallus before we quit the city at dusk. I was astonished at the old man's confidence in his authority over the maddened ruler. I certainly was in no position to convince the Constantine of anything.

Meanwhile, Roxana and I entrusted Leo to the affectionate care of a doting Meroveus. We two found a quiet corner nearby. It was no one's business where—least of all Apodemius'—and for two brief hours of friendship and affection we comforted ourselves in each other's arms. She wore Constantia's diamond necklace—and for a delightful half hour next to my eager body— absolutely nothing else. Around my own neck, there was only my cord with its tiny Manlius ring-key and the remaining ring of Marcellinus, that futile bribe promised to Barbatio.

Afterwards we re-dressed and downed an intimate supper together of *puls* and fruit salad in a tavern dining room downstairs from our rented room.

She looked as beautiful that last stolen evening in Constantinopolis as on that first and secretive night in Roma when I'd peeked at her naked body as she swam alone in the *agentes*' swimming pool. She was still lithe and fascinating, and still one step ahead of me and my clumsy loyalties.

But in the intervening years, the spitfire girl who set out to shame us fellow students for our slow wits and thick muscles had grown more gentle and wary in demeanor. Tonight she wore a shimmering rust silk robe and an orange *palla* that set off her gold hair trinkets and chestnut waves. She tucked Constantia's priceless diamond collar back in her purse and safely out of public view. We amused ourselves with gossip having nothing to do with Antiochia's woes, the Lord Chamberlain, Clodius, or the dreadful imperial husband and his late wife.

Escaping Antiochia had already lightened her heart. She was playful and flirtatious as she regaled me with stories of Leo's curious, mind. She loved the boy. I cherished her all the more for that. But I noticed that evening a certain tension in her gaiety. There was still something she wasn't telling me.

I thought I knew what it was.

'You wrote reports to the Emperor, reports that exposed the Caesar and his wife.'

Roxana said nothing. She didn't deny she was the third witness in the 'trinity.'

'Thalassius knew, didn't he?'

'Was he the one who betrayed me?' Her eyes flashed as bright as her hair ornaments. 'I never received an answer to my reports, not even a sign that they had been received or read.'

'Thalassius never betrayed you. But your letters were intercepted before they left the Palace.'

'Eusebius,' she sighed. 'No wonder he sent his eunuchs on my trail when I left the island. That's when he discovered my hideaway. He wanted to see if I met anyone in a conspiracy against Gallus.'

'How ironic that it was where you went to be alone. How frustrated he must have been, letting you run off on his long leash and finding nothing at the end of it but a one-room shack.'

Only as we hurried back to Constantinopolis's imposing palace where Apodemius was finishing his preparations for departure under the sullen, confused eyes of Gallus and his 'escorts,' did Roxana discuss Leo's future.

'I'll take him home to Roma and deliver him to this Verus he talks of nonstop. With a small boy, the trip may take almost a month. He's already worn down to nothing, but he's as safe with me on the main route as with anyone. I haven't forgotten my assassination and defense lessons at the Castra.'

'There is no one else, absolutely no one else you can trust him to, but Verus. Promise me you will not let go of that boy until Verus has locked him in the Senator's study with a good book on his knees. And make sure Verus repays you for any costs this doesn't cover.'

I placed most of the coins I had left into her soft palm.

'Yes, I understand. Not until I see him sitting on the little reading bench the Senator built for you. It was the one place in the house that truly belonged to you alone.'

She gave me an indulgent smile. I must have had bored her with my anecdotes of happier days in the Manlius study.

'Exactly. And then where will you wait for me?'

She looked away and watched Apodemius supervising fresh horses being harnessed up for her departure. Leo was already asleep in the imperial carriage Apodemius had set aside for Roxana's return to the old capital. In addition to that diamond treasure, her small purse hid the most powerful road permit any Roman citizen could carry on the *Cursus Publicus*—a *diploma* scribbled out by the *Magister Agentium* Apodemius himself.

'Roxana?'

She hadn't answered my question.

'Roxana! You're going to wait for me, aren't you?'

'No, Marcus.' She avoided my startled scrutiny.

'But Apodemius said he would debrief you in Roma. He promised to consider re-enlisting you in the service.'

'I've changed my mind.'

'If Apodemius agrees to take you back after all this, you can't refuse him now.'

'I've told Apodemius. He has already agreed. He understands my change of heart. You see, after delivering Leo in Roma to your majordomo Verus, I'm travelling on, to the northwest of Gallia.'

'*Gallia?*'

'To find Silvanus' garrison and see if he'll take me back.'

'General Silvanus? But he's married, Roxana. Surely you knew that.'

She wouldn't look me in the eyes.

'It's your new assignment, isn't it? Roxana, you can tell me.'

'No, it's not an assignment. It's a simple desire to see him again. Don't be angry.'

'I'm not angry. It's that I don't want to see you disappointed or hurt.'

'Marcus, did you think I would stay with you? You toss and turn in your sleep, obsessed and distracted. You're not married, but you are tied down—by the past.'

'I know. The men who died—'

'Have nothing to do with my feelings. You cry out her name in your sleep.'

She didn't say whose name. She didn't have to.

It was no use. I went to take a last look at my son and to lay at his side a toy sword I'd picked up from a stall on my walk back through the market with Roxana. I had also bought a gold belt buckle for Verus and a comb for Lavinia. The teeth were set into a pale green stone that the vendor said came along caravan routes from a country far beyond Persia.

I kissed the sleepy boy good-bye with a prayer that the gods would watch over them all until I returned to the Manlius house. As Roxana's carriage rumbled off, he was curled up in her arms.

⚔⚔⚔

'You'll want to wear these for warmth,' I told the Caesar as we prepared to resume our westward journey. It was now a few hours before midnight. I handed him clean underclothes, a warm tunic, and a pair of the simple riding trousers our western cavalry favored.

There were no imperial insignia.

'Give them to our slaves. They look after our clothes.'

'Your slaves aren't coming beyond this point. And you'll want to change out of those red shoes into these.' I added a pair of army boots to the pile.

'My slippers are fine,' he said. 'We'll ride in our carriage.'

'The carriages are gone. And the legionaries of the East are already on the way back to their garrisons.'

'On whose orders?'

'The Emperor Constantius. For your safety, we're finishing the trip incognito by horse relay,' I said.

I lied.

In fact, Constantius had authorized ten carriages maximum, but Apodemius didn't want to risk twenty more days in carriages when five or six days on horseback by fast relay was safer. Escorting a Caesar was a delicate task at the best of times. It was a dangerous one if the Caesar was a disgruntled Constantine, ready to balk at every turn.

Now that Constantia's devious wits were absent and Eusebius nowhere in sight, all we had left to fear was Gallus' unpredictable temper. He remained a dangerous figurehead with implicit power for any wily opportunist who could get at him. It was important to keep him from rallying any armed support along the journey.

'We act on the urgent invitation of your sovereign who seeks your help,' I said.

Gallus made no move to remove his embroidered tunics and brocade robes meant for ceremonial processions.

'We stopped trusting you, *Agens*, when we arrived here to that dismal reception. We would still see you dead. We believe nothing, absolutely nothing you tell us. Does Constantius really ask for our advice? On what matter, precisely?'

'I am too low in rank to know the details.'

'Why is there such urgency? Is there another letter for us? That old man told us nothing, but waved some imperial papers insisting we hurry on to some town called Petobio.'

'Then we must hasten to Petobio.'

'But why should our cousin write to that crippled old codger and not to us? Why don't we head straight to the court at Mediolanum? Why? Why?'

'New orders. That's all I know.'

'You're a liar.'

He rose from his sulky couch, took the trousers from my hands and threw them down on the tiles. 'And a spy and *a murderer.*'

I picked up the trousers and placed them on top of the boots.

'You killed our cousin Constans. Oh, you think we didn't know? We heard the truth about you from Eusebius. The *Basilissa* didn't believe it, but we do.'

He looked around the lavishly decorated chamber as if he had never seen it before. 'Where is Constantia? Send her to us now. We *command* her to come.'

'Her body lay in state too long. The climate here is dry but warm, even in winter. She had to be buried without further delay.'

He stared at me.

'You attended the rites yourself, Caesar.'

'Yes, of course.' Gallus looked out the window at the bright city roofs outside and dismissed me with a wave of his hand. Apodemius' guards took over. From that moment on, Gallus was never alone.

We rode out under a full moon, waving good-bye to a haggard and saddened Honoratus. We had an escort of only twelve men handpicked by Constantius to fetch his cousin.

'We want no one that Gallus knows or can bribe,' he had stipulated.

It seemed Apodemius had no intention of stopping until we reached the very end of the Empire itself. I could not have guessed the old man had such stamina in him, but with our westward relay race through Hadrianoupolis, Philippopolis and Naissus, he rode as well as a man half his age. Arthritis had crippled his joints but his seat on a horse was sure.

I knew he was famous for crisscrossing his network of hideouts in disguise faster than even his most experienced couriers. No one could explain how he did it. Now I got to see the *Magister Agentium* in action. Of course, for the most part we followed the *Cursus Publicus*, the most reliable paved network of roads in the Empire, always keeping the horses on the verge of soft ground to one side for the sake of their hooves.

But Apodemius wanted no one to know of our mission. He cut small detours around the comfortable *mansiones* meant for high officials riding across the Empire. He took side roads, even goat paths and canal tracks, without hesitation, and thus eliminated crucial hours from our journey.

Above all, no one must recognize Apodemius, our armed escort, or the Caesar *en route*. He stayed in full disguise as a travelling Greek for as long as we were in the East.

The army used flames at night to signal from garrison to garrison, across deserts, mountain ranges and river valleys. Apodemius had ingeniously adapted this trick for his secret purposes. He had devised his own network of signal lights, sent by the humblest of affectionate villagers and trusted minor town officials. By this he ensured there were always fresh horses and meals ready on our arrival.

For Apodemius, there was no gossip as he washed, no straddling a bench for a second cup of wine and no visiting a favorite girl in the alcove out back. For the rest of us, that also meant little sleep. We were back on the road within thirty minutes of stopping anywhere. We were beating the speed of even the fastest rider wearing the feather of 'urgency' in his cap by an hour or more at any of the official state stopovers.

As long as we were in the East, the Caesar's name might garner support from an unguarded quarter. Apodemius persuaded him that rough roads and the dangers of the West meant the kind of stately progression he had made through Syria was out of the question now. Gallus had no experience of the West whatsoever. If he had tried to muster support before it was too late, he might have made things difficult for us. Instead, he seemed foolishly hopeful that Constantius intended to save him.

We were on a forced dash aiming for a rendezvous at Petobio on the eastern border of Noricum province. Gallus may have been bewildered, but he was still proud enough to try to hide his confusion. We *agentes* and soldiers were trained up for it, but he had to be roped into his saddle in case he dozed off.

The petulant Caesar also refused to eat. Constantius' soldiers took to feeding him lentils on a spoon like an idiot child. For an instant or two, in the pleading and confusion in his dazed eyes, I recognized the resemblance between father and daughter. No one ever mentioned Anastasia. I suspected the child would disappear, utterly lost and unmourned in the annals of the Empire.

At last, even Apodemius needed to sleep. After sneaking the Caesar by a detour around the great city of Sirmium that marked the partition of the Eastern Empire from the West, we continued on for hours and hours but now it was dusk and even the old man seemed ready to stop.

I was too exhausted to pay any attention to a town in the distance that could well have been familiar. After all, for many years I'd ridden this route as a cadet rider. No doubt by morning the name would come back to me.

Apodemius sent two soldiers into the market before the sun disappeared to bargain for food. The rest of us took a humble cow track up to a hillock surrounded by vast fields that lay brown and untilled in the final slanting light. A river flowed past our stopping place and we refreshed ourselves in its cool, clear flow. The current was fast, dangerous and deep. We didn't linger on its slippery banks for long.

It was a peaceful spot. The gurgle of the water lulled my anxious heart. I wanted nothing more than to lay down my head and sleep. As usual, a trusted guide finally arrived and greeted Apodemius with a serious but familiar expression of recognition. As night fell, our party was shown where to bed down—a clean barn just within sight.

I was overcome with exhaustion and melancholy. For once, I begged off the first shift of the evening guarding the Caesar. The night was far from balmy but I collapsed with grateful relief on a clump of grassy plain sheltered by a ridge of low bush. I had once slept rough on a nightly basis as an army slave. Perhaps it was that fond memory of a simpler time that blessed my slumbers that night under the stars. Not a single bleeding, grasping spirit tormented me. I felt as though my soul was finally sinking, sinking down, and falling to the very bottom of a soft nest lined with velvet. Everything was dark and silent.

Apodemius woke me up a few minutes before dawn when the gray sky was lightening to the color of a sword blade and the birds had started rustling. The matted grass under my back was moist and the unbuckled armor lying within my reach was moist with dew.

'Did you sleep all right? I let you skip your shifts,' the old man said.

He had washed the blacking out of his white hair and changed back into the soft wool robes he wore against the chill of the Castra's faulty heating system. I realized we were safely in the Western Empire, for all its poverty and neglected monuments.

I nodded and shook off my sleep. The sensation of such deep and dreamless rest was like the balm of a good wine or the relief of a woman's caress—rich and satisfying.

'They didn't haunt you, the dead of Mursa?'

'They left me alone, for once.'

'Because you've come back to them, Numidianus.'

He stretched his bony arms wide toward the rolling hills that slept a little longer at our feet.

I jumped to my feet. 'Here?'

But already I didn't need Apodemius' confirmation that I had just slept through the night on the battlefield of Mursa.

The quiet hills sprang to life in my memory's eye. The sky darkened. The roar of screams and clashing arms flooded my ears. I scanned the fields for signs of that barrier of corpses that had blocked my progress as I carried the dying Commander toward the triage tents in the vain hope of saving his life. But there was no palisade of bones within view.

Where had the Commander lain? Where had I witnessed the noble hunter Gaiso fall to his death? Where had I stumbled across that dismembered hand of the power monger Marcellinus and removed his priceless rings to return to his widow?

I fingered his remaining ring on my cord now, hanging next to *Matrona* Laetitia's ring-key.

The grassy weeds over these men stretched brown and thick all around my boots. In silence, Apodemius and I stood in Mursa together. Perhaps he knew more about war memories than I realized. Taking me by the arm, he urged me to show him, yard by yard and blow by blow, where and how the great armies of the empire, East and West, had slaughtered each other long into the night on this very plain.

I finally found the slope where the medical teams had heard the grateful news that in a gesture of civil reconciliation, the victor Constantius II promised assistance to the usurper Magnentius' surviving wounded.

We marked off the line of medical tents where an occasional stake still protruded. Suddenly, we reached the spot where I had found the Commander dragging himself, still strapped to his shield, through the mud. I fell silent mid-sentence as I gulped back my tears.

'It was a noble gesture, but Constantius had no choice but to issue an amnesty. Without the Western Army, the Empire had no future and he knew it,' Apodemius commented.

But it was a gesture too late for fifty-four thousand good men, with no grievance against each other, who had fought for Constantius or Magnentius and now left no trace of themselves. I searched as we walked. Only now and then did the glint of a harness bit or a rotting leather sword belt betray the dark secret of this peaceful land.

'Where did it all go?' I wiped the tears off my cheeks with embarrassment.

'The weapons and helmets? You didn't expect they would be left lying here, did you, Numidianus? Not in Pannonia, the very crossroads of the Empire. This isn't the remote Teutoberg Forest, you know,' Apodemius chuckled. 'These are good fields, ready for plowing next spring and there's a ready market in Sirmium for secondhand materiel.'

'But the bodies? I can't believe they're all gone. They stretched forever, up into those hills, and all along the riverbanks, and filling the shallow water. Where are the remains?'

'Oh, what the animals left undisturbed made for rich compost years ago. The bones lie buried in mass graves. But their *souls* are at peace, Numidianus. You see? They have gone to their rest.'

He patted my shoulder and helped me refasten my padding and slip on my armor.

'Let them go, boy, and they'll let you sleep from now on.'

⚜⚜⚜

Petobio waited for us with desultory streets basking in the last rays of dusk along a slope overlooking the rushing Dravus. The town looked like a provincial maiden still shivering outdoors, long after the best men are safe around their own home fires, in the vain hope of a little passing trade.

But its slightly shabby air and modest size belied its former dominance. Less than a hundred years earlier, Petobio had been the base camp for the *Legio XIII Gemina*, the soldiers who conquered and controlled Pannonia in centuries past. The legionaries had been reposted long ago, but the merchants and matrons who closed their shops and called their children to dinner as we rode past surely carried *Gemina* veterans' blood in their veins.

'Who's meeting us here?' I asked Apodemius once we had traded in our horses.

'The Master of the Guards, Barbatio.'

'*Barbatio*? How—?' I could not hide my dismay.

'He was one of the men who started this affair. The Emperor Constantius has ordained that Barbatio be part of what happens next.'

'But he was leaving Antiochia to join Ursicinus!'

'He could not have told you that. He had instructions to leave Antiochia only hours after your imperial convoy and make no stops on his way here.'

So that was what the imperial courier Probitus had passed to Barbatio back in Antiochia. Barbatio had told me had no intention of remaining in the vicinity of Eusebius, but I had jumped to the wrong conclusion. That 'especially thick' packet

325

containing the love letter from a nagging wife had been padded out with secret imperial orders to proceed to the West.

Our small party waited at the tombstone of Marcus Valerius Verus in the very center of the town's forum. It was a marble monument with a beautiful carving of the goddess of the moon, Selene, leaning over her dead lover Endymion. The goddess was trying to awaken him from his eternal sleep with the kisses of her beams. It was a tribute to love after death, made more poignant as the moon itself shed an eerie cold light on its relief.

On the other side of the huge stone block, a carved Orpheus played his lyre in sorrow for his lost Eurydice.

Gallus stood off to one side between two guards, sullen and unresponsive under their constraint. He said nothing and in fact, I don't think he overheard Apodemius mention Barbatio's name. His Constantinian cow-eyes with their long lashes were transfixed by the carved figures on the tombstone, especially by the sorrowful Orpheus.

Suddenly he broke down, wailing, 'She was our Eurydice.' He threw himself against the chiseled marble and started banging his head against its sharp corners. 'Constantia, Constantia!' he wailed.

Our escort yanked him away before he drew his own imperial blood.

'We can't keep him in an open square like this. Someone may discover us,' I said. 'Leave a man for Barbatio and find us a refuge.'

'Yes, we won't wait for him any longer,' Apodemius made a signal for us to leave the exposed square.

'You won't have to wait, *Magister Agentium*. I'm a man who stands behind his word.'

It was Barbatio's voice some fifty feet away. He appeared in the doorway of Petobio's main tavern, silhouetted like the brutish giant he was by the flickering oil lamps within. He might have been a demon from Hades, appearing there in the shadows although, as he stepped forward to greet us properly, I saw he was quite human, if a little thinner. He had just made a journey that no doubt cost him as many sleepless nights and saddle sores as we had suffered.

Barbatio stepped up to the sobbing Caesar crouched at the foot of the monument. He pulled off his own rough soldier's cloak and wrapped it around Gallus.

'Get up at once, *Domine*,' he ordered.

Barbatio had an unadorned carriage standing by. We forced Gallus into it against his will. It took four armed men of the trusted escort to get the door finally bolted shut. We mounted fresh horses and galloped out of Petobio, not even stopping over for the night.

We were racing against time, discovery, and a common enemy. Dragging the single carriage roughshod as fast as if we were all on a horse relay of the greatest imperial emergency, we moved southwards along the *Cursus* for the rest of the night and all of the next day.

With only three stops for horse changes, we finally pulled into Pola, Istria in the early hours of the third day. I had feared that the carriage, reinforced for military uses but only as fast as any carriage could be, might well lose a wheel or worse, one of its team.

But Barbatio was nothing if not an expert when it came to vehicles and horses. This leg of the journey was the highlight of his career so far. He had planned the logistics well. As we drew within sight of Pola, I saw legionaries surrounding the town walls and guarding its gates. On a promontory overlooking the Sea of Adria, a grim stone fortress awaited us.

There was no longer any hiding the purpose of our journey from the terrified ruler of the East. Within the hour, the Caesar Gallus had arrived at his true destination.

'What is this place, Master of the Guards? Are you here to protect or harm me? Tell me you've come to save me.'

Barbatio ignored the Caesar's shouts from his carriage prison. We clopped past the great arena and through silent streets, heading up the paved road to the great castle. The town of Pola slept on, ignorant of its imperial guest.

The fortress walls were manned by dozens more troops standing on alert. None hailed the Caesar or even broke the silence of the chilly night.

Under their frigid gaze, we dismounted and marched through passages behind a grim-faced sentry until our travelling party descended down narrow stone steps and into a corridor lined with windowless cells well below ground. At this level of the fortress, we were closer to the sea. The sound of the tide crashing on stones outside echoed through the walls.

A large iron door stood unbolted. We filed into a small room dank with the moisture of salt water and moss.

'This is Colonia Pietas Iulia Pola Pollentia Herculanea,' Apodemius explained to Gallus in a calm voice, as if the cell were a comfortable suite furnished with cushions and central heating under the floor.

'I've heard of this place,' Gallus mused, as if it were a mere setting for some mythical bedside tale he'd heard in childhood.

'I'm not surprised, Caesar. This is where your uncle Constantine executed your cousin Crispus for plotting against him twenty-eight years ago. I thought it might make you feel at home.'

The old man pulled aside his travelling cloak, lifted an oil lantern, and passed the light along the wall.

There, revealed by the feeble flame, we all read a line of graffiti scratched into the granite with a sharp point by Constantine's ill-fated eldest son by his first wife Minervina. Flavius Julius Crispus had been accused of sleeping with his stepmother Fausta and imprisoned in this very cell.

Was the charge true? No one knew, but the old Constantine had shown his son no mercy. The condemned boy's jagged letters looked still fresh, even after almost three decades in dank obscurity.

They read, '*Innocens ego sum.*'

Gallus shrunk back from the lettering. He stared at Apodemius with a wild expression. 'But we're as innocent as Crispus was! We're no conspirator! The Emperor has promised us elevation.'

He made a futile dash for the door. It was firmly bolted. Guards stood in the corridor outside. Gallus turned on Apodemius and flailed at the old man with his fists until Barbatio pulled him off and tossed him down on the damp stone floor.

'What are we doing here? Where is our cousin?' he spit the words out at us.

'On orders of his Imperial Highness, the Emperor Constantius II, we have been asked to investigate the judicial decisions and administrative policies carried out in Antiochia during your reign as Caesar,' Apodemius said, readjusting his rumpled tunic.

He pulled a sheaf of notes from the battered satchel buckled to his belt. 'I would advise you to sit down, Caesar, on that stool over there. Please answer our questions.'

Apodemius dragged a second stool close to Gallus and eased his bones down with visible relief.

'Let us rest! Let us alone! Get the Emperor. The *Imperator* must hear us!'

'He is listening. He is listening to you now, through us. First, I'd like to talk about the execution of the Egyptian merchant in Antiochia, one Clematius.'

'We don't know anything about that. Ask the *Augusta*. Bring her to us.'

At this Apodemius paused and glanced at me, then resumed, 'Perhaps you'd prefer to talk about the sudden deaths of a number of very senior imperial officials posted to your court.'

We heard footsteps outside the cell door and a murmur of men addressing the sentry. Apodemius' head shot up from his papers, his eyes narrowed, and his ears cocked. He had given orders that we weren't to be interrupted.

'Who's out there?' Barbatio shouted through the bolted door.

His sentry answered, 'Three visitors—Lord Chamberlain Eusebius, Imperial Secretary Pentadius, and Tribune Mallobaudes.'

Apodemius closed his eyes and lifted his chin to the dripping ceiling, taking a stiff, sudden breath of resignation. He said nothing, but at that moment, when he opened his eyes again, I read defeat.

For we had just lost the race. We had lost unimpeded control over the Caesar. Quite possibly, we had lost salvation of the Eastern Empire from a truly evil man.

The bolts slid open, one by one, and the oak door swung open on its iron hinges. Eusebius' brocaded bulk filled the doorway. Taking in the sight of his frail, bent opponent still wearing his rustic travel tunic and cloak, the eunuch waved a silken sleeve across his face as if to ward off the uncomfortable closeness of men who had ridden too long and hard without baths.

The trio of officials joined us in that small cell. Within seconds, our own nostrils filled with the pungent aromas that surrounded the Lord Chamberlain. It was the same waft of sweet rotting scent that had sickened my stomach in his offices in Sirmium, even as he saved me from the torture instruments of Paulus Catena.

'You call an imperial trial without the Lord Chamberlain or a secretary to record your deliberations? Where are your witnesses? Who are the judges?'

'I carry instructions from our Emperor,' Apodemius said.

'To arrive at the truth, I'm sure. And we are here to listen and none too soon, I see,' Eusebius said with an unctuous smile for everyone, even Barbatio and myself. 'We are here to defend what needs defending and to condemn the crimes, *if any*, to which the Caesar confesses.'

And so Apodemius' questioning resumed as the newly arrived Pentadius scribbled furious notes on a large wax tablet.

'We were discussing the conviction of one Alexandrian trader, a certain Clematius.'

Gallus mumbled, 'He raped his mother-in-law. He confessed under torture.'

'Was he framed?'

'We have no idea. We never saw the man,' Gallus blurted out, looking up at Eusebius. 'We only did what Constantia told us. She watched the interrogation to the very end. She said he admitted everything. She sent that woman's complaint to the *Comes* of the East, Honoratus. If he were here, he could confirm what we say.'

'Yes, go on.'

'The Prefect Thalassius handed down the death penalty. That makes two high officials who stood behind that execution.'

'Which was carried out before the *quaestor* Luscus' opinion calling for an appeal could be taken up.'

'We had nothing to do with it. We had more important duties as Caesar than to meddle in a petty family scandal.'

Apodemius passed quickly through two minor cases of miscarriage of justice, but in both instances, Gallus seemed unclear about any details, even though the original complaints had come from the Imperial Suite after reports had passed through the secret back gate into the Palace.

Eusebius had settled on a bench along the wall by now. He seemed satisfied with the lack of progress Apodemius was making.

'Caesar, why did you instigate a starving mob to tear Theophilus, the Governor of Syria, to pieces?'

'We hardly gave an order for murder! We simply laid the hunger of the people at Theophilus' feet. The results were out of our control.'

'Surely you knew that by blaming Theophilus for the shortages, the people would turn on him like the hungry animals they were?'

'How could we know that? We don't know where you get such accusations.'

Gallus kept his eyes fixed on the dripping flagstones before he rallied, 'Unless you listen to the lies of a thick-headed, ambitious Horse Guard thug who licks the asshole of that upstart Ursicinus.'

Barbatio lurched forward and punched Gallus with a swift upper cut to his handsome jaw. He sent the Caesar slamming into the wall behind his stool. Apodemius rose with painful difficulty on his bad knees and helped Gallus back to his stool.

'Keep that Dacian animal off us or we'll have him beheaded,' Gallus snarled. He was sweating hard, despite the cold air of the cell. His golden curls were matted from travel and sleep. He glowered at Apodemius through those famous eyelashes that wooed his admirers but had failed to fill empty bellies.

Eusebius looked on, still smiling. The less the eunuch said, the more I worried. He was waiting for Apodemius to make a mistake that would get him caught in one of those tacky webs that only Eusebius could weave.

'Why did you condemn Domitianus and Montius to a cruel death by quartering?'

'Constantia told us to do that. She said we must make people fear us. Put your questions to her.'

Eusebius allowed one eyebrow to shoot up but said nothing. I knew it was no lie, for I had been the last one to see the *Augusta* there on the parade ground after the excitement and horror had died away. She had shone with triumph as she uttered those words to me, '*It's all going to be all right from now on. They'll fear him after this.*'

She had set him up to it, after all.

Apodemius stayed cautious. 'What else would Constantia tell us if she were her? Come, Caesar, we wouldn't want your wife to see you like this until it's all sorted out. Let's leave her out of it. What did Constantia say?'

'She said we had to punish insolence and rebellion in public or we'd lose all our authority. Then that little creep Montius showed his true colors. We only did it to frighten them! We didn't mean to carry it out!'

'Did you poison the Prefect of the Palace, Thalassius?'

Gallus looked wild. 'The Prefect? Of course not! We wouldn't know how! Why would we kill *him*? Because he refused to lower the grain prices? We knew Thalassius was trying to regulate the speculators out of business. Thalassius was an honorable official.'

Apodemius glanced over at Eusebius and muttered, 'No, Flavius Claudius Constantius Gallus, I believe you didn't kill Thalassius.'

Gallus pointed his swelling jaw at his Lord Chamberlain. 'You have the Emperor's trust. You have his ear. We demand to know on whose authority this cripple interrogates us like this! You know the truth. You were there in Antiochia! Tell him! Tell him and send word to Constantius, immediately.'

Eusebius said nothing. Gallus only panicked more. Sweat was dripping down his face. Barbatio's boulder-like fist had split the Caesar's lower lip open, making his protests sound thick and drunken.

'Look, we're telling you the truth. Constantia was the one who listened to all the complaints. She encouraged people to sneak in and tell us what was really going on in the city. Constantia said Antiochia was stinking with corruption. We were going to clean it out. We tried to meet the people, not only inside the Palace in secret, but out in the streets where they lived. We wanted to do good. She was the one who took money and jewels, but those were gifts of thanks for settling disputes and obtaining retribution for the victims.'

His lip was thickening fast from Barbatio's blow as he appealed to us. 'Gifts for her, not for us!'

Before I realized what was happening, Gallus had leapt up and made for my throat with his soft hands. Pressing his bruised face into mine, he hissed through his bloody lips, 'S . . . s . . . spy, S . . . spy, dirty spy, you let her die like a dog in the road,' sending red spittle spattering my cheeks. I worked to get his furious fingers off my neck.

Barbatio pulled him back again and called the sentries for a rope. With their help, he bound Gallus' hands and feet.

Eusebius' eyes bulged at Apodemius as if my superior had just made a particularly stupid move in a board game. He murmured to Pentadius and Mallobaudes, 'Take that down. There will be an accounting for all this. I guarantee it.'

'Tell me more about this corruption,' Apodemius continued softly, as if he were a priest at a sacred ritual whispering prayers over a condemned sheep. 'Tell me about the jewels and the bribes.'

'We don't know any details,' Gallus muttered. 'All we know is that you're blaming us for things we never understood. The problem was not that we abused our power. The problem was that *we had none.*'

Apodemius went on with his gentle questions, but now Gallus refused to answer in any way for the criminal cases the old man raised, point by point, death by death. There were names I didn't recognize and fresh tortures that turned my stomach.

The interrogation had now lasted for more than an hour. Eusebius gave an ostentatious yawn, placing his well-cushioned hand over a pair of generous lips. He patted down that cap of fawn-colored fuzz covering his brow and heaved a sigh.

'I'm tired, *Magister Agentium.* My boat trip here was rather rushed and difficult in this winter weather but I did it for you, Caesar.'

Gallus blubbed through his pain with as much dignity as he could muster. 'We won't forget your loyalty, *Praepositus Sacri Cubiculi.*'

'Without more evidence than this, only empty questions, they can't hold you for long. You and I will return to Constantinopolis within the week.'

'Why don't you continue on to the Emperor in Mediolanum?' Apodemius gave a wry chuckle.

Gallus jerked his head up in confusion at his chief eunuch.

'Yes, Constantius has promised to elevate us to Co-Emperor.'

Eusebius swept his long robes clear of the grime-encrusted floor and made for the bolted door. Pentadius and Mallobaudes rose to follow him with a nod to Apodemius out of respect for his *schola.*

Barbatio drew his sword, unable to contain his disappointment at seeing months of mounting disgust and ambition stymied in one hour by the arrival of this neutered intrigant.

'Wait, Lord Chamberlain. Denials must be refuted with facts,' Apodemius said in a calm tone.

'We see you have none, Apodemius. Within a week, I'll have Constantius' counter order to restore this young man to his rightful place.'

'And promote us! He owes it to us, now more than ever!' burbled Gallus through his bleeding lips.

Apodemius lifted his hand to stay their exit. 'You'd like that, wouldn't you, Eusebius? So you could go back to ruling this half-demented boy as your puppet without any interference.'

'My reports were true,' Barbatio growled across the small cell at the departing eunuch.

Misled by my superior's quiet manner and patient questioning, the Dacian brute had lost faith in Apodemius. His dream of higher office under a future Caesar Ursicinus of the East was slipping between his calloused fingers.

He couldn't contain his frustration any longer. He grabbed Gallus by his shirt and slapped him hard across the face, back and forth, again and again, roaring, 'Tell the truth, you incestuous little freak!' until Apodemius shouted at him to stop but Barbatio kept on. 'You robbed and maimed and killed hundreds of innocent people.'

'Let him go, Barbatio. I want to ask him something in particular. Caesar, tell me about the case of one Epigones, a construction manager contracted to repair earthquake damage to state buildings and monuments.'

'Epigones? He was some kind of cheat,' Gallus mumbled.

'How do you know?'

'There was a trial.'

'Did you attend the hearings?'

'Of course not. We had better things to do.'

'Yet Epigones was tortured in the cruelest ways possible and condemned.'

'What of it? He confessed. He was as corrupt as all of them.'

'Who told you?'

'The *Basilissa*, of course.'

'Yes, but *who told her*? Who sent all these unhappy subjects through your secret door, Caesar? Who told them they could expect no less than the cousin of the great *Imperator*, not to mention his sister, to bother with such petty squabbles and disputes? You're a clever young man, Caesar. Didn't you ever wonder why so many dozens of strangers came knocking in the night, bringing you their complaints about the rich merchants and landowners of Antiochia?'

'They knew we would listen.'

'Yes, but how, Caesar? Why? Who first gave them that understanding? Did you post placards outside the baths? Did you send out proclamations? Have your scribes prepare brochures? Dispatch imperial criers into the streets?'

'I've heard enough,' Eusebius said. He rose off the bench and knocked on the iron door to be released from our stinking enclosure.

'You've lost, Apodemius, *you've lost it all.*' Eusebius said as he pounded on the door again. 'I predict a long retirement for you, if you're very lucky, in the wilds of some Celtic wilderness. It's a pity how constant rainfall can be so bad for arthritis.'

The sentry opened the door as Pentadius tucked away his stylus and tablet.

'Wait!' I blurted out. They all turned and stared at me.

'Caesar Gallus, you said that Thalassius was an honest man.'

'He was,' mumbled Gallus. 'Too good to be in the same room with men like you.'

'Perhaps, but I think, Eusebius, you might like to stay to hear what Thalassius had to say in evidence, the evidence you still claim is missing.'

Eusebius' large eyes blinked but he didn't exit the cell.

Apodemius watched me. He had been working from notes based on Barbatio's incomplete reports and my own hurried reports to him, coded messages from which he had the gist of Gallus' crimes, not more. He had hoped to force a confession from Gallus but the Caesar's mind was now too weakened, angry, and confused to cooperate.

Besides, even in his hysterical fear, Gallus smelled escape as long as Eusebius stayed near. We wouldn't get anything more out of his deranged memory.

I drew my sword from its scabbard.

'Put your weapon down, Marcus Gregorianus Numidianus,' Apodemius warned me.

'I had no intention of using it, *Magister.*' I carefully placed it next to my boots and knelt by the light of an oil lantern. The jagged wet flagstones cut into my knees.

From within the scabbard, I carefully extracted the roll of Thalassius' secret reports I had rescued from its hiding place under Athena's mattress before leaving Antiochia. Apodemius gasped with palpable hope.

'You will find these much more complete, *Magister.*'

Apodemius took the bundle of fine vellum sheets from me, unrolled them carefully, and began to scan their titles.

'The case of Clematius of Alexander, merchant and husband, resident of Antiochia,' he started and then paused. 'I think you might want to take your seat again, Lord Chamberlain.'

Eusebius slowly lowered his heavy bulk back down on the bench. He nodded to Mallobaudes and Pentadius to do the same.

'Pentadius, you'll want to take notes,' Apodemius said with a tight smile on his thin lips.

He read in a calm voice, exactly in the determined spirit with which Thalassius must have methodically recorded the sudden arrest of the popular Clematius, the public announcement of the charges, the furious scandal on everyone's lips, the frantic denials of the Alexandrian youth, the passionate pleas for clemency from his wife matched by the condemnations of her own mother, the *quaestor*'s failed appeal, and even the impersonal expression on the *Augusta*'s face as she followed the boy off to the torture chambers.

Thalassius had omitted no detail.

Gallus mumbled, 'We don't recall any of this. We weren't summoned to these events.'

'I would recommend the final observations made on each case,' I interjected.

Apodemius said to Eusebius, 'But of course you knew all this, because I see here that the Prefect of the Palace then records, "Following the conviction on all charges and the subsequent torture and execution of the Egyptian, the costs of prosecution were covered from the proceeds of sale of all his assets, including his home and profitable cotton trading business, by *the office of the Lord Chamberlain.* His wife received a partial sum out of damages awarded to her mother".'

Apodemius shuffled through Thalassius' notes, 'Here's the case of the construction chief; "After the conviction of Epigones on all charges of bribery and fraudulent billing, the costs of the engineer's trial were paid out of the proceeds of sale of his assets—his offices, tools and trained slaves, city house and country villa which were put into the receivership of *the office of the Lord Chamberlain*".'

Apodemius flipped the pages to scan case by case. 'Each case seems to offer variety when it comes to the crime, but somehow Thalassius' final comments start to look a bit repetitive. For example, "Following conviction on all charges of fraud and dishonest trading, and the subsequent sentence of Seleuceus Pogon and two of his four sons to permanent exile from the borders of the Empire, the costs of the state's investigation, gathering of witnesses, trial as well as compensation to the injured parties were paid out of the proceeds of sales of the convicted man's company holdings—including partnerships in construction enterprises in Tarsus, Damascus, and Jerusalem",' Apodemius looked straight at Eusebius before reciting, '*by the office of the Lord Chamberlain.*'

Gallus had started sobbing, 'What did you do with her? Why doesn't she come to help us now?'

Apodemius looked square at the eunuch looming in the shadows. 'I thought the imperial bedchambers were your official department, *Praepositus*. Judging from the dozens of comments here, you seem to have gone into a sideline in the confiscated property business.'

Eusebius' flabby face had darkened in the shadows cast by lanterns set into the merciless walls.

The eunuch laid a hand to still the scribbling fingers of Pentadius. 'We can reinstate the Caesar by agreement. I guarantee there will be a review of appeals in all those cases. If restitution is in order, it will be made.'

Gallus lifted his face, 'Can you do that, Eusebius? Can you get us back to Antiochia?'

He ran his shaking fingers through his dirty blond curls.

'As soon as we get back, we'll arrest all those traitors of the Senate and this time we'll make sure they die. We won't leave a single official left to betray us. We'll kill them all ourself, by hand, personally.'

A terrified expression crossed his handsome face from ear to ear, his imperial smile turning into a vicious grin from Hades.

'We're sorry we didn't listen to you more, Eusebius. The eunuchs have always been my friends, even back in the fortress at Marcellum. They were the only friends of my youth.'

'But how can you return to Antiochia a mere Caesar when you've already declared yourself Co-Emperor?' Apodemius asked, keeping his eyes fixed on Eusebius.

'That's right,' Gallus said. 'We have to come back as *Imperator*. We'll declare ourself Emperor, that's all, like we did in Constantinopolis. We'll be Divine. And we'll suppress the conspiracy of General Ursicinus. He and his tribunes will all fall before our swords.'

Gallus leered up at Barbatio. 'And we'll make sure that the *Basilissa* watches your torture.'

There was a long and potent pause as we all took in the full measure of Gallus' insanity. Eusebius cleared his throat and re-fastened his high cloak collar. 'I trust you carry orders from the West, *Magister Agentium*, in the event of any conspiracy to claim the throne.'

'As a matter of fact, I do.'

'Then I would hardly be one to interfere with the will of the *Imperator*.'

Eusebius signaled to his two companions and sharply rapped again on the iron door.

'Eusebius, don't leave us!' Gallus screamed. 'We need you to carry out our plans for the East!'

The door swung open. The trio swept out in their thick robes leaving a cloud of cloying perfumes. The door bolted shut behind them.

'Carry out the order,' Apodemius murmured to Barbatio.

I couldn't have stopped the Dacian if I had wanted to.

Barbatio drew his sword. He tossed the young man, stomach across the stool and face toward the floor, and pressed one boot down on the Caesar's shoulder blades. He lifted his weapon and without further hesitation, sliced off the Constantine's head.

The ruler who only a month ago had been a terror across Syria now bled at our feet a twitching, headless corpse.

But then it got worse. Like a mad man, Barbatio sliced again and again at the imperial face. The head rolled back and forth across the cold stones.

'Stop him!' Apodemius shouted to the sentries outside. They pulled Barbatio away, shoving the volcanic giant up against the wall. Had Apodemius planned on delivering the late Caesar's body to his brother as proof the orders of execution had been carried out, it was now too late.

Barbatio had mutilated Gallus' beautiful features beyond recognition.

I heard Apodemius' condemnation through a wave of revulsion that rose up from my stomach at Barbatio's barbarism.

'I supposed you had hoped to return to the East, Master of the Guards,' the old man said with an asperity he reserved for enemies, not friends.

Barbatio's great chest still heaved with the enjoyment of his savagery. 'That's right. I'll serve under the new Caesar, General Ursicinus.' He beamed at us, his crooked teeth catching the oil lamps' flickering light.

'Perhaps not. Such excessive zeal seems wasted on our effeminate, ornate Eastern courts,' Apodemius declared. 'You show the kind of rare enthusiasm for manly physical effort that should be applied where it can make a real difference.'

Barbatio's grin began to fade as Apodemius continued, 'Barbatio, you can count on my recommendation that you be transferred immediately to the northern front facing the Rhenus. General Claudius Silvanus is fighting a losing battle up there against barbarian incursions. It's a desperate situation and we're losing many good Romans in defense of the Empire. Silvanus needs . . . *men* like you.'

CHAPTER 22, ONE LAST
CONSTANTINE

—THE ROAD TO MEDIOLANUM, 354 AD—

Apodemius turned his back on Barbatio. With a grunt of pain, he dropped to his knees on the stone floor, leaned over the throbbing corpse, and removed Gallus' red slippers. He tucked them into his leather satchel along with Thalassius' reports.

I helped the old man back to his feet.

'We're taking the slippers to Constantius, Numidianus. Thanks to the Master of the Guards here, there is little else of the Caesar that the Emperor would recognize. We'll leave in ten minutes.'

He turned to Barbatio. 'No doubt you have orders from your commander to stay here overseeing the troops surrounding this fortress until further instructions.'

Barbatio mustered an obedient nod, though he was fuming at the prospect of service on the remote Gallic borders.

Adjusting his mud-spattered cloak, Apodemius left the cell, trailed by the sentries.

Barbatio and I were alone.

Panting steam into the frigid air, Barbatio stood a few feet from me, with only the corpse and the upturned stool between us. Blood streamed out of Gallus' torso. It pooled, dark and warm, near our boots.

For a moment I wondered if indignation at his sudden demotion, even to serve under a renowned officer like General Silvanus, would trigger a second violent death—mine.

For over a year in the intrigue-riddled court of Antiochia, Barbatio had dodged the wiles of the Lord Chamberlain and guarded the welfare of an unstable and unpredictable weakling with only the absent Ursicinus as his navigational star. He'd risked his position to write those clumsy reports to Constantius. He'd dodged the fatal whims of Constantia and kept his own counsel—a military man to the last—pinning his bets on a new regime with himself at the right-hand of the battle-hardened general.

Now he stood there snorting like a bull, his dream of promotion in the wealthy East slammed flat on his horns. Up on the Lower Rhenus, General Silvanus already had his staff of trusted Franco-Roman officers commanding Frankish auxiliaries. These forces had been weathered and tested by constant skirmishes with raiding parties from other Germanic tribes. Silvanus' officers knew northeastern Gallia as their own, and their fellow Franks were all but confederates with the Roman army in defending the borders against rival barbarians.

Barbatio would be an outsider and he knew it.

'Do I have you to thank for this?'

'You have that to thank.' I pointed to the mutilated head staring at us from the corner of the cell.

'You're glad to see me sent up there,' his low voice rumbled. 'You're no friend of mine. You accused me of slave trading. You tried to blackmail me. But why destroy me? Did you give that old bastard a bad report of me on the way here as well?'

'How could I? Your orders to meet us here were secret, even from me. You always took a joke too far. Now you've let your greed for quick profits from slave-trading cloud your honor. And you bungled a death sentence, turning it from an execution into an atrocity.'

I pointed at the unsightly corpse. 'You did this to yourself. Why, Barbatio, why?'

'He mocked me, this play-Caesar who had never fought a battle. He never issued one order that didn't harm or ruin someone. I kept him safe, night after night, as he toured that sewer of a city, trapping people into their own betrayals and tortures. He didn't care about the poor. He taunted them with a few handouts as they starved to death right under his nose.'

'You hid your hatred well.'

'I'd had enough. Finally, I let him go out into the streets with those so-called guards of the *domestici*. He was no *Caesar*. I found it hard to believe he was even a Constantine. Why didn't you let them kill him that night in the theater quarter? But you're always the clever one, aren't you, slave-boy?'

He was still holding his bloodied *spatha*, waving its point in the air. He was trying to decide how far to go. He lifted its tip in my direction once or twice, swinging it up and down. My own sword still lay on the floor. I reached down and in a studied move, slowly slipped it back into its scabbard.

'We're old acquaintances, Barbatio. You fought well with the *Legio IIIA* in the Battle of Bagae against the Circumcellions. You're not ready for a fancy uniform and a lot of paperwork. Don't tell me you would really miss Antiochia's fancy carriages and riders in those silk tunics? Judging by this,' I touched the Caesar's cooling shoulder with the toe of my boot, 'you miss the smell of blood.'

'Are you insinuating I'm afraid?' He threatened me again with his sword.

'No!'

'I can handle any bunch of *bagaudae* marauders, but I've earned better than that.'

He shook his dripping weapon at the door through which Apodemius had disappeared. 'That old man carried an imperial death warrant. He knew the facts before we entered this cell. He wanted Gallus killed, Constantius wanted him killed, and half the East wanted him killed. So I killed the bastard. I'm a servant of the Empire. And I get a posting in the frozen north as my reward?'

He gave Gallus' head a final kick, smashing it into the wall like a melon. 'I only want what's coming to me.'

'I can't change a posting on the Rhenus. But I made you a fair offer back in Antiochia. I've still got one ring. Bring back the

Domina Kahina. Up north, you'll need lots of money to win over new friends.'

I pulled Marcellinus' ring out of my shirt so he could admire its glittering promise by the oil lamps.

'Look at those stones. They're worth a lot.'

He heaved with frustration at the turn of the Fates against him. In the rough garrisons of the Gallic *limes*, where men jostled for privileges, comfort, and allies, any extra cash would come in handy. Seeing the bitter scowl on his thick features, I realized he would have produced half a dozen commanders' refugee wives at that moment in Pola—if it had meant pocketing a small fortune like the one I dangled in front of him.

'Just tell me where she went, Barbatio. I'll do the rest. I'll go fetch her. You won't have to bring her to Roma. I'll go wherever she went—even to Persia or Armenia—tell me, *who bought her?*'

I slipped the ring off the cord and held it out, tempting him with it. 'Tell me, Barbatio. Where is she? Who sold her? Who bought her?'

The towering soldier looked at the stone floor and said nothing.

My heart sank as I digested the truth. Barbatio couldn't help himself or me. His slave inventory had dried up over a year ago with the end of Paulus Catena's rich harvest of captive rebels hiding in Britannia. Barbatio was no longer useful to the middlemen who funneled the civil war prisoners to their new lives of enslavement. He had lost his contacts and all his pull.

But if he was powerless to help me, Barbatio was the last the man to admit it.

'Every war produces slaves. Julius Caesar took prisoners as slaves,' he equivocated.

'Roman *citizens* are not sold into slavery after a civil action between Romans—no matter how violent or disastrous. It's against every law and custom of our Empire. It is only for the Emperor himself to decide what happens to the rebels—not for you to send them to castration and life in foreign mines and fields before they even get a hearing.'

'I was never one for studying law but I forgot, you're only a freedman thanks to some fine print, a mere clause, right?'

'I think a man under such scrutiny as General Ursicinus suffers will be very careful with whom he rides. He was hauled before Constantius once last year over treason rumors. He needs to keep his tablet very, very clean.'

'You can never prove I had anything to do with selling citizens, Numidianus. No one has ever seen me trading slaves. There are no records, no accounts. You have no witnesses to bring before Ursicinus or anyone else who can testify I dirtied my hands with that kind of thing.'

'But I'm right, aren't I? You know who sold *Domina* Kahina.'

'You and your fine Numidian whore lady.'

He reared up and spat full in my face. Before I could react, he had grabbed the ring and swallowed it whole—bulky as it was. Fighting off his gagging reflex, he forced the jewel down his gullet. When it was finally secure from my grasp, he threw his head back, roaring with laughter.

'I hope I never see you again,' I said. 'You can rot up there from frostbite, for all I care.'

'Oh, you'll see me again, Numidianus, you can be sure of that. From now on, you'll wish you had eyes in the back of your head, because I won't be happy until I've revenged myself on you for this. We're not even yet.'

The lamps had run out of oil and were sputtering. It was time to escape this room of imperial despair and death.

'Bring the body upstairs,' I said. 'You can bury it yourself.'

⚔⚔⚔

Apodemius and I didn't linger. There was no trace of Eusebius or his associates. We left ten minutes later, without food or companions. The winds scouring the promontory of the fortress of Pola roared in our ears. The waves pounded the cliffs below us over a deafening gale. We descended a vertiginous trail out of town to an isolated assignation point on the shoreline where Apodemius negotiated an unseasonal and dangerous crossing of the Adria westward to Patavium.

Hugging the shore as best he could manage, our navigator kept his small boat under taut command, reassuring an anxious Apodemius that we could outrun any horse relay through Aquileia by entrusting him with our lives on such a risky route.

We committed the entire success of our mission to his skill. We hoped that even in a race for imperial influence, Eusebius would take some short rest at the imperial palace in Aquileia before continuing his journey onwards to pour venom into the Emperor's willing ears.

We curled up in our travel cloaks and clung to the coils of ropes we had for pillows. The captain shouted to us with relief as the dawn rose behind us.

The eastern shores of Italia heaved up on the horizon across the whitecapped water. Our crew of six were lean, hard-eyed men with sinews running down their arms like knotted hemp. They shared their flatbread, olives, and diluted wine as we closed in on the harbor over the final hour.

They had seen this austere, white-haired official with the knobby knees, heavy wool cloak and painful feet shod in his goatskin boots before. As we disembarked, I noticed that Apodemius paid them well with a word of thanks and a grasp of the shoulder for every sailor in turn.

Not for the first time during the extraordinary marathon from Constantinopolis with Apodemius, I wondered what it had taken him to build up such a vast and reliable network as our *schola*'s. The answer seemed to be nothing more than this—an impeccable memory for names, respect for a job well done, and one bulging bag of coins at a time.

We disembarked and made straight for a stable in Patavium where a selection of fast horses had been standing by for us for over a week. Apodemius was pushing himself to the utmost to reach Constantius before Eusebius' tentacles could find a new way of wrapping them around my *Magister*'s neck and strangling him into silence.

We went on and on, riding hard into a ferocious wind through the day and into the dusk, the sound of leather harnesses on horseflesh audible over the thrash of the trees in a high wind. We were moving faster even than the gusts of rain we cut through on roads soon emptied of traffic as the moon reached its zenith. We kept going through the hours remaining until dawn.

This was why we trained, I thought, not only to cover the long-distance postal routes or conduct ceremonial escort services across the face of the Empire. We also trained for desperate rides like this, where the fate of imperial families rested in a satchel and powerful men vied to poison the well of favor out of jealousy, avarice, or spite.

Only an hour before we reached Verona, my heart stopped at the sight of Apodemius' mount ahead of me sinking to its knees onto the soft verge of the *Cursus*. The old man fell sideways as the horse sank full-length under him onto the cobbled stones. It was still dark. Apodemius lay still, sprawled across the road, stunned by the crash.

'Are you all right?'

The old man didn't answer.

I leapt off my horse and pulled his right leg free from under the horse's flank where he might have been crushed. The horse shook his great sweating body and thrashed its legs in agony, then dropped its head on the road, and lay motionless.

We were lucky. Apodemius suffered no broken bones but he was shaken. I laid my ear to the horse's chest, but to our astonishment, the powerful animal had stopped breathing altogether and its pulse was gone.

Apodemius had ridden him to his death.

I checked and saw that my own horse was in danger of failing as well. We walked him forward in despair until we spotted the lights of a village ahead. I dashed through the gray fog of dawn with my *pugio* ready and within twenty minutes I had cut loose a workhorse to share until we could reach the next state stables.

From there, we stopped only to change horses in Verona, dispatch the stolen horse back to its owner, and seize a bit of food. Then bucked up by the fresh breezes lifting the fog away from a cool, sunny morning, we reached Mediolanum by the late afternoon, only three days after arriving in Pola.

We hastened through the bustling market streets of the imperial capital to announce ourselves to Ahenobarbus and request an audience with Constantius. We waited at a *thermae* near the inner gates of the Palace where we could quickly wash and shave. If I say we took a bath before presenting ourselves to the imperial reception rooms, I should add that your average Egyptian cat spends more time on his forepaw than we spent on our toilet that morning.

But I did lean my head back against the blue tiles of a steamy corner in the main room and close my eyes for a precious minute.

I let myself imagine Verus greeting Roxana and Leo in a few weeks' time down in Roma. I vowed to leave an offering at the Castra Peregrina's temple to Jupiter Redux, the holy altar where *agentes* from afar offered prayers for a safe return to the provinces and *agentes* from Roma gave thanks for a safe homecoming.

I would lay my offering to Jupiter with resignation for the one homecoming the Fates had denied me. Leo was saved but Kahina was lost. I should be grateful that Leo was in one piece and that his cousin Clodius could threaten his future no more.

Soon I'd be home again in Roma. Leo had no one else now. Only I carried within my heart all the Manlius memories and beliefs that were his legacy. Wherever I was posted next, Leo came before the *schola* in importance.

Apodemius broke into my thoughts: 'I commend you for your conscientious service, Numidianus.'

'Thank you, *Magister*.'

'I didn't envisage famine and earthquake as part of your assignment. I knew that Eusebius would be sufficient danger once he realized you were not his double agent.'

'He had that figured out soon enough. But I was left in the dark about so many other things. Your messages to us in Antiochia were ambiguous. I conducted the imperial escort thinking that Gallus really was invited to Mediolanum for promotion. For a little while, I confess I even wondered if you'd capitulated to the Lord Chamberlain's ambitions.'

'Oh, ye of little faith, as those Christian cultists like to say.'

'The *Augusta* suspected a ruse from early on. She died virtually alone for her courage in trying to tackle her brother in advance. She knew he was erratic and violent. I believe she intended to plead for her husband's life to be spent in retirement as an imperial madman.'

'That female was never a coward. Being widowed so young by her own brother's ruthless hand twisted a beautiful young woman into a Fury. I believe she never truly loved anyone else after Hannibalianus. Certainly, she never felt safe again, not for a single hour.'

'How do you know that, *Magister*?'

He shrugged. 'Because I've read so much of her private correspondence, of course. Years and years of it.' He shook his head, 'Lurid stuff at the best of times.'

'But why leave me in the dark?'

'It was easier for you to play your part and get the Caesar moving west that way. Oh, don't look at me like that. I felt no pleasure in any of this task. Of all the Empire's servants, only the *agentes* are immune from prosecution when it comes to an unpleasant duty of this magnitude. Still, the less you were personally implicated, the better.'

'Constantius hopes his cousin was innocent.'

'Indeed, there will be no joy on the Emperor's face this morning when he sees those red slippers, Numidianus, nor should we expect a reward for carrying out his order.' Apodemius sighed. 'But I promise you, there will be enormous relief.'

'Was there any chance Gallus could have been kept under control? Might he have been spared?'

'I believe there was no hope in the end. Gallus committed too many crimes, many of them entirely without Eusebius' prompting. And the only Achilles heel by which we could rout the growing corruption of the East under the reign of eunuchs was to fasten on their greed and the way they used the Caesar's gullibility. We had to threaten to expose it in front of the chief eunuch himself. As I said, we had to wait for the chariots to round the *meta*.'

We walked together to return our towels and reclaim our clothes from the boys who had promised to clean them.

'But *Magister*, Eusebius is still in power. He still holds the ear of Constantius. One way or the other he will continue to pile up his secret fortune.'

'Oh, I think Eusebius may have reached the apex of his influence. Perhaps we're about to see a new set of lips gain the divine ear. I have high hopes for the new Empress Eusebia.'

We dressed in a hurry and settled our bill.

Apodemius smoothed down his straggling white hair and rubbed his hands. 'Ah, there's Ahenobarbus, coming for us. It's time for our audience with the Emperor.'

The copper-headed senior *agens* was signaling us from the arches of the bathhouse's central lobby. We crossed the Forum and entered the Palace of Mediolanum.

⚔⚔⚔

We found Constantius in the middle of a heated council meeting. We waited behind a row of praetorians for the discussion to finish. The *praefectus praetorio praesens*, the highest civil servant of the Emperor, was pushing for a new campaign against the Alemanni tribesman descending on Roman territory from their stronghold around Lentia. He argued with the *consistorium* whether the Emperor should make the journey to Rhaetia as far as the *Campi Canini* to the east of Lake Verbanus or proceed all the way to the Lake of Brigantia.

The sentries announcing us broke in on their debate. As our heavy travel boots echoed across the polished marble floor, the Emperor slowly turned in that rigid manner of his, his whole torso turning like a statue come to life between the arms of his wide *cathedra*.

As he swiveled, the eyes of officials, secretaries, and personal attendants slowly followed, landing on us as if Constantius' gaze was some kind of invisible net he dragged behind his powerful ship of state, and we were two insignificant fish caught in its knotted strings.

'Ah.' Constantius held up a large hand to silence the discussion. 'You have returned, *Magister Agentium.*'

I detected no discernable welcome in the Emperor's tone. Apodemius reached into the satchel hanging from his belt, extracted the red slippers, and laid them at the Emperor's feet. He nodded in respect and then stepped back to join Ahenobarbus and myself.

We waited.

'You have carried out our request.'

'Yes, *Imperator.*'

'You did not receive our last message rescinding that order?'

Apodemius stared up at the dais, shocked at the Emperor's question. The implications were horrific.

'No, or we would not have proceeded, *Imperator,*' he whispered.

'But we clearly addressed our change of heart to the Lord Chamberlain in time. We understood that Eusebius wished to be there as witness to the inquiry.'

'The Lord Chamberlain was present. He seems not to have known of any new orders. He said nothing during the proceedings.'

Constantius' face drained of what little color it had. No one present dared move so much as an eyebrow in the silence.

'And there was no lingering doubt?' the Emperor asked, after a deep breath. 'You found no mitigating circumstances? The reports were uniformly negative? The charges were true?'

'This *agens* collected supplementary records and additional witnesses bearing out your decision, *Imperator.*' Apodemius nodded at me.

'He did not suffer?'

'No,' Apodemius lied. I gave a curt nod of confirmation.

'It is very important to us that he did not suffer.'

'The end was clean and swift.'

'Well, there is something to thank God for,' Constantius said.

There was a long silence as the mystified councilors slowly grasped the significance of the conversation they were witnessing without any warning. A chain of whispers circled the table, 'Gallus. It's the Caesar Gallus.'

'You are freed of a scourge, *Imperator*,' whispered the Prefect of the Praetorians, Lampadius.

'A difficult deed done with dispatch and discretion,' ventured Mattyocopus or 'Skinflint,' the Superintendent of the Emperor's Privy Purse was sitting at the end of the table.

'You're unchallenged, now, *Imperator*,' added Aedesius, the Master of the Rolls. 'Congratulations on putting the interests of the Empire before family sentiment, as always.'

Constantius gave a shiver as his eyes fixed on his dead cousin's slippers. 'Thank you for your endorsement and praise, but it is a large empire. We cannot control every corner of it without help. We are now short one caesar.'

'But who could we ever trust?' one Arbetio asked. 'There are no more Constantines.'

The councilors shook their heads in condolence and glanced at each other under lowered eyelids with expressions marking regret and ambition in equal portions.

'We still have one, actually,' Constantius said, pulling his heavy eyes away from the slippers with difficulty, 'the half-brother of the deceased Gallus, the little bookworm Julian. He lives as a scholar and recluse. He is the last cousin. Our Empress is a great advocate for the boy. But he's barely twenty-one, untrained for leadership, untested in battle, and ill favored for administration. He devotes himself to philosophy. He wears hair shirts and doesn't even shave.'

'Not exactly a leader of men,' sniffed Aedesius.

'We're afraid not . . . Need we sign anything?' Constantius looked slowly over to Apodemius with an enormous sigh.

'Yes, *Imperator*.'

Advancing with the order of execution in his hand, Apodemius required that Constantius initial it for a second time, beneath his original signature.

It should have been the work of a minute, but we had to wait while Constantius was supplied with a large pen and special ink. An imperial secretary scrambled for the writing supplies. Constantius gazed at the trio of *agentes* in front of him with those unblinking eyes of his. His cousin had had similar Constantinian eyes, but Gallus' expression had danced with the sparks of madness and the exhilaration of violence. His sister Constantia's large, dark-lashed eyes had been lined with makeup, Belgican-style, to camouflage the traces of her permanent grief.

But at least the Caesar and his hellish *Augusta* had betrayed some signs of human life in their regard. I detected no vitality, emotion, or imagination in the eyes of our implacable sovereign.

At last everything was ready. The Emperor rose to his feet. Leaning over the ornate marble council table, he signed the death warrant again with a long flourish.

'If you would be so good as to countersign, *Magister*.'

Apodemius took the document from Constantius. I detected one white eyebrow shoot up in surprise before he took up the outsized pen and obeyed with his signature.

He handed the document to Constantius' notaries. We three bowed and exited the Presence with a shared sigh of relief.

'Eusebius must have known! He must have got that last order in time! He was trying to trap you in a murder, *Magister!*' Ahenobarbus protested. We were hurrying to bedchambers he had set aside for us.

'No, no, he didn't get the counter order in time. Or he could have saved Gallus for his own ends,' I argued.

'Gods and goddesses, I had to see it to believe it!' Apodemius exploded under his breath as he hurried ahead of us, pulling away from Ahenobarbus' shepherding arm. 'The hubris of that man!'

'What? What?' Ahenobarbus and I asked him in one breath.

'His signature! He had the audacity to sign himself, "Our Eternity, The Lord of the Entire Universe".'

'Is there such a title in the history of the Empire, *Magister*?' I asked.

Ahenobarbus rubbed his wild hair. 'Unfortunately, there is now.'

Chapter 23, Settling Accounts

—Roma, Spring, 355 AD—

I was home at last and for the first time not as a slave child, a returning freedman, or an unwelcome guest. I was the master of the house in which I grew up. I was fully in charge of affairs simply because there was no adult around with a better claim. Sadly, I was finally free to confirm my suspicions that this venerable house was not what it once was.

In my boyhood, I'd been one of dozens of slaves working in the Manlius House under *Matrona* Laetitia's watchful eye, and one of hundreds, perhaps even thousands, owned by the clan to work their vast holdings. I'd never visited the more distant properties to count heads and neither had Verus. Now we two asked ourselves just how much had been lost or saved over the last ten years?

Who and what did Leo actually inherit, if and when deeds could ever be found?

Somehow, the Manlius 'property,' such as these nameless souls were, still lived and labored outside Roma in offices, warehouses, pastures, and farmlands. Month after month, revenues trickled in through some combination of inertia and tradition, still directed to a business manager long gone. I suspected that foremen and rapacious tax collectors siphoned off most of the earnings, yet they made sure that token income reached us in the capital in fits and starts, if only to ensure that nothing in this conveniently opaque arrangement changed at our other end.

As soon as I returned from Mediolanum, I settled my accounts with the Castra paymaster—salary, expenses, and even a bonus regularly attached to 'imperial escort duties.' Verus and I made the most of every silver coin. It wasn't much to rebuild on, but Clodius' sleazy depredations hadn't completely destroyed us—only because the deeds stayed missing. Whatever our tiny heir to the Manlius House owed the world, we had reason to believe that Leo still possessed a great estate as well, if only we knew where to find the proof.

On the understanding that Clodius was unlikely to return, Verus spent a week cleaning out his 'improvements.' He tossed out the vulgar cushions and tacky decorations, tore down the tawdry window hangings, and rolled up the cheap rugs. During the Commander's absence on the battlefield, his pregnant North African provincial bride Kahina had struggled to learn the ways of a Roman matron and keep up appearances. The blind old Senator had supervised her choices for as long as he was able, but his sinking health—not fraying brocade covering the *triclinium*'s dining couches—had preoccupied her days before the civil war overturned the calm of Roma.

Now we ripped, scrubbed, and scoured. Some of the plaster walls around the garden were crumbling. We found the ancestral masks and house gods, all chipped and scratched, jumbled together in storage crates. We repaired the *lararium* and got the fountain flowing again.

We used our remaining slaves to scrub clean the old-fashioned black and white tiles of the public rooms. I called in an expert to re-grout or replace the most damaged sections. He wanted to put in modern colored mosaics, but I said no, we didn't even have enough cash to cover his repair fees. We loaded him down with early eggplants, pine nuts, and honey from the countryside, promising cash after the harvest.

The weeping Lavinia had dried her eyes and come back smiling from the apartment in Ostia to look after Leo. He was too big for a wet nurse but still too young to attend school. My boy was bright, but I couldn't afford a private tutor.

I put in long hours at the Castra Peregrina. On some days, I had to endure lengthy debriefings with specialists monitoring the East. On other days, I drafted a long report summarizing the end of the reign of Gallus as I had witnessed it.

My Castra supervisor ordered me to use the rest of my time on refresher lessons in updated coding, the latest route expansions, and Germanic border dialects.

I returned home late each evening with mixed feelings of worry over our finances and contentment with the boy. Leo always waited up for me. I delighted in reading at his bedside or devising new games and toys for him. But this wasn't enough to offset my gloom at his dreary prospects as the Roman scion of a great house in the final stages of decay.

Germanic language skills seemed less than useless these days, but those tedious lessons I'd taken in the Castra before the war, when I had angled for a posting close to home in Accounting and Customs, finally came in handy.

For many long nights by the light of an oil lamp, I reviewed the mess in which Clodius had left the Manlius estate. Our accounts were in deeper than that trench he'd sunk himself into on the night of his ludicrous *criobolium*. Even if Clodius' bookkeeping was an indecipherable tangle of confused I.O.U.'s and abandoned ledgers jammed onto a high shelf, the number of debtors turning up at our front gate each morning told the story clearly enough.

Many reputable Romans had extended Clodius credit on a promise that the finer points of legal appropriation would inevitably come with time. Until Clodius could locate the ownership papers, such lenders were prepared to gamble on his inflated promises of rich takings and higher social position.

I tried explaining that any loan to Clodius had been nothing more than a bad bet, an investment in nothing more than hot air, but they still demanded their cash back. Every time I headed down the streets of the Esquiline to remount the Caelian hill for the safety of the Castra on the summit, I had a pack of these greedy hounds flourishing Clodius' signature in my face and baying at me with foul language. Their rates of interest were criminal and now their threats were bordering on criminal as well. I began to worry for my physical safety.

I gave up my pleasant evenings at the Tavern of the Seven Sages with Cornelius. I couldn't afford to pay for the rounds at the rate of his drinking and anyway, his veteran's gossip from the field depressed me. For every repulse of the Frankish raiders up on the Rhenus our side won, it seemed there was another successful toehold by Alemanni mountain bands across our border from the northeast.

The Manlius household was sticking out a siege of its own. We kept the heavy oak gates bolted fast against our creditor parasites and their hired thugs. We even left the branches of the spreading fig tree outside unpruned, in the vain hope that by summer, the ancient tree's massive foliage would completely obscure access to our bankrupt home.

I was under personal siege in more ways than one. I dreaded the day I would be summoned to discuss my next assignment. I had privately faced up to the truth, that it was now—not later—that a choice between guarding Leo's welfare and moving to a new field posting must be made. He was too young to accompany me and he needed an education first. Whenever the next assignment came, I would be forced to refuse it and resign from the *schola* to look for work in Roma that would pay our daily bills, if not our debtors.

I hadn't spoken to Apodemius for almost two months when I got a summons to go to his office at the end of another workday—an early start for the nocturnal spymaster.

His back was turned to the door as his deaf assistant ushered me in. The old man was marking Alemannic incursions into Noricum by moving little painted pins across that much-pierced wall map. His hands were more claw-like and distended than ever. Some of the pins slipped through his fingers and scattered on the floor. I knelt down and gathered them up, holding them out in my palm as he checked reports on his desk and shifted the little markers around.

There were more barbarian pins than Roman military along the northern garrisons of the Lower Rhenus. Barbatio and Roxana would both be up there by now, attached in their separate fashions to General Silvanus. Looking at the clusters of enemy pins massed across the wide river, I could only hope the situation looked better on the ground than it did on Apodemius' wall.

In the East, I saw that General Ursicinus had advanced legionaries of the *Fretensis* and *Flavia* in a defensive string closer to the Persian front.

By contrast, my home province of Numidia Militaris looked downright serene, its rectangles of pins neatly lined up in towns I knew well, like Lambaesis and Theveste. I thought of the humdrum duties of the aqueduct architects and irrigation plumbers of the *Legio III Augusta* with affectionate envy.

Finally Apodemius finished his poking and piercing and settled down behind his broad desk.

'You've been dodging your immediate superior, Marcus Gregorianus Numidianus. Sit down, sit down.'

I took the well-worn stool opposite.

'I attend all my courses.'

'You missed your evaluation meeting.'

'I had a scheduling problem. I have responsibilities and distractions at home.'

'Come live at the barracks.'

'The child, Leontus—'

'Ah, yes. I'd forgotten. Roxana left him here in Roma when she joined Silvanus, didn't she?'

'He belongs here in Roma, *Magister.*'

'You're saying that he belongs with you and you need more time.'

'Yes, *Magister.*'

Apodemius tinkered with one of the ivory pieces that always sat on a *latrunculi* board next to his desk. He had never asked me to play the 'game of brigands.'

'Finished your report on Antiochia?'

'Yes, *Magister.* I submitted it to the scribes two days ago for copying, but I'm not sure what my simple observations are good for.'

'All observations are important. I've summoned that Frank, Meroveus, to dictate a full account of his time in the Palace as well.'

'I found Meroveus very reliable. I'd be happy to see him restored to dignity and usefulness.'

'Good. I may find further uses for the man, if he's willing and does a thorough job. It's important that the record is absolutely complete, from the beginning of Thalassius' accounts to the last instant of Gallus' death.'

'Why? Have you found out what happened to the Emperor's last command? Did it ever exist or did he invent that to avoid blame for his cousin's death?'

'I have been able to find out nothing, not even who allegedly carried this mysterious counter order. It makes me very uneasy. Given his history, it's understandable the Emperor is highly sensitive to having more Constantine deaths laid at his door.'

'But the order was addressed to Eusebius, so can't you—?'

'Eusebius is the last person I intend to query for clarification about the missing order. Perhaps it never existed. In the meantime, the official archives must contain the fullest possible story as political insurance.'

'Surely what's done is done. You can't reverse the shadows on a sundial or make a water clock flow backwards. Gallus is dead. Is there anyone left to care?'

'Yes, his half-brother Julian.'

'You heard the Emperor yourself. Julian is a kid with his nose stuck in books who will never amount to anything.'

'Have we taught you nothing, Numidianus? Outside that window may be nothing more than another ordinary Roman day in the reign of Constantius II, but inside this office, on that map up there, on this desk, and in our heads, we keep our eyes fixed on the horizon for *whatever* might lie ahead.'

He *was* worried and moreover, he was allowing me to see it. For a moment I waited in silence for what I hoped wasn't coming—a transfer out of Roma.

'By the way, how are the Germanic lessons coming?'

'Slowly. One thing's for certain—it's not a language with a future. Surely they'll learn Latin soon enough, so it feels like a waste of time.'

'Well, practice up while you can.'

'A writing system would help.'

'Well, you're in luck. The Germanics master tells me we have a new teaching tool—at least for Gothic dialect. It's a translation of the Christians' stories and whatnot from Greek into Gothic by some barbarian missionary, a bishop named Ulfilas. He comes from a colony of Greeks captured by Goths years ago. He must be a very clever man. He devised a new alphabet for them. I supposed it's a bit late to hope we might recruit him to our service.'

'Probably, *Magister*.' I gave him a wan smile, but I felt as listless as I sounded. I realized Apodemius was assessing me, judging my spirits and resilience for a new posting. Making idle conversation about this Ulfilas character was long enough for him to determine that I wasn't ready.

'Anyway, we've recently acquired a partial copy for our library. Look it over. You never know what you may need for the next posting.'

I was about to say that I'd be resigning the moment any such posting came up, but he was already selecting fresh memos off a pile near his mouse cage for his next meeting.

'Oh, Numidianus, our man in Carthago, Jovan, should be waiting outside by now. Send him in as you go, will you?'

ᚠᚠᚠ

On my way out that evening, I stopped at the Temple of Jupiter Redux on the western edge of the Castra compound to offer up a private prayer for the dead, especially one gentle Numidian woman who would never return.

The temple had once faced the street but was now smothered behind a modern building constructed only a few feet in front of its classical facade. The temple was falling into serious neglect and little visited these days by the preoccupied *agentes* who hurried past on duty. Most working agents didn't go in for the Christian state cult and in the meantime, even bloodless pagan rituals had fallen out of fashion.

Inside the dark marble chamber, the altar stood naked of flowers or offerings. The close air hung stale with lingering traces of centuries-old incense. With housecleaning preying on my mind, I resolved to return with rags to polish down the ancient plaques mounted by grateful *peregrini* of the past.

I hesitated before leaving the Castra compound in order to check the traffic along the darkening street but I saw no creditor to harangue or threaten me. I headed north along the Vicus Cyclopus for home.

It was a tranquil evening. Mothers called their children from play in nearby parks to supper. Housewives shouted to each other over my head as they resolved some humorous drama of the day and slammed their shutters shut with a friendly wave. Guard dogs barked as I passed their door and were silenced with a scrap tossed from a kitchen window.

I saw slits of light appear behind the shutters as these city folks lit their lamps. The hours were lengthening from 'winter hours' to 'summer hours.' The spring was drawing to a close. Perhaps we'd have some early harvests and new shipments to ease the credit crunch that furrowed Verus' brow each night as he unbolted the back alley gate to the servants' entrance so I could slip in unobserved.

The chill of the old temple had lodged in my heart. For weeks on end, I'd been detouring, dodging, and ditching shadowy figures on my tail. Sometimes when I stood fast and challenged them, they were no more threatening than another tailor's lackey clamoring for back payment for a set of Clodius' fringed tunics. But sometimes they were more persistent and shouted that if I didn't pay up, they knew how to treat bankrupts like me once and for all, so I 'wouldn't forget.'

I hurried along with the stream of people heading out to dine or off to the theater in the crowded valley below the Castra.

As I passed with the crowd under the great Claudia Aqueduct that ran the length of the Caelian Hill, I stopped in the shadow of the massive stone arches overhead and checked behind me from sheer habit.

Nothing seemed amiss until I spotted a tall man in a dark hooded cloak mingling with light-dressed pedestrians. His heavy coverage looked out of place on this balmy evening.

I was growing as fretful as an old woman. After all, the man showed no interest in me. He might well be nothing more than a guard from the *Cohors V Vigilum*, the security forces that were headquartered a few blocks away. Still, he made me nervous. Not that I didn't have the fighting skill to take on one man, or even two, but I hoped I didn't have to.

I measured my steps more carefully now and slipped once or twice into a doorway or wine stall to see if the stranger passed me by. He kept an even distance between us. Whenever I checked, he had his back turned to peruse some cobbler's sign or a brothel's billboard of rates and services. Now I sped up my pace and finally lost him in the narrower, quieter streets of the Esquiline.

It had all been just a figment of my jumpy imagination.

The next evening I worked late, double-checking the scribes' finished copy of my report on Antiochia to be sent upstairs. The streets would be empty and just to feel safer, I exited by a portico that sat at the back end of the compound, the *Aedicula Genii Castrorum*. It shut off our main courtyard from the foundations of the great aqueduct next door. No road penetrated the waterworks' massive foundation at this point, so the gate was inconvenient and little used. I even had to borrow the key to unlock it.

I clambered in the dark through refuse and past a collection of drunks sheltering in the aqueduct's arch to find myself in a maze of obscure alleys and underlit back streets on the other side. I was sure that any common gangster hired to harass me for repayments would be flummoxed by my disappearance.

But my doubtful instincts had not been so misguided, after all. The tall man in the hooded cloak caught up with me twenty minutes later, tipped off by some watcher no doubt, as I strode up through the night toward our alley entrance. Realizing I was on to his surveillance, he gave chase and was only about five hundred feet away when I pounded on the back gate and eased through, breathless, to the safety of Verus' worried embrace.

I was safe, but the stranger had now seen where I lived and how to corner me. I had no doubt that might be his object, and for some reason, I felt, none of us in the household was safe now.

I slept in the barracks all the next week in the hope that my hefty pursuer would conclude I'd been transferred out of Roma. I communicated with Verus by messenger but perhaps the messengers carrying my notes back and forth tipped him off, because the first time I ventured out again at dusk to slip home in the lingering flow of sedan chairs and pedestrians, I thought I spotted him again.

My nerves weren't fraying—I was too seasoned an *agens* for that—but I confess to a heightened sense of prudence. I was now the only protection Leo had against the world. I couldn't afford to play loose with my life, enjoying a single youth's bravado in the face of some thuggery over debts. Whatever happened to me from now on might be at Leo's permanent expense.

I raced to the Porta Aurelia to ask Cornelius for backup. He was the kind of rough-and-ready drinking pal who wouldn't be tempted years later to dredge up the story of an ugly creditors' brawl as a foothold over me for the next rung in promotion.

But Cornelius wasn't hanging around the tavern, the serving girl Delicia told me.

By the time I reached our back alley again, no one lay in wait. It was all a mirage, like those visions that appear to Roman soldiers patrolling the western desert.

But there *were* suspicious scuffle marks all over the paving stones at our back gate, as if muddy feet had scraped and struggled for a foothold. Someone had tried to enter our property and ambush me within our very walls.

I circled the block and hid myself, watching the front gate. Cornelius arrived just then, armed up to his jug ears, but for once sober as a Vestal. We crouched down and waited together, just as if we were back in an army camp on late night sentry duty.

'We've waited at least an hour now,' he growled. 'Nobody's trying to break in. My knees are getting stiff.'

'Something's up, I'm sure of it.'

'I'm counting the drinks you owe me.'

'Shush.'

As the moon reached its fullest point, we spotted a man slipping along the walls from the other end of the street. We wouldn't have noticed if it hadn't been for a dog barking in a courtyard a couple of houses away. The hound had stuck his snout underneath his gate as the stranger passed him by on his way toward our fig tree.

Only this time the tall man was accompanied by a smaller man in unseasonable trousers and heavy wrappings around his head. I glimpsed very dark-skinned arms and a bad limp to this second man's gait. The two of them were more conspicuous now and even if the second man was lighter in build, his movements seemed more sinister and unpredictable.

I guessed that one of our creditors had decided to exact a price for the tens of thousands we still owed—either through outright burglary, kidnapping, or worse. The tall man had failed to gain entry to the house by the back wall and now he'd gone and fetched a light-footed accomplice.

I waited, peering around the base of a statue, but they were too far away for us to notice much more.

Then the taller man pulled his hood off in the warm night. The moonlight flooding the street shone full on his head.

It was Barbatio, his oiled black hair reflecting the light of a street torch.

Cornelius was ready to jump on him, but I put a cautioning arm out.

'I know this man,' I whispered. 'He's no mere burglar.'

We slipped forward to near where he'd stopped and I prayed that bloody dog wouldn't start up howling again.

Barbatio spoke to the other fellow, but I couldn't make out what he said. His accomplice nodded but said nothing.

'What's he doing?' Cornelius asked. 'What's all the mystery for, if he knows you?'

'The gods only know but obviously he doesn't want to be seen here. He's supposed to be serving up on the Rhenus, not skulking around Roma. He says I've ruined his career.'

'So, when you float past on the Tiber face down tomorrow morning, he'll say the Fates gave you what you deserved, while he has some alibi cooked up for himself back in the north?'

The smaller man tested the front gate, which was firmly bolted. This alarmed Barbatio, who drew back into the shadows and quickly covered up his face with his hood, in case someone should see him.

Then he gestured for the small man to go up the fig tree.

Not for the first time I saw how the tree's generous, thick branches, so useful in fending off pesky creditors and their persistent hooligans, spread into a handy staircase for anyone who dared climb up the trunk. I'd done it myself as a boy and earned many a scolding from Verus. It was an easy means of scaling the Manlius walls and dropping down into the front courtyard leading to the atrium within but it was something only a true scoundrel would tackle.

Barbatio and his pal had figured this out now. They circled the tree. Its thick foliage hid their silent gesticulations from our sight.

Barbatio prepared to hoist the other into the depths of the leaves. The smaller man took hold of the lower branches and lifted himself up, getting a solid foothold at the crook of a limb and the trunk. They were as noiseless as thieves. We waited but it seemed that Barbatio was too heavy to follow up the tree.

It was our only chance to bring down Barbatio first and then tackle his lighter pal before he got inside the property. Cornelius saw it as fast as I did. The two of us sped down the street along the wall. We pulled out our daggers and caught Barbatio in a pincer move, with Cornelius circling the man's thick neck and yanking him backwards to expose his broad hairy belly underneath the cloak.

'I've got him!' Cornelius grunted. 'Get the little guy.'

But I couldn't risk leaving Barbatio to Cornelius like that. I knew where his armor gave way to his tunic. I placed the point of my *pugio* deep into his thick stomach just short of cutting the thick skin.

'If you want to save your reputation, Barbatio, you'll take a quick ride out of Roma tonight. General Silvanus must be missing you by now,' I said.

'Not before I finish my business with you,' he growled. He made a grab for me and missed. He wore the precious ring he'd swallowed back in Istria. It was the only thing that caught the moonlight in the thick leafy shadows.

'Killing me won't help your reputation. And smarter men than you have tried to harm the child.'

He gave a malevolent chuckle from that wine vat he called a chest. 'It's not killing you I had in mind but you've slandered me and I'm getting my own back. We're settling our accounts, here and now!'

He gave a sudden wrench and nearly got free of Cornelius' grasp, so I dug the *pugio* back into his brawny hide.

'I didn't decide your assignment on the Rhenus.'

'No, but you called me a slave trader, a flesh vendor, and a pimp.'

'You broke the law. You sold Roman citizens. Nobody would blame me if I sliced you in two right now.'

'If you know what's good for you, you won't say what you saw or heard tonight. I'm getting even now, but I had nothing to do with this, right? As far as you know, I'm in Mogontiacum,' Barbatio spit at me. 'You heard me? I'm in Mogontiacum. I had nothing to do with this!'

He wrenched himself again, desperate to get free of Cornelius' expert hold.

The dark assassin crouched, frozen on the ledge by our threats. I heard the leaves rustle above us as he hastened back down to Barbatio's aid. Heaving himself clumsily down by the arms from a branch, he dropped to the street on small feet, half falling onto the pavement.

'Please stop,' he said.

Only it wasn't a man. I whirled around and saw two familiar eyes welling up with tears out of a face completely blackened by relentless sun and weathered by the winds of some harsh and foreign fields.

I was staring at Kahina.

'Let this man go. He spent all his savings to get me back . . . and waited for my delivery for weeks. I'm home, Marcus, I'm home.'

CHAPTER 24, THE READING BENCH

—THE *DOMUS* MANLIUS—

Ulysses returned to Ithaca from decades of war and exile so changed by hardship that even his own wife wasn't sure it was her husband. Only when he corrected Penelope, as she instructed her servant to carry in a bed he had carved for them himself from an immovable oak tree, did the faithful wife recognize that this stranger must be her hero, returned at long last.

Kahina had changed, too, and not just in appearance. Our Leo looked at her with quiet courtesy, expressing no joy or even recognition of the mother he hadn't seen for three years. She smiled at him from across the room or over a table, but with a look filled with sadness at the missing years. Lavinia urged the little boy to kiss his mother and to show her his toys. He was obedient. Kahina turned away then, her eyes wet with tears of hurt and loss.

The relentless Hispanic sun had creased her smooth olive skin into roughened mahogany. Her hands were crisscrossed with thickened veins, her nails broken and peeling, and her palms covered with a horn-like callous. The soles of her feet were thickened into a flat and shiny crust by months of trodding over rough brush. Her delicate ankles bore white stripes, thick scars where the shackles had torn her skin again and again and healed over. Her thick hair had turned a strange red color, not from henna, but from hunger.

For the first few hours of her homecoming, I struggled to find the graceful Numidian maid, mother, and matron, in this unkempt and almost inarticulate slave woman. I drew her out as slowly as the army doctor Ari used to withdraw darts or arrow shafts in soldiers fresh off the battlefield.

I fought off my urge to embrace or even touch her. It was as if her mind, as well as her body, was wounded in many secret places. She pulled away from me and even looked on Verus, the cook, and Lavinia with distrust. She was afraid any one of us might betray her to slave drivers hunting for her in far away Hispania Nova. For the first few weeks, she wanted to sleep with the slaves in their plain quarters behind the kitchen.

Gradually we pieced together what had happened to her. Along with other officers' wives and families, Kahina fled the conquering forces of Constantius II after the decisive debacle in Mursa. With a large party of other refugees, she trudged her way northwards, making a dangerous night crossing of the sleeve of water separating Gallia from the diocese of Britannia. Magnentius had been popular with the colonists up there and some of the refugees had contacts and guarantees of help. Until Paulus Catena arrived on his campaign of retribution and province-wide terror, many Romans of Britannia sheltered and fed the noble escapees.

But Catena demolished the Britannic resistance, the provincial leadership, and with his indiscriminate cruelty, Roma's reputation in a few short weeks.

It was my nightmares come true. Catena had captured Kahina. She was a prize among women as the wife of the famous Commander Atticus Manlius Gregorius, but Kahina was wise enough to disguise her complete identity. Catena regarded the young Numidian lady with personal disdain. He was too ignorant or stupid to realize that the wife of Magnentius' *magister militum* would have been a dazzling trophy to present to Constantius' court.

We didn't get many more details from her from that point in the story on, as if she had ceased to be herself once in Catena's custody. All she would say was that one morning, somewhere on the southbound road before reaching Arelate, she had been separated, along with a handful of other able-bodied prisoners, from the main convoy of prisoners.

They were trundled off in a train of wagons with their backs to the morning sun. The weather grew warmer and her spirits lifted. It felt as though she was returning to her North African home. She had asked the name of the road. It was the Via Domita, the road to Hispania. Their final destination was Gallaecia.

Her hopes sank that night with the setting sun. She'd been sold through a dealer to a notorious *latifundium*, one of the enormous estates that put Italia's small farmers out of business centuries ago in the race to feed Roma.

The Gallaecian foremen didn't care whether their slaves had a past of any kind, much less a political or aristocratic one. They didn't even care if they had once had a name. They shackled Kahina afresh and threw her into the fields to join the thousands of other tormented souls fated to sow and pick until they died right there among the sheaves of wheat and barrels of olives. She was told that if she made trouble, the next stop would be the mines from which no slave resurfaced.

At that point in the story, Kahina always turned her blackened face away from me. Her expression turned inward and even though her lips continued to move, she had stopped using words I understood. If she was trying to tell me how brutal it had been, these were not Latin words, only the strange dialect of her owners. I assured her that it was safe now, she could tell me in Latin or the dialect of our beloved Numidia, but she sat there silently mouthing and shaking her head.

Her shoulders, once flawlessly alluring and soft, bore long, shiny scars of lashes—crueler than any I'd had to suffer, even when whipped to fake my cover as a runaway for my first mission. When I saw how deep their whips had cut into her back muscles, I wondered how she had survived at all. She had been flayed like a fish in the market, but still she had lived.

After a time, I realized that talking to us about her enslavement was upsetting her over and over again. We left her to sit in the garden watching Leo play in the good weather but sometimes we caught her pulling up the flowers, as if she thought she would please Verus by harvesting his garden like a wheat field. I realized her mind was as scarred as her body. Would she heal with time?

In my spare time at the Castra Peregrina, I called up the *agentes'* reports from the mail circuits in Hispania. Toiling over maps of their routes and delivery registration books, combined with Kahina's piecemeal comments about harvesting in view of the mountains with the smell of sea winds, I pinned down her captors to one of the biggest of the coastal estates.

On the map it stretched for miles and miles. The riders reported an enterprise that herded sheep and cattle, as well as exported olive oil, wheat, and wine to Roma. I wondered how a beautiful and valuable prisoner-of-war with no hope of rescue had ended up there broken and abused, sleeping only a few hours a night in a crowd of hundreds of unwashed slaves in an open-air barn.

Even more curious, after all his bluff and bluster, how had Barbatio located Catena's dirty-handed chain of middlemen through which he'd negotiated her release? Of course, Catena himself was a Hispaniard, and that might have made tracking his crime network somewhat easier.

I discovered the answer where I least expected one day, on the huge map hanging over Apodemius' desk.

Kahina's final incarceration wasn't far from the Castra Legionis, the permanent headquarters of the *Legio VII Germina Felix*, one of the toughest outfits in the service. Barbatio and his slave links must have been tied to someone in that legion.

There was nothing I could do, for now, but Roman justice, even the amateur variety, has a long memory. I wrote down what I knew for the archives and vowed to wait for the day of reckoning I was sure would come.

At night, Kahina finally consented to sleep alone on clean linens in the Commander's great bed, as big as the one built by Ulysses for Penelope. This had been their marital bed, where she'd given birth to our Leo. But the emptiness and luxury of her old bedroom frightened her. She screamed in her sleep and kicked her legs free of invisible shackles. Lavinia would rush to her with warm drinks, clean sponges, fresh pillows, and a word of comfort, but the oblivion of sleep only lasted a few hours before the nightmares returned.

In the garden, I asked her why she so often woke up engulfed in terror.

'I dream I'm still in Gallaecia. I feel the chains and the whips. I reach for my ankles and then I feel faint with relief.'

'The dreams will fade,' I promised. 'You will come back to us.'

But what might have worked for me in Mursa was too great a risk in her mental state. I wasn't about to take her back to Hispania to put her phantoms to rest.

⚔⚔⚔

'Here's a court order demanding we hand over the deeds to one of Clodius' creditors,' I told Verus one night. 'We might be within a month of eviction.'

We had known that sooner or later it would come to formal legal actions. Our days of outrunning indignant gamblers and cloak-makers couldn't last forever. Even the lowlife of Roma had friends in high places, debts to call in, and ready cash to pay lawyers.

'We looked everywhere,' Verus said.

'We'll just have to look again.'

'We ain't going to find nothing. No deeds and no deed box. The whole place was just turned upside down by them plasterers we got in, wasn't it?'

'Clodius must have looked hard and he couldn't find it.'

Verus nodded. 'Clodius asked the old man before he died, more than once, but the Senator would ask, "Surely Marcus knows?" and smile.'

'Well, I don't, Verus. The Senator was taunting Clodius. How could I know?'

'Well, of course not. You was off in the field with the Commander. It drove Clodius nuts.'

We sat, disconsolate, over yet another bowl of *puls*. Even our wine was diluted to baby's swill.

'The last time we had plasterers in was when Leo was born,' Verus said, 'and they was a lot cheaper then, I'll tell you.'

'Why?' I would let Verus ramble. After so long alone, he liked having company.

'Repairs in the old man's library, as I recall. You was away, of course, off riding up and down the Empire with that mailbag of yours. The lady was still lying in and the baby was about three or four days old. It seemed a strange time to start in on house repairs, but no, nobody listens to ol' Verus about peace and quiet for the newborn and his mum. Anyway, in comes all these men with their buckets of powder and pastes and sandpaper and what not. Batty old coot, the Senator. Had to have his way, no matter what kind of a mess it made.'

This was Verus' way of reliving the happier days. I smiled and said, 'I miss the Senator as much as you. Maybe more.'

'Oh, sure, but lordy, what a to-do! There was a little bit of rain that week and he comes out of his study down them steps all of a sudden, and says that plaster was crumbling onto his precious books.

'"Get me some repairmen, Verus", he says, but if the roof was falling in on him, he didn't look all that fussed about it. In fact, he looked happy as a faun with his pipes.'

'Where was Clodius in all this?'

'Out. Whenever there was work to be done, even *watching* work to be done, Clodius made sure he was "out." Well, of course, he was in a big snit about the little boy taking his place in the line-up, you know. Poor ol' Clodius, panting after his Manlius money to come, like a charioteer just about to bust out of the cage and grab all the laurels, when little Leo turns up, and all. He got drunk for days.'

Verus was a little drunk himself, although it was hard to see how our harmless retainer could get inebriated on just a few cups of pinkish fountain water. I sent him off to bed.

I felt sentimental after all that chat about the Senator. Oil lamp in hand, I crossed the atrium garden with no one for company but the lonely trickle of the fountain as I mounted the steps to the Senator's study at the back of the house. With Clodius gone, the books were safe from sale for the moment and Verus had left the key hidden on the lintel. I unstuck the swollen door and entered the stuffy room.

I sniffed traces of the old man himself, his mix of bath oils and ink, leather and dusty upholstery. I felt eight years old all over again.

I went over to the bookshelves and scanned the beloved volumes I'd read to him as his sight faded. Verus' vigilance had saved the precious volumes from Soren the Bookseller's eager clutches. Here, right where I expected, was our own copy of Plutarch's *Parallel Lives*. By the time we'd got to the estimable Plutarch, we two were old friends—the slave boy and the famous blind orator, the Numidian bastard and the wise old aristocrat who had dared to take a Gallo-Roman noblewoman for his second wife.

Unlike Verus, I would never have called the Senator a batty old coot, but he had been an obstinate, hard-driving, and noble soul. Of course, he must have been upset that plaster was falling on his beloved books.

I looked up at the ceiling to examine it for damage. For a minute, I stared, my brain not taking in the conundrum, for the ceiling wasn't made of plaster at all, but carved wood. Of course it was. The Senator had always been very proud of his study's expensive wooden ceiling.

It was a strange story, Verus' tale tonight, of plaster crumbling off the ceiling onto the Senator's valuable library.

It couldn't be true.

I sat down in my grandfather's leather seat and pondered. Verus must have meant that the stucco *on the walls* was flaking. Here and there, I saw, the murals depicting a garden in ancient Greece peopled by mythical birds and animals were dented and scratched.

But they weren't flaking. Verus had distinctly said plasterers, not painters.

The old carpets bought from an eastern merchant decades ago still covered the tiled floor. I couldn't help but make a mental note that they needed a hard beating by one of the slaves. But there were no plaster flakes on the floor.

Shoved along the walls was the same old step stool for pulling books off the upper shelves and in the corner stood the same basin on a tripod for the Senator to wash his hands before coming down to dine. Verus had left the old man's writing desk just as it was when he died, with his old wax tablets and *stili* of bone, iron, and brass waiting for his erudite hand to jot down a quotation or two. Once his eyesight was gone, they had waited in vain.

I had learned to write with that iron one.

Long before his sight had finally disappeared and long before I'd learned the Latin and Greek classics by heart, I would sit down on the solid bench, built like a step sticking out from the wall for me. There was that same rug laid across it now, that worn out rug that always scratched my bare thighs as I worked hard to learn my words.

Then the Senator had checked each letter, by tracing his finger across the wax, reluctant to admit that his vision wasn't what it had been . . .

Anyway, in comes all these men with their buckets of powder and pastes and sandpaper and what not. Batty old coot. Had to have his way, no matter what kind of a mess it made.

Had to have what way?

The rug was still there covering the low-slung protrusion along the wall. Thinking of how long it had lain there, I decided that it was time to shake off the sentiment and clean the study out. If strangers' hands were invading us soon to tally up our worth and auction us off to slavering cronies of Clodius and their claims, I'd be the first to salvage and pack up what might mean something someday to the last Manlius heir.

And anyway, no one would want a forgotten Senator's lap rug worn thin by a little slave's squirming.

I pulled up the long rug and folded it, gasping as a cloud of dust exploded up my nose and left me blinking through tears. It was late. Tomorrow I'd do an inventory of the books we could keep for ourselves and the ones we'd pile up for Soren's collection wagon. We'd save the Senator's inlaid desk and his busts of Pliny and Cicero, but have to sell off the set of marble and onyx chairs that had been in the family for centuries. We'd give away the basin and the—

I held up the lamp and walked back across the room, dropping the old rug to one side with a thump that sent up another puff of dust.

The bench on which I'd sat for ten years had been finished off with plaster. Smoothed and sanded, the hard surface was not only not flaking, but as fresh as the day the Senator laid the rug over it.

But was it the same plaster on which I'd first sat?

I went to the Senator's desk for his iron stylus and jabbed at the corner of the bench, scratching a thin line, then stabbing, then working away in futile digs and dents at the crumbly surface.

The lamp sputtered out and I dropped the stylus and ran to the servants' quarters.

'Verus,' I shook him awake. 'Verus, get me a hammer and chisel!'

'Thieves? Burglars?'

I laughed and said, 'No, just a crazy idea, a crazy, crazy idea!'

I ran back across the garden and ran up the steps to the study with a fresh lamp from the hall.

Verus followed me, wrapped only in his underclothes, his little potbelly like a melon hanging on his withered frame. As he watched, I slammed down hard on the corner of the seat. A chunk of white plaster fell away.

'Get yourself some tools, man! He said I would know, he said *I would know. This was the only place in the house that belonged to me alone.*'

Verus came back with an iron wedge used to pound meat.

'The cook'll kill me if I break this, she will,' he warned me.

'It's here, Verus. It's got to be here. He knew that only I cared about this spot. Clodius would never touch it.'

We slammed again and again at the plaster, sending shards of it flying as I destroyed the most precious corner, the most cherished memory of my entire childhood to pieces. I worked away in the half-light and finally, my chisel hit harder than plaster.

'I've found it, Verus, I've found it!'

I hugged the old bird and he ran off to get more tools.

An hour later, we stood back. What had been a long solid platform about a foot and a half high jutting out of the wall was now a mound of plaster rubble piled high on three sides of a metal box with iron bindings.

'It's the old deed box, my boy,' Verus said. 'I ain't seen it since *Matrona* Laetitia kept that ring-key on her finger. But has it got anything in it? That's the question, son, that's the question.'

There was nothing left but the suspenseful moment when I pulled out the ring hanging on the cord around my neck, the same ring the Senator had imbedded in my childhood *bulla* as security. I inserted it into the old-fashioned padlock clamping the box shut.

I was twisting the key when the rusting padlock fell into two pieces in my hands. The key still fitted neatly into it, but the hinge just gave way.

It would take us the rest of the night to scan the papers inside. On top were the documents for the Sardinian cornfields, the Calabrian beehives, and then papers concerning shared ownership in pastureland with lumberyards attached in Cisalpine Gallia inherited by the Commander's mother.

Below that were the deeds and old accounts for five hundred acres of Falernian vines—significant vineyards in Sicily, and a minor one in Setia—as well as a small estate on the banks of the Liris and two oyster beds in Baiae.

I smiled to see three rough African certificates for silver workshops in Africa that the Commander had acquired during his first tour. It was on that tour that he met my mother.

There was a pig herd in Parma from which we still received a few hams out of the hundreds it seemed we were owed and yet more hives in Hybla, the famous home of bees in Sicily, from which, I guessed offhand, we were getting only one tenth of the revenues due. The deeds to the docks and apartment in Ostia were bundled in a leather pocketbook with deeds to a villa overlooking the Gulf of Naples. The last rent on that had been paid seven years ago.

'I assumed that place had been sold off,' Verus said in wonder. 'It's got a view worth a million *solidi*.'

The light cracking through the windows told us how long we'd sat there, transfixed by relief. It was enough joy for one night.

It was enough joy for one year.

At the bottom of the box lay a sack of red silk velvet tied up with a golden cord.

'Gods of Olympus,' Verus said, 'That's the old man's will.'

There, in a handwriting I had thought I'd never see again, witnessed by seven citizens of Roma, the Senator had bequeathed all these riches to the Commander, his son.

In the event of the Commander's untimely death, the entire estate was to go to 'the freedman Marcus Manlius Gregorianus Numidianus.'

I gasped to see he had included the clan's name in his bequest to me. My last doubts were silenced. The Senator had known indeed that I was his bastard grandson.

But under that there was a codicil cancelling out the bequest to me. It was initialed by one of his previous witnesses, none other than the wily old Picenus who had done Clodius out of his hopes.

The two old men had been friends. Perhaps the two old men had even been confidants.

Had to have his way, no matter what kind of a mess it made . . . I imagined the old Senator on that glorious day he had called in the plasterers. He had been so eager to enshrine his legal heir's fortune on paper he had not even waited the traditional nine days for his daughter-in-law to rise from her birthing couch for the Ceremony of Recognition.

I read to Verus by the rising light of dawn, ' ... to my grandson, Gregorius Manlius Leontus, to be administered under the trusteeship of the freedman Marcus Manlius Gregorianus Numidianus, until he comes of age.'

It was exactly as I would have wished it. There was still a generous stipend for me to ensure my lifetime as trustee. The Senator had laid his plans and only his sudden murder had kept us from understanding in full his wise and secretive precautions.

Verus wanted to rush and wake Kahina and tell her everything was going to be all right after all.

But Kahina was sleeping late this morning. She had suffered no nightmares at all during our fevered hours of happy demolition.

'No, Verus,' I said. 'Let her sleep. Let her sleep as long as she wants.'

The End

A note from the publishers:

Have you read all of the *Embers of Empire* adventures by Q. V. Hunter?

The Assassin's Veil, Embers of Empire, Vol. I
Usurpers, Embers of Empire, Vol. II
The Wolves of Ambition, Embers of Empire, Vol. IV
The Deadly Caesar, Embers of Empire, Vol. V
The Burning Stakes, Embers of Empire, Vol. VI
The Purple Shroud, Embers of Empire, Vol. VII
The Treason of Friends, Embers of Empire, Vol. VIII
The Prefect's Rope, Embers of Empire, Vol. IX

If you are enjoying the *Embers of Empire* series, please post a review on your blog or reading platform, e.g. Amazon, Goodreads, Smashwords, or Library Thing.

Corrections should be sent directly to this address: eyesandears.editions@gmail.com

Would you like to know when new Q.V. Hunter novels come out? Just send an e-mail address to:

eyesandears.editions@gmail.com
subject: Q.V. Hunter Updates

Your information will not be used for any other purpose.

Our warmest thanks,
Editorial Department
Eyes and Ears Editions

PLACES AND GLOSSARY

agens, agentes in rebus—the imperial department of road inspectors, couriers, and customs regulators (also intelligence gatherers)

Aila—Aqaba, Jordan

Alemanni—a Germanic tribe, the principal forerunners of modern Germanophone Swiss

Antoniana colonia Tyana—Kemerhisar, Turkey

Archelais—Aksaray, Turkey

Arelate—Arles, France

Antiochia—Antakya, Turkey

bagaudae—peasant insurgents rebellious over landlord abuses in the remoter areas of Late Roman Gallia and Hispania

Bononia—Boulogne, France

Britannia—Britain

bulla—amulet worn by Roman children for protection from the gods

domesticus, domestici—imperial household assistant and guards

caldarium—the hottest room in the regular sequence of bathing rooms; after the *caldarium*, bathers would progress back through the *tepidarium*, moderately warm room, to the coolest room, the *frigidarium*

Camulodunum—Colchester, England

Campi Canini—a region in the area of modern-day Bellinzona, Switzerland

Carthago—Carthage, Tunis, Tunisia

Castra Legionis—Léon, Spain

Castra Peregrina—the barracks on the Caelian Hill in Rome, Italy build for the *peregrini*, soldiers detached for special service in Rome from the provincial armies. The Castra later became the headquarters for the military couriers and then the Empire's secret services, the *frumentarii* until their disbanding by Emperor Diocletian. They were

succeeded by a reformed service, the agentes in rebus.
The ruins of a part of the and several inscriptions
connected with them we *castra* re found in 1905 under
the Convent of the Little Company of Mary, just
southeast of S. Stefano Rotondo.

carceres—starting cages used in chariot races

clarus—a medium rank of imperial official.

clarissimus—the third rank of imperial official

Colonia Pietas Iulia Pola Pollentia Herculanea—Pola, Croatia

Coenum Gallicanum—a lost Roman station in what is modern
 Anatolia, Turkey

contubernalis—tent mate

cornicen—a junior army officer in the class of *aeneator,* or horn
 signaller, playing a *cornu*

criobolium—pagan rite sacrificing a ram (see *taurobolium*)

curiosus, curiosi—an insulting nickname for the *agentes in rebus*

Cursus Clabunaris—the part of the state road network reinforced
 to carry heavy cargo

Cursus Publicus—the Roman Empire's state road and stopover
 network

the Dravus River—the Drava River

the Danuvius River—the Danube river

diplomata—imperial travel certificates for use of the *Cursus
 Publicus*

peregrinus, peregrini—foreigners, aliens, here referring to non-
 Romanborn agents

Diocaesarea—Tsipori, Israel

Diospolis, Colonia Lucia Septimia Severa Diospolis—Lod, Israel

dispensator—majordomo

domina—lady, honorific for mistress of household

domus—house, household

elogia—traditional elegy

essedarius—chariot fighter

evectio—permit to travel by public post

fibula—shoulder fastener or brooch

flamen—Roman priest

Forum Julii—Fréjus, France

frumentarius, frumentarii—precursors of the *agentes in rebus*, disbanded by Diocletian for corruption

furnus, furni—cooking ovens of brick or stone

Hadrianoupolis—Edime, Turkey

Hephthalites—'Hunnish' tribal invaders of the mid-fourth century harassing the Persians' northeastern border

honestiores—privileged classes of Roma, persons of status and property

hordearius—meaning 'barleyman,' an athlete on a carbohydrate-heavy diet

Gallia—Gaul, the Roman province approximating modern France

Genua—Genoa, Italy

Lake of Brigantia—the Lake of Constance or the Bodensee, bordering Germany, Switzerland, and Austria

Lake of Verganus—the Lago Maggiore, Italy

lararium—shrine for the house gods

lares—house gods protecting the residents

latifundium—giant agricultural estate

latrunculi—board game akin to checkers

Lentia—Lintz, Austria

Londinium—London, England

magister officiorum—one of the most senior official posts in Late Roma, created by Constantine, in charge of the palatine secretariat

magister agentium—the Master of the Schola of *Agentes in Rebus*

mansio, mansiones—state run inns on the *Cursus Publicus*

mappa—a cloth dropped to signal the start of a game or race

Massagetae—nomads from the plains east of the Caspian Sea, variously described as precursors of the Huns or Alans

matrona—matriarch of family/household

Mediolanum—Milan, Italy

meta—the turning post at one end of a racetrack

Mogontiacum—Mainz, Germany

Naissus—Niš, Serbia

Neapolis—Naples, Italy

negotiatores—negotiators

Nicomedia—Izmit, Turkey

Palaestina—Palestine

palaestra—exercise area of a public bath house

Patavium—Padua, Italy

petanus—a peacetime riding helmet made of thick leather rather than metal

Petobio—Ptuj, Slovenia

Philippopolis—Plovdiv, Bulgaria

Pola, Istria—Pula, Croatia

Pisae—Pisa, Italy

prima—the first hour of the Roman day

pugio, pugiones—the standard-issue military dagger of Late Rome

puls—soup

pultarius—caldron

quadriga—team of four chariot horses

Rhaetia—the home of the Rhaetians, an Alpine tribe in eastern and southeast Switzerland, southern Bavaria, the Upper Swabia, Vorarlberg, the greater part of Tirol, and part of Lombardy.

the Rhenus River—the Rhine River

the Rhodanus River—the Rhône River

schola—a distinct body within the Roman government

scutarii—well-equipped light infantry armed with swords, shields and heavy javelins

the Sea of Adria—the Adriatic Sea

silentiarius—courtier assigned the job of keeping silence and order

spatha—the long sword carried by Late Roman soldiers

spina—the center divider or 'spine' of the chariot racetrack

spectabilus—the second rank of imperial official

stoa—roofed walkway

strigil, strigiles, tool for scraping skin in bath

stilus, stili—pointed instrument for writing on wax-covered tablets.

taurobolium—pagan rite of bull slaughter performed in the honor of emperors until discouraged by the Christian state

Tiberias—Tiberias (also Tverya, Tiveria), Israel, historically the largest Jewish city in the Galilee and the political/religious hub of the Jews of Palestine

Thamesis—the Thames River, England

tiro, tirones—beginners, trainees

triclinium—formal dining room

vexillatio—during the Empire's Dominate period, *vexillatio* means a cavalry unit of the Roman army. In the fourth century, the *Vexillationes Palatinae* and *Vexilationes Comitatenses* of the Roman field armies were between 300-600 men.

vicarius—a Late Roman judge or jurisdictional official, possibly acting in outer dioceses in the place of the *iudex ordinarius*

Vosporus—the Bosporus, Turkey

HISTORICAL NOTES

The brief and lurid reign of the Caesar Flavius Claudius Constantius Gallus and his consort cousin, the *Augusta* Flavia Constantia (sometimes known as Constantina,) received the close attention of the fourth-century historian Ammianus Marcellinus. Edward Gibbon of *The Decline and Fall of the Roman Empire* nicknamed Ammianus 'my faithful guide,' but Ammianus' lively account is also corroborated by the Greek scholar Libanius, (a victim himself of slanders alleging sorcery using decapitated girls,) as well as other historians and commentators.

Ammianus gives us a vivid account of Gallus' habit of touring his brightly lit Antioch at night in ineffectual disguise to consort with the lowborn and roust out traitors. He also describes the mounting paranoia spreading through the city's high society. The elites turn on and turn in each other in their haste to pass spurious reports and bribes to the imperial couple via a back door to the Palace.

Ammianus records how the stiff-necked Prefect of the Palace, Thalassius sent terse reports to Constantius II in the West and how the *Comes* of the East, Honoratus, attempted to counter Gallus' execution of the weak-willed Antiochene 'Senate.' (This may well be this same Honoratus who pops up again as Constantinopolis's first recorded Prefect of the City who took office on December 11, 359 and held it until 361.)

Ammianus also records the ambition of the Master of the Guards, Barbatio, the hysterical dismemberment of the Governor Theophilus at the hands of a hungry mob aroused by Gallus' taunts, the exhortations of the doomed *Quaestor* Montius, and the short, provocative speech of the arrogant Prefect Domitianus during his only meeting with the Caesar, which ended with his murder.

In short, many of the most incredible scenes in this book are drawn from Ammianus' lively history.

Ammianus enjoys the knack of the best historians in including highly visual tidbits that make his horrific tale come alive, such as the Antiochene who complains that his bedroom seems to have ears, or the deceased Caesar's red slippers that Apodemius places at the feet of Constantius, having killed at least one horse in his race back to Mediolanum. (The speed of travelling at maximum high-speed by the imperial system of horse relay has been calculated by Stanford University in their Orbis Via project, but obviously Apodemius overdid it and was later held to public account for his destruction of state animals.)

Ammianus also records the sad story of the case of Clematius and the diamond necklace bribe with the skill of a modern detective writer.

However, the story of Gallus' disastrous rule was so rich in incident that Ammianus himself finally begs off from further recitation of horror stories of false charges and cruel tortures. He apologizes for getting waylaid by so much scandal and wrongdoing.

I hope readers will forgive my own compression of the factual time frame of the story of Gallus, done purely for narrative pace. This is particularly true toward the end in the treatment of the final journey that the ill-fated Caesar made from Antioch to his final destination in the fortress in Pola. For example, Gallus' hubris in anticipating his 'elevation' and his awarding the laurels to Thorax from the imperial box as if he were already an emperor was reported to Constantius, who then stripped him of his military escort *only* after the Gallus travelling party had left Constantinopolis and reached Adrianople.

Moreover, the records of the interrogation of Gallus were sent to Constantius for review before the execution order returned from the imperial court.

But when it comes to the individual fates of these powerful politicians and the drama behind their battle for power and the stability of the Empire, the truth needs no embellishment or modification.

Ammianus dwells also on the property greed and power abuse of the Lord Chamberlain, the eunuch Eusebius. The only liberty I have taken in weaving together his loose and somewhat disjointed facts is blaming Eusebius for specifically prompting and profiting by the 'back door' stream of calumnies polluting Antioch. On the other hand, his presence in the judgment and execution of Gallus is not only historical fact, but also a critical action that would come to haunt him later.

Along with the Gallus tale, Ammianus treats the reader of Book XIV to a discursive detour around the former imperial capital Roma as it fell into decline under the Prefect Orfitus. He paints for us its fashionable ladies, ne'er-do-well toadies, decaying elites—all of them displaying decadent styles of dress and travel through festering streets teeming with the unemployed. Years later, Ammianus adds, Orfitus was convicted for the kind of embezzling our fictional majordomo Verus suspects all along. Yet Orfitus survived his punishment in exile to return to Roma.

Faithful guide he may seem, but of course Ammianus was a political player himself; he served some of his career as a military officer under General Ursicinus and modern historians view him as less than objective—or at least, he makes little effort to sound objective.

For example, he describes Constantia as nothing less than a Fury in human form. We could only wish he had more information about her death by fever on the lonely road ending in Caeni Gallicani, a place of no other discernable importance.

Ammianus also describes the historical *agens* Apodemius as 'a friend to no good man.' There is savage relish in his vivid scene wherein Apodemius conducts the interrogation of 'the trial' before supervising the carrying out of Constantius II's orders to execute the Caesar Gallus.

Again, Ammianus is the source of the historical detail regarding the mutilation of Gallus' face. (Ammianus also blames Apodemius for later events that threaten to turn Emperor Constantius II against his ally General Silvanus.)

Yet viewed from a distance, the overall historical record speaks in Apodemius' favor; the Caesar Gallus was certainly himself 'no good man.' The historian Zozimus cites the court prefect Lampadius and citizens Dynamius and Picentius as also defaming Gallus (although he hews to the party line that these were merely ambitious slanders for personal gain.) As for the Franco-Roman General Silvanus, he was already famous for his eleventh-hour betrayal of his Emperor, the usurper Magnentius, on the battlefield of the century's bloodiest battle at Mursa. History favors the winners, but Silvanus' vacillation and defection to Constantius II's side speaks more for his political canniness than his loyalty.

Constantius II himself cannot have been an easy man to serve nor a happy man to know, preoccupied as he was with fending off attacks by Persians and Alemanni, struggling to balance ferocious religious controversies over the nature of Christ, and trying to rule an empire overstretched from London to Carthage to Palestine with no reliable partner.

Within two years of this tale, we find a new cast of characters installed in Antioch under the Emperor Constantius. He has now returned from his anti-barbarian campaigns in the West to resume his struggle with the Persians. Antioch is also the base for the deliciously named Strategius, the Praetorian Prefect of the East running an agent, coincidentally named Clematius, across enemy lines to spy on Shapur II. This is one of the rare recorded instances of an *agens* dispatched on a *foreign* mission and I borrowed it to explain Apodemius' presence in Constantinopolis just in time to save Marcus.

Religious preoccupations don't feature much in our story, but they were constantly in the Arian Christian Emperor's imperial in-box. Constantius' outright ban of pagan sacrifice in Roma only came in an official sense much later than our time frame here.

However, there was a constant attempt by Constantius to erode the religious nature of the lingering pagan rituals while preserving their links to the secular public Games and holidays so vital to Roma's social calendar. The practice of bull or ram sacrifice was briefly revived as a last-ditch demonstration of pagan resistance in Late Rome.

Students of Gibbon may also recognize my fictional eunuch-master Einku's description of Constantius II as 'feeble, etc.' as lifted directly from the historian's own assessment. We get various contemporary descriptions of Constantius as nervous, susceptible to rumor, and swayed by eunuchs as he worked to stay in command of a difficult situation.

Some experts even suggest that in pulling his last remaining male relative out of obscurity in 355, Constantius would have been just as happy if—rather than morphing from scholar to popular commander—Julian had died on the battlefields of Gaul.

Fortunately for history lovers, the story of 'Julian the Apostate' is far more interesting than that.

ACKNOWLEDGEMENTS

Ammianus, Marcellinus, *The Roman History of Ammianus Marcellinus during the Reigns of the Emperors Constantius, Julian, Jovianus, Valentinian, and Valens, Book XIV*, translated by C.D. Yonge, Henry G. Bohn, London, 1862

Banchich Thomas, Eugene Lane, *The History of Zonaras: From Alexander Severus to the Death of Theodosius the Great*, Routledge, New York, 2009

Barnes, Timothy D., *Athanasius and Constantius, Theology and Politics in the Constantinian Empire*, Harvard University Press, Boston, 2001

Barnes, Timothy D. *Ammianus Marcellinus and the Representation of Historical Reality, Volume 56*, Cornell University Press, Ithaca, N.Y. 1998

Brown, Peter, *The World of Late Antiquity*, Thames and Hudson, London, 1971

Potter, David S., *The Roman Empire at Bay, AD 180-395*, Routledge History of the Ancient World, New Ed. Edition, London/New York 2004

Bury, J. B, *The Cambridge Medieval History, Volume I*, M. Gwatkin, J. P. Whitney ed. Cambridge University Press, 1936

Cameron, Averil, *The Cambridge Ancient History Volume XIII: The Late Empire, 337-425 AD*, Cambridge University Press, 1997

Champlin, Edward, *Final Judgements, Duty and Emotion in Roman Wills, 200 BC-AD 250*, University of California Press, Berkeley, 1991

Echard, Laurence, *The Roman History from the Removal of the Imperial Seat by Constantine the Great, to the Taking of Rome by Odoacer K. of the Heruli and the Ruin of the Empire in the West to its Restitution by Charlemagne*, Vol. III, Christ's College, Cambridge, 1696

Faas, Patrick, *Around the Roman Table*, Macmillan, London, 1994

Gibbon, Edward, *The History of the Decline and Fall of the Roman Empire*, ed. J.B. Bury with an introduction by W. E. H. Lecky, Fred de Fau and Co., New York 1906, The Online Library of Liberty

Kelly, Christopher, *Ruling the Later Roman Empire*, Harvard University Press, Boston, 2006

Knapp, Robert, *Invisible Romans*, Profile Books, London, 2013

Kuefler, Mathew, *The Manly Eunuch: Masculinity, Gender Ambiguity, and Christian Ideology in Late Antiquity*, University of Chicago Press, 2001

Goldsworthy, Adrian, *How Rome Fell, Death of a Superpower*, Yale University Press, New Haven, 2009

Goldsworthy, Adrian, *The Complete Roman Army*, Thames & Hudson, London, 2003

Heather, Peter, *The Fall of the Roman Empire, A New History*, Macmillan, Oxford, 2005

Jones-Lewis, Molly, *The Heterosexualized Eunuch in the Roman Empire*, Austin College, Academia.edu, 2013

MacDowall, Simon, *Late Roman Cavalryman AD 236-565*, Osprey Publishing, Botley, Oxford, 1995

Philostorgius, *Epitome of the Ecclesiastical History of Philostorgius*, compiled by Photius, Patriarch of Constantinopolis, Edward Ealford, translated by Henry G. Bohn, Covent Garden, London 1855

Shambaugh, John E., *The Ancient Roman City*, John Hopkins University Press, Baltimore Maryland, 1988

Rüpke, Jörg, *A Companion to Roman Religion (Blackwell Companions to the Ancient World)*, Wiley-Blackwell, London, 2011

Stambaugh, John E., *The Ancient Roman City*, The John Hopkins University Press, Baltimore, 1988

Wace, Henry, William C. Percy, Ed., *Dictionary of Christian Biography and Literature to the End of the Sixth Century A.D., with an Account of the Principal Sects and Heresies*, Little, Brown and Company, 1887

Zosimus, *New History, Book II*, ed. Green and Chaplin, London, 1814

Also: deepest thanks to the online communities of:

Romanarmy.com, Jasper Oorthuys, Associate Webmaster, and Jenny Cline, Founder

LacusCurtius at the University of Chicago, web master Bill Thayer

ORBISvia, Stanford University

Forum Ancient Coins

Academia.edu

Any errors are my own and I welcome corrections.

ABOUT THE AUTHOR

Q. V. Hunter's interest in classical history began with four years of high school Latin followed by university courses in ancient religions. A fascination with Late Antiquity deepened when Hunter moved to a two-hundred-year-old farmhouse near an ancient Roman colony. The farmhouse is easily reached by modern road, but also by a Roman road running more directly down to the *Colonia Equestris Noviodunum.*

Noviodunum was founded around 50 BCE as a retirement community for Julius Caesar's cavalry veterans. It's listed as the *civitas Equestrium id est Noviodunus* in the *Notitia Galliarum,* (the fourth-century directory listing all seventeen provinces of Roman Gallia.)

Noviodunum became Rome's most important colony along Lake Leman—with a forum, baths, basilica, and amphitheater. Potable water came via an aqueduct running all the way from present-day Divonne, France. Noviodunum belonged to a network of settlements radiating out from Lugdunum (Lyon, France) around the Rhône Valley. Roman colonists were encouraged to supervise the Celtic Helvetii who had been transported to the area against their will after their defeat at the Battle of Bibracte in 58 BC.

As a result of Germanic Alemanni invasions in 259-260 AD, much of Roman Noviodunum was razed but it flourishes again today as the Swiss town of Nyon.

Hunter is married to a self-proclaimed 'Ur-Swiss,' a descendant of those very Alemanni barbarians who settled farther north of Nyon in the Alpine lake region that gave birth to the three founding cantons of the Confederation Helvetica, i.e. Switzerland, in 1291 AD.

They have three adult children.

Made in the USA
San Bernardino, CA
10 July 2020